Ameerah

Rebekkah Ford

Copyright © 2015 by Rebekkah Ford

Printed in the U.S.A.

Interior formatting by Tugboat Design

ISBN: 13: 978-0-692-60903-3

First Edition January 2016

Table of Contents

Acknowledgments

I'd like to thank Tarnya Rutheford and Veronica Williams for helping me create two characters in this book—Aidan Logan and Sylis Doyle. Both gals are part of my street team and took the opportunity I gave them to come up with a character for Ameerah's story. They did an awesome job, and I'm grateful for their support and friendship.

Thank you Crissy Sutcliffe, Debb Lavoie, and Rosemary Hendry for being my beta readers and a huge support of my books. You girls rock!

I'd like to thank my street team for your support. I appreciate it. You're awesome.

I'd like to give a shout out to my cover artist Stephanie Flint, my editor Chase Nottingham, and Christina Pollard Escue. You three were a huge help in making this book what it is today, and I appreciate you and your dedication. You're awesome!

I'd like to thank my awesome formatter Deborah Bradseth from Tugboat Design. I appreciate you and all of your help.

I'd like to acknowledge my wonderful husband Kevin Ford. You are my best friend, and I can always count on you to make me laugh and give me huggles.

Also, I'd like to thank my fans. I appreciate you more than I can say. Y'all rock!

Some birds cannot be caged, and I'm one of them.
~Ameerah Arrowood 1925

Chapter One

Present Day

This human had exquisite taste. I sure knew how to pick them. I mentally patted myself on the back, even though the truth of the matter was after my heinous death in the insane asylum, I'd been possessing soulless humans for damn near ninety years. I had loads of experiences in choosing the best apple in the orchard.

The four-poster bed was lovely in the moonlight. The bottom edges of its sheer curtains lifted off the floor, causing the delicate fabric to ripple and bow in the center, creating a complete circle. The cool breeze had a smoky, nutty aroma.

The smell of fall.

I draped the black garment bag over the back of a chair and flicked on the elegant floor lamp beside it. The beautiful cone shade had a Tiffany-style stained art glass that shed a warm glow throughout the room. Goosebumps rose on my bare arms. The temperature outside was dropping. I closed the window, pulled the blind down, and sighed. Plain and simple, I was in a pissy mood. I wasn't up for the roaring 'twenties party Derek was orchestrating for me and me alone. He knew when I was human, I was a flapper gal and had the time of my life. He thought maybe his little shindig would cheer me up, but frankly it was doing quite the opposite.

A high-pitched scream issued from my purse that hung across my body. I retrieved my cell from the side pocket and smiled, recalling my recent trip to a swanky department store.

While I was shopping earlier today, I noticed the customer service attendant had paid no attention to the patrons whose attire were far less than what she sported, which looked like a Ralph Lauren maroon silk blouse and a black ruffled skirt. Then, her quick, brown eyes spotted me browsing in the lingerie aisle.

I was her cash cow.

The Armani black leather pants I wore, along with my red Manolo Blahnik high heels, were unmistakable to one who knew fashion. I was sure this thirty-something-year-old worked on commission, and she wasn't about to pass an opportunity to collect. As she headed my way, a plastic Barbie doll smile plastered on her face, my phone screamed as it did now. I smiled at that recent memory and pushed the talk button with the image bright in my mind of the horrific look the sales lady had thrown at me, and then her doing a beeline in the opposite direction when I smirked and winked at her.

I laughed as I brought the phone to my ear.

"You sound in bloody good spirits," Derek said. I could hear the smile in his voice.

"Let's not use the word *spirit*," I grumbled, my mood reverting back to pissy.

"Why the hell not?"

"Uh, because we are one, and we're not good," I reminded him.

"Speak for yourself, love. I'm a fence-sitter and quite enjoying it if I do say so myself."

"Straddling the line between Heaven and Hell. I'm right there with you," I said, but then fell silent.

"Your troubles are getting the best of you," he said. When I didn't respond, he continued. "Why don't you slip into that gorgeous dress you bought and come join the party? It starts in an hour."

I glanced at the garment bag. He knew I had fine taste and purchased a flapper dress. My heart ached, and a deep longing followed. It would be nice to listen to some jazz and have a few drinks, I told myself. "Very well," I sighed.

"Splendid." He sounded happy. "Now, go tidy yourself up."

We said our goodbyes, and I got busy getting dolled up. After my shower and drying off my shoulder length dark hair, I curled and pinned it up. Carefully, I placed a thin lace headband over it, loving the short, white feather sticking up its side. The whole process took me longer than I intended, because the next thing I knew, I was running twenty minutes late.

Shit.

I threw on my T-strapped high heels and gave myself a once over in the mirror. A beam of light swiped across my sad hazel eyes, reminding me, though I became a dark spirit ninety years ago, I was considered young. Once I reached maturity, my eyes would glow, brought on by an inflection of different emotions. Only certain beings could catch the anomaly we somehow created when we dwelled in the human flesh. I closed my eyes, then opened them, focusing on my costume. The dress was stunning on this thin, curvaceous body. The pale pink, ivory, and silver embroidered lace-type pattern, along with the soft colors of pearl beading and sequins, intertwined throughout the material. The fringes that were touching my knees paid homage to the height of my existence once upon a time ago. I needed one more thing to set off my outfit.

Red lipstick.

I applied some, smacked my lips, and grabbed my chain beaded purse.

Twenty minutes later, I entered an underground club called *Chameleons* on the outskirts of Astoria, Oregon. Derek owned and operated the business. It was a place where our kind could unwind and indulge in our hedonistic ways. A live jazz band was already playing on the elevated platform in the back. The large room had a whiff of decadence from the rosewood walls to the fine oak bar stationed in the corner with red cushioned retro barstools lining its length. In the center was a dance floor, and beyond it were tables and booths. A second level circulated the entire area where patrons sat or danced.

"Ameerah," Derek called when he spotted me. He motioned for me to join him at the bar where he sat with a Guinness bottle in hand, looking dapper in his black fedora hat and suit. "You are a vision, love," he gushed, giving me an appreciative look.

I offered him a weak smile and glanced around, absorbing the entire atmosphere. It was as if I stepped back into time. My time. I wrapped my fingers around the long pearl necklace dangling from my neck, admiring the ladies in their fringe flapper dresses. Some wore cloche hats, while others chose headbands with a feather like my own. The men wore either pinstriped suits with vests or tuxedos, setting off their black shirts with a black or white tie. Of course a lot of them followed suit with Derek, wearing the ever-so-popular fedora from back in those days.

My heart bled.

If only I could return to the 1920s. If only I ran away before my parents got their filthy claws in me and stuck me in that horrid place. If only I had taken extra precautions to hide my journal so my pompous, stick-in-the-ass mother wouldn't have discovered it.

If only–

"Ameerah?"

I blinked and turned to Derek. His piercing, ocean-blue eyes held a deep concern. It was for me. I knew it was. The corners of his mouth turned down, giving the unmistakable expression of worry for a dear friend. Not wanting him to think I lacked gratitude for his generous attempt to cheer me up, I took a seat beside him and ordered a bloody Mary with extra olives. "I'm fine," I said, extracting a silver cigarette case from my purse. He stroked a match and held it up, lighting my ciggy. I inhaled deeply and then exhaled, blowing smoke rings in front of us. Boy, did I love a good smoke and drink.

"You're a terrible liar," he said, pushing his caramel colored bangs out of his eyes. "You know what you need?"

"What? Salvation? It might be too late for me, but nonetheless, I'm seeking it." I took a sip of my drink. The spicy, peppery tomato juice tasted wonderful. I popped an olive in my mouth.

"No, love," he said. "Salvation comes from within not from without."

"So I heard," I said with a sigh.

"From whom, may I ask?" He raised his eyebrows, prompting me to elaborate.

The rich tones of clarinet and tenor sax played in the background like a scenic backdrop in a Leonardo da Vinci painting. The atmosphere was charged with continuous chatter and laughter. The smell of alcohol and tobacco played a familiar cord in my heart along with the music and the hotsy totsy outfits.

I took a long drag off my ciggy and slowly blew the smoke up between us. "A light walker," I said with a smirk.

The tip of his beer bottle rested at the edge of his bottom lip, ready to be tilted to release the firewater onto his palate. In shock, he set it down instead. "You engaged in a conversation with a bloody light walker?" His stared at me, wide-eyed, mouth agape.

"Be careful what you say, Derek," I said and continued in a sarcastic tone. "Humans revere them as angels. You mustn't disrespect these heavenly beings." I was still pissed off about my earlier encounter with one, who interestingly enough looked like a young Bob Dylan.

"My arse," he snorted. He took one last drag off his smoke before putting it out in the already overflowing ashtray and picking up his drink. I looked at him, knowing by his hurried gestures he was about to make a suggestion. "I propose we go to the backroom where we can have some privacy." He rose and paused when I remained seated. "Shall we, love?"

I wasn't sure if I wanted to divulge more tales of my life or problems, but the alcohol was going down quite well . . . Oh, hell, why the fuck not?

I caught the eye of the pretty blonde bartender who was wiping the counter down a few feet away. "Can I have a fallen angel cocktail, please?"

Derek guffawed, catching my snarky sense of humor and ordered himself a whiskey and water on the rocks.

She smiled. "Of course." She grabbed the crème de menthe, gin, and lime, sneaking coy peeks at me while making my drink. I caught the beam of light flash across her brown eyes. She was a young dark spirit like me.

Derek leaned in next to my ear. "We can talk later if you'd like to take her in the back room for a bit of snogging. It sure would remedy your sour mood."

I had to admit the idea was quite appealing. Her luscious kisser was painted a dark crimson, accentuating her pout. Her black cloche hat looked adorable on her with blonde, chin length curls framing her round face. Yes, I could definitely have a go with her, but now wasn't the time. Besides, I had Nadia who was stuck in a state of confusion in the lower world to think about. There was no way I could get there to awake her from her stupor—unless I overcame my issues . . . or so I had been told by a light walker. It didn't mean a hill of beans that I was changing my ways. I had to fight and overcome my own demons to move on, or accept his offer and get rehabilitated in the afterlife, which wasn't going to happen, not after what happened to me when I was human.

"It's a tempting offer," I said to Derek. "However, I have a story I need to tell and would like for you to be the one I share it with."

The bartender handed me my drink. When I took it, her fingers softly brushed against mine. "If I can help you with anything else, don't hesitate to ask," she told me, her eyes lingering on my face. She bit the corner of her bottom lip when I held her gaze, silently telling her I might seek her out before the sun rises.

"I won't," I said with a flirtatious half-smile, then turned on my heel to follow Derek to his private quarters.

We weaved our way through the crowd, stopping a couple of times for short, polite conversations with a handful of slightly intoxicated, freewill-loving people. The night was still young. I imagined they'd all be snockered in a few hours.

We entered a comfortable room with a stamped-tin ceiling and plush maroon couches and chairs. On the far wall was a miniature bar, lit by small bulbs along the top of its black metal base. I noticed as soon as he closed the heavy oak door how the noise from the party disappeared. We were shut in silence. I sat in the armchair facing the loveseat where he parked himself and placed my drink on the claw foot cherry wood end table. The room smelled like stale cigarettes and alcohol. I loved that smell. It reminded me of the pubs I used to frequent years ago in England after I became a dark spirit.

"So tell me about the light walker and why the hell you were conversing with him," Derek said. "By the way, rumor has it you're quite chummy with Nathan Caswell and Paige Reed. Is it true?"

"They're my friends," I admitted. When he opened his mouth to object, I raised my hand to shut his trap. I knew he would object to me having any friendly relations with our enemies—the immortals who cast us out of the humans we possessed. Nathan was the best dark spirit tracker of his kind. "Trust me. They're good people."

"You're bloody daft," he said, shaking his head. "You're treading in dangerous waters, love. If Bael were to discover you were mates with them . . . or Volac got wind of your dealings, either one would charge you with treason and banish you to The Sheol of Glass."

I'd heard of that dark, swampy realm where your only hope of escape was to have your captor release you through the same dark ritual he enslaved you with or by a witch in the living. Like the lower world, there were many compartments to the Sheol of Glass. It was not one place. Bael, the oldest dark spirit of us all, knew how to wield the blackest of magic. The spell would be considered a deadfall, which was one of many traps to capture a spirit. Volac, who was another ancient entity, may not be as powerful as Bael, but he had his own tricks up his sleeve and was not one to underestimate or provoke.

"Volac already knows," I admitted. "He caught me performing a ritual with Paige and Nathan not too long ago. I wanted to show them where that bitch Aosoth was, where her black soul went after Anwar had cast her out." Derek was clearly at a loss for words, because he stared at me, slack-jawed. "I don't want to talk about that now," I went on. "This party tonight made me realize I need to unburden myself by sharing my story with someone. I would like it to be you." I shifted in my seat and took a drink of my cocktail, eyeing him over the rim. My stomach rolled. The only other person I shared my tale with was Nadia—a human whom I fell in love with decades ago. Then, Aosoth killed her.

"I'm flattered to be invited into your confidence." Derek popped a ciggy into his mouth. He pulled out his Zippo from his pants pocket. When he tilted it, the silver caught the light just so, the flat surface giving the appearance of a tiny mirror. He flicked the top with his thumb. A short, clicking noise fell between us. "We've been friends for half a century," he continued. "It's no secret I adore you." He motioned to the door where beyond it, the party was in full swing. "But why me? Why unload your baggage on a chap like myself?"

"I trust you, and I need your help," I answered. "You know some of what I endured while I was human . . . but not all. I would like what I tell you to be kept between us, and then afterward, I have a favor to ask of you."

"Ask it now. There is no need for you to pamper my ego with entrusting me with tales of your life as a human." He took a sip of his whiskey; the ice knocking against the glass seemed to amplify in my ears.

I was on edge, I realized. I twisted my fingers in my lap. When I made the snap decision to tell him the details of my existence, I hadn't realized how difficult it would be to wheel myself back to that time. However, the pinching in my gut dared me to follow through.

No, not dared.

Urged.

I opened my mouth, and in a rush I spoke before the fear set and curdled inside my stomach. "I'll ask you the favor when I end my tale." I took a deep breath and continued, still twisting my fingers in my lap. "I need to get the story out before I lose my nerve. I think . . . I think possibly it'll help me find peace. At least, I hope so."

Derek sat back and rested his ankle on his knee, understanding softening his features. "Well then, love, I'm all ears."

And so, I began my story.

Chapter Two

1925

I was born into a prominent family in 1907. My father was a businessman who worked in the financial district of Manhattan in New York City. He also dabbled in industrial activities such as construction, oil, and steel. He rubbed elbows with the best of them and invested wisely in the stock market. I was an only child, a robot who my stick-in-the-mud, narcissistic mother would attempt to program into her perfect offspring. She had no interest in my needs, unless she was bored and lonely. Then, she would acknowledge my presence to fill the empty hours where, God forbid, she might grow a conscious if she were left without some sort of companionship.

In 1925, I was eighteen years old. Rebellious. I was against the exorbitant, snobbish behavior my parents and their cronies defecated on whom they quickly determined were lesser than them. Their eyes held a critical glint that bred uneasiness within me whenever I had the misfortune of being in their presence. I resented all of them for what I felt was deplorable behavior and for treating me like an ornamental figure, only to be displayed when it suited their personal agendas. This was my life growing up until finally I had enough.

We lived in Washington Heights, a picturesque town in upper Manhattan. I have to admit our house was breathtaking. It was part Queen Anne style and part colonial revival with a dash of Romanesque.

A wide wraparound porch with classical white columns, arches, and gambrel roofs was pleasing to the eye. The round tower on the south side with the arched windows, overlooking our sprawling lawn and apple orchard, was my bedroom—very fitting considering my station in the family was almost a reflection of a twisted fairytale story. My name, Ameerah, should be a clue. It meant princess. Its roots were Arabic, and though not an ounce of Arab blood ran through my veins, my mother named me for that very reason alone. At least she didn't dub me Cinder-fuckin'-rella . . . but I digress.

I graduated high school in May of 1925 and had been sneaking about all year with my best pal, Betty, to jazz clubs to hear the likes of Louis Armstrong and Fletcher Henderson. We learned how to do dances such as the Charleston and Bunny Hug. We drank from small silver flasks, not giving a shit about prohibition, but we still hid it beneath our dresses by attaching it to our garters. We did what we could not to draw too much attention from the authorities. We smoked and made new friends every time we hit the entertainment scene on weekends when my parents thought I was at Betty's house playing cards or baking cookies.

But then one afternoon, a week after I graduated, the cat was out of the bag. It was my own decision of course. I was tired of the false pretense I enacted in the presence of my parents to satisfy their expectations on how I should behave and dress. I decided to go to a barber and have him cut my long hair into a stylish bob. I loved it. The natural curl to my dark tresses brushed against my chin beneath the cloche hat I wore. I came home that evening wearing my knee-high gold and white brocade, drop down waist fringe dress. Though my mother had recently graduated from the outdated and yawn-worthy floor-length dresses to mid-calf ones, I knew without a doubt her disapproval of my ensemble would be epic.

"Ameerah, is that you?" she called from the kitchen when I closed the front door.

"The one and only," I said, smiling at my reflection in the hallway mirror. I had lined my hazel eyes in kohl and painted my kisser in dark red, just like I always did when I went out at night with Betty.

"Your father will be home soon. Set the table while I finish making supper," she said, sounding exasperated.

In our household, my mother was famous for her theatrics. My father thought it was an endearing trait. I found it annoying. She refused to hire a maid, even though her friends employed at least one, claiming they were doing their civil duty to society by their charitable contribution to hire a negro—or jigaboo as they were known to call them—to keep house. My mother had another perspective on the matter. She didn't want *those* kinds of people on our property, let alone in our house. They came from the jungle, for Christ's sake. They were aboriginals. I detested her narrow-minded views of the black race, even more so now that I'd seen how talented and innovative many were. It always made me wonder how well they would excel as bankers or lawyers. If only she knew how I envied them whenever I'd watch their performances at the jazz clubs in Harlem and how glamorous I thought they were.

"All right," I answered as I stepped into our dining room. The dishes were already stacked on the table with the silverware on top. I proceeded to do as she requested, putting my father's plate in front of the captain's chair for starters. I could hear my mother mumbling something on the other side of the door to the kitchen. Her image flitted past the tall, narrow, French window beside it. I squared my shoulders and held my head high.

She came out with a platter of sliced roast beef, roasted potatoes, and glazed carrots. Her gaze met mine, and she stopped cold in her tracks. Her lips parted, but no words escaped. Then, the skin around her brown eyes tightened, and her lips puckered. She set the platter on the table and turned to me, her expression now dark and angry. "What on earth possessed you to cut your beautiful long hair and dress so perversely?" She made an up and down sweeping gesture in front of me. "You look like one of those . . . those flapper gals. My word, Ameerah, what will our friends think?"

"I don't care what your high-hat friends think," I said with an indifferent shrug. "They're a bunch of wet blankets anyway."

"Baloney," she said. "They're a swell class of spiffy people. *Our* type of class." The snobbery in her voice fueled my conviction to stand my ground. I loathed how she segregated us and others like us from those who were less fortunate.

"Here's a news flash for you, Mother . . . I'm not like you or your friends. I *never* will be," I spat.

"Bite your tongue. You—"

"What is all the commotion?" My father entered the room, looking ducky in his three-piece suit and fedora hat. He set his briefcase down, took one look at me, and frowned in disapproval. "What the devil are you thinking, dressing and painting your face like some Jezebel?"

Sure, bring a character straight out of the Bible to make a point that I found utterly ridiculous. We were Roman Catholics but only went to church on holidays or when it suited some twisted social agenda. My pal Betty was Catholic, and I'd gone to church with her family more than I'd ever been with my own damn family. Personally, I loved going to the old gothic church, dipping my fingers in holy water, making the sign of the cross on my chest, and looking in gross fascination upon Jesus, his limp body hanging on the huge cross behind the altar. I always marveled at the whole communion ritual. You ate the body of Christ and drank his blood. It reminded me of Bran Stoker's *Dracula*. To me, the Catholic faith from priests speaking Latin down to the rituals parishioners followed was dark and inviting. At the time, I was ignorant about the true history of it all. I never thought about the fate of my own soul, or if the world would grow bleak with each passing decade.

"This is who I am," I finally said after squirming beneath my father's critical gaze. "I'm a flapper," I proudly announced.

"Like hell you are," he said, placing his hat on the high back chair in the corner. His black hair was neatly parted on the side, not a strand out of place. "You are a member of our family and will act accordingly."

"Well, then," I said, "I will gather my effects and be on my merry way."

My mother was dishing out the food I'm sure she would have any poor bastard believe she slaved over for hours. She paused with a spoonful of glazed carrots and looked at us. "Wait. Where would you go? What would you do without the allowance we provide you?"

"I'll get a room and work at one of the clubs in Harlem," I said, envisioning myself working in a cabaret where I could possibly meet Ethel Waters or Fletcher Henderson.

My mother set the spoon down. It clanked against the plate. I watched the color leech from her face. "Not my princess." She turned to my father, who was standing with his arms tight against his chest, glaring. "Do something, Henry."

He sighed and wiped a hand across his face. "What do you want from us, Ameerah?" He sounded businesslike, as if he were making a deal with one of his competitors. I didn't like it. I was his daughter, yet he had the air of an entrepreneur who was forced into a corner.

"I want you to accept me for who I am. I want to be treated like an individual instead of a prop in your puppet show," I countered.

My father took his seat at the table and picked a ciggy out of its bronze case. He lit it, took a drag, and slowly released a cloud of smoke above us. "Would you be willing to compromise?"

I sat in the chair next to him, plucked the butt from his mouth, puffed on it, and blew perfect smoke rings toward him. The look on my parents' faces was priceless: eyes wide, mouths agape. I smirked, handed him his ciggy back and said, "I'm all ears."

My father cleared his throat, attempting to recover from the shock of his daughter smoking. It was looked down upon for a woman to smoke, yet it was okay for a man. I found the double standard annoying and refused to live my life inferior to the male species.

"What if we turned a blind eye to this outlandish behavior you adopted and in return you restrain it during the day and when we're in the company of others in our social standing."

"It's a phase she's going through," my mother said to him. "I'm sure it'll pass."

"Indeed, Cornelia. It very well could be." He patted her hand and looked at me, waiting for my reply.

I quickly weighed my options. I could get a job and a place to live in Harlem. In fact, I wouldn't have to work for a while. I'd been saving my monthly allowance for years. It would get me by for a bit. Hell, I probably could even buy a Model T with all the dough I had. The idea was quite appealing. Then, the thought about doing a little bootlegging on the side entered my mind. A thrill went through me at the prospect of becoming an underground distributor of the finest hooch in town. However, if I accepted my father's proposition, I wouldn't have to concern myself with a job. They didn't want me to—

"Ameerah?" my father said, interrupting my mental chatter. The timbre in his voice held an inflection of sternness I didn't appreciate. "Do we have a deal?"

I blinked at him. "I'm not one of your business associates," I replied. "I'm your *daughter*." I took a drink of my water, swallowing against the unexpected tears rising in my throat. My heart felt heavy when the realization came that he never treated me as such. Sure, he threw endearments my way, but his love was shown through materialistic means instead of willingly sharing my company. Sadly enough, he and my mother only knew me through their own tunnel vision on how they wanted to perceive their daughter. It bothered me. A lot.

"Of course you are, dear," my mother said in a soft, placating tone. "We love you very much and only want the best for you. Why do you think your father works so hard? He does it to give us all of this." She swept her hand in the air, indicating to all the fine things we had, including the four tiered crystal chandelier hanging above.

I swiped the back of my hand across my wet cheeks. "I don't care about what assets we've accumulated. I've seen people who had far less than us, and they seemed much happier."

"Horse feathers," my father grunted. "If those people had the slightest opportunity to increase their standard of living to where they could afford a nice house, they would not only be happy, but would also have a sense of security."

"I don't know," I replied, wondering if what he said was true. I guess it depended upon the individual. Money and ranking high in the social network of the ritzy class would change a lot of people. I think it would take a special person who was true to himself, not to sacrifice who he was for the glory of being the envy of his peers.

"You're only eighteen, Ameerah," my father said and sighed, suddenly looking older than he was. "I'm making allowances for your youth. Your mother and I don't want you to be subjected to a lower standard of living. We want you to get married to a successful gentleman who can provide a comfortable life for you and your children. I realize you can go to college and become a teacher or a nurse, but if a woman has the opportunity to take care of a man's castle and the man, she should do so. Not to mention, if they had children. To become a wife and a mother and do it well, is the most admirable job a woman can do in this life."

I disagreed, but I kept my trap shut. His prehistoric thinking was beyond conversion. Women were much more than housemaids and bottle feeders. He couldn't figure that out and probably never would. I dug my nails into my palms, making half-moon impressions.

"Your father and I have something else we would like to bring to the table," my mother said, giving my father a look as if to silently ask for his approval. He nodded, and she went on. "Since you're out of school now, we thought this would be a great opportunity for you and me to try something new."

I narrowed my eyes. "What?"

She shifted in her seat and folded her hands on the lace tablecloth. "Your father has several business meetings lined up this summer in Chicago, San Francisco, and Reno. I would like to accompany him."

My thoughts raced. The first one was, what about me? I bet they never even considered taking me along with them. I could feel my throat tightening as I questioned why they wouldn't want me around, that maybe they didn't love me. But then a second thought quickly followed. I would have the whole house to myself. I could come and go as I pleased. I would have my autonomy. I bit the tip of my finger to try to keep myself from smiling.

"You would keep house while we're gone," my father said, not missing a beat after my mother paused. "We don't want any funny business here while we're away, and who knows? We might be home sooner than expected. As you're already aware, sometimes my business meetings get cancelled or cut short. Therefore, I suggest you respect our wishes." He gave me an uncompromising look to emphasize his statement.

"Okay, but then what?" I asked, trying to appear bored when really I wanted to jump up and down from the excitement of being independent of them for the first time in my life.

My father took one last drag off his ciggy and snuffed it out in the copper ashtray next to his glass of water. He didn't answer right away. Instead he proceeded to cut his meat. While we ate in silence, I had the distinct feeling he already knew his answer, but he was teaching me patience. I was fine with it and allowed my mind to wander to all the things I could do while they were away. Basically, it would be the same things I'd been doing almost every weekend, minus the sneaking around. Although I could have Betty spend the night, and we'd have the freedom to do whatever the hell we wanted.

"After this summer," my father finally said, "if you have conducted your behavior in a suitable fashion in our absence, I will consider you adult enough to make important decisions for your future."

It's my future, and you have no fucking say in it, but what the hell, I'll play along.

"What about Abraham?" Mother asked, her hopeful eyes addressing me.

"He's nifty and all," I replied, "but he's Betty's older brother . . ."

"The boy has a bright future," my father said. "He's following his old man's footsteps in becoming a doctor."

"I know," I sighed, "but can we talk about it some other time?"

"Very well." My father nodded. "So do we have a deal about your behavior and this summer?"

Oh, boy! Do we ever.

I stretched my hand across the table. A small smile crossed my father's face. He placed his hand in mine. "Deal," I said, shaking it, making a list in my mind of all the fun things I planned to do while they were away. This summer was going to be the bee's knees.

But little did I know the summer of 1925 would be my best summer ever and my worst nightmare.

Chapter Three

June 1925

The visions started after my eighteenth birthday, which was in April. Actually, I'd been having them since the age of six, but they were few and far between. I thought nothing of them as one would who, on rare occasions, could guess the person behind the knock on the door. But now, the visions were coming to me more frequently. I began paying attention to the flashing pictures in my optical mind and thought it would be a splendid idea to write the details in a journal. It was my way of keeping track of them and to see if they would come to fruition. The only downside to this gift—if you wanted to call it that—was every time a vision sprang forth, I received a horrible headache in its wake. Whomever bestowed this ability on me had a sick sense of humor. I could hear the bastard now: *Ameerah will have the good fortune of knowing the near future, but she will pay a price for my generosity. She will have an ache in her head afterward. It will be sharp between the eyes and painful.* Hell, I wouldn't be surprised if there was a devious laugh attached to that statement.

Asshole.

Of course, I could be completely out in left field and no godly being had anything to do with it. I didn't even believe in a god or an afterlife. But considering the circumstances, it certainly felt like I was being fucked with. Even Betty, who was the only one who knew about the visions, thought the same way.

"Ameerah," she said while I rubbed the spot between my eyebrows and groaned. "Whoever did this to you is one sick son-of-a-bitch."

I laughed, though nothing was funny. "I agree." I opened my eyes when most of the pain lifted. Betty was standing in front of my bureau, her deep blue eyes flashed with anger, then concern. Like me, she was wearing a conservative drop waist dress, the hemline touching more than a couple inches below her knees. The light yellow with the fabric white belt complimented her golden locks. It was too warm to wear a cloche hat, so she wore her bob style haircut in finger waves. "But maybe nobody did this to me."

"Baloney," she said. "You know as well as I there are other forces at play."

I took my leather-bound journal out of my bedside table drawer. Not wanting to mess with a fountain pen, I decided to use a pencil instead. I wanted to jot down the vision before it escaped me. It was nothing to be alarmed about; it only involved my parents coming home early because of my father losing a deal that could have been quite lucrative for him. "I don't know what to believe," I mumbled.

Betty flopped beside me on the bed, causing me to bounce sideways. I steadied myself and became hyperaware of how being close to her made my heart race. I ignored the nervous, excited feeling she stirred in me, like I have for the past six months and proceeded to write in my journal.

"Well, we can change that, ya know?"

I continued to write, not wanting to lose my train of thought.

Betty leaned closer to me, silently reading what I wrote, her arm pressed against mine. I focused my attention on the task at hand instead of the strange sensation in my stomach, which was comparable to when I rode the Ferris wheel at Schenck Brothers Palisades Park in New Jersey. It was annoying to say the least, and I had no idea why she was making me feel this way. I had gone on a couple dates with her older brother Abraham during Christmas break and even kissed him a few times. He was a fun fella to be around, and like me, he loved to go to jazz clubs, but not once did my body react to him like it did to Betty.

Betty reached beneath her dress and pulled out a small silver flask from her garter. She unscrewed the cap and took a swig. "Your father is going to be a bear to be around," she said, smacking her lips and making a face. I put the journal away, and she handed me the hooch. "It's whiskey, but I watered it down some," she admitted.

I took a sip, remembering how Abraham taught me how to drink the giggle water: cup the liquid in the center of your tongue so it didn't touch the edges. Push it up to the roof of your mouth and swallow. The whiskey had a honey and caramel taste to it. As it slid down my throat, a warm burning sensation followed. I handed the flask back to her. "Where did you get this?"

She smiled. "Abe."

I gawked at her. "Your brother is a bootlegger now?" I knew Abe, as we called him, loved to have a good time, but he was a premed student, destined for great success. I never pictured him to go against the glossy image society viewed him as and to blend in with the shadows of law-breaking citizens such as myself.

Impressive.

Betty's smile grew into a grin. "He is, but don't tell him I told you. In fact, don't mention it. He's on the dean's list and doesn't want to ruin his perfect record in school."

"I won't say a word," I promised, still reeling from this bit of information.

"He's going to pick us up at eight and take us to a speakeasy on 53rd Avenue in Harlem," she said. "He knows the person who runs it."

We'd been to a speakeasy several times, but if this was the one I was thinking of, we were in for a treat. I'd heard the best hooch in town was served there. We were going to have one hell of a night.

I hopped off the bed and pulled Betty up with me. "It's two hours from now. We should get ready."

"I heard the big cheese who runs it is trying to emulate Al Capone," Betty said, placing her pink and silver suitcase on my bed. "Al is from Brooklyn, ya know, but lives in Chicago now."

I opened my armoire, where I kept all my dresses and picked my favorite one: an elaborate lace and embroidery swirl pattern in light shades of pearl and iridescent beads. There were layers of fringes throughout the material, ending an inch below the knee. "I've heard many sordid tales about him, but I also heard some good ones. Rumor has it he's generous when it comes to charity. But regardless, he's one fella you don't want to get on his bad side."

Betty nodded. "To be frank, I'm not one to meddle in the affairs of gangsters." She lifted a silver and light gray chiffon beaded dress. The beadwork was in a design of leaves and flowers. The bottom of the dress had thin hanging beaded panels of fabric. It was gorgeous.

"Where did you get your dress, Betty? It's beautiful," I gushed, draping my outfit over my arm and touching the material on hers. I loved the feel of the sheer silky fabric and imagined how it would feel against my skin.

Her gaze was locked on the V-neck collar, like she was too embarrassed to look at me. "I made it." The corner of her mouth lifted into a tiny smile.

I stared at her in stunned silence. I never knew she could sew like this, let alone create such a spectacular piece of work out of fabric and accessories. "You're fooling me?"

She slowly shook her head and peeked at me from out the corner of her eye. Her smile widened. "Nope. What you're looking at is my latest creation. Do you really like it?" She touched the dress with great fondness.

"Wow, Betty. Your dress is better than the clothes at Saks Fifth Avenue. Why didn't you tell me you like to sew things other than a button or mending a garment?" I think I was in shock, because I couldn't stop staring at her.

Her cheeks bloomed a pinkish red color. "I didn't want you to think I was turning into one of those women we always squawked about." She looked up and met my gaze. "I admire you, Ameerah," she said, suddenly appearing shy and vulnerable. "You're a strong and confident person. I . . . I think I'm . . ." Her eyes dropped to my lips, then to my face again. I wanted to comfort her but didn't dare. A torrent of emotions I didn't understand kept me on guard. "I don't want to disappoint you," she finally said, looking away, although I could tell there was something more she wanted to say.

"You're not." I pointed to her dress while tossing mine on the bed. "This is the cat's meow. It's brilliant."

"Really?"

"Oh, my God, Betty. You have talent. Talent I wish I had. Don't ever feel guilty about something you love to do and what makes you happy. In fact"—I turned her around by the shoulders so she was facing me, and I looked her straight in the eyes— "I think you should become your own fashion designer and start up your own clothing line."

"Like Coco Chanel," she said, beaming.

I grinned and nodded.

She squealed and threw her arms around me. "Ooooh, I love you, Ameerah."

I hugged her back, feeling both awkward and elated. She only loved me as a friend, nothing more, I told myself. I was startled at that revelation and released my arms, taking a couple small steps back, suddenly conscious of the crushing feeling I felt in my gut. Then, it hit me like a ton of bricks.

I was in love with her.

But how could this be?

I was supposed to have those feelings toward a man, not a woman. The way I felt for Betty was wrong on so many levels. It wasn't normal. *I* wasn't normal. Maybe because my parents lacked the ability to show me affection, I hungered for it. So maybe I wasn't a lesbian or in love with her. I was merely starved for affection, any affection. I perked up at the idea. Yes, it seemed reasonable.

There was a loud knock at the door. Betty and I looked at each other, smiled, and bolted out of my room. Laughing, we raced for the front door. I stumbled into her, and we were giggling as she opened it.

"What are you two dames doing?" Abe asked, raising his eyebrows in question.

"Betty was showing me the nifty dress she made," I said as we stepped out of the way so he could come in. He looked spiffy in his black suit and bowtie that offset his white shirt. His fedora, tilted on the side of his head, embodied his cool, ritzy demeanor.

His charming smile reached his cobalt eyes. "She showed me earlier. I daresay she is the talented one in the family."

"Stop," Betty said, playfully smacking him on the arm. "I may be handy with a thread and needle, but your wits far exceed mine."

"You need to apply yourself more," he answered. "Don't sell yourself short, little sis."

"Anyway," she said, ignoring his comment. "Why are you so early? We still need to get dolled up."

"I was bored." He shrugged. "Schmoozing with the likes of our kinfolk is not my idea of a good time."

"Mom and Dad had their pals over again?" Betty asked.

Both of our parents were good friends and associated with the same crowd of yawn- worthy people. I didn't blame Abe for skipping out. I would have done the same.

"Of course," Abe replied, not hiding his distaste for them. "Their snobbery clouds their vision of what is truly important in life."

"Explain," I said, wanting to hear his take on the matter.

"I don't blame them for wanting the finer things," he said as we moseyed to the living room. He sat on the high wingback chair while Betty and I parked ourselves on the couch. "I want the same thing, but I'm not willing to sacrifice who I am and become one of their cookie cutter figures in order to appease the ridiculous ideologies of small-minded people."

I impersonated a golf clap. "Well said. I'm impressed."

He reached inside his suit jacket and produced a silver thin case. It flipped open, exposing a row of cigarettes. He plucked one out and popped it in his mouth.

"Butt me." I made a gestured toward the ciggies.

"Me, too," Betty said, leaning forward, stretching her hand to him.

He gave us a devilish smile, handed us one, and lit it for us. A cloud of smoke rose above us as we enjoyed Mother Nature's gift of the tobacco plant. I could feel the chemicals running their course through my system, relaxing me. Normally, a man would frown upon a woman smoking, but Abe was different. He was for equality, a trait I found attractive. Too bad my body didn't react to him like my mind did.

"I'm famished," he announced when a short silence fell between us.

"There are cold cuts in the ice box. You can make yourself a sandwich if you like," I offered.

"There's also fried chicken," Betty added. "Ameerah and I made some earlier. You can heat it in the oven while we get ready."

"You're welcome to anything you can scrounge up in my kitchen," I said, rising. "Betty and I shouldn't be long." I pulled Betty to her feet. "Make yourself at home. In fact, you're invited to stay the night if you like." My parents wouldn't mind, I told myself. They were practically rooting for Abe to court me. Besides, they'd been away for only two weeks. I was almost certain they were having too much fun to come home this early.

"Thanks for the generous offer." He smiled and winked. "Food comes first, and we'll see what the rest of the night will bring."

"Ameerah," Betty whispered as we headed back to my room. She slipped her arm around mine and leaned her head on my shoulder. "I think you should tell Abe about your visions."

Where did that come from? "Why would you suggest such a thing?"

"He's smart and might know why you're getting them."

"I think he has too much on his plate to deal with my bizarre problem," I said, closing my bedroom door behind us.

"He knows a lot of people." She sat on my bed and proceeded to take her shoes off. "I think he can help."

"I'll consider it," I answered, shifting my attention to my dress lying in a half moon position next to her. I picked it up, suddenly feeling uncomfortable. Her presence filled the room, coating me like an extra layer of skin. I knew she meant well, but I wasn't sure if it was a good idea or not. Refusing to look at her, I went to my bureau where I kept my undergarments. The thin elastic girdle I chose would flatten my breast and stomach, though my midriff was already tight, flapper gals like myself preferred our bosoms to appear nonexistent under our outfits. "Actually," I went on, taking what I needed and stepping behind the ornate wooden dressing screen to give us both some privacy, "now that I think about it, I don't believe it would be a good idea."

"I was afraid you'd say that," Betty replied. I could hear the frown in her voice. "But really, Ameerah, you can trust Abe."

"Maybe so, but I want to keep it between us, okay?"

"Sure. My lips are sealed," she promised.

She must have been already applying her makeup, because her voice carried from across the room where my vanity was. I sat on the small red settee to slip my beige stockings on, trying not to get a snag.

She gasped, making me pause. "I have a marvelous idea."

"What?" I hoped she wasn't going to suggest we ask Abe about what he'd do if he were having visions of the near future, just to see what he'd say. It would be way too obvious.

"How about seeing a medium?" Her excitement was palpable in the bubbly tone of her voice.

"Houdini thinks they're frauds," I said. "He's done shows debunking them and even offered to pay ten thousand dollars to anyone who could prove their supernatural abilities that he couldn't mirror." I slipped my dress on and adjusted it.

"Yeah, yeah, everybody knows about Houdini, but what about Edgar Cayce?"

I'd read about Edgar Cayce and his clairvoyant abilities in the newspapers. He was a popular figure who would go into a trance and help cure illnesses. He once said he could see auras around people, could hear voices of departed loved ones, and could speak to angels. I didn't know how I felt about those things, but apparently he was phenomenal in aiding those in poor health.

I smoothed out my dress and did a little shimmy, causing the fringes to swing back and forth. "Edgar Cayce," I replied, stepping around the dressing screen, "helps heal . . ." I stopped short when Betty turned away from the mirror to look at me, a tube of red lipstick in her raised hand. Her lips were painted in it, which accentuated her pout and went well with her golden locks. Kohl liner made her dark blue eyes appear seductive. I noticed they were slowly drinking in my body as I was doing the same to her. She looked breathtaking in her silver and gray beaded dress. The leaves and flower design shimmered in the light when she made the slightest of movements. I met her gaze. Something sparked in her eyes. Hunger? She bit her bottom lip. A shock of heat flowed through me. My train of thought was lost. She was staring at my mouth, I noticed. Her chest was rising faster than normal. My heart was pounding. Oh, God, I think I wanted to kiss her. No, this was wrong. I blinked and quickly gathered myself. "You look ravishing," I breathed. There, I broke whatever spell I was under.

She sent me a coy smile. "So do you."

I laughed, waving it off. "I haven't even dolled up my face yet."

"You're beautiful, Ameerah," she said. "With or without makeup."

"I'm glad you think so." I moved close to her so I could freshen my face. Reluctantly, she stepped aside. Something between us was shifting; I could feel it. Maybe it began months ago in a subtle way. I had gone out with Abe a few times. We even kissed and did some heavy petting. I thought about Betty's behavior back then. She had become quiet and reserved around me. I remembered it clearly now. She didn't want to talk about her brother but would ask me how I felt about him. When I'd told her he didn't curl my toes, she crawled back out of her shell and things went back to normal. At the time, I thought it had to do with the weirdness of me dating her brother, but now I wondered if it was something more. I severed those thoughts and filled the silence that fell between us. "Anyway, back to Mr. Cayce. I'm not ill unless—"

"I didn't mean something is wrong with you," she quickly said. "I was only making a point."

"Which was?"

"Not all psychics are charlatans."

"Well, if you think it might help me, I'm onboard."

What the hell. What's the worst that can happen?

"I do," she said, delighted, hugging me from behind and kissing my cheek, confusing me even more with the way my body reacted to her.

There was a loud knock at the door. "Are you dames almost ready?" Abe's voice rang out.

Betty released her arms, and I turned, facing her. She was smiling. "Let's go." She grabbed our beaded purses off the bed and handed me mine. I followed her out of the room, determined to shelf the feelings she aroused in me and to have a grand time.

Chapter Four

The Charleston

"You should let me drive the Tin Lizzie," I said to Abe when he pulled into a lighted parking lot behind a row of brick buildings.

"Show some respect, Ameerah," Abe said, clearly joking by his lighthearted tone. "What you're sitting in is the *new* Model T Tudor Sedan."

Betty leaned over my lap so Abe could see her. "You're such a bigshot." She made a face and stuck her tongue out, making us both laugh.

He pretended to brush dirt off his shoulder. "I'm going to be a doctor and have to live up to a certain standard."

"What a bunch of hooey," Betty replied.

"You're full of shit," I said.

His eyes widened, and his mouth dropped, feigning disbelief. "Ameerah! How can a poor little bunny such as yourself spew filthy words from those luscious lips?"

"Easy, I don't take any guff from wannabe bigshots. You keep it up. There's a lot more where that came from, baby." I winked at him and grinned.

"Neither do I," Betty piped in between giggles. "We'll tell you to scram if you ever start acting like an elitist pompous ass."

I nodded in agreement. "Like our parents and their so-called-friends"—I did air quotes—"which by the way, I think would double-cross them if a better opportunity came around."

"Absolutely." Betty nodded. "But so would our parents . . . well, maybe not my mom. There is hope for her, I think."

I looked at Betty. Like me, she wore an embroidered headband with a white feather sticking up on the side. She opted for a chain necklace that hung past her breasts, whereas I wore a long string of pearls. There was a happy glint in her ocean blues, which made me smile. She was right; her mom was more down to earth than the rest of them. I imagined she had to play the part of an obedient wife to keep the peace in the household. Personally, I wouldn't tolerate being in a position where I had to sacrifice what I stood for or who I was to appease another or the masses. I hoped Betty had the good sense not to fall into the same pattern as her mother.

"I would never double-cross you two," Abe said, frowning. "I'm not like them."

"I know you wouldn't," I reassured him, and for a split second I almost told him about my visions but bit my tongue instead.

"I have to put the persona on, to fool those who expect me to act accordingly," he explained. "In all honesty, I detest narrow-minded false people who would sell their souls for a prestigious life, instead of earning it by being true to themselves."

"We know, Abe," Betty said in a hurried, let's-get-on-with it tone. "I want you to tell us where we're at."

He pointed to the lit exposed blue bulb above a door on the back of the building. "We're going to Sam's Pharmacy, where a speakeasy is hidden beneath the building. The owner is known as Slim."

"And you're acquainted with him how?" I asked, raising my eyebrows with a silly, mocking expression.

Abe tapped his thumb on the steering wheel, a small smile tugging at his lips. "Let's just say, I have . . . connections when it comes to transporting the finest liquor in the state of New York."

"Wow. My noble brother is a bootlegger in disguise," Betty said, pretending to be shocked.

Abe opened his door, the smell of gasoline and garbage from a nearby trash bin, wafted in, causing me to wrinkle my nose. "I like to think of myself as an enforcer against the stupidity of the establishment." He shot us a devious grin and stepped out.

"This is exciting," Betty gushed as we followed behind him.

Abe rapped his knuckles in short, uneven patterns against a brown wooden door. There was a small black square in the center. I heard a click, and then two eyes peered out.

"Panther sweat," Abe said.

The door swung open, giving us access. I had no idea what to expect. I'd been to many clubs before, and even a few speakeasies in Harlem near Jungle Alley, but none of them were as mysterious as this one. I quickly realized they were less elegant lap joints as police were known to call them, compared to where we were going, and this was the blind pig I'd thought about earlier that served the best hooch in town.

A burst of excitement sent my pulse racing when my mind conjured thoughts of what sort of illicit behavior we'd be engaging in besides drinking. I glanced at the gentleman who granted us access. He was a tall, lanky fella who appeared to be a clerk in his plain black trousers and gray button-up shirt. His outfit and stoic demeanor was a nifty masquerade to the hidden treasures within this establishment.

We followed him down a long, narrow hallway lined with shelves stacked with boxes of medical supplies. At the end on the right was a whitewashed door that one would presume was a broom closet. We halted behind him. After he opened the door and pulled the string to the overhead light bulb, we moved closer, crowding at the threshold. The tiny room housed cleaning products: a mop bucket, broom, and dustpan, which all were on the concrete floor in no certain order. Betty and I watched in fascination as he slid the back wall to the side, revealing a dimly lit corridor. He stepped aside and ushered us forward.

Abe slipped a bill in the fella's hand, who gave him a slight nod in return. After we entered the cellar-type room, the door closed behind us.

"How much dough did you give him?" Betty wanted to know. I could see a door a couple yards ahead. The rocky walls and enclosed area we were in felt medieval to me. The musky, mildew smell added to the sudden impression of a dungeon that was in my mind. "I didn't know you're supposed to tip him," she added as an afterthought.

"None of your beeswax," he answered. "And to answer your second question, you always tip the doorman. It's called etiquette, Betty." He paused in front of a worn oak door and turned, facing us and catching Betty sticking her tongue out at him. I smiled at Betty's childish, silly gesture. "Your infantile behavior is unbecoming," Abe told her, trying to keep a straight face but then laughed and planted a quick kiss on her cheek. "I have some business to attend to, so be good while I make my rounds."

"Yeah, yeah." Betty crossed her arms and playfully rolled her eyes. "Whatever you say."

Abe opened the door, and we were at once engulfed in a cacophony of high-spirited jazz music and laughter. We descended the stairs through the haze of smoke. Uproar of conversations from all directions reached my ears in excited confusion. There were couples dancing on the polished oak dance floor near the elevated platform where the band performed in the back. The African heritage musicians were wearing brown suits and bowler hats, enthusiastically playing their horns, trumpets, clarinets, trombones, and one at a piano.

"Abe!" someone shouted when we were halfway down the steps.

"Who's calling you?" Betty asked, looking about.

In the corner of the room were tables roughly pushed together and fellas seated around them, gambling. No one seemed to be paying attention to us. They appeared to be having too much fun to take notice of our arrival or anyone else in the room for that matter.

"Abe!"

A fella wearing a white Panama straw hat and dressed in a nifty tight-waisted black jacket and matching skinny trousers, waved and smiled when we made eye contact with him. Abe raised his hand to acknowledge him.

"Is he the big cheese you're going to talk to?" Betty asked when we stopped at the foot of the stairs and waited.

"Yes, he's one of them," Abe answered out the side of his mouth, then smiled and offered his hand to the fella who happened to approach us at that exact moment.

"I didn't know you were going to bring a couple dolls with you." He slapped his hand in Abe's while giving Betty and me an appreciative once over. His honey-colored eyes twinkled with a contagious nature of loving to have a good time, and I had the sudden feeling that those in his company couldn't help but be infected by his charms and fun-loving demeanor. He was the type of fella you instantly liked.

"Frank, this is my baby sister, Betty." Abe indicated to Betty with a nod. "The lovely lady next to her is Ameerah. She's a longtime family friend."

"Hello, sweethearts." He winked at us and shot a quick glance at the crowded bar tucked inside a large arched alcove where several bartenders were mixing cocktails. "Why don't you two go order yourselves a southside while I take this old boy off your hands for a while."

I'd heard of that drink before. It was gin, lemon, mint, and a simple syrup. Rumor had it, that was Al Capone's favorite cocktail, and he would order the beverage whenever he was in town from Chicago. I'd never had the giggle water before, but I was willing to try something new.

"I'll catch up with you later," Abe told us when Betty and I stepped away from them.

"Tell the bartender Highball sent you," Frank said. "Drinks are on me."

Betty turned and flashed Frank a dazzling smile. "Thank you!" she exclaimed, her voice pitched in excitement and gratitude.

I blew him a kiss and linked arms with Betty. We maneuvered our way through the sea of mixed cultures and scantily-clad women in their beaded dresses with shimmering, plunging necklines that left little to the imagination. I couldn't help but revel in our surroundings and the joyful energy animated by each small group we passed.

"Highball suggested we have a southside," I told the bartender when we reached the bar. I had to admit, he was an adorable fella in his tweed newsboy cap and matching brown vest and bowtie. He was in the middle of mixing a cocktail, and I noticed his biceps that strained against the rolled-up sleeves of his white shirt. I also took note of how unresponsive parts of my body were toward him, whereas when I looked at Betty or some of the other gorgeous women in our presence, desire tightened my stomach. I pushed my dysfunctional hormones aside and focused on having fun instead.

"Good choice," he said with a friendly smile, finishing what he was doing. He then turned to grab some alcohol and ingredients in a tall glass case behind him.

"Frank . . . I mean Highball is paying for our drinks," Betty told him.

I took a couple ciggies out of my purse and handed one to Betty. She gladly accepted it. "Let's see if we can find a table when we get our drinks," I told her. I tried to look through the space between people, but then someone would step in my way. I stood on my tiptoes to try to get a better view, but being five six and in low heels, I couldn't see over the hats and bobbing heads.

"I think I want to order a bee's knees after we finish this one," Betty said, rolling the ciggy between her thumb and index finger. "Unless I fancy the southside better."

Bee's knees was Betty's favorite cocktail. It was bathtub gin, honey, lemon, and orange juice. I was quite fond of it myself, but I had my own top choice that I planned on ordering after this one.

The bartender set our cocktails in front of us. "Enjoy."

"I'm sure we will," Betty replied, taking hers and handing me mine. She sipped it, and I think she made a pleased sound, but I wasn't sure because the music and chattering patrons drowned out whatever noise issued from her. But by the delightful expression on her face, I gathered she approved of this newfound alcoholic beverage we could now add to our collection of home runners.

I raised the glass to my lips, immediately smelling the wonderful minty aroma. Once the liquid reached my mouth, I kept it on my tongue for a few seconds and then swallowed. The citrus in the gin gave it a light and refreshing taste. Not bad. I could see why Al Capone fancied it. "I can get use to this," I said to Betty, "especially on a warm summer day."

"Me, too." She jerked her head toward the other room and moved in that direction. I followed her, trying not to bump into anyone. "There's a table," she said over her shoulder. "The one Abe and Highball are sitting at."

"We might be intruding," I said, not wanting to interrupt their meeting.

"Then, they can conduct their bull session somewhere else." She flashed me a silly grin, and I couldn't help but laugh while wondering if Abe would regret bringing her along. I stopped short when we approached the table and heard part of their conversation that I was sure wasn't meant for our ears.

"He was making a lot of noise running a load, and the feds took it away," Abe was saying to Frank. His gaze swept to Betty. He cleared his throat and shifted in his seat. "We need a few more moments if you don't mind?"

Betty took the seat across from him. "I do mind. We're here to have fun. You can take your business somewhere else." She stuck the ciggy in her mouth. I sat beside her and mirrored her gestures. Frank lit our ciggies. After he blew out the match, he tossed it into the ashtray in the middle of the table, all the while staring at Betty. I coughed, which seemed to snap him out of his trance. At the same time, Betty released airy rings of smoke between us, seeming to be oblivious to her new admirer. "Thank you."

"My pleasure," he said and pointed to our cocktails. "Does the southside meet your approval?"

I nodded and at the same time Betty said, "It's lovely, but I have to admit, the bee's knees is still my drink of choice."

He turned his attention on me. "And what about you, Ameerah?"

I took a drag off my ciggy. "I'd order it again, but I favor the tuxedo #2 over anything else . . . at least for now." I raised my glass as if I were toasting him. "This is quite good, though. Have you tried it, Abe?"

Abe nodded. "Of course. In fact, I ordered one, and here it is now."

An attractive brunette wearing a cloche hat and a black dress with rows of fringes, held a glass in each hand. She handed one to Abe and the other to Frank.

"Thank you, Camille," Abe said.

"You're welcome, Mr. Hollingsworth. Is there anything else you or your party would like for me to get?"

"I'll take a bee's knees," Betty piped up before Abe could utter a response.

"I'll have a tuxedo #2," I said.

Camille nodded and shifted her attention on Frank, waiting for further instructions.

"Tell the bartender whatever Betty and Ameerah fancy tonight, to charge it to my account," Frank told her. His attention shifted to Betty who was grinning from ear to ear. It then occurred to me that his generosity wasn't pure. He had a self-serving agenda, which was to win Betty over. And although my assumptions could be wrong, his behavior and body language suggested he was carrying a torch for her, and it left a sour taste in my mouth.

"I appreciate your chivalrous gesture, Frank," I said, "but it's not necessary." I turned to Camille and dug into my purse. "How much are the cocktails?"

The corner of her mouth lifted into a tiny smile. "Fifty cents each."

"Ameerah," Betty said, the timbre of her voice mixed in shock and disbelief. "If Frank wants to be a gentleman and buy our beverages, by all means allow him to do so."

I handed a dollar to Camille. "This will cover our order."

"Ameerah," Betty said again, leaning her elbow on the table, turning to me. "Why are you doing this?" she mouthed.

There was no way I could answer her with our present company hanging on our every word. So instead, I gulped down my cocktail, handed the glass to Camille, and said, "I'm simply exercising my right to step out of the shadow of the Victorian mindset our parents are holding fast to and demonstrating my ability as a nonconformist woman to take care of myself."

To my surprise, Camille's professional demeanor cracked, and her face brightened. "Well said, Ameerah." Her eyes darted to Frank, then to me. "I'll have your cocktails in a jiffy."

"Take your time. Betty is still . . ." I glanced at Betty who was downing the rest of her drink. Frank and Abe were lighting their ciggies. Frank whispered something to Abe who shrugged in response to whatever he said.

Betty handed her glass to Camille. "You can have mine, too."

Camille looked at me, her features softening. "You can call me Cammy," she said and then turned and left.

I watched her disappear in the crowd toward the bar while I took another drag off my smoke. The black, silvery fringes on her dress glistened with each movement she made. "I hope I didn't insult you, Frank," I said, blowing smoke above the table. "I do appreciate your kind gesture, but if I have the means to provide for myself, I certainly am going to do so. Besides, this way there are no strings attached or a hidden price to pay."

Abe let out a lighthearted laugh and gestured toward me. "As you can see, our Ameerah is a strong-willed gal who has no problem speaking her mind."

"No offense taken," Frank said in an easy manner, waving it off. "I admire a gal who won't comprise her character to appease those who only view the world in black and white."

"Why, thank you," I said. "I'd like to add that I think it's nifty to be treated like a lady and the gentleman pays for the drinks and a nice meal, if he's the one who initiated the date that is. I'm also not opposed to someone buying me a cocktail. However, I'm not one to take advantage of such kindness." I wanted to say more, but I left it at that to spare Abe any further embarrassment. Betty and I had already caused him enough in front of his friend.

"Ameerah is the cat's meow," Betty said, bumping her shoulder with mine, making me blush. "She has a way of seeing things I don't."

"You're a creative designer." I pointed to her dress. "She made this."

Frank's eyebrows rose in surprise. "You did?"

I nodded. "Hell, she even designed it."

"And here you are not even crowing about it," he said to Betty, clearly flirting with her.

Betty's gaze dropped to the table. "Why should I?"

"Betty is too modest to flaunt her first masterpiece in front of the masses," Frank said.

"Ameerah knows how to do the Charleston better than anybody I've ever seen," Betty interjected in an attempt to get the attention off herself.

I cringed inside. Like Betty, I hated to be the center of attention. I was the type of person who liked to watch other people and keep in the shadows as best I could. Unless, of course, I was dancing in a group of other hoofers.

Camille appeared with our drinks and made a point to slip a piece of paper in my hand. Covertly, I placed that hand on my lap and pretended to look for something in my purse, sliding the note inside it.

"You sweethearts are full of surprises." Frank held his glass up, and all three of us raised ours. "But so am I. To a newfound and lucrative friendship."

I wasn't sure what he meant by what he said or what he had up his sleeve, but nevertheless, I clinked my glass against theirs and toasted to it.

Betty took a swig of her bee's knees. "What do you mean by lucrative?"

"Yeah, Frank, what do you have in mind?" Abe had a nervous look on his face. I gathered he was worried Frank would involve Betty in their underground bootlegging business.

Frank laughed and clapped a hand on Abe's shoulder. "There's no need to be concerned, old boy. What's between us"—he moved his finger back and forth—"stays that way." He looked up at a dark-haired fella passing our table and wearing a similar newsboy hat as the bartender. "Hey,

Johnny." The fella stopped and glanced at Frank, a lit ciggy dangling out the corner of his mouth. "Tell James to play 'The Charleston.'"

Johnny nodded and backtracked his steps to the band. I watched him break through the crowd and craned my neck to see him approach a black fella sitting at a piano. I had no doubt the pianist knew how to play stride piano. I'd been to Harlem plenty of times and have heard this jazz style of playing where it was highly rhythmic with a swinging beat. Most of the time, the musicians used their improvisational skills with a more modern style than succumbing to the old ragtime beats.

I took a sip of my cocktail, savoring the hint of orange bitters and gave Frank a questioning look, even though I had a feeling why he made this bold move. He wanted to see me dance, but why?

As if he could read my thoughts, he smiled. "Slim and I are toying with the idea of employing some gals for entertainment purposes. If you're as good as Betty says you are, I might have a job offer for you."

"Oh, she is," Betty said, nearly popping out of her seat with enthusiasm, upsetting her half empty drink. She grabbed a couple napkins stacked in the center of the table and sopped up the small pools of liquid splattered around her glass.

My heart skipped several beats. I absolutely adored dancing. If I could make a decent living as a hoofer, I'd be over the moon. "Betty is good as well," I said, not wanting her to be excluded from this opportunity. Besides, I loved when we danced together.

Betty grunted and shook her head. "I'm not nearly as good as you, Ameerah." She drained what was left of her cocktail and released a little hiccup. Covering her mouth, she giggled, her body jerking a couple times as more hiccups followed.

Abe indicated to the empty glass in front of her while sticking a ciggy in his mouth and lighting it. "I think you need to take it easy on that stuff."

"Butt me," she said. After Abe handed her a ciggy and lit it for her, she took a long drag, blew a thick tunnel of smoke toward him and said, "Mind your own beeswax."

Frank smiled, stuck a ciggy in the corner of his mouth, lit it, and with his eyes partly squinted said, "You two remind me of my older sister and me. She used to boss me around, and I in turn would tell her to beat it." He looked at Abe. "My suggestion to you is leave her be. If Betty gets tanked, I'm sure Ameerah will take care of her."

"Absolutely." I nodded, finishing off my own drink.

"Don't worry about me," Betty told us. "I'll be fine."

The jazz music stopped, and the people who were on the dance floor dispersed. I watched as some of them headed to tables where they struck up conversations with the occupants around them, while the others made a beeline for the bar. Then, an off-beat sound in a variety of syncopated patterns boomed from the piano.

Frank looked at me. "Let's see what you can do."

I scooted back my chair, stood, and placed my hand on Betty's arm. "C'mon."

Betty looked at me and shook her head. "I don't want to embarrass myself. You go ahead without me."

I wasn't about to let her off that easily. I took her hand in mine and nudged it toward me. "You're not going to make a fool out of yourself. We're here to have fun. You've danced with me plenty of times in public. Don't be a wet blanket."

"You have no reason to be nervous," Abe said to Betty. He jerked his head to the dance floor. "Go, and keep in mind if you allow your fear of other people's opinions to keep you from being who you are, you'll never be truly happy."

"Great advice," I said, smiling as a rush of excitement poured over me from the rhythmic music resounding around us. I could hardly stand still and found myself moving my body to the beats.

Abe shrugged. "I have my moments."

Betty rose from her seat, and as we were walking away, she shot back in a loud voice so Abe could hear her. "Yeah, this coming from a fella who is leading a double life."

We were the first to step onto the dance floor, and I was hyperaware of a hundred plus eyes on us but paid no mind to them. On the other hand, Betty gave me an apprehensive look. She had no reason to doubt herself, I thought, but I knew why she did. We were in a much classier juice joint than the ones we normally frequented, and her insecurities were getting the best of her. I sent her an encouraging smile, trying to relay in my expression that she'd do great. She bit her bottom lip, her dark blue eyes alert and brimming with life. She nodded. We began performing "The Charleston" like we had many times in the comforts of her bedroom when we would practice dance moves for hours on end. We kicked our heels outward, then bent and straightened our knees in time to the music, all the while throwing our arms and legs in the air with reckless abandon. Then, we squatted forward with our hands on our knees, waggling them in and out, crossing our hands in the middle. More gals joined us, and soon after, wolf whistles from the audience reached us.

I was having the time of my life, loving every second of it. In fact, I was smiling so much my face was hurting. Little did I know this glorious night would forever be seared into my memory for many reasons, and performing "The Charleston" was the first one.

Chapter Five

Deal of a Lifetime

Slim was the real McCoy—the genuine article. I felt it when Betty and I went back to our table after performing "The Charleston," and there sitting between Frank and Abe was a dark-haired fella wearing a black fedora with a four-inch contrasting band wrapped around its base. By no means was this fella slim like the doorman who had granted us access to this hidden gem. So at first I had no idea who this new occupant at our table was; however, by his spiffy black suit and the way he held his broad shoulders straight and the direct gestures he made with his hands while in conversation, his energy was one of confidence and authority.

There were cocktails waiting for us. I was too thirsty from dancing to give Frank grief over not respecting my wishes to pay for my own booze. Besides, I was making a point at the time that I felt was well received. He now knew I had boundaries, and I wasn't a dumb Dora. If he wanted to treat us the rest of the night, so be it.

Frank must have misread my curious expression regarding our new visitor, because he raised his hands up as if I pulled a gat on him. "Slim ordered the drinks. I took no part in it. I even warned him of your stark truthfulness and how much you prided yourself from breaking free of the constricting, out-of-date morals forced onto females."

"No need for apologies," I said, taking my seat and a sip of my drink.

"You're Slim?" Betty asked, staring wide-eyed at him.

He nodded, a pleasant smile crossing his face. "The name is misleading, I know, but I've had it since I was a young boy when I was scrawny and going through that awkward stage we all go through. Since then, the nickname has stuck with me, even through college."

Abe handed Betty and me each a ciggy and lit it for us. I thanked him and returned my attention to Slim. "If you don't mind me prying, what is your actual name?"

He extended his hand, and I shook it. "Clyde Kelly, but I prefer to be addressed as Slim."

"Ameerah Arrowood." His grip was firm and tight but not crushing. I met it with my own strength. "I will respect your wishes, of course."

"I appreciate it. Obviously, I haven't extended the same courtesy to you." He gestured to my beverage. "However, I knew you'd be parched after your magnificent performance, so I took the liberty of ordering you and Betty a cocktail."

"Thank you," Betty piped up. "It sure hits the spot." She then turned her attention to Frank. "I told you Ameerah is the cat's meow. I bet I looked like a fool compared to her." She laughed. It was an easygoing sound, silly and unpretentious. "I have to admit, dancing is not my forte." She shrugged and finished off her cocktail.

"You did great," I told her. "Don't sell yourself short."

"I have to agree with Ameerah," Frank said. "Never once did I see you stumble."

"Oh, believe me," Betty said, eyebrows raised, head slightly bobbing. "I fouled up some moves. I'm good at covering them . . . that's all." She looked around and half stood, trying to see over the sea of heads.

"Who are you searching for?" I picked up my glass when I saw her hand was dangerously close to it and could have easily knocked it over.

"Camille," she said. "I want another drink."

"Frank, would you be a gentleman and go get these dolls another one?" Slim asked.

Frank stood and shifted his gaze to Betty and me. "A bee's knees and a tuxedo #2, right?"

"Perfect," Betty answered at the same time I nodded. "Thank you."

"My pleasure." He flashed her a flirty smile and headed to the bar.

"I told Slim about you designing and creating the dress you have on," Abe said to Betty.

Slim's eyes darted to Betty. The golden brown color warmed with appreciation as they focused on Betty's outfit and then Betty. "It's quite striking, which brings me to a question I would like to ask you two sweethearts." He folded his large hands on the table and continued after Betty and I exchanged curious looks. "I would like to offer you both a job working here for me on Friday and Saturday nights. I'll pay you handsomely, and the drinks and food will be on the house, as long as it doesn't hamper your performance."

My heart raced and three words kept ringing inside my head: This is it! This is it! This is it! I knew what type of job he was offering me because of what Frank said earlier, but I had to be sure and wanted to know what Betty's part would be. "What type of gig are you suggesting?"

Betty took my hand beneath the table and squeezed it. She always did that when she was nervous. The last time was when we got our long hair wacked off and cut into the bob style we sported now. My palm was hot and sweaty against hers, but she didn't let go, and I caught her shooting a quick glance at me out the corner of her eye.

"Dancing," he answered. "I already hired five gals, and I have to level with you Ameerah,"—he leaned forward so he was closer to Betty and me—"you're the best hoofer out of them all, and I'd like for you to teach them what you know." He leaned back and withdrew a thin ivory case from his jacket and picked a ciggy out. He stuck it between his lips, lit it, and blew out a cloud of smoke. "I'll pay you fifteen dollars a night to start. As my business grows, so will your salary."

Abe's mouth dropped open, and a dumbfounded expression entered his face.

This time I squeezed Betty's hand and did the unthinkable.

I laughed.

Maybe it was the giggle water, but I found Abe's reaction pure funny papers. Or it could possibly be those two things along with the hilarious fact that I was being given an opportunity of a lifetime to do what I absolutely would love to do for a living. Betty looked at Abe when I pointed at him and joined in my laughter. I had no doubt that Betty and I appeared like a couple hysterical hyenas with our shoulders jumping up and down and our mouths wide open. I wrapped an arm around my stomach to subdue the sudden muscle cramp I was getting.

"What's so funny?" Frank asked, setting my cocktail in front of me. "What did I miss?"

Still snickering, I held a hand up and took a couple deep, slow breaths. "I'm sorry, Slim. I mean no disrespect." Betty had her hand over her mouth in attempt to stifle her giggles. I bumped her shoulder with mine. "And neither does Betty."

"Ameerah is right," Betty managed to say. She coughed a couple times and cleared her throat, doing everything in her power not to look at Abe. "I hope you don't think we were insulting you, because we weren't."

"There is no need for your apologies," Slim said, an easygoing smile crossing his face. "I wasn't offended in the least. Besides, the look on Abe's face was priceless."

Frank's eyes darted among the four of us, probably trying to gather whatever information he could to make sense out of what we were talking about. I decided to save him the trouble of repeating his earlier question. "Slim offered me a generous deal to dance here, and Abe's reaction to how much dough I'd be making was hilarious."

Abe looked at Frank. "It caught me by surprise 'cause I know fellas working in factories fifty hours a week make far less than what Ameerah will be making in two nights."

"This is the face Abe made." Betty mirrored Abe's expression perfectly, which created laughter around our table.

"You're full of baloney," Abe said, trying to be serious but failing miserably. "My eyes weren't bugged out like that."

Betty tapped the table a few times with the heel of her hand. "They were."

I offered my hand to Slim. "I accept the job."

He slapped his hand in mine. "I'm happy to have you onboard, but I'm not finish yet." He turned to Betty. "Would you be interested in being a substitute dancer, as well as designing and making the costumes?"

Betty was in the middle of taking a sip of her drink. She swallowed and slowly set her glass down. "Would I get to pick the patterns and material?"

"Of course. I trust your taste. You're clearly a gifted designer with a talent that shouldn't go to waste. Write a list of the materials you need and where to purchase them, and I will make sure you get them."

Betty took a swig of her drink and stuck her arm out in front of mine. "Pinch me."

I gave her a funny look. "What?"

She giggled. "Pinch me. I must be dreaming." I pinched her. She grinned and swung her attention back to Slim. "What are my wages going to be?" She hiccupped a couple times and pressed her lips together. It looked like she was holding her breath by the constipated expression on her face. I wondered if it was to get rid of the hiccups or because she was anticipating Slim's answer.

"If you're dancing," he said, "you'll receive fifteen dollars a night. If you're not, for each dress you make, you'll get five dollars. So on top of what I'll already be paying you, you'll also be paid for entertaining the customers on the nights you're needed."

Wow. Betty would be raking in the dough during some months when one of the girls couldn't make a performance. I wondered how she would pull this gig off without tipping her parents off. Regardless, I was sure she would find a way to make it work.

Betty abruptly stood and took Slim's hand in hers. Enthusiastically, she shook it. "You have yourself a new employee."

Chapter Six

Disturbing Vision

I was on my fourth cocktail, and my thoughts and hopes were reeling from Slim's offer to pay me fifteen dollars a show to dance at his club on Friday and Saturday nights. With that kind of dough, I could quickly save up, add it to the stash I already had from my allowance, and get the hell out of my parent's house.

As I took my last few drags off my ciggy and finished my drink, thoughts of grandeur excited me. I could be like Gilda Gray, famous for her shimmy dance and was picked up by a talent agent, then went on to do feature films. I envisioned appearing in the Ziegfeld Follies, a chain of elaborate theatrical productions here in New York City on Broadway. Working for Slim was just the beginning to a prosperous and glamorous life. The life I thought I'd never have. The life I was now bound and determined to live.

Slim laid out the details for us, and his plans to make his club one of the most popular speakeasies in New York City. The rest of the gals and I would get together here on Tuesdays, Wednesdays, and Thursdays, to practice our routines. The band would already know which songs to play. We would start out small—two dance performances a night, but eventually there would be four, and he talked about getting comedian Moms Mabley as another side act. She was already performing at The Cotton Club, but he had high hopes and an ambitious vision of the future of his club, and he was confident she would perform here. When he rattled off the names of the gals who would be under me and mentioned Camille, I suddenly remembered her note still tucked away in my purse.

"Excuse me, gentlemen, but this flapper gal needs to use the john," I said after agreeing to meet my coworkers later tonight and doing our first show a week from today. Normally, I'd tell him we'd need more time, but since we were starting out small, I felt like we'd be ready by then. Betty, on the other hand, would require more time. Thankfully, Slim realized that and said we'd get by with our own dresses for the time being. "Can you please tell me where it is?"

"I'll join you," Betty said.

Frank pointed toward the back to a half wall past the stage and band. "It's down a short hallway. You can't miss it."

"Take your time," Abe said as we were leaving. "We have our own business we need to discuss."

Betty wrapped her arm around mine and hugged it while releasing a little squeal of excitement. "Can you believe our good fortune? I almost can't."

I shook my head and laughed.

When we entered the restroom with its black and white tiles in a checkered patterned, I stuck my arm out. "Pinch me." I couldn't help but imitate her earlier response.

In a quick motion, she squeezed my flesh. "Nope, it's certainly not a dream."

"This whole night is so surreal," I said while we went into separate stalls and did our business. Betty didn't respond, so I continued, "I never thought in a million years such an opportunity would come my way. I had no doubt that you would get yours because of how gifted you are at designing clothes, but me . . . no, not a chance in hell." I flushed and went to wash my hands. In silence, Betty stepped beside me, a morose expression clouding her face. "What's eating you?"

"What are we going to tell our parents?" Whatever buzz she had a few moments ago was gone, along with her silly giddiness that was stolen from her by a frown now planted on her pretty face. "I've never told you this before, but my dad won't pipe down about me dating one of Abe's classmates. He thinks I should get married, have kids, and be a dutiful wife, but I don't want that. As Clara Bow says, 'Marriage ain't no women's job no more.'" Both Betty and I loved Clara Bow. She was a famous Hollywood movie actress and flapper. Like us, she was from New York, which made her even more appealing to us.

"What do you want?" I asked, even though I knew. I thought if she said it out loud, it would fuel her determination to live the life she craved.

"I want to be like Coco Chanel and have my own clothing designs. I want to be an independent woman, own my own automobile and house, and travel around Europe." She took her lipstick out of her purse and touched-up her lips. "My mom is aware of my desire to accomplish those things, but she won't dare challenge my father and his way of thinking."

"I have the same problem, only my mother agrees with my father. In fact, she wants me to date Abe, which I won't because I don't have romantic feelings for him."

"So what are we going to do?" She turned away from the mirror above the ceramic basin, and her gaze dropped to the folded piece of paper in my hand. "Who is that from?"

"Cammy slipped it to me earlier. I forgot all about it until Slim mentioned her name."

"She doesn't even *know* you." There was a note of jealousy in her voice, but I ignored it, because she had no reason to feel that way. "What does it say?"

"She's inviting us to go to Jungle Alley with her later tonight." I handed the letter to Betty. "I wonder when her shift will be over. I can use a bite to eat. What about you?" Earlier I saw a waitress bringing out stuffed mushrooms and finger sandwiches. I decided at that moment to order something to eat and another cocktail while we waited for Cammy.

Betty shrugged and handed the letter back to me. "Why not? We've only been to a few clubs there. We can check out some new ones."

"Are you hungry?" I asked again, checking my makeup in the mirror.

"I'm starving."

"Let's go find Cammy, order some food and drinks and ask when she's off for the night."

Cammy walked in with four other girls trailing behind her. They were chatting about a clam house or something. All of them were dressed similar to Betty and me. They even had their hair bobbed; however, they styled theirs differently than ours. "Good you're here," she said. "Slim told me you had to use the john. Did you read my note?"

I nodded. "We were heading out to look for you to see when you're done here for the night."

"Slim gave me the rest of the night off." She shimmied her hips, surprising me with how uninhibited she was compared to her reserved behavior when she was serving our drinks. "He wants us all to get acquainted since we'll be working and performing together. Eleanor here"—she pointed to a gal a couple inches taller than me with black hair shorter than ours and styled with a curl next to each ear—"can drive us wherever we want to go."

After Cammy made some quick introductions, and Betty told Abe we had a ride home, all seven of us gals piled into Eleanor's black convertible. It was the berries. I loved her automobile, which she told me was a Lancia Lambda. I'd seen those before but never had ridden in one. I liked it much better than Abe's Tin Lizzie. My father had a couple nifty automobiles, but this one spoke to me of freedom and a new exciting way of life.

Jungle Alley was on 133rd street between Lenox and 7th avenue in central Harlem. The whole block was lined with businesses geared toward entertainment and good food. Ruby, who was the shortest and chattiest one in our group, suggested we go to The Cotton Club since Betty and I had never been there before, and it would give us more of an idea of what Slim had in mind for the future of his joint. It didn't take much persuasion to sell us on the idea. In truth, we had already made plans to hit this hot spot in the near future. Besides, we didn't need a password to get in, and it was never raided, probably because all the right palms had been greased. I'd heard rumors The Cotton Club was owned by a gangster who catered to the Mafia and politicians. I'd mentioned it on the way there, and Hazel, who sat in the front with Eleanor, turned in her seat and fixed her big green eyes on me. "It's true," she said, plucking a ciggy from between Delores' fingers. She took a drag and gave it back to her.

"How do you know?" Betty asked.

Delores swiped a piece of her brown hair off her cheek. The warm breeze from having the top down had my own hair tickling on the side of my face. I mimicked her gesture while watching a smile spread across her face. "She's a moll."

"You're a gangster's girlfriend?" Betty blurted.

Hazel laughed, apparently enjoying Betty's reaction and proceeded to tell us all about it and how he showered her with gifts and the finest hooch around. He was away on business for a few days, she told us when Cammy asked her where he was tonight. Hazel boasted that before he bade her a farewell, he handed her a wad of dough, which she proudly informed us she would use to pay for our meals and drinks at The Cotton Club, since the items on the menu were pricey. I had the urge to pipe up that it wouldn't be necessary, but bit my tongue instead. I quickly got the impression she was the type of gal who got a charge out of impressing others with her shocking tales, and she craved attention. I wondered if we'd have a problem working together because people with those qualities vexed me. It reminded me of my parents and their friends who always tried to outclass the other or stay neck-and-neck in the derby race of fine living. But I pushed those feelings aside, determined not to allow it ruin the opportunity I was given. I politely nodded and played along, pretending to be in awe of her involvement with a gangster and the benefits that went along with it.

We pulled up to The Cotton Club's marquee, and I saw a doorman in a black top hat greeting the customers. When we approached the entrance, he ushered us in and another fella directed us to a large horseshoe-shaped room with jungle décor, right down to the artificial palm trees placed smartly around the room. I was taken aback at how lavish this club was and kept looking at the elegant murals of southern plantation motifs lining the walls. The tables, situated on two tiers ringed by banquettes, were crowded together and dressed in white linen. We were lucky to claim one, and shortly after we sat, a handsome waiter in a red tuxedo took my order: a chicken salad and cocktail. The other gals followed my lead. We ate, drank, smoked, and told stories while listening to the house band playing on the veranda. A couple steps down was the dance floor where people were stepping in time to the music. I imagined that was where they did their floorshows as well.

"What time is it?" Delores asked a waiter walking past. I recognized him as the one who served our liquor in tea cups earlier.

"Half past ten," he answered, balancing a tray of food on the palm of his hand.

Ruby was about to take a bite of her Chinese chop suey when she frowned. "The floorshows don't kick off until midnight. I should have thought about that earlier. We could have gone to Sugar Daddy's first."

Betty and I had been there before. You had to enter through a narrow underground passage at the bottom of some steep steps into a cellar. It was a subterranean haunt in Harlem's low-down district that consisted of mostly Africans, but they had no problem with us joining them, and we made a few friends that night.

As the gals discussed what we should do, the room suddenly shifted out of place, and a vision of me being chained to a metal bed bolted to the floor engulfed me. I dropped my head into my hands and moaned when a piercing headache followed.

"Ameerah." Betty placed a hand on my arm. "Are you okay?"

"What's wrong?" Cammy asked. She was on the other side of me and shifted in her seat. Leaning in, she touched my forehead. "You don't feel hot. Are you going to be sick?"

My body shook as a chill crested inside my bones. I had plenty of visions before but nothing like this one. It was quick but vivid and felt so real. I told myself it wasn't, and I'd never be in a situation such as that.

I couldn't fathom how I would be, and besides, who would do such a thing?

"Here, give her this," I heard Eleanor say.

Betty gently removed my hand from my face and handed me a cold glass of water. "Drink this."

"Why are you shaking?" Ruby asked, sounding annoyed. "If you're sick, we should take you home. I don't want you to *infect* us all."

"She's not sick," Betty snapped. "She gets bad headaches sometimes."

I took a deep drink of the water, feeling the cool liquid slide down my throat. I set the glass on the table and rubbed my throbbing temples. "I think I'm going to call it a night." I rose from the table. "I'll get a taxi cab."

"So am I." Betty took one last swig of her drink and stood.

Eleanor was kind enough to offer to take me home, but I politely refused and apologized for being a wet blanket. We made arrangements to meet on Tuesday afternoon at Slim's to practice our routines and so Betty could get their measurements for the dresses she'd be making.

As we were leaving, I heard Ruby say to the others that if I got a headache during our performance I'd not only make a fool out of myself but them, as well. It struck a nerve, and my tolerance level for her was quickly waning. Before I could turn to confront Ruby, Betty grabbed my arm and told me it wasn't worth it. I gritted my teeth and balled my hands into fists, digging my nails into my palms. She was right, but I wanted nothing more at that moment than to storm back to our table and wring Ruby's scrawny little neck.

Chapter Seven

I Kissed a Girl and I liked It

I finally told Betty when we got home about my vision and how it made me feel. She was as dumbfounded as me as to why I'd have such a disturbing startling revelation. We both tried to come up with reasons.

"I know why," she said after we hashed out several off-the-wall ideas. She picked Mary Shelley's book, *Frankenstein*, off my nightstand and tossed it on the bed, puzzling me. "This would give anyone nightmares."

"Have you read it?"

"No, but I've heard about it, and from what I know of the story, I'm guessing that's the reason you had the vision. Your mind is probably pulling up images from what you've read and using it metaphorically to get a message across to you."

"Makes sense," I mused. "I wonder . . ."

Betty was getting some of her things out of her suitcase and paused with a hairbrush in her hand. It was a round, silver-plated one with fancy swirly designs on it. "You wonder what?"

"If the chains mean I'm bound to my parents, and the bed bolted to the floor is a symbol of me still living under their roof."

"It's a good possibility and seems like the most logical explanation." With her arms full of supplies and her nightgown, she headed to take a bath.

I took a deep, calming breath, feeling the muscles in my body relaxing.

There was nothing to be concerned about, I told myself. We solved the riddle, and now I'd write it in my journal for future analysis, along with tonight's events. I propped my pillow against the headboard of my bed, got into a comfortable sitting position, and wrote.

After Betty finished her bath, I took mine, and when I entered my room, wearing a peach silk and ruffled nighty, she looked up at me from the chair in the corner of my room and slowly rose. Her powder blue, sheer nightgown accentuated her curves in all the right places. I couldn't help but notice her hard nipples straining against the material. I diverted my attention, trying not to gawk, surprised she wasn't wearing a robe like she normally would.

"I read your journal," she confessed. There was no apology in her eyes. "Did you mean what you wrote about me?"

My mind raced with all the things I'd written, and then my heart sank. Oh, God, I mentioned how I felt about her and how she made my body react. I stared at my bare feet, searching for a way out of this awkward predicament. I could find no words and wanted to crawl inside a hole.

"There's nothing wrong with it," she said, gently lifting my chin. "I feel the same."

"You do?"

The next thing I knew, her lips were on mine, soft and eager. A rush of heat flowed through parts of my body in poetic sequence with the fluttering sensation in my stomach. When I parted my lips and our tongues intertwined, our kiss deepened. Gently, my hand skimmed her inner thigh beneath her gown. Her skin was smooth like silk. When the tip of my fingers pressed in easy circular motions against the damp, delicate lace material between her thighs, a soft gasp escaped her lips, followed by a low, guttural moan. The sound of her pleasure almost threw me over the edge. My breaths became quick and uneven. I never knew such a sexy noise could arouse me so, and the heat and wetness between my own legs was throbbing. Tenderly, I separated her slick folds and plunged my fingers inside. She broke our kiss and threw her head back, releasing a loud, drawn-out moan. Backing her against the wall, I kissed her neck and collarbone while she moved her hips back and forth against my fingers so they were penetrating her deeper. Still moaning, she kissed me with such intense abandonment, huffing in my mouth, that I was shaking. I think I groaned. I wasn't sure. I was in the moment, savoring the luscious feelings she awakened within me. We undressed each other and ended up on my bed with Betty straddling me. She ground her sex hard against mine while she sucked on my nipples. The sounds of panting and whimpering filled the silence. The extreme friction of our rubbing clits took me to greater heights than fingers could ever do, and we both cried out as we exploded into ecstasy.

Tonight was the first night I'd ever kissed or made love to another female. The pleasure and feelings were beyond anything I could have ever imagined. I'd had sex with fellas before, and although I enjoyed it, nothing compared to this. As I lay in Betty's arms, our legs tangled together, I finally admitted to myself that I, Ameerah Arrowood, was a lesbian and in love with my best friend.

* * *

Betty and I were inseparable, hiding our love affair from our new friends and family. My mother called to let me know they were in Chicago and of course to make sure I was being their shining star daughter. I assured her I was behaving, spending my days with Betty, lounging around the house, learning how to cook better—my culinary skills weren't the greatest—knowing my father would approve of that information. I continued satisfying Mom's curiosity by informing her we'd been staying home at night, playing cards, and gossiping about the cute fella working at our local supermarket. Mother's guarded mood toward me shifted into a delighted one, so I pulled the wool further over her eyes and laid it on thick when she asked me what he looked like and if I knew if he was going to college or had a girlfriend. I played along, creating a fictional character who was nifty and would suit her standards.

The days bled into each other. Never in my life had I felt such joy and love. Betty and I met the gals at Slim's during the week. We practiced our dance routines in the afternoons, and sometimes at night, we'd all go to Jungle Alley and party. Ruby was still being her pain-in-the- ass self, but I was too happy to allow her jealousy to ruin my mood. Eventually, Betty and I would find our way back to my house, and we would spend hours necking and petting in a half- drunken state.

Our first show was a huge success. I was in my element, and word quickly spread about our dancing performances. Our next one was even better, and the glamorous, flashy dresses Betty created for us were the cat's meow. The ladies in the audience displayed a deep interest in Betty's unique designs. They wanted to know where they could purchase the likes of ours. The next thing we knew, Betty was elbow deep in orders to fill. During the day, I'd help her measure and cut out the material, so she could keep up with production. We were living our dreams and would have conversations about what we were going to do about our relationship and life in general. We decided with all the dough we were making and what I already had saved, we'd rent an apartment and continue with our new professions. If our parents didn't approve, so be it. It was our life, not theirs, and we were damn sure to live it the way we wanted. Their approval no longer mattered. We felt liberated in so many ways and would not trade our freedom and happiness for our family's acceptance.

One night after an exhausting but grand show, Betty and I went off on our own while the other gals headed to a rent party. Betty had discovered that a homosexual nightlife where everyone could flaunt their sexual orientation without being persecuted thrived in Harlem. The Clam House, which I vaguely remembered Delores and the other gals chatting about when we first met them, was a popular hangout for people such as us. We went there to see an African entertainer by the name of Gladys Bentley. She was a large, gregarious woman who wore a tuxedo and top hat while playing the piano and singing the blues in a raspy, deeply rich voice. She'd take popular songs and would add her own bawdy lyrics, which always had us in fits of laughter. She was marvelous. We also checked out similar haunts where we didn't have to hide our relationship in other Harlem nightspots and Greenwich Village.

It had been five weeks since our first night at Slim's and kiss—the best night of my life. We'd decided to share with Abe our plans to rent an apartment and purchase an automobile, which Betty and I would share. Of course, we kept our relationship under our hats but had decided that eventually we'd tell him when the time was right. Abe supported our decision and even offered to help us find a suitable place to rest our heads and a nice set of wheels within our means. Our parents wouldn't get wind of our future endeavor to leave the nest until the end of the summer when all our chess pieces were poised to put into place, and we could strategically make our move. Literally.

The day after we told Abe our scheme, he showed up at my house while Betty was taking a break from sketching out dress designs and me having a rest from choreographing a new dance routine.

"I'd like for you two to meet someone who is special to me," he said when Betty and I greeted him at the front door. A woman with black, bushy, chin-length hair stepped out of the shadows. When she moved farther into the pale light of the porch, each strand on her head showed as a tiny spiral, and her café au lait skin was flawless. "This is Anyah. Anyah, this is my baby sister Betty and her best pal Ameerah."

We said hi and invited them in. Abe had brought along some fine whiskey, so I poured us each a shot over a glass of ice and added water while Abe told us Anyah's father came through Ellis Island from the Caribbean. He later met her mother. I noticed while we were sitting in the living room chatting, Anyah was throwing side glances at me. I ignored it and listened to Abe come clean about their relationship and how he knew his parents wouldn't accept the fact he wasn't dating within his same race, but he didn't care. They were in love, and before school started, he would confront them about it.

Betty slipped her hand in mine and squeezed it, silently telling me we should inform Abe about our relationship. I wasn't sure if it was a good idea, but then I caught Anyah's gaze dart from our hands to our faces.

She smiled. Her expression was warm and filled with understanding. She knew. Then, her gaze rested on me, and her chocolate colored eyes grew sad. A haunting feeling stirred inside me like one gets when about to receive some grave news.

"Abe, I have something to confess," Betty started to say, but I held a hand up to halt her.

"Sorry," I told her and planted my attention on Anyah. "Why do you keep looking at me like I have some fatal disease?" I made sure to keep my tone light so no one would interpret my question as accusing.

"I apologize," Anyah said, "but . . ." She closed her eyes and fell silent.

"Anyah is a clairvoyant," Abe piped up. When Betty and I looked at him, he continued, "She can perceive things outside our senses."

"No, kidding?" Betty asked, delighted. "We had talked about seeing one, but we've been too busy to pursue it." She turned to Anyah who was now staring at me. "What information are you receiving about Ameerah?"

"Do you mind if I sit beside you and touch your hand?" Anyah asked me.

"Not at all." I moved closer to Betty on the couch to where our thighs were touching.

Anyah rose. She sat on the other side of me and held my hand. The minute our palms touched, mine tingled. "You have psychic abilities, as well."

"Interesting." Abe scooted to the edge of his seat and leaned forward, resting his forearms on his knees. "Is it true, Ameerah?"

Betty smiled and nodded before I could answer. "She has visions and gets horrible headaches afterward."

"I used to think this stuff was a bunch of baloney," Abe confessed, "until Anyah proved me wrong. Now, I'm a firm believer and seriously contemplating changing my major to psychology . . . or parapsychology as Max Dessoir coined years ago. I know Stanford University has conducted tests on extrasensory perception and psychokinesis. Maybe I can do the same thing at NYU."

Betty placed her fingers on her lips. "Dad will flip if you don't follow in his footsteps, and when he and Mom meets Anyah . . ." She turned to Anyah. "Sorry, I don't mean to be rude, but Abe already told you how they are, so you already know. Ameerah and I aren't like them."

"It's okay," Anyah said. "I understand, and Abe speaks highly of you and Ameerah."

"I don't care what they say," Abe said darkly. "I'm going to live my life the way I want to."

"Why is my palm tingling against yours?" I asked her.

She removed her hand from mine and placed it in her lap. "When two people who possess a psychic ability touch palms, they will experience a prickling sensation."

"Nifty," Betty said.

Anyah looked at me. "Your last vision was a disturbing one. Was it not?"

I nodded. "It was." The words to tell her all about it rose in my throat. I closed my mouth before they could roll off my tongue.

"She had a vision of–" Betty began to say, but Anyah interrupted her.

"It's not necessary to tell me." Anyah let out a heavy sigh and touched my arm in a manner one would in an attempt to comfort someone before revealing grievous news. My heart raced. "Your spirit is in danger of wickedness, and I see pain being inflicted upon your body." Tears glistened in her eyes.

I could feel the color draining from my face. "Don't you mean soul?"

Slowly, she shook her head. "They're two different things." When she saw the confusion on my face, she continued. "Your spirit is attached to your soul. It builds and creates it through each incarnation or tasks on the other side. We all have freewill, and if your spirit chooses to live an existence of debauchery, it affects the soul accordingly."

Betty stiffened beside me. I glanced at her, and her lips were pressed into a tight line. She rose and stood in front of me and Anyah. "Is this because we're lesbians?"

"What?" Abe made a gesture between Betty and me. "Are you two having an affair?" He laughed. "Oh, boy, our parents are surely going to disown us now."

Betty rounded on him. "I don't care. I'm in love with Ameerah. If you or them or anyone else can't deal with it, then scram."

Abe held his hands up in defense. "I have no problem with your sexual orientation. I love Ameerah, too, but in a sisterly way, and I support your relationship. It's just you surprised me. I never suspected you two carried a torch for one another."

"Your relationship has nothing to do with Ameerah's fate," Anyah said, grabbing Betty's attention. "The soul is neither female nor male . . . it just is."

"Then why?" I managed to ask, still disturbed with this information. "Why am I a target of such bad luck? I'm not an evil person."

Anyah frowned. "I don't know why, but I'm certain if you can get through this tribulation that awaits you, your spirit will be fine, and the storm will be over."

Danger.

Pain.

Suffering.

Tribulation.

Those four words chimed in my head. No matter how hard I tried to focus on listening to Abe tell us more about his future plans and making some rum runs for extra dough to invest in the stock market, my thoughts kept reverting to what Anyah told me. I wanted them to stop and knew a way to silence the mental chatter and numb the dread that had settled in the pit of my stomach.

More whiskey.

I got drunk and so did Betty, probably for the same reasons. We played cards while we consumed the giggle water, smoked, told jokes, and laughed. I played some jazz and attempted to show Abe and Anyah the new routines I was working on but couldn't stay steady on my feet. Betty looped her arm around mine to perform the new dance with me, but we ended up tripping over each other's feet. We crumpled to the floor in a heap of laughter.

Abe took our hands and pulled us upright. "C'mon, dolls. You need to sleep." He led us to my room. We fell into bed, our bodies bouncing against each other on the mattress.

"Whoa. The room is spinning." Betty covered her face. "Make it stop, Abe."

I was experiencing the same sensation, with a dash of nausea added. Betty turned on her side, and I curled against her, pressing my forehead to her back. My thoughts scattered, and a deep heaviness sprouted throughout my body. Sleep was claiming me, and I welcomed it. In the distance, Abe's amused yet nurturing voice told Betty this wasn't the first time she had bed spins, and it certainly wouldn't be the last. Something warm and comforting covered us. A blanket? And that was the last thing I could remember.

Chapter Eight

August 1925

Everyone loved the new routines I choreographed and the outfits Betty designed and made. Slim's business grew exponentially, and so did our salaries. Everything happened at lightning speed, and we were quickly making a name for ourselves. I didn't even mind Ruby's attempts at stealing the show to be the center of attention. I was enjoying myself too much to care. I couldn't fathom how Anyah's prediction could come into play with the abundance of good fortune Betty and I were having. We had finally put our worries and concerns to rest by chalking it up as a bunch of hooey. The visions even stopped, and I was certain stardom was in my future.

Boy was I wrong.

Since Betty was spending all summer at my house and only going home to exchange clothes and pick up some miscellaneous items, her parents requested she spend some time with them. Reluctantly, she agreed but only because she was caught up with her work. Abe still hadn't told their folks about his plans, but I imagined it would be any day now since he was due back in school in two weeks. I wondered what the outcome would be, but I was sure it wouldn't turn out well.

I woke early on a Sunday morning, got dressed, had breakfast, and spent the day with Delores in the city. I didn't get home until well after suppertime. Exhausted, I was looking forward to a relaxing soak in the tub. Grabbing my purchases off the floor of her automobile, I thanked her for a wonderful time and stepped into the night in front of my house. The sound of chirping crickets surrounded me. Delores smiled and said she enjoyed herself, and we should do this again sometime. I agreed and waved goodbye, pleased that we were becoming good friends. As I watched her drive away, a falling star blazed across the black sky, bright and silvery, and several more followed. I closed my eyes and made a wish that Lady Luck would continue to bestow good fortune upon Betty and me. Turning on my heel, I paused in my tracks and stared at the white columns and arches of our extravagant house. For some reason, it suddenly appeared dark and brooding—haunting even. I recalled what Betty had told me about reading *Frankenstein*. Maybe she was right. Horror stories had a way of creeping into your life and conjuring irrational thoughts during times like these. I shook the uneasy feeling off and climbed the steps to the porch. When I reached for the door, it swung open. I jumped back and screamed at the same time the porch light popped on, and the house lit up.

"We need to have a family discussion," my father said, opening the door wider. There was no amusement or apologies in his eyes for startling me; instead they were hard, just like his expression.

Shit.

My mind raced, trying to remember what condition I left the house in this morning. Were there dirty ashtrays on the tables or cigarette butts in the garbage? Did I carelessly leave evidence of my alcohol consumption in their absence?

My stomach fell out from under me.

I did.

"Get in the house, Ameerah," my father ordered when I didn't move. His tone was stern, unyielding, causing my heart to pound heavily against my chest.

There was no way out of this. Whatever solution I tried to think up wouldn't suffice. I had to come clean and tell them they would no longer rule over me. I now had enough dough to move out and had actually found a charming apartment in Greenwich Village today I planned on showing Betty and was sure she would adore. Not to mention Greenwich Village was a haven for creative people such as ourselves. It would be perfect for our new lifestyle.

I marched inside the house, set my bags down near the staircase, and went into the living room. Mother was sitting on the couch with a sour look on her face, and my father moved beside her, still standing. He was tall and liked to use his height to get his point across by intimidating others so they would be more prone to listen to him. I knew his game. I knew it quite well. His behavior was an effective tactic that I grew to resent because no matter how hard I fought to resist it, I was always reduced to the fearful child I once was.

"Take a seat." He nodded to the chair across from them.

I sat and remained quiet, trying to think of a suitable way to tell them my future plans.

"Were you having cigarette parties?" Mother asked.

"No," I answered. "Not unless you count having a few friends over to play cards and smoke while we entertained ourselves."

"What about alcohol?" My father wanted to know.

"What about it?"

Mother shifted in her seat with an annoyed look on her face. "It's against the law!"

Father sat beside her and took her hand. She leaned against him, submitting to his silent gesture that he would have words with me now. "We know you've been drinking in our house." He shook his head in a pitiful manner. "We trusted you."

A sad, crushing feeling knotted in my chest. I should have at least respected their wishes not to have allowed my friends drink and smoke under their roof. Yeah, Betty and I had done those things in this house before, even when my parents weren't out of state, but we were both conservative and cautious not to get busted. "I'm sorry."

"I noticed you haven't been taking care of the apples," Mother said.

"When's the last time you attended to them?"

The apples.

Damn. I forgot about our orchard. With everything going on, it never crossed my mind. There was no way out of this screw-up of mine. I shrugged.

"Answer your mother."

Her arms were crossed tight around her chest, and she was glaring at me.

"I haven't. I can't remember the last time I've checked on them. I've been too busy and forgot."

"I saw that today," she said, seething. "Most of them are rotten. No good. Because of your neglect and irresponsibility, it's quite possible I might not be able to make my famous apple pies for the ladies and gentlemen who are eager to purchase them. How could you do this to me, Ameerah? Lots of people might be let down because of you, and I'll be the laughingstock among our friends."

"They're not your friends, then," I said.

My father shot me a reproachful look. "Watch your tongue." I dropped my gaze and stared at my lap. "Tomorrow you will spend the day in the orchard seeing what apples you can salvage. You will then collect and bring them to your mother. Understood?"

I had a sudden fiery urge to tell him no, and whether it was right or wrong, I wasn't going to be bullied into doing what he demanded of me. However, the guilt they laid on me was too thick to break through. I should have been more responsible and taken care of the apples and not have had my friends over to drink. I would comply this time and try to make up for my mistakes.

"Yes, and I'm sorry."

Mother sighed heavily. "I'm tired of hearing those two words." When I raised my eyebrows in question, she continued in a mocking, childlike voice. "*I'm sorry. I'm sorry.*" She waved her hands in the air for added drama.

Instantly, my face blazed hot. I rose from my seat and straightened my shoulders. "Well, after tomorrow, when I fulfill my obligation to you, you'll never have to see the likes of me again."

"Ameerah," my father said when I turned to leave the room, "our family discussion is not over."

"Let her go," I heard Mother say. "We both need to cool off."

I grabbed my bags and went up to my room. As soon as I entered, I closed my door, threw my purchases on the floor, and crawled into bed. Silently, I cried myself to sleep under the weight of humiliation crushing me.

* * *

The next morning I avoided my parents and spent the whole day in our orchard, picking through apples and putting the ones that were firm and bruise-free in baskets. I did a lot of daydreaming and planning during those hours of solitude and decided to call Delores that evening. I'd ask her to give me a lift and see if I could stay with her tonight. Tomorrow, I'd sign the lease for the apartment we looked at yesterday. Slim knew the owner of the building and had pulled some strings for me. He was the one who tipped me off about the rental, and the lady who showed it to me confessed the owner hadn't advertised it as a favor to Slim, and I should count my blessings for this opportunity. She promised to keep it under her hat until Betty had a chance to see it. Originally, I didn't want to sign the lease without Betty's approval since she'd be paying half the rent, but I was sure she'd think it was the bee's knees. Besides, she'd understand my hasty move once I told her why.

I had three large baskets full of apples by the time the sun dipped into the horizon. I didn't know what the hell Mother was talking about last night when she said most of them were rotten. I sighed as I pulled the red wagon I placed the baskets in to our house and chalked her behavior up as another one of her theatrical displays to overdramatize a minor situation to gain attention.

"Ameerah," I heard Mother say after I entered the kitchen to get a bite to eat before I called Delores. I was famished and needed to get some food into my belly. "I apologize for my behavior last night."

Surprised, I turned away from the icebox and faced her. Never in my life had Mother ever said she was sorry to me. It was an epic moment, and I blinked at her. Part of me wanted to reenact the very conduct she was speaking of, so she could get a taste of the turmoil I felt during those moments of her belittling me. However, the disturbed sadness in her brown eyes halted my quick tongue. So instead I said, "Okay."

She gently placed a hand on my arm. "I was tired and disappointed." She cupped my cheek. "You're my daughter, and I love you. I only want the best for you. Your father and I don't want you to leave us on bad terms."

"Your mother is right," Father said, entering through the kitchen doors. "I realize we can't make you stay here, but we still would like for you to be part of this family."

"I have three baskets of apples outside by the steps." I motioned to the back door. "They're all good, so you can still make your famous apple pies, and no one will be disappointed. Your popularity will remain intact."

A warm smile crossed Mother's face. "Thank you, my sweet princess."

I hated when she called me that. I ignored it like I always did and looked at my parents expectantly when Mother took a step back from me and glanced over her shoulder at Father. It was obvious they had more to say. He crossed the room and wrapped an arm around her shoulders. She hung her head and sniffed.

My heart went out to her, and I wondered if it was because I decided to move out, and she would actually miss me, or were her tears purely for selfish reasons? "What's eating you?"

"Your grandmother Etta is in the hospital," Father said, looking down at Mother, rubbing her shoulder. "We received word today while you were in the orchard, and we plan on leaving first thing tomorrow morning to go see her. We think you should come along, just in case . . ."

A small sob escaped Mother's lips. She covered her mouth and nodded.

My grandmother was a spunky old gal who lived in the country near Salem, Massachusetts. I used to spend summers with her when I was a child, and the times we shared were precious memories I kept tucked away. She used to tell me stories about the witch trials that I never grew tired of. Mother, on the other hand, didn't approve of her own mother telling me tales that would surely haunt my dreams. They never did, and I'd always prod grandmother Etta with questions to keep her talking. A memory of when I was six and helping her in the garden where she spent most of her time, fluttered across my mind: her gloved hands, warm smile, and straw hat to keep the sun off her face. She always had so much energy, so much life, and now she wasn't doing well. "What's wrong with her?"

"She has pneumonia," Father said. "She also lost a lot of weight and has been feeling fatigued for quite some time now, complaining her bones hurt. Her doctor and his hospital staff are running tests to see what's ailing her besides the virus she has."

My hand went to my chest. Grandmother was a tiny woman as it was. She was barely five feet and couldn't have weighed more than a hundred and ten pounds, maybe less. This was disturbing news. "How much weight did she lose?"

"Twenty pounds," Mother said, dabbing a lace handkerchief at the corner of her eyes.

I gasped, and my hand flew to my mouth. "Oh, my God." I had the sudden need to see her as soon as possible. "Can we leave tonight . . . or at least get there so we can visit her first thing in the morning?"

"It's four hours away," Father answered. He looked at his watch. "It's after six now, and we haven't had supper yet. Your mother has been too upset to cook. We'll leave at seven tomorrow morning, spend the day there, and come back."

He was right. It would be nonsensical to leave now, arrive in Salem at midnight, and find accommodations so late. Besides, I needed to call Mrs. McNeely—the lady who showed me the lovely apartment yesterday—and tell her I'd take it. I also wanted to get hold of Delores and tell her what was going on. The gals were already aware we'd be performing the same routines as last weekend, so there was no need for us to practice this week. However, if they had any questions, they could farm them to Delores until I was back in town.

I offered to cook supper and even made Mother a cup of tea so she could relax in the study with Father while he read through a business proposal. I felt sorry for her. She was an only child, and her father died when she was young, so her mother was all she had. The least I could do was make things easier for her tonight.

While the potatoes were boiling and the meatloaf was in the oven—one of the few things I knew how to cook well—I made my calls. Afterward, I felt relieved and elated at the same time. Relieved, because Delores was a gem. She told me not to worry and everything would be okay. She offered her support and made me feel better about the whole situation. Elated, because when I confided to Mrs. McNeely about my current situation regarding my grandmother and then told her I would take the apartment but wouldn't be able to sign the lease until I arrived back in town, she was quite understanding about my ordeal. She offered her condolences and welcomed me to the neighborhood. She had no doubt in her mind I would thrive in the community and be an asset, as well. I was on cloud nine when our conversation ended and was flitting and twirling in the kitchen like a giddy little girl. I longed for Betty to be here with me to enjoy the grand news, but it would have to wait until I saw her in a few days.

We were now the proud renters of a charming abode where we could come and go as we pleased and be together. I clapped my hands and jumped up and down until I thought I caught a shadow moving past the tall, narrow French windows beside the kitchen door that led to the dining room.

The door opened.

It was Mother.

I wondered if she saw me acting like a silly schoolgirl. I still hadn't told her or Father my plans, except that I was leaving, but they never asked, which was odd now that I thought about it. I did a mental shrug. Like I cared. I wasn't going to tell them everything anyway. It was none of their beeswax and not part of my scheme to break free from their clutches.

I faced Mother. She was frowning, and the look in her brown eyes appeared almost frightened—or maybe disturbed. I wasn't sure which. Sometimes her moods were hard to figure out.

"I came in here to get the dishes, so I could set the table," she said in a cold, detached tone.

She saw me. I could tell by the sudden uncomfortable vibe in the room. I guess I should spill the beans. I didn't want her to think I wasn't upset about my grandmother. I was. I'd only had a temporary reprieve from my worries and was enjoying the moment.

I handed Mother a stack of plates. "I know you saw me dancing around the kitchen."

"I don't have a clue on what you're talking about," she said, clearly playing dumb.

I decided to let sleeping dogs lie. Two could play her game. A moment ago, I was willing to tell her my good news but now not so much.

A half hour later, we ate our supper as a family in the dining room, listening to Father idly chat about work and the stock market. I caught Mother and him shooting nervous glances at each other, and when I called it to their attention, they feigned ignorance. Annoyed, I abruptly told them I'd received fabulous news, which explained why I was dancing in the kitchen. Again, they proceeded to insult my intelligence by snubbing me, treating me like an idiot. The back of my neck burned. I rose from my seat and slammed a fist on the table, causing the dining ware to jump and rattle. I demanded to be treated like an equal instead of a dumb Dora. They gawked at me as I told them my concerns for Grandmother, and I'd be moving out as soon as we were back in town. I stormed from the room and got ready for bed, planning on writing in my journal before I went to sleep. I opened the drawer to my nightstand where I normally kept it beneath some magazines. There it was on top, upside down, something I'd never do.

My heart dropped.

I picked it up and clutched the leather book to my chest.

They knew.

They knew *everything*.

Chapter Nine

Danvers, Massachusetts

1925

We left early the next morning in my father's 1924 black Studebaker sedan. I loved this automobile with its nickel-plated bumpers and classy style. Not to mention how roomy and comfortable it was to ride in. In the past, I'd hoped he would have allowed me to drive it someday, but now it no longer mattered to me. What counted most was seeing Grandmother and getting through this long drive without blowing my top over them invading my privacy. I'd finally decided late last night when I was tossing and turning in a fitful state of worry that I'd pretend I didn't know about their shamelessly bold act of prying into my personal life. I'd put aside my profane feelings and act like the Puritan daughter they expected me to be.

The four-hour journey was long and boring, and I was ever so grateful to have had the presence of mind to take along a book to pass the time. I tuned out my parent's conversations and got lost in Bram Stoker's *Dracula*. Earlier, I had to smile when I grabbed it for our trip, imagining Betty razzing me for reading horror stories that could possibly be the culprit for the disturbing vision I had. Maybe so, but I was drawn to those types of stories—a dark gothic world where monsters and immortality secretly existed alongside humans—I didn't know why, but I was.

"Where are we going?" I asked after we entered Massachusetts, and I noticed we weren't heading to Salem.

"Danvers," Father said. "We're going to a hospital and care facility that's one of the best in the nation."

I dog eared my page and set the book down. "Why?"

Mother turned and looked at me. Her expression was warm but a bit sad. "We want your grandmother to be back to her old self again, so we'll be talking to a doctor on how we can accomplish that goal."

I frowned. Was Grandmother in worse condition than they originally told me? "Why would she have to go to a care facility? Can't we take her home with us instead?"

"She might have tuberculosis, and Bandbridge has a TB ward she can stay at if she does," Father told me.

"I thought she had pneumonia," my voice cracked. I knew what tuberculosis was. It was a death sentence. Tears sprang from my eyes. "When will we know if she has TB?"

Mother handed me a handkerchief. "They're running tests now, but we want to be prepared to give her the best treatment possible, just in case the news is grave."

"There's no cure," I said, drying my face. "And we won't be able to see her because it's highly contagious."

Silence.

Mother glanced at Father and turned back in her seat, facing away from me. I couldn't understand why they weren't up front with me from the beginning about Grandmother's possible fate, and I could feel my temper rising. But I had an act to perform, so I halted my anger, along with the mounting charges I held against them and sat back, crossing my arms tightly over my chest.

Father sighed. "Let's not get all worked up just yet. I'm sure whatever is ailing your grandmother, can be cured with the right care and treatment."

I kept quiet and closed my eyes, silently praying for Grandmother to be okay. I must have dozed off, because the next thing I knew, I heard

Mother calling my name.

"Ameerah. Wake up, sweetheart. We're here."

My eyes flew open, and I squinted against the bright sun. I sat up and winced from the kink in my neck. "Where are we?" I asked stupidly, massaging my collarbone.

"Bandbridge," Father answered.

I rubbed the sleep from my eyes and peered out the window, blinking a couple times to adjust my bleary vision. I was astonished at the massive Victorian structure in front of us. It sprawled across acres of farmland with scenic vistas of lush green grass, dotted with looming oak trees, and lined with thick shrubbery. The ornate architecture had a gothic flair with its rising spires, towers, and peaked gables. I counted thirteen buildings and estimated more lurked behind the complex.

Father parked opposite of the buildings, beside a row of automobiles. He adjusted his black Fedora, tilting it just so on his head, and exited along with Mother.

"C'mon, dear.'" My door opened and Mother stood before me with the corners of her mouth curled tightly. I wondered if her forced smile was a gimmick to coerce me to believe Grandmother would be all right. "The doctor is waiting for us."

I stepped out and smoothed my drop-waist raspberry dress, feeling the whimsical crochet lace pattern against my fingertips as they skimmed the material and the ruffled edging past my hips. I loved this outfit, not only because of the design, but when I walked, it flounced about my body in a proper, ladylike fashion so I wouldn't receive any grief from my parents like I would in my flapper ensemble.

"This way." Father nodded to one of the center buildings with a tower. He took Mother's hand, and she leaned against him as if she were exhausted and needed his support. I imagined she was emotionally drained from the turmoil of not knowing what would befall her own mother. Her contradictory behavior for the past twenty-four hours was a red flag, which told me more was going on than they led me to believe.

We entered into a small, enclosed, softly lit entryway. A small window glared down from the top of a heavy wooden door. Father pushed a red button next to the brass handle. A loud buzzing sounded, announcing our arrival I presumed. I thought the measures of security enacted in this facility were odd. Maybe they were concerned TB patients would try to vacate the premises and risk the health of the unaffected. I imagined the tuberculosis ward was one of the wings attached to this building. The vastness was both impressive and intimidating at the same time. One would need a map or a box of crumbs to find the way back to point A.

"I'm Henry Arrowood," Father said to the woman who appeared on the other side of the window. "We have an appointment with Doctor Stratton."

The door opened into a large carpeted area. Several benches and plastic chairs lined the walls between rooms. The air had an artificial metallic smell I didn't care for. I followed my parents into a comfortable sitting room and waited while the woman alerted the doctor of our arrival.

Twenty minutes or so later, she stepped into the room, brushing a lock of brown hair off her plain features. "Doctor Stratton will see you now." Despite her stoic demeanor, her golden eyes softened when they caught mine, and I felt a sense of pity from her. I quickly gathered the news we were about to receive regarding Grandmother would be bad.

I held my arms tight against my chest and swallowed back the tears rising in my throat while she led us to a room across and down the hall. When we approached the office, a balding man with a dark horseshoe pattern on top of his head greeted us with a friendly smile and invited us in to take seats. We sat, and Father introduced Mother and me to the doctor.

"Ameerah," the doctor said while settling into his seat behind the desk. "It's nice to meet you."

"Likewise," I answered, wondering why all of a sudden his attention was focused on me. He was only being polite, I told myself, even though he had an inquisitive expression on his face, and he seemed to be studying me. I shifted my gaze to the cross hanging on the wall behind him and then to a picture of a beach with only one set of footprints. Although, I wasn't close enough to read the verse written on the photo, I knew what it said.

Doctor Stratton glanced over his shoulder, and then his dark eyes fell on me. "Footprints in the Sand. Have you read it, Ameerah?"

I nodded. "I have."

"The good Lord is always with us and even more so through troubling times. Do you agree?"

"I don't want to be carried," I said and elaborated my statement when he gave me a funny look. "If someone were to carry me through the trials in my life, how would I emotionally and spiritually grow? I don't want to lean on some phantom deity as a delusional crutch who I would, in turn, give credit to for overcoming something I simply did myself. It's like giving a patient a sugar pill and telling her it's a miracle drug that'll cure her illness. She believes what is being told to her, takes the medicine, and is suddenly cured."

Mother let out an uncomfortable laugh. "Sometimes Ameerah's tongue runs away from her."

"You don't believe in the Bible?" Doctor Stratton asked, ignoring Mother's comment. He frowned, not hiding his disapproval.

"I don't believe in talking snakes. So no, I don't. It's a history book written by lowbrow people."

"Ameerah!" Mother gasped.

Father cleared his throat. "We're not here to have a religious debate, and by no means is Ameerah's attitude toward the good book a reflection of how her mother and I feel, which brings us to why we're here."

"Yes, of course," Doctor Stratton said, shuffling some papers on his desk.

I wondered what Father meant by that, but when I looked at him, he wouldn't make eye contact with me and neither would Mother.

"Do you know why you're here?" Doctor Stratton asked me.

Now it was my turn to give him a funny look. "Yes, I do. My grandmother is sick and might have tuberculosis and . . . " I could feel the color draining from my face when the sudden realization hit that we were here for me and not my grandmother.

My parents double-crossed me.

The whole grandmother-being-sick story was a ruse to get me here. Grandmother was fine. It was me who they'd been referring to all along, which explained Mother's behavior and everything else in between. My mouth dropped, and I looked at my parents. "You lied to me."

Mother was wringing her hands in her lap. "We had to, sweetheart. You need help. You're not the Ameerah we raised."

I narrowed my eyes on the woman who gave me life and was all too willing to take it away from me. I said one word, "Grandmother."

"She has the flu," she answered, reaching for Father's hand.

I raised my eyebrows and voice. "The flu!" I stood and rounded on my parents.

"Sit down, Ameerah," Doctor Stratton ordered.

I shot him a dirty look. "Don't tell me what to do. This is family business." I swung my attention back on my parents. Angry tears sprouted, which made me even more furious. They didn't deserve my tears. "You betrayed me. Your own flesh and blood. How could you?"

"You're sick, Ameerah," Father said, "and mentally unstable."

"What?" I said, half-laughing in a you-got-to-be-fooling-me kind of way. "And how do you propose to back up a ludicrous statement such as that?"

Unfazed by my outburst, Father responded in a clear, unfeeling tone, "You butchered your beautiful long hair and started dressing in a perverse, shameful manner. You smoke. You drink alcohol, which is illegal, so you're breaking the–"

"Just because I stood up to you and Mother after years of being your puppet and finally showing you who I really am doesn't make me a nutcase. It makes me somebody you don't like."

"The visons," Mother said.

The visons.

What could I say to that? I had no rational answer to why I received them. My mind raced, searching for a logical retort to her statement.

"How long have you had them?" Doctor Stratton asked.

I ignored him and replied to Mother's simple but crucifying declaration regarding my sanity. "Having visions doesn't make me a fruitcake. John of Patmos had them." I threw that one in, knowing the doctor was a religious man and could relate it to my situation.

"John was a holy man," the doctor said. "Do you go to church?"

"With my best friend Betty I do," I answered.

"The one you're having a sinful relationship with?"

My face grew hot, stung with a mixture of anger and embarrassment. I pointed at my parents, jabbing my finger in the air. "You had no right to invade my privacy. Shame on the both of you."

"They're your parents, Ameerah," the doctor said. "Any loving parents who are concerned about their child's welfare would have done the same thing. They're only looking out for your best interest."

"Hah," I said. "They have you snowed."

Mother opened her purse and pulled out my journal. "It's all here in Ameerah's own writing. What she's written is proof of her mental instability, from her poor judgment in the company she keeps, such as jigaboos and lawbreakers, to having visions and impure inclinations, which includes sexual relations with her best friend Betty."

I snatched my book out of her hand. "You keep Betty out of this. The both of you have stepped way over the line, and as far as I'm concerned, we're no long–"

"We feel it's our duty—not only as friends with Betty's parents but also a moral obligation to inform them about your relationship with their daughter," Father said. "But rest assured, everything else will be kept under our hats. I've worked too long and hard to allow you and your antics to tarnish our good name."

I was livid. They didn't care about me. What it boiled down to was they were afraid the lifestyle I'd chosen would reach their swanky crowd and in turn cause them to lose their social rank. I wouldn't be surprised if they had conspired to frame me all along to either get me out of the picture or in their twisted way of thinking, have me rehabilitated so I could be the cookie-cutter daughter who was prim and proper—molded by their ideological hands to suit their pompous asses.

Then there was Betty. I had to warn her before it was too late. I clenched my jaw, and all my muscles tightened when the thought of what her parents would do if they discovered the truth about us entered my mind. Truthfully, I had no idea what the repercussions would be, and I was sure she'd have Abe's support. It would get ugly, though, and the thought of her being in turmoil at the hands of others coupled with my own parent's betrayal made me snap.

I leaned forward into my Father's face. "If you or her"—I pointed harshly at Mother—"breathes a word to Betty's parents about our relationship, I will do *everything* in my power to ruin you."

Mother paled and shrank back in her seat.

Father stood, towering over me, attempting once again to use his size as a tool of intimidation; however, I was too angry for it to have any effect on me. He glared. "Are you threatening us?"

"It's not a threat. It's a promise," I half-yelled.

"Calm down, Ameerah," Doctor Stratton said. "Or I'll have to take drastic measures to cool you off."

I swung my attention on him. "Fuck you!" When I turned back to Father, I was met with a blow across the cheek and a loud slapping sound. An immediate burning, bruise sensation, pulsed across the right side of my face.

"You do not disrespect your el–"

On impulse, and fueled by a rage I'd never felt before, I shoved Father's waist with all my might. He stumbled backward. The heel of his shoe caught the leg of a chair, and he fell hard against the wall.

"Henry!" Mother screeched, jumping to her feet at the same time a buzzer went off. It sounded different than the one at the entrance door—more of a long, drawn out, high-pitched noise.

I rushed past her, heading for the door, still gripping my journal. My plans were clear and straightforward: grab my purse out of the Studebaker, find a telephone, and call Betty. I'd have her and Abe get my belongings out of the house as fast as they could, and hurry my ass home.

"You're not leaving, Ameerah," Doctor Stratton said, now standing beside his desk.

The door swung open, and a rough-looking burly fella blocked the doorway. I could see through the gap beneath his arm a woman standing in the background to his right. She wore a white cap and a black dress with a white apron. She was reaching for something in her deep pocket.

I was trapped.

I looked at the doctor. "You can't hold be against my will. I'm an adult. I have to give my consent, so release me now."

"You have proven to me that you're mentally unstable and not fit to make rational decisions," he told me. "Therefore, I have every legal right to withhold you, unless your parents suggest otherwise." He made eye contact with Father, who was now standing, rubbing his backside.

"Absolutely," he answered. "The Ameerah you encountered today is not my daughter. Do what you must to bring her back to us."

I had no choice but to fight my way out of here. I kicked the attendant as hard as I could in the crotch. When he doubled over, I squeezed by him. Once again, the buzzer sounded. The nurse attempted to grab me, but I darted out of her reach and ran for the entrance. When I reached it, I turned the handle, but the door wouldn't budge. I twisted the knob back and forth. Nothing.

Shit!

My heart pounded hard against my chest, and the right side of my face throbbed.

Two large fellas stormed my way. The nurse followed them.

There was no escape.

I felt like a canary being cornered by ravenous felines.

I dropped my journal and slipped off my shoes, planning to use the heels as weapons. I knew I wouldn't get out of this situation. I was now a hostage. But I'd be damn if I were to fall to my knees and beg for mercy. I wouldn't go without a fight.

The fella on my left stepped forward, reaching for my arm. I brought down the heel of my shoe hard on his forearm. He immediately pulled away, cursing as he did so. The other one on my right tried snatching my wrist. I turned and with great force, swiped the edge of the heel across his cheek. He let out a painful cry and stumbled sideways, cupping his face, grunting *bitch* between his teeth. The next thing I knew, my left wrist was being bent backward by the first attendant I struck. I dropped the shoe and before I could defend myself with the other one, my feet were kicked out from under me. My back and head smacked the floor. My lungs tightened, and a sharp, aching sensation gripped me. Gasping for air, I turned on my side and stretched out my hand in a poor attempt to latch onto an ankle and bring the asshole down with me.

Wicked laughter laced with anger broke free from the fella who took me down when he noticed even with the wind knocked out of me, I wasn't giving up. He moved his foot out of my reach and straddled me. His weight stole whatever oxygen I had from my lungs. A pitching, rasping sound escaped me in quick intervals. The room spun. Something sharp pierced my arm, and a cold sensation flooded my veins. A pair of ice-blue eyes hung over me—unkind and calculating. Cracked lips formed the words *Nighty, night*. My vision became hazy. I could feel myself slipping into a dark void. My last fleeting thoughts were they might have caught me this time, but some birds could not be caged, and I was one of them.

Chapter Ten

Bandbridge Insane Asylum

August 1925

The straps were tight around my wrists and ankles. The bed was hard, uncomfortable. Every muscle in my body ached. A thin white blanket covered me, and a flimsy blue gown replaced the dress I'd worn when I entered this facility.

What the hell.

I tried moving my arms and feet, but they only budged a little.

I didn't know how long I'd been in this position or how long I'd been out cold, but my bladder was full, and I had a raging headache. The inner edges and corners of my eyes were also crusty. I wanted desperately to wipe the gunk away.

With all my strength, I tugged on the restraints again. The leather dug into my flesh. The realization then hit me that I was anchored to this bed, and I couldn't do a damn thing about it. My first reaction was to panic. Anyone would if she woke up like I did now in an uncompromising, degrading, and nightmarish situation. But even though my pulse was racing, and I had a strong desire to scream at the top of my lungs to be released, I had the presence of mind not to do so.

Once upon a time ago, Mother locked me in a coat closet because I wasn't minding her. She kept me there all afternoon, only to release me before Father came home from the office. I learned then to do what I was told and play the part she wanted me to act.

The events that led to my imprisonment were fresh in my mind and reminded me of that awful childhood memory. If only I would have kept my anger in check in Doctor Stratton's office and portrayed myself in a different light, I could have avoided this nonsense. But who was I kidding? My parents betrayed me in every possible manner. There was no way I could have stifled the rage they evoked inside me, especially when Father mentioned informing Betty's family about our relationship.

Betty.

I had to figure a way out of here so I could reach her. If that meant playing the good patient and doing what they said, I needed to do it. The quicker I pulled the wool over their eyes the better.

"Hello," I called out, looking around the tiny, windowless room. A lamp on a small table in the corner was the only source of light. A wooden chair was stationed beside it, and the closed door leading out was on the opposite wall. I could see a shadow moving beneath the gap between the bottom of the door and floor. "Hello."

The shadow paused. I held my breath. The knobbed turned, and a nurse I'd never seen before but dressed in the same black dress and white apron as the one I encountered earlier entered. She had a wary look on her face. "You're awake. How do you feel?"

"Hung over and like I'd been hit by a train," I answered. "I have to use the john, and I'd like to clean myself up. May I do so?"

"I don't know." She nervously looked around. "I heard you were quite the handful yesterday."

Hope sprung to life inside me. I'd only been here a day. If I could quickly find a way out, I'd have a chance to get to Betty before her parents punished her or tried to ruin her life.

"You're denying me the opportunity to relieve myself?"

She shook her head and waved her hands in the air. "Oh, no, no. What I meant was I don't know if I should take you myself." She glanced over her shoulder. "Maybe I should get one of the attendants to escort you."

"What's your name?"

"Ann."

"I'm sure you know mine."

"Yes, Ameerah. A lovely name." A soft smile crossed her face. Then it was chased away by a deep frown when her eyes rested on the right side of my cheek. "You have an ugly bruise."

I made a move to touch it, but the restraints prevented me. My whole body throbbed and ached and where my father struck me was part of it. "A mark of my father's love," I said.

"My father had the same kind of love for me." Her eyes widened, and she touched her lips. "I shouldn't have told you that. Sorry. Today is my third day here, and I should mind my tongue around patients. We're not supposed to get personal with them."

"Listen," I said, "I promise you I will not act out if you untie me from this bed and allow me to use the john and wash myself." I released the full power of my pleading and honest eyes on her.

"I have to accompany you . . . even when you . . . excrete your waste," she said, trying to frame in a diplomatic way that she had to watch me pee and take a shit. "But I'll do the best I can to give you some privacy."

I didn't like the idea of being shadowed.

How dare they strip my human rights away from me.

How could my parents do this to me?

I could feel my anger heating to a boil, but I managed to put a lid on it for the sake of gaining Ann's trust.

"I'd be a liar if I were to tell you being under watchful eyes didn't bother me," I admitted. "However, you have a job to perform, and I won't cause you any trouble. You have my word."

She nodded and undid the cuffs on my wrists first. I rubbed and massaged them while she worked on releasing my ankles. My whole body was stiff and sore. Slowly I pushed myself into a sitting position. The room spun, disorienting me. I held onto the edge of the bed and took slow, deep breaths to ward off the nausea.

"Are you okay?"

I hung my head, still taking slow, deep breaths. "I'll be fine. I feel a little nauseous."

"It's the medicine they gave you last night." She took my hand and gently guided me across the room. "Lunch is about to be served. You'll feel better once you get some food in you."

We entered an uncarpeted, vacant hallway that branched out on both ends. Several metal doors with bolts lined the walls. The blue paper booties I wore crinkled against the bottoms of my feet sliding across the shiny white floor.

"What did they give me?" I asked when we stepped into the restroom straight across from the room I was in.

Ann led me to a stall with no door, only an off-white partition that separated it from the other johns. "It was a barbiturate used to sedate patients. Sleep therapy is what some doctors dubbed it." She continued to talk while I emptied my bladder, keeping her word to give me as much privacy as she could.

Once I finished, I went to the sink and cringed at my reflection in the mirror. The right side of my face had a purple, yellowish bruise across my cheek, and the luster in my hazel eyes was gone. My complexion had a grayish cast. Whatever was injected into my body created a carbon copy of myself.

Ann handed me a washrag, and I realized there was no hot water when I went to dampened it. After I cleaned off my eyes and face, we headed down the north side of the hall. I listened to Ann tell me that most of the residents were in the common room, which explained the eerie silence.

"There you are," a manly nurse with thick forearms and a broad forehead said when we rounded the corner from another corridor. She was heading our way and seemed quite annoyed.

Ann stiffened but held her head high. "Ameerah caught my attention. She needed to use the lavatory, and now I'm taking her to the dining room for lunch."

"I realize you're new here, Ann," the other nurse said, "but we do not call patients by their first name in their presence. Each one has a number." She pointed at me. "This one is number sixty-four."

A laugh of disbelief escaped my lips. I couldn't help it. What type of place was this, sedating people, tying them to a bed, and calling them by numbers instead of their names? I found being called Sixty-four another check in the box under the dehumanization category. "Excuse me," I said when they looked at me, "I don't know what type of facility I'm in, but regardless, I have a name. It's Ameerah. To refer to me by a number is demonizing my identity, so I'd appreciate it if you would stick with my name instead."

The coarse nurse scowled. "We will do no such thing."

I made a face. "Why? What's the purpose in such a demoralizing act? And what the hell is this place?"

Still scowling the nurse snapped, "Watch your mouth."

"You're in an insane asylum," Ann said.

I stared at her, dumbfounded. "What? I thought this was a hospital to treat TB patients and some sort of rehabilitation facility."

Ann touched my arm. She had a nurturing nature about her that I found comforting, despite Helda the sea hags' glaring presence. "There is a secure wing off this building where people struck with tuberculosis go."

My head was pounding, and this bit of news seemed to amplify it. I rubbed my temples. My parents had me committed to a mental institution. How could they do this to me? I was their daughter. Their only child. But I knew why. They cared more about their social status than their own flesh and blood. I always knew it, but I never imagined they'd have me locked away. And although a newfound hatred for them brewed inside me, I couldn't stop the crushing blow to my heart. Tears spilled down my cheeks.

I looked at Ann through watery eyes. "I'm not crazy. You have to believe me. My parents double-crossed me, because they feared I'd ruin their reputation."

"Ann," the other nurse said in a warning tone when the new nurse was about to hug me. Ann stepped back. "This is why we call patients by their chosen number, instead of their name. It's a preventative measure for staff members not to get too personal with patients, unless you have the authority to do so, which you do not."

Ann nodded like an obedient child to a tyrannical father. Her behavior reminded me of myself while growing up. I detested it.

"You're needed in section B," the charge nurse said to her. "You'll no longer be assisting Sixty-four. Your behavior has compromised your position to do so."

"Yes, Norma." Ann muttered an apology and scurried past me without giving me a second glance.

I wiped the tears off my face, careful not to press on the bruise. In silence, I followed Norma down the hall. We made a right turn to another corridor. A metal gurney with straps hanging off its sides stood against the wall, waiting for its next occupant. I noticed a dark stain on the flimsy mattress where the head would lie and shuddered. I was in a living nightmare, and my earlier hope of escaping vanished when Ann was dismissed from my company. The only thing I had to work with was trying to convince Doctor Stratton that I wasn't insane.

"When will I get to visit with Doctor Stratton again?" I asked Norma when we stopped in front of a wooden door with thick slats across its length.

She pulled a ring of keys from her pocket and picked through them. I had the sudden urge to knock her out and snatch them from her. But I resisted and decided if my first plan didn't work, I would resort to any such violent behavior in order to gain my freedom.

She found the one she was looking for and slipped it in the lock. "He wants to see you after supper."

"Why so late?"

"You're not the only one in his care," she said in a clipped voice.

We entered a spacious dining area with a table stretching the length of the room. There were several entrances, and a group of women of all ages and dressed in drab clothes filed in. I caught the eye of a disheveled middle-aged woman. She flashed me a maniacal grin and made lewd gestures. I glanced at Norma to see if she witnessed what I saw, and she met my gaze.

"Go on, Sixty-four," she said. "Eat with your peers."

"Ameerah. My name is Ameerah. Did you see what that gal did?" I pointed in the direction where she now sat. "The one with the dark, wild hair."

Norma stepped in front of me. Her massive frame blocking my view of the table. The hard lines around her mouth deepened. "I will not have you question or disrespect my authority. I'm well aware of what your name is, but from now on, you will respond in a pleasant manner when I or any of the other staff members address you as Sixty-four. Is that understood?"

I wanted to tell her to go to hell, but bit my tongue instead and nodded.

A wicked smile crossed her face. My expression must have given away the defiance raging inside me, because she leaned forward and said in a low voice next to my ear, "Your treatment plan in Bandbridge will be based on my daily reports of your behavior to Doctor Stratton. So in essence, your fate is in my hands. I suggest you mind me and what I have to say"—she dropped her voice to a whisper—"as of right now . . . I don't like you." She faced me, her voice back to normal. "But you can change my mind. Do as I say without question, and my opinion of you might change."

I stared at her, too stunned to reply. Her admission was another blow to my chest. The thought never occurred to me that part of her job was to turn in detailed reports to my doctor regarding my conduct in this hellhole. I could see the promise in her dark eyes that she would spin lies about me if she desired. I was like a chained dog, outside in the eye of winter, shivering, left to starve and freeze to death. My only hope was my master to have a sudden change of heart and release me or someone to discover my wrongful imprisonment and save me.

No one was going to rescue me.

Norma was now my master.

Chapter Eleven

Dr. Stratton

To say lunch was unsatisfactory would be an understatement. We were served unsalted beef broth, a piece of unbuttered bread, and a cup of plain tea. I sat at the end of the long backless bench and kept to myself, trying to avoid eye contact. The gal beside me hummed quietly to herself while she rocked back and forth. Curiosity forced me to peek out of the corner of my eye in attempt to size up my company. The patients opposite me seemed to be in their own little world. Most of them were focused on their meal. I wondered if there were a few sane ones suffering the same plight as me. A skinny gal with long, straight hair the color of ginger was having a lengthy conversation with herself. She prattled on in mostly gibberish, and at intervals, she'd burst out in laughter as if she were told a funny joke. The one who had made an obscene gesture at me earlier sat at the other end of the table. I wasn't about to risk calling her attention to me, so I kept my eyes on my plate.

After lunch, Norma came back. I remained with her while the other patients were herded away by other staff members.

"Follow me, *Sixty-four*," she said, stressing the number.

Pressing my lips together, I walked beside her as we exited through a door into a hall. An overwhelming feeling of hopelessness ignited and burned what little optimism I had left inside me. There was no way I'd be able to escape on my own, even if I were armed with a ring full of keys. Bandbridge was a labyrinth of corridors and doors that I had no idea where they led. My only saving grace was to convince the doctor I was sane, so he'd release me.

Norma escorted me to a room where another nurse was thumbing through files in a metal cabinet. When she found what she was looking for, she turned and met me with a warm smile. She had a kind face and appeared to be in her early thirties. I wondered if she would help me.

"Good afternoon, Sixty-four," she said. "I'm going to take your measurements and give you a simple and painless exam." She set the chart she held on a counter lined with glass containers filled with cotton balls, band-aids, q-tips, and the like.

I returned the same pleasantries and didn't put up a fuss when she measured and weighed me. She also took my vitals and had me stick my tongue out.

Norma remained in the room the entire time, shadowing me while the nurse performed her job in a methodical, professional manner. When she inspected the bruise on my cheek, prodding it with her fingertips, I winced. She moved to the back of my head, touching a lump.

I jerked forward. "Ow." My hand automatically reached behind my noggin. "It's sore. Sorry, I didn't realize until now."

"I can give you something for the pain," she offered.

Norman shook her head. "Leave her be. Sixty-four needs a reminder of what can happen if she disobeys."

I loathed her.

Not long after, Norma left me in the common room, which was down another endless passageway. There were patients scattered in this living room-type setting, doing their own thing. Some sat at a long table near the center of the room, resting their heads on their arms, while others looked at magazines. One gal stood nearby, staring at the floor. Her lips moved in constant silent conversation. I didn't spot obscene gal and was grateful. I didn't want any trouble and wasn't sure if she would instigate something to get a rise out of me, but either way, I wasn't up to finding out.

I went to a barred window about five feet from the floor and sat in a cushioned chair next to it. I noticed more than a few of my peers who occupied couches and chairs such as mine had vacant eyes. A chill crawled up my spine when a thought occurred to me that any one of them could have been sane. But now as I watched their behavior, it was clear to me if they were sound minded upon entering Brandbridge, the treatment here changed it—changed them. I'd be damned if I would allow that to happen to me, but what if they were a reflection of my fate? I thought about the vision I had chained to a bed. Was it a premonition? What was Betty doing? I wondered what my parents told Delores. We had a show this weekend. What was Slim thinking? Abe was a smart fella. I wondered if he'd realize how fishy my disappearance was. If he did, I was sure between him and Slim, they'd be able to bust me out of here. Maybe there was still hope for me. Maybe.

"What's your name?" a soft female voice asked, startling me out of my mental chatter.

I looked up to a pair of wide, golden doll-like eyes and a wholesome face to match. "Ameerah," I answered. "What's yours?"

"Elizabeth or Liz for short," she said, mindlessly twirling a piece of her long light brown hair around her finger. "You're new. I've never seen you before."

"It's my first day. How long have you been here?" She seemed normal. I wondered why she was committed, and if she'd been double-crossed as well.

The corner of her mouth dipped. She looked at the ceiling. Her splayed fingers on her right hand moved up and down as she counted softly on each one. "Three months, I think. Maybe two."

"Have you ever tried to escape?" I couldn't imagine myself being in here for that long. I would surely go nuts. I glanced at the gal chattering and laughing to herself near the table. Maybe that was what happened to her.

Elizabeth shook her head. "There's no way out of here. It's completely secured."

A noise caught my attention—part crying, part whimpering. I glanced in the direction it was coming from. A young gal about my age sat in a corner with her knees drawn up, and her face pressed against them. My heart went out to her. I made a move to go to her.

"I wouldn't if I were you," Elizabeth said, halting me.

"Why?" I ask, not taking my eyes off the poor gal.

"You'll only irritate her, and she might go berserk."

I sat back down. "Why are you in here?"

"Our house caught fire and burned to the ground," she said, rubbing the side of her cheek. "My husband and I made it safely outside. Our five-year-old son, Samuel, didn't."

My hand flew to my mouth, covering it. "Oh, my God. I'm so sorry." I didn't know what else to do other than express my sorrow. What could you say to someone who lost a child?

She looked past me. Her expression fell into a deep sadness. "Yes, so am I." Her eyes met mine, and she smiled. "He's not gone."

"Yes, he'll always be with you, and you'll–"

"No, no," she abruptly said, waving her hand back and forth. "Sammy is with me most of the time. I told my husband this, but he wouldn't listen to me, stubborn man. Anyway, after he grew impatient with me, he had me committed here. But he's coming for me. My husband that is. I should be released any day now."

Her admission to seeing her dead son intrigued me. I wasn't sure if I should continue this conversation, but my curiosity got the best of me. "Does Sammy talk to you?"

"He does," she said with an enthusiastic nod. "He told me not to feel bad. It wasn't my fault, and he's having fun playing in the meadow with the other children and happy doggies."

"Did he describe where he is?"

She nodded again. "He said the flowers and grass are much prettier and brighter than here." Something caught her attention, and she laughed. "There's my Sammy." She pointed to the center of the room. "Do you see him? He's waving to me." She waved back and blew him a kiss.

Of course I didn't see anything, but that didn't mean he wasn't there. Maybe she had the ability to see spirits, like I had visions. Who was I to say she was full of baloney?

Norma entered the room along with a few staff members. Her immediate presence was like a black cloud in a gray sky.

While Norma was looking the other way, Elizabeth made a face directly at her. "That one," she said to me, "is a wicked woman. You don't want to cross her."

I frowned. "I know. I discovered that earlier when she threatened to falsify reports regarding my behavior to Doctor Stratton if I didn't mind her."

"She's the doctor's beloved aunt, ya know?"

My stomach dropped, and a sudden quake of despair caused my hands to tremble. I could feel my brittle emotions trying to hold it together crumbling. I took a deep, shaky breath, refusing to break down in public.

"Are you okay?"

I threaded my fingers, locking them together. It was time to eat, and we were ordered to get in line.

I rose from my seat. "No, Elizabeth, I'm not," I said. "In short of a miracle, I see no way of me getting discharged from here."

We were escorted into the dining area where we ate flavorless boiled meat, a plain baked potato, cold beans, and weak tea that had a pinkish tint to it. I picked at my meal and gave most of it to my neighbor who was a large woman that made grunting noises every so many minutes. Elizabeth sat on the other side of me, talking to her invisible son. She introduced him to me, and I played along, which delighted her.

Finally, it was time to visit with Doctor Stratton. If I could convince him I wasn't insane, I might be able to get out of here by Friday. At this point, he was my only hope.

Norma guided me to his office. I walked in silence with my hands clenched behind my back. The only thing she said to me was I better be on my best behavior, or she would personally make my life a living hell.

"How was your first day at Bandbridge?" Doctor Stratton asked me after Norma left his office.

I took a seat opposite him, the same one I was in yesterday. "Educational," I answered honestly.

"How so?"

"There are patients here who clearly need psychological help," I said. "I've never been subjected to such odd behavior or in an environment like Bandbridge."

He folded his hands on his desk and slowly nodded. "You come from a privileged background, so what you're saying is understandable."

"I feel bad for them," I admitted.

"You don't see any similarities with your own behavior?"

"No."

"Tell me about your visions?"

I shifted in my chair, my mind racing for a quick answer to throw at him. I grabbed the first one that came to mind because of the way he was looking at me, as if he were studying a foreign object, which set my nerves on edge. "I don't have visions," I lied. "I made it up."

"Why would you do such a thing? What could you possibly gain from it?" His skeptical expression told me he wasn't buying it. I could see this was a mistake. I should tell him the truth and be honest with him.

"I lied," I said with a heavy sigh. "I do have visions. I've had them since I was a child."

Doctor Stratton pushed his black, round cheaters up on the bridge of his nose and narrowed his eyes at me. "Why did you lie, Ameerah? I'm only trying to help you."

"I'm sorry," I said. "I don't want you to think I'm insane because I'm not. Just because I have visions doesn't mean I'm mad. Like I told you yesterday, John of Patmos had visions, and he wasn't considered looney."

"Yes, well," he said, "like I told you yesterday, John was a holy man. You're far from being an apostle of Christ, and as a Christian, I personally take offense to your comparison." He broke eye contact with me and busied himself with shuffling the papers on his desk.

"I didn't mean to offend you," I quickly said. "I was only trying to get you to understand my point of view on the matter."

"I'm a trained professional," he retorted. "From what I've read in your journal, what your parents and Norma told me, and from what I've seen with my own eyes, you need psychiatric help. You suffer from social transgression and–"

"What the hell does that mean?" I blurted, hearing the annoyance in my voice, but at this point I didn't care.

"Your behavior is not of the norm. You smoke."

"My father smokes, and so does just about everyone else, including gals such as myself."

"You drink alcoholic beverages."

"I'm not the only one. I realize it's prohibited, but that doesn't stop our politicians from abstinence."

"You dress in scanty outfits."

I laughed at the absurdity of his reasons for holding me against my will, and his compliant about my choice of attire was the icing on the cake. It was clear I wasn't going to be released and that his mind was already made up about me. I'd have to find another way to break out of Bandbridge.

"You find this comical, do you?"

"I find your examples regarding my social behavior ridiculous, and I think you're reaching for reasons to keep me here," I said.

His expression turned dark, and his thin lips tightened. "You're in no position to question or mock my assessment regarding your case. As a courtesy to you"—he pointed at me with a harsh jerk of his hand—"I made allowances which I rarely do and revealed why I'm keeping you here. You're morally insane, Ameerah, and are prone to delusions because of your visions and false beliefs in them."

"Why did you decide to tell me those things then?" I asked.

"Because you made a conscious decision to tell me you lied about not having visions, which proves to me you can be rehabilitated." He smoothed his black tie against his white shirt and looked long and hard at me. I stared back, refusing to look away. Finally he spoke: "I failed to add one glaring defect in your behavior with the other ones I already mentioned."

His disgust for whatever it was he hadn't mentioned thus far coated the air between us. It grew thick in a matter of seconds. My heart raced, but somehow I found the courage to respond, despite the repulsiveness gleaming in his dark eyes. "And what might that be?"

"Your sinful relationship with your best friend, Betty," he spat as if he had a bad taste in his mouth. I wanted to punch him in the face.

"Don't bring religion into this or my treatment plan," I shot back, digging my nails into the leather seat. "You nor anybody else has a right to judge me. What I do in my personal life is my business. If you take your ideology out of the equation, you'd realize what a foolish mistake it is to keep me locked up here. You know as well as I do I'm not mad. Sure I have visions. Why? I don't know, but look at Edgar Cayce. He's known as the 'sleeping prophet' and look at all the good he's done. He's not crazy."

Dr. Stratton rose from his desk and crossed the room. He opened the door and glanced into the hall where Norma was standing nearby. "We're done here."

I stood. "So that's it? You're not even going to consider what I said? It's wrong keeping me here, and you know it."

He ignored me and kept his attention on Norma. "See to it that Ameerah gets a good scrubbin'. She's covered in filth—inside and out. And if she gives you any lip, wash her mouth out with soap."

"You son-of-a-bitch!" I hollered, jumping to my feet, my hands clenched into fists.

Norma stepped into the office, her thick frame and broad shoulders swallowing the threshold, blocking my way out. She marched toward me while Doctor Stratton watched with an entertained expression on his face. I darted around the desk, flinging books, papers, and files at her.

"Stay away from me. I'm not crazy, and you know it," I said to Norma's ugly mug that had a hateful expression on it. She was determined to subdue me or squash me like a bug, maybe both. I wasn't sure, but she was focused on taking me down. The way her jaw was set in determination and her eyes narrowed on me left no doubt in my mind.

Two large fellas entered the room, flanking me. I grabbed some sort of trophy off a shelf next to the corner they were backing me into. I flung it at one of the attendants. It hit his shoulder, which caused him to yelp. He slapped a hand over it and backed away, allowing the other fella ahead of him. Norma pulled something out of her pocket. A needle. My first impulse was to snatch it from her. I reached in her direction, but she was too quick. Her meaty hand latched onto my wrist, yanking me to her. I was pulled off my feet and smacked the floor—a replay of yesterday's fiasco. The air was knocked out of my lungs. A continuous strained, raspy sound escaped my lips as I desperately tried to catch my breath. A sharp pain stabbed my arm. Despite my sudden disorientation, I kicked and swung my arms about with everything I had. Large hands latched onto my throat, choking me, starving me of oxygen, and then everything went black.

Chapter Twelve

A Living Hell

The side of my face was pressed against something cold and wet. My body shivered.

I was freezing.

Curling into a fetal position, I moved my hands close to my chest. My wrists felt heavy, and a rattling noise caused me to force my eyes open. My vision was blurry, and my head felt like it had been stuffed with cotton. My thoughts were sluggish.

I closed my eyes.

Tired.

I was so tired.

I could feel myself slipping beneath dark waters. How easy it would be to give into it, to be spared the daily doldrums of life by unplugging from it all. I'd live in my own little world where nothing could harm me and there would be no strife, only peace. Maybe that was how the patients with the empty eyes felt.

Patients.

Empty eyes.

Bandbridge.

Insane asylum.

My thoughts cleared, and a horrible wailing sound snapped me out of my stupor. My cheek was in a puddle of my own drool. With a start,

I sat up and felt soreness between my legs. My head swam and ached. My wrists and ankles were bound by steel clamps attached to a metal chain anchored to a bed bolted to the white tile floor—just like the vision I had. I pulled a tattered yellow blanket off the thin mattress and wrapped it around me in an attempt to stop my body from shaking. The wailing continued, followed by broken sobs. My stomach churned, and a fierce nausea ravaged my body. I turned my head, braced my hands on the floor, and vomited what looked like brown liquid in the dull light. My abdomen contracted, and once again my mouth fell open; an awful choking sound came out, followed by more bile. My throat burned, and I had a rank taste in my mouth.

"Please let me out of here," a female yelled, followed by more heart-wrenching cries.

The tiny concrete room I was in only had a bed, a sink, a small wastebasket, and a wooden chair in the far corner. There was a rusty pot within arm's length with a roll of toilet paper inside it. I had no doubt my detainment was Doctor Stratton's twisted game of punishing me. He read my journal, and this was his way of bringing my vision into fruition.

Bastard.

"Please let me out of here," the tearful voice repeated.

I didn't have much to work with and knew it wouldn't do me any good to plead for mercy like the poor gal across the hall. Not that I would anyway. I'd be damned if I'd give them the pleasure of breaking me.

There were no towels to clean up my vomit, so I took the pillowcase off a pillow on the bed and used it to mop up the mess. The chains rattled with every move I made, unnerving me. After I rinsed the pillowcase in the sink and hung it on the edge to dry, I scooped a handful of cold water into my mouth. Swishing it around, I spit it out in an attempt to get rid of the rank taste, wishing I had mouthwash. Unfortunately, I had to pee, so I took the toilet paper out, thankful at least I was given that luxury, and squatted above the bowl. The sound of urine hitting the pot echoed around me. Afterward, I tossed the used paper into the trashcan and dumped my waste in the sink, turning the water on full blast.

"Let me out." The cries continued.

My head was still pounding, and I wasn't feeling quite right. I didn't dare lie down in fear I may fall back asleep. I had no idea how long I'd been sedated, but I was determined to keep my wits as sharp as possible.

Wrapping the blanket back around me, I slumped on the floor against the bed. My thoughts scattered to where I couldn't focus on one subject for more than a minute. My parents got my first attention and their underhandedness to imprison me here. They would pay. I'd make sure of it. Before I could grasp a plan on how I'd carryout my revenge, I found myself musing about Betty. Was she okay? Would she or Abe search and find me? Then, clips of me being bound in a white jacket and sitting in the common room flashed before me. Needles being poked in my arm that were attached to a tube with liquid flowing to my veins pressed against my memory. I held out my arm and discovered little bruising track marks.

What the hell have they done to me?

How long had I actually been here?

The man with the ice-blue eyes came to me. A fuzzy memory of him on top of me, spreading my legs, saying something about after he was through, I'd be a converted woman only wanting dick, whirled around me along with distant laughter.

Dropping my head in my hands, I rubbed my temples. I could hear Elizabeth in my mind saying, "Ameerah. Ameerah." snapping her fingers next to my ear. I closed my eyes, holding fast to her voice calling my name. I could see the worry in her face, but the picture shifted in and out of focus. "They're drugging you too much," she whispered in my ear. "You need to find a way to get them to stop. You don't want to be a zombie for the rest of your life, do you?" I must have showed some small sign that part of me was still there and somewhat aware, because she smiled, nodded, and cradled my cheeks in her hands. "Yes, Ameerah, you're a fighter. I can see it in your eyes. You can beat them at their own game, but you must come back in order do it." With gentle fingers, she wiped the tears from my cheeks. "Don't cry. Do you want to see Sammy?" A white-haired boy of about the age of five appeared in front of me beside Elizabeth. His eyebrows knitted. He looked worried. He reached out, like he wanted to touch me. His image kept flickering, and I could vaguely recall my sluggish thoughts in those moments as being fascinated that along with Elizabeth, I could see her child's spirit.

The door opened, causing me to look up. Norma stood at the threshold. The hall light hung behind her, framing her massive body. I wanted to wrap the chains around her neck and choke the bitch to death.

"You're awake," she said in a gruff voice. She entered the room and surveyed our surroundings. "My, my. Sixty-four is resourceful, using the bedlinen to clean up whatever vulgar mess she created."

"How long are you going to keep me chained to this bed?" I asked, watching her every move. "And how long have I been sedated?"

She clapped her hands, and a taunting grin crossed her wide face. "You're in luck. It's bath time." She bent over and placed her hands on her knees. We were eye-to-eye, but she wasn't near enough for me to touch her. "Only if you promise to behave. Otherwise, you'll have to remain in restraints." She looked away and then back at me, her eyes wide like she remembered something exciting to tell me. "Oh! You've been in sleep therapy for about three weeks. It's now September."

Three weeks! How could someone dehumanize another person like that? I was appalled.

"What will it be, Sixty-four? Chained to the bed or a bath?"

The thought of having a bath and clean clothes appealed to me more than I wanted to let on. My whole body felt dingy and gross, including my hair. I wasn't a dumb Dora and would play along in order to get what I wanted.

"I promise," I said.

She went to the open door and waved someone in. A husky gal stepped into the room. She had a square jaw and thick black eyebrows that reminded me of a caterpillar. She wore the same nursing attire as

Norma and seemed equally as abrasive.

"This is Florence," Norma told me. "She will be the one bathing you."

"Bathing me?" I didn't think I heard her right. I was perfectly capable of washing myself. "What do you mean?"

Norma laughed, not bothering to answer. She pulled a ring of keys out of her pocket and picked through them until she found the right one. "If you make one strike against me or anyone else or even attempt to, I won't be so generous next time," she warned before she reached for the shackle on my wrist.

"I understand," I replied, wanting desperately to be free from these chains and the grime washed away from my body. I pushed the blanket off and offered my wrists to her.

She unlocked the clamps. They fell, making a heavy clattering noise when they hit the floor. Rubbing my wrists, I rose after she freed my ankles and followed Norma out of the room into a long, narrow, yellow corridor. Like an armed guard, Florence stayed behind me.

"Please don't keep me here," the sobbing gal begged on the other side of a metal door, across from the room I was in.

My heart broke for her. I almost asked why she was locked up and if she could join us, but the way Norma kept eyeing me, like she was waiting for an opening to pounce, I thought it best not to.

We halted at an iron door, which Norma unlocked. She yanked it open, and a whiny, creaking noise filled the silence. With both nurses on either side of me, we entered a large area attached to a network of underground tunnels—six to be exact. A sudden realization hit me that we were beneath the complex, and I'd been made more helpless by being tucked away from the other patients and attendants. They could do whatever they fancied, and no one would be none the wiser. The more I discovered about Bandbridge and the people who ran it, the more evil I thought they were.

We took the farthest tunnel to the right, which made me wonder where the other ones led. A pungent rotten cabbage odor lingered in the air in certain spots we passed. I was cold and wished I still had the blanket. Norma and Florence chatted about the weather and the new restaurant in town. I had a feeling they were purposely mentioning how great the food was as a not-so-subtle dig. They knew how rotten the meals were here and how hungry I must have been. Then, they went on about the horrible flappers and how they were a festering sore in society that needed to be cleansed before they contaminated the poor, innocent youths. I caught myself several times biting my lip and at one point, stuck my knuckle between my teeth and bit that, as well.

The tunnel merged into a basement. We climbed concrete stairs and passed through a door into a large, uncarpeted hallway with white-tiled floors almost too bright to look at. I continued to follow Norma until we stepped into a large bathing room.

"Take your gown off," Florence ordered.

The bathtub had brown water in it. A layer of dirt, hair, and what looked like bits of dried skin, covered the top. "Aren't you going to drain that and put fresh water in it? I don't want to bathe in someone else's filth."

"If you don't get in the damn tub," Norma snapped, "we'll chain you back to the bed, and you can live in your own filth."

A lump formed in my throat, and tears stung my eyes. I was reduced to being at their mercy because the grime on my own body, including between my legs, was too unbearable for me to deny even this unfavorable opportunity. I had made a promise to myself not to allow them to take my dignity, and they already had and were doing it again. I hated myself for this. I hated them.

Gritting my teeth, I released the gown from my body and stepped into the cool water. I held my hand out for the soap, but Florence ignored me. Instead, she took it upon herself to lather a thick scrub brush and proceeded to rub it against my skin in a firm manner. My hand went up to stop her, but then I saw Norma extract a hypodermic needle from her pocket. She waved it, taunting me with a wicked grin. I stopped myself from batting Florence away and endured the whole process of scrubbing my skin almost raw, straight down to her washing and pulling my hair.

The tears continued to flow.

I hated humans.

I really did.

I began doubting Betty's feelings for me. If she really loved me, she would have found me by now. The same with Abe, Slim, Delores, and even Cammy. They were my friends. Why hadn't they made an effort to save me? If anybody could have busted me out, it would be Slim. He was the big cheese and knew a lot of influential fellas.

Why?

My heart broke at the realization I wasn't important enough to be rescued.

After the horrid bath, Norma threw a towel at me, along with a gray and black checkered cotton dress, white undergarments, gray socks, and black slippers. I put the clothes on, refusing to look at my tormentors. Afterward, Florence took a comb to my hair. Closing my eyes, I endured the rough tugging the best I could, but when the teeth of the comb touched the sore spot on the back of my head, along with Florence's rough pulling, I hollered, "Ow!" and my hand automatically knocked her hand away, my palm covering that sensitive area. The next thing I knew, I was being yanked backward by my hair.

"You will not disrespect me," Florence said, gripping my tresses harder. "You will take what I dish out. Period!"

Something snapped inside my brain. The fear of all the consequences I'd have to bear for my actions was gone.

I had enough.

I backed into her in quick steps, and with all my strength, I shoved her into a wall, driving my elbow as hard as I could into her stomach. She let out a sharp gasp and released her grip. Norma charged me, her manly features contorted into a mask of anger. I dodged her and went to grab a wooden chair near the tub. I could have run out of the room, but then what? I had no way of unlocking the doors, so my plan was simple: knock Norma and Florence out with the chair, take the keys and everything else from them, and bust out of here. But when I picked it up, I could hardly lift it. I hadn't realized how weak I was from the lack of nutrition. I turned and was met with a hard blow square in the face. A loud crunching noise came from my nose, and blood poured out like a running faucet. My hands immediately went up in front of me, and I couldn't see anything because my eyes were watering from Norma's punch. The sudden pain almost blinded me.

"We need to teach Sixty-four to respect her elders," I heard Florence say.

I was roughly shoved backward into the bathtub. The sound of water splashing onto the floor surrounded me when I fell in. I was sitting sideways in the middle, my feet sticking up, my clothes soaked.

I swung my feet in while flinging water at them. "Get away from me!"

"It's too late for this one," Norma said, pushing my shoulders down into the soiled liquid and then my head.

My arms flung up to stop her, but Florence snatched my wrists and locked them to my sides. I kicked my feet as hard as I could and in panic, my body twisted back and forth in a struggle to survive. I ran out of breath, and my mouth opened, allowing the water to pour inside me. My chest and lungs were on fire, and everything became yellow and started to fade.

Some birds cannot be caged, and I'm one of them.

A sudden blackness followed, along with a fierce hate that swelled in my heart toward humanity. I detested humans, and mark my words, I would get my revenge on those who wronged me.

Chapter Thirteen

Recruiting Station

I was in a black void.
One Mississippi.
Two Mississippi.
Three Mississippi.

Three seconds later, everything turned bright white, but it didn't harm my eyes. Silhouettes of people stood in the distance. There were a couple fellas wearing top hats among the group. I could hear them inside my head; their voices were much clearer and brighter than on earth. It was as if the sun shined on each spoken word. They were talking about my arrival. Curious. But then someone said murder when another asked how I died. The anger in me boiled when sharp images of my demise took hold of me, and the thread of communication between us distorted. The air swirled around me. A grayish, black funnel formed, incasing me inside its belly.

Don't be afraid.

I wasn't, I told the phantom voice. The resentment I harbored was too intense to bother with such frivolities. My state of being was wound tightly with sinews of hate, revenge, disgust, and the like.

Good.

In a matter of seconds, I found myself in a dreary realm, standing on a wooden bridge. A wrought iron lamp post was positioned on both ends. A golden hue lit its glass case. Mist rose from the dark water below, and tall ebony trees stretched across the landscape, their bare limbs webbing the greenish, yellowish sky.

"Where am I?" I wondered out loud, more intrigued than scared. In fact, I felt a sense of elation rather than doom, like I was on the cusp of a once-in-a-lifetime opportunity that could elevate me in ways I'd never imagined.

"You're at a recruiting station."

My eyes darted around me, looking for the owner of the voice I heard. A tall fella appeared through a break between the trees. I crossed the bridge and met him halfway. His attire reminded me of the bartender at Slim's speakeasy: brown trousers, matching suspenders, newsboy hat, and an off-white long sleeved button-up shirt—a familiar sight that warmed my heart. I instantly liked him.

"Recruiting station?" I was off the trolley, because I didn't understand what he meant. "I see no one here but us?"

His welcoming smile reached his deep blue eyes. "I have a lot to teach you, lass, but before my manners run away from me, I'm Aidan Cain Logan to be precise. If you accept my offer, I'll help you along." I opened my mouth to introduce myself, but he spoke before I could, his Irish accent sprinkling each word. "Ameerah Arrowood. No middle name. I know all about you, so there is no need for you to layout your biography."

"How?" I was dumbfounded he had knowledge of my existence and wondered if he really did know everything about me and my life on earth or if he was fooling me.

He moved his hand above his head clockwise. The trees vanished, revealing a vast, endless field of crushed wheat. Groups of shadowy figures in pairs were scattered across the planes. He repeated his gesture; only, this time his hand went counterclockwise instead. The image disappeared, replaced by the prior one.

"Just because your eyes cannot see what's around you, doesn't mean it's not there," he simply stated. "On the matter of me knowing who you are, the best way I can explain it is each recruiter is assigned a certain area on earth. When a spirit harbors and emits an energy, much like our own, we're drawn to it. We watch it."

I wasn't sure how I felt about his admission. Was he the cause of all the turmoil in my life? "Did you have a hand in my demise?"

His brown hair brushed back and forth against his collar when he shook his head. "Nah, I've never toyed with your life. I like your spunk. Besides, recruiters can't possess soulless humans or humans who allow us passage into their bodies unless we're on duty with a newbie."

"Soulless humans?"

"There are people born without a soul," he said as if it were old news. "Dark spirits can dwell in these soulless humans, live the life they desire, and enjoy the pleasures of being back in the flesh, such as sex, alcohol, drugs, food, and whatnot. It's quite fun actually. I'm looking forward to jumping into the game again."

My thoughts spun.

Dark spirits?

Soulless humans?

Possession?

Normally, I would think he was full of baloney, but considering where I was and what I'd seen thus far, I had no reason not to believe him.

"You want revenge on your parents. Am I correct?" he asked and at the same time snapped his fingers.

A motion picture screen materialized beside him. Clips of my life from infancy to my father and mother abandoning me at Bandbridge appeared. Not every situation was displayed but enough to awaken the sorrowful and angry emotions alive within me. Honestly, the events during my childhood I could easily let go, despite my heartache. However, my parents double-crossing me by having me locked away in an insane asylum where I was abused, drugged, and bumped off I couldn't swallow. When I watched the part where Father told me I was sick and mentally unstable, I had enough.

"Stop," I said, balling my hands into fists, tears wetting my cheeks.

Aidan snapped his fingers twice. The screen disappeared. A fierce animosity intertwined with rage and vengeance aimed directly at my parents gripped me. I'd made a promise to Father I'd do everything in my power to ruin him, and now I might get my chance.

"Ameerah, do you still want–"

"Yes," I replied, and for some reason when he said my name, I thought about Norma addressing me as Sixty-four and why she did so. I'd find a way to take care of her, as well. "Yes, I want revenge. Tell me what I need to do in order to accomplish it, and what the fuck is a dark spirit? Is it a demon? Does Hell exist?" I was in an irritable mood so those questions flew out of my mouth. I wrung my hands, then stretched them out before balling them into fists again.

Aidan laughed in an absurd sort of way, like I was full of baloney. "Human's definition of demons and Hell is rubbish. Hellfire and eternal damnation does not exist. There is, however, the Sheol of Glass, which is a dimension with large pockets of darkness where some spirits go until a witch or the person who sent them there frees them. There are also other dimensions, such as the lower world, that could be considered a Hell-like existence, but nothing like you were taught in bible school."

"I'd like to know about them," I said, my interest piqued at the thought of multiple prison realms and how I could avoid being sentenced to one.

"If you would like, I'll teach you what you need and want to know," he said. "On the matter of what a dark spirit is, we're anarchist. The only authority we have to answer to, which is rare by the way, is the "old one" who is the first of our kind. He's the reason I'm here, because I have to prove myself in order to join his ranks." Aidan flipped his hand in the air in a sweeping motion, indicating the realm we're in, his handsome face twisted in annoyance. "But for the most part, the "old one" allows us our freedom. He only intervenes when he absolutely must."

"Why are spirits such as yourself called a dark spirit? Is it because you're evil?" Aidan didn't seem wicked to me. I liked him and wanted to get to know him better.

"We're called dark because we do whatever the hell we want," he said, "and if the light walkers don't like it, they can stick it up their arses." He curled his first two fingers and jerked them in the air, emphasizing his statement.

I laughed. "You slay me." He was a funny fella, and I imagined he'd be a riot to have a few cocktails with.

"Humans call them angels, but we can chat about them later. Anyway," he continued, "dark spirits can be ruthless and considered evil, but like I mentioned earlier, for the most part, we're all about having fun and enjoying the pleasures of being in the flesh. We have the ability to manipulate situations to our advantage and experience whatever life we wish."

"Sounds wonderful," I said. "But what if I decided not to become one? Then what?"

He frowned. "You'd have to do what the light walkers said in order for you to move on. They would council you on the life you led and the experiences you went through. You also wouldn't be able to get your revenge on your folks."

I loathed authority I was forced to follow, and I couldn't allow my parents to get away with what they'd done to me. I wanted them to suffer as much as I had, but there were a couple more questions I had to ask before I made my decision.

"What if I change my mind and no longer want to be a dark spirit?"

He looked me straight in the eyes and said, "You'll have to seek salvation, then."

My gaze was locked onto his. I blinked. "Oh, and I'd have to perform whatever duties the light walkers told me in order to crossover?"

"Correct."

After my whole ordeal in Bandbridge, the thought of being forced to do something I didn't want to sickened me. "Will I be selling my soul if I were to become a dark spirit?"

He laughed and shook his head. "No, Ameerah, your spirit and soul are two different things. You cannot sell your soul. The closest thing is a blood oath, and we're not performing one."

I thought about everything he told me and all the things I'd need to learn. I could experience anything and everything a human life had to offer and live the rest of my existence the way I wanted to. The earth would be my playground.

The elation I felt when I entered here returned, and so did the revulsion and hate toward my parents and everyone who did me wrong.

"You said you'll help me along and teach me what I need and want to know," I said more as a statement than a question.

"Correct," he answered and placed a reassuring hand on my shoulder. "I won't throw you to the wolves, lass. I'll teach you an entertaining new way of life that's quite simply brilliant. Trust me on this."

His sincerity was all I needed to cinch my decision. I smiled. "You have yourself a new dark spirit, then."

Chapter Fourteen

A New Existence

Aidan wasn't one to instruct me in a classroom setting where I'd take notes on what I needed to know in order to exist in this new life I'm about to embark on. I agreed. I was more of a hands-on type of gal and had no qualms with getting dirty. Besides, he'd told me that showing how to possess a human was the only time he had permission to dwell in the human flesh while paying his dues as a recruiter. He wanted to dive into that part straightaway, because frankly, he was dying for a good Irish whiskey and smoke. No pun intended.

He took my hand, and the next thing I knew, I had an aerial view of a picturesque town surrounded by forest, mountains, rivers, and ocean. It was spectacular. I felt like a seagull flying through the pinkish, lilac sky, scouring the land, so I could settle down for the evening. When I was human, I had a fear of heights, but as a spectral being, there was no terror—only exhilaration. I could feel the weather shifting. Rain. Soon the sky would open up and weep. Strange I could not smell it. In fact, I had no sense of smell at all.

Aidan lofted us high above a wooded peninsula jutting into a wide river. A ferryboat belched black smoke while approaching a small town below. "Astoria is built on the oldest settlement in Oregon and is known for its logging industry and fishing where the Columbia meets the Pacific Ocean."

I looked at him. A wave of dull, doting hues of black, gray, brown, and green, floated beside me. A rippled extension of those colors connected to me. My mind compared what I saw to a group of dust motes but bigger and luminous. I glanced at my form. It mirrored his, only the shades were muddied red and green. There were also pink, orange, yellow, and gray in the mix.

"Those are parts of your soul," Aidan told me, obviously sensing my curiosity. "As your current spirit changes, so does its colors. The soul is pliable and reflects the state of the spirit attached to it."

"Amazing." I thought about it as I watched a fishing vessel down below move across the water. There were docks ahead of us with boats moored around it, and it looked like groups of fellas unloading cargo or fish. I couldn't tell. "We're made up of energy, then?"

"Yes," he answered, then changed the subject. "See the large building over there? It's a bunkhouse for the lads who labor in the cannery. They're mostly Chinese workers seeking a better way of life for themselves and families."

"Is that where we're going?" We turned left over the docks. "I guess not."

"I'm taking you to an underground club . . . a speakeasy, where my pals are. Soulless humans like to meander around that area. If we're lucky, we'll find a couple to use as part of your training."

"Nifty." I could hardly contain my excitement. I was not only intrigued by being able to inhabit a soulless individual but was also looking forward to the experience. It made me wonder if I ever knew a person without a soul. Were my parents some of them? Then, I thought about Norma, Florence, and Doctor Stratton. If so, was my torment and misery caused by a dark spirit? Since Aidan had been watching me while I was human, I asked him.

"Your Ma, Da, and the others do have a soul." he said. He tapped his finger on the side of his head. "They're just off their nut."

We landed on a street between rows of colorful shops that were connected. A few had metal signs poking off the building: Astoria

Electric Co., Furniture, Drugs. The lampposts were evenly spaced down the sidewalks and already lit. Vehicles were parked alongside the street, which gave me hope that our choice in a host would be plentiful so I wouldn't have to practice dwelling in an unattractive rag-a-muffin.

"Off their nut?" I made a face, at first not understanding what he meant, but then it clicked. "You mean crazy?"

"You got it, lass." His eyes widened, and he made a swirling gesture near his ear. "Bonkers. Mad." He paused and tilted his head like he was trying to hear a distant noise. He smiled and slapped me on the shoulder. "We're in luck, although I wish there was a soulless lad nearby I could occupy." He shrugged. "No matter. We'll have to get by for now." He pointed to a gal in a white polka dot dress, strolling down the sidewalk. "You hear it?"

"Hear what?" There were people getting in and out of vehicles, some were leaving, while others headed to different shops. Their conversations were muddled because I wasn't close enough to eavesdrop.

"The dull, low humming noise," he said. "The soulless emit such a sound. It's how we can identify them. Their energy is similar to ours."

We moved closer to the gal, to where I could see the round, brown curls pinned around her head in a feminine style. As we approached, an auditable, monotone noise reached me. How odd.

"I can hear it now." I had the sudden desire to possess her, to own the body. There was no need for me to ask how I could accomplish such an act; he saw it in my expression.

He smiled and nodded. "As you grow accustom to your new existence, there will be no hesitation such as you're displaying now. Rest assured, little bird, all will be second nature to you soon enough." He nudged me with his elbow. "Step into her energy field and imagine being inside that voluptuous body. Her vitality can be yours if you take it."

I did as he instructed. I stood in front of her, and she halted. I waved a hand in front of her face. She couldn't see me. Her brown eyes appeared like empty-mirrors, only reflecting the outside world instead of taking everything in and absorbing her surroundings. She was a meat suit with a pulse. I wondered what it would be like to be inside her, looking out through those eyes. What sort of vision did she have? What about memories? Would I be bombarded with her life history?

"Go on. What are you waiting for?"

I looked at him, hesitant, yet anxious at the same time to possess her. "What if I get overwhelmed with everything that has happened in her life?"

"You won't, lass," he said. "The only information you'll acquire is the basics, nothing personal. You'll see."

"How do I leave the body?" The thought never occurred to me until now that I had no idea how to leave if I wanted to.

"A fledging like you won't be able to dwell inside the human flesh for long," he answered. "Your spirit will vacate on its own. I'll go into more detail about the mechanics of it later. But for now, your first lesson is to merge with that body." His gaze darted over polka dot's shoulder. A cheerful smile spread across his face. "The lad exiting the drugstore is soulless. This is grand." With the back of his hand, he tapped the side of my shoulder. "Watch what I do, then follow suit."

He crossed the short distance between us and the fella in quick strides, like a feline charging a field mouse. As soon as he stepped in front of the fella, Aidan's face and chest latched onto the human while his back stretched outward, as if he were a rubber band being pulled away from the body, disfiguring his profile. Then, he slammed into it, disappearing from sight. The fella, who was now occupied by Aidan, rolled his shoulders and shook his arms out. He looked in my direction and with a sly smile, winked.

"Now or never, Ameerah," I said to myself. Taking a deep breath, I visualized inhabiting this gal and what it would feel like to take up residence inside her body. A tingling sensation took hold of me. Then, it felt like someone was pulling my arm back until I jerked forward in an abrupt manner, causing me to gasp. Everything went black. The next thing I knew, I was looking out of someone else's eyes, thankful to see clearly.

"Ameerah," Aidan said, sounding unsure, his voice much deeper in his new host.

I raised my arms above my head, locked my fingers together, and stretched like I used to before dance practice. "Mission accomplished." I clucked my tongue and breathed in the thick earthy smell of rain lingering in the air, savoring the aromas I hadn't realized I missed until now.

I suddenly became aware this human's muscles weren't as flexible as mine were when I was alive, and her frame was wider. Not fat by any means, just more voluptuous, to quote Aidan's earlier description. The heavy full kind of feeling and stiff joints had me flexing my fingers and twisting my torso from side to side.

"Within a fair amount of time, you'll adapt." Aidan hooked his arm through mine, turning me toward the row of businesses. "Once inhabiting humans becomes second nature to you, the discomfort you're experiencing now won't be so potent." He gave me a sidelong glance. "How you feeling?"

I squirmed against him as we sauntered on. "Uncomfortable, like I have an itch I cannot scratch."

"To be expected, lass, but–" A couple fellas in nifty suits and fedora hats passed us, chatting about oil prices. When they were out of earshot, Aidan continued. "When you bust out of this vessel,"—a beam of light, swiped across his hazel eyes—"stay nearby. I'll be there as soon as I can."

I stopped in my tracks and untangled myself from him. I blinked, questioning if what I saw was real or if it was some sort of side effect from possessing another being.

Aidan's eyebrows knitted. "What's the matter?"

I told him what I saw. He smiled and shook his head, assuring me my eyes hadn't betrayed me. What I encountered was real. He went on to explain that when a dark spirit inhabited a human, a laser beam would flash over the iris or part of it or the whole eye would glow. Each condition determined the age of the entity. The older you were, the more brilliant your eyes would be.

"Are we the only ones who can see it?" The smell of burgers and fries wafted in the air. My stomach rumbled and pinched with hunger. I almost had forgotten the feeling of having an appetite. I then realized if I were to crossover, the desires, needs, and pleasures of the human body would only be a distant memory and nothing more. It was a damned shame, and I was pleased with my decision to become a dark spirit, although at the moment I was feeling a sharp tightness around this body too unbearable to ignore.

"No," he said. "People who are marked for immortality and the immortals can see the an–" He clutched my arms in a desperate manner, startling me. "Hold on, lass. Don't let go yet."

The shocked look on my face must have alarmed him, or somehow he could tell I was losing my grasp on Clara.

Hold up.

How could I possibly know–

As if a waxed seal on a letter had been broken, trivial information regarding Clara and her life unfolded. I remembered my conversation with Aidan regarding the host's memories. What he told me proved to be correct, which strengthened my trust in him even more.

Still gripping my arms, Aidan's eyes peered into mine. They darted back and forth, possibly checking to see if he could spot my spirit. "You're still there." It wasn't a question. He knew. The anxious expression on his face melted into a relieved one.

"I am, but I can't hold on much longer." I narrowed my gaze while attempting to ignore the horrible, constricting, and itchy feeling invading my entire spirit. "Immortals, Aidan? Really? Are you going to tell me Dracula exists, too?" Honestly, I wasn't sure if he was fooling me, but for some reason the notion immortals existed was hard for me to swallow. I knew the knowledge I'd obtained and the wondrous things I'd seen thus far made my doubt seem silly. However, I couldn't change how I felt and would voice my skepticism whenever I saw fit to do so.

He laughed. "No, lass, vampires don't exist." An elderly couple, both wearing hats and smartly dressed, crossed the street and headed our way. Aidan lowered his voice, "Leave this vessel, and we will chat about the immortals. I should have told you about them from the start, but my desire to have a glass of fine Irish whiskey got the best of me. My apologies."

The older fella touched the brim of his hat and nodded when he and his companion walked past us. "Good evening," he said.

"Good evening," Aidan and I answered in unison.

Aidan turned his back on them and stepped closer to me. "Can you smell the rain? It's going to be pissing soon. I suggest we leave these vessels and chat somewhere else."

When he said the last word, a sudden suffocating feeling rushed through me. Claustrophobia settled in. I bent over and opened my mouth to gulp in some air.

"Leaving a vessel gets easier, lass," Aidan said, wrapping his arms around me and guiding me to a bench nearby. "Relax and give into it. Your spirit will eventually acclimate to possessing humans, but right now it's a bit knackered from struggling to hang on. You need to regain your energy. Let go, so we can crack on."

I was able to get enough air into my lungs and stop myself from panicking. With Aidan's arm draped around my shoulders, we sat, and I relaxed. I gave into the squeezing pressure around the head, throat, and chest area. In a matter of seconds, a whooshing noise reached my ears. My stomach flipped. Everything went black. A loud popping sound echoed around me. Then, I found myself standing in front of Clara and the human Aidan was dwelling in. A tired heaviness weighed upon my spiritual form. I was exhausted and needed to rest. My only thought at the moment was a nice comfy bed.

"Way to go, lass," Aidan said from behind, startling me.

I turned around and slapped his shoulder. "Don't sneak up on me."

He flinched back and held his hands up in surrender. "Sorry, I didn't mean to frighten you. I thought you saw me leave."

"No, I didn't."

"I gather you were too preoccupied at the moment to have noticed."

"Wow, you're brilliant," I said, sarcasm dripping from my voice.

He laughed good-heartedly. "Beautiful and sassy, just how I like my women."

"Can we go somewhere I can rest?" I asked in a middle of a yawn, ignoring his comment. "I also want to know about the immortals."

"I know where we can go that'll suit our energy." He took my hand, and when we blinked out of downtown Astoria, the image of Clara on the bench with her head against the fella's shoulder—both appearing sound asleep—faded away.

Chapter Fifteen

The Immortals

The white moon was bright and full, its rays breaking through the canopy of trees. Like splayed fingers, the beams touched the clearing we occupied. The energy field we were in was soothing, reminding me of soaking in a nice, hot tub of water after a long, strenuous day. I sat on the ground and leaned against a log. I breathed a sigh of comfort while Aidan stood before me, animated as ever, showing no signs of fatigue.

"There are hot spots around earth where we can go to reenergize," he told me, "such as this area"—he swept his hand in the air in a round circle, indicating the perimeter—"deep in the forest."

"What about the immortals?"

"I'll get to them in a minute," he said and continued. "When immortals cast you out of a human, your spirit automatically catapults to an unsavory territory where you will feel pain before you can regain your energy. The agony has to do with the incantations they say while they're driving you out of the body. A spell of some sort. Once you're in tiptop shape, you have to wait until a soulless person enters your area in order to escape your confinement."

I frowned. "Have you ever had the misfortune of such an experience?" I didn't know who the immortals were, but from the sound of them, I wouldn't want to cross one. I wondered if I'd be able to tell when one was around. Then I thought, how would they know when one of us was dwelling inside a human?

Aidan rubbed the side of his face and nodded. "Unfortunately, I have. Not a jolly good time if I do say so myself. Eventually, you'll learn how to evade them, and the older you get, the bolder you'll become due to knowing each one and their personalities. It's a game of cards, lass, where you'll learn which one to put down, when to call their bluff, and when to leave the table."

I was good at reading people and understood what he was saying. Hell, my whole damned childhood was like what he described. I could feel a cockiness growing inside me as I imagined an immortal approaching me with the determination to cast me out. Fuck him or her. What I did and how I chose to live my life was my own damned business. What right did they have to encroach their standards upon mine? As long as I did no harm to anyone . . . well, one's who didn't deserve to suffer . . . what business was it of theirs? None.

Aidan sat beside me and rested his arms on his knees. "Now you know two different places you can go to regain your energy when you exit a vessel. You can also jump from body to body if there are soulless ones around or a human with a soul invites you in. Oh, and one other thing." He looked at me, a caveat expression marring his features. "If you're scared, you'll be trapped inside the flesh, which is fucking horrible."

"Why is that?"

"Because you can be tortured. You're possessing a human; therefore, you feel everything. Also, if the human dies, you will be sent directly to one of these spots."

I sat up and turned to him. "How does an immortal know when we're around?"

He touched his ear with the tip of his finger. "Their ears ring, and remember they can see the beam of light flash across our eyes or if our eyes glow."

"Nifty for them, but not so swell for our kind," I said, hearing the disappointment in my tone.

"But they have to be within close proximity in order to detect us," he added.

"Well, it's nice to know they do have restrictions." Rubbing my forehead, I sighed. I could feel the exhaustion loosening its grip, but my head swam with everything he'd been telling me. The information was a lot to take in, and I was sure we hadn't even scratched the surface yet. But nonetheless, I was intrigued and wanted to know more. Of course, I was realistic. I'd forget some of the things Aidan had told me and would have to discover them on my own. I was okay with it, and the fact that Aidan would more than likely overlook helpful information I could use to aid me in this new existence.

"When we possess a human, we have powerful strength," Aidan said. "The immortals on the other hand, have remarkable strength, and they're fast."

"How fast?"

He raised his eyebrows and half-smiled. "Like a bullet."

My mouth dropped. "No way."

"I'm telling the truth, lass." He crossed his heart. "You'll see it for yourself one day, and regardless of them being our adversaries, you'll be amazed by it."

"Why do they have so many advantages over us?" I picked up a stone and tossed it aside. "Seems unfair to me."

"Indeed, it is," Aidan said. "Some lads are born with a silver spoon in their mouths and get everything handed to them instead of earning their keep by the sweat off their brows. Whereas others are born with a wooden spoon and are forced to carve out a living for themselves. However, in the process they learn how to be self-sufficient and adaptable."—he tapped the side of his temple with his finger—"thinkers."

"Survivors," I chimed in and smiled.

"Yes." Aidan nodded, mirroring my smile. "The immortals may have several advantages over us, but we have more than a few tricks up our sleeves."

The sound of leaves rustling behind me caught my attention. A doe paused at the edge of our clearing. She raised her nose and sniffed the air. Her brown eyes met mine. She stared, acting like she could see my presence. She then blinked and turned around, leaving the way she came.

"Can we possess animals?" I asked, wondering what it would be like to look out from inside another species.

"No, lass," Aidan answered. "However, there is a cat named Zeruel. His energy is pure and has never been tainted. What dwells inside that feline is the light of creation. Mortals who have been marked for immortality will discover Zeruel on their front doorsteps. He protects them from us until the human decides which path to take."

Intrigued, I sat up and crossed my legs. "What can he do to us?"

Aidan picked up a stick and drew the shape of a cat into the dirt. "He emits a powerful light we can see. If we go near it, we'll get trapped inside his radiance." He shrugged. "Or so I was told."

"What does he look like?"

"His face and paws are black," he said and used the tip of the stick as a pointer on his drawing while he continued Zeruel's description. "His body is dark gray with black markings throughout his fur. There's also a large black star on his back." He drew a star on his picture, for visual purposes I supposed.

I lay back, leaned my head against the log, and closed my eyes. "Interesting. Who would have thought a powerful entity would choose a cat to dwell in."

"Witches have familiars, and ninety percent of the time they're cats."

"True." I opened one eye and peeked at him. "Are there really witches who can perform magic? My grandmother used to tell me tales about the witches in Salem and about the witch trials."

"Yes, and gaining their friendship greatly benefits us. So when you come across one, I suggest you make a pal." He stood. "How are you feeling?"

"Better." The exhaustion had lifted and a newfound source of revitalizing energy had me jumping to my feet. I was ready to possess another human and was determined to hang on longer this time around. My goal was simple: accomplish dwelling inside a vessel for as long as it suited my purposes. Then, I would devise a plan to ruin my parents' lives. My revenge would be sweet justice, and I was anxious to get on with it. "I'm ready for another go," I said.

"Atta girl," Aidan said with an adorable grin that would cause any straight female to be weak in the knees, whereas I appreciated the view but was immune to his boyish good looks.

"Where are you taking me now?" I offered my hand to him.

"Back to the same place as before, lass." At his touch, we blinked out of the forest before I could respond.

* * *

We were in a club with tables evenly laid out around a square dance floor. Swirls of cigarette smoke clouded the air. The jewelry the women wore twinkled beneath the dim lights. A cacophony of laughter, conversations, and high-spirited jazz welcomed me like an old friend, invoking a bittersweet longing to be back at Slim's speakeasy. Even the band playing on an elevated platform in the back of the room brought back fresh memories of countless hours of practicing routines with my gals. I couldn't help but wonder who was leading them now and if any made an effort to contact me. I doubt they had, which left a bad taste in my mouth for humanity. Then, I thought of Betty. What in the world had become of her? Could true love be fleeting when outside forces slams its disapproving will upon the blissful couple? I wasn't sure, and the thought of Betty abandoning what we had broke my heart. To be honest, though, the same feelings I'd experienced before I was bumped off in Bandbridge regarding Betty not caring about me still remained; however, a small sliver of hope that I could be wrong kept me from falling to pieces. Maybe not all humans were bad seeds upon this earth. I reminded myself that I wasn't, so there had to be some exceptions, right?

We stood in the back, away from the crowd. Despite the jazz playing, I could hear the dull, low humming noise soulless people emitted. The sound came in all directions. I nudged Aidan with my elbow. "I thought we were returning to downtown Astoria."

He was scanning the crowd, appearing to be looking for someone in particular, his expression bright with excitement. "We did, only we're in a secret juice joint beneath the barber shop." He shrugged. "I figured why not take you to where the action is instead of fucking about? Besides, this is a haven for the soulless, our kind, and of course humans who don't have a fucking clue they're flirting or conversing with a dark spirit." He laughed. "We could be rattling their kidneys with our budgin' and they wouldn't know it was one of us."

"True," I said, sharing in his laughter, wondering if any of my friends had and didn't know it. The whole idea was both creepy and deceptively comical in the sense that most so-called normal men and women were either too self-involved or sleepwalking through life to notice what was really going on in front of their own eyes. I saw nothing wrong with such devious acts on our part. I no longer had respect for them, and if I ever did, the individual would have to earn it. Yet in this moment of time, I despised humankind.

Aidan kept peering about. I followed his scattered line of vision among the sea of faces. "Who are you looking for?"

"A lad whose characteristics are similar to mine." He glanced at me. "Think of this as being in a sweetshop where you can choose whatever suits your fancy." He pointed to a pretty blonde flapper holding a cocktail in her hand and laughing with a group. "What do you think about that one? I'd poke her." He waggled his eyebrows.

I bumped my arm against his. "Not if I decide to possess her, which I'm thinking I might." She had my style—from the feminine dress of dusty, rose chiffon to the light shades of pearl and iridescent beads that were part of an elaborate lace pattern throughout the material. The overlay of fringe set off her flapper ensemble perfectly. I loved it and wondered if she was a hoofer like me.

"Haven't you ever been poked by a lad before?" Aidan asked.

"You should know. You've been watching me for quite some time," I answered.

"I didn't watch your every mooove," he said, drawing out the last word. "I had other souls to attend to."

"Well, then, yes I have if you must know." I kept watching the blonde gal carrying on a conversation with a fella in a newsboy hat similar to what Aidan wore. She had a nice body that wasn't too thin and looked like she was about five-six. Perfect.

Aidan's eyes widened, and the tone of his voice pitched in disbelief. "And you didn't like it?"

I scrunched up my nose. "No, it wasn't a good experience."

He laughed. "Of course it wouldn't be. A lady's first time being poked is always the worse."

I frowned and held up three fingers.

"With the same lad?" He sounded skeptical, like maybe the one fella wasn't a good lover, and I needed to broaden my horizon. "Maybe he didn't know how to use his flute properly."

"No, with three different fellas." The trio of times were black check marks in a box labeled *not attracted* with a list of categories I'd created inside my head. Sure, I'd expected my first experience to be laden with pain, but it also didn't help matters that I wasn't in the least bit attracted to the fella. But perhaps I was just being fickle. Or so I thought. My hope was to cure myself of my unrelenting attraction toward the female form. My girlfriends would gush about the petting parties they'd attended and what a thrill they were. Their constant chattering on the subject raised a new consciousness within me. I was different from them. I had no desire to allow a fella to passionately embrace me and open myself to him, so he could pillage my body with his hands, tongue, and organ. But my yearning to be normal had trumped my reservations to be intimate with the opposite sex. In the end, I discovered some things about myself: being penetrated and stimulated was the cat's meow. The ultimate. I loved it. Being penetrated and stimulated by a fella, not so much. In my secret fantasies, another female did those things to me. I'd touch myself, imagining it to be her instead of me. My breathing would become erratic, my soft moans adding to the erotic visual inside my head. But they were her passionate moans, created by me pleasing her. She'd arch her back, her breast perfect, beautiful mounds. She'd cry out in ecstasy, which always sent me into an explosive orgasm. I was a hopeless case. But despite me knowing those things about myself, I lived in denial until that fateful day with Betty where my fantasies became reality. I sighed. "I'm not attracted to the opposite sex. At all."

"Well, I can't really blame you there, lass." With a nod of his head, Aidan indicated to the blonde I'd been eyeing. "Why don't you take over that show pony, and I'll do the same with the lad in the newsboy hat."

"He's chatting with the blonde now and has a cocktail in his hand," I said more to myself than him. "I wonder what they're drinking."

"We're about to find out, lass." He placed his hands on top of my shoulders. "Please try to hang onto the body for as long as you possibly can. I think we both deserve to have some fun tonight." He must have seen the uncertainty in my eyes when the thought of him leaving me on my own entered my mind, because a promising expression brightened his face. "I assure you I won't get plastered . . ." He paused and flashed me a crooked smile. "Well, maybe a wee bit shit-faced, but if you leave your vessel, stay where you're at. I'll be along shortly after."

"I'm sure I can manage on my own," I said, not wanting him to feel like he had to babysit me.

"I have no doubt, lass." He winked, then asked, "You see that molly over there?" He pointed to an attractive gal in a black sequined flapper dress. "I want to poke her. I'm horned up and hope the lad I choose has a massive flute."

I laughed. "If he doesn't, you can always leap into another host, right?"

He nodded. "C'mon. Let's go have some well-deserved fun."

Chapter Sixteen

Acclimating

The dull, low humming was louder when I stood in front of the blonde. I glanced at Aidan. He waved as he merged with the fella in the newsboy hat and disappeared. Just like that. No stretching or distortion of his spirit like before. Now inside the human, he straightened his shoulders and tilted his head from side to side. I was clueless about how he managed to make eye contact with me since I was still in the spiritual form, but he looked directly at me. With drink in hand he smiled, and drained the last of the caramel colored liquor.

I longed for a cocktail and a ciggy and had a sudden determination to ace this test and not muck it up. I focused on the gal, imagining dwelling inside her gorgeous body. She was listening to the party around her, beating their gums about I didn't know what. I had no interest in their idle chatter. I moved closer, so close I could see the red lipstick fading on her bottom lip. The image of me looking through her amber eyes burned bright inside my mind. A tingling sensation spread across every inch of my form. I relaxed and submitted to the feeling, unlike my first time when I was nervous and unsure. I decided to try Aidan's move, hoping to avoid being yanked back and jerked forward like before. Lifting my foot, I stepped inside her, as if she were a doorway into another room. Like a black cloud passing over the sun, darkness followed and then warmth and a giddy, easy feeling I remembered quite well. I breathed in, the smell of cigarettes and alcohol enveloped me, and for a few staggering seconds, I thought I was at Slim's in my own human body.

"Do you want another drink, Gracie?" a male voice with a moderate Irish twang asked.

I blinked, confused at first because the question seemed to be directed at me. My gaze fell on the fella who was wearing the newsboy hat. Then, I realized I possessed the blonde and knew her basic information, such as her name was Grace Depree, age nineteen, born and raised here in Astoria, Oregon, to a middle class family. Her father was a fisherman, mother a housewife. Grace had an older sister who was married with a baby on the way. She lived in the state of Washington and was the golden child of the two. Much like myself, Grace was the typical flapper gal, except she was soulless with artificial feelings of love and compassion. She only had one priority. Herself.

I looked at the tumbler in my hand. Empty. "Yes, I would love to have a tuxedo #2, Aidan," I said. Then, out of nowhere, the fella's name came to me through the limited information I had of Grace's life. "I mean, Preston," I quickly added.

He smiled, revealing an adorable dimple in his left cheek. "Stay here, lass. I'll go fetch you one."

I handed him my glass and watched him disappear into the crowd. Stretching my arms above my head and bending both knees into a squatting position, I was pleased to discover Grace's limbs were flexible. She had the body of a dancer, and the tightness I felt around the chest and upper back was due to her bandaging her breasts to make them flat—one of many fashion statements flappers practiced to break free from the Victorian era, which stifled women.

The gal in the black sequined fringe dress Aidan wanted to poke looked up from a conversation she was having with a fella in a blue pinstripe suit and met my gaze, but then her attention fell back on him. She said something and lightly touched his arm. He pinched the brim of his straw boater hat and nodded. Making eye contact with me again, she stepped away from his company and headed toward me.

I knew her name. Sally. Fragmented information about her seeped into my consciousness like a thin layer of smoke beneath a door. She was the same age as Grace, soulless, and loved to have a swell time. Aidan was in for a treat, unless—

"Grace." She smiled, and at the same time, a laser beam swiped across her hazel eyes.

I finished my thought—unless Sally had a dark spirit dwelling inside, who was a flat tire. But that was unlikely since dark spirits thrived on indulging themselves in the pleasures of the flesh. Now, I was one of them, and the endless possibilities thrilled me.

She stopped in front of me, pausing long enough to scrutinize my face. I gathered she saw the same anomaly in my eyes since she kept staring into them.

I leaned in next to her ear. A floral, alcohol scent reached my nostrils. I was never a fan of flowery perfume and was glad the booze leaking from her pores dulled the smell. "My name is Ameerah, a newborn into this supernatural world. This is my second time possessing a human, and I'd appreciate it if you'd stop staring at me."

A pinkish red color bloomed in her cheeks. "Sorry. I was taken by surprise. I didn't expect a dark spirit inside of Gracie." She stuck her hand out. "This human's name is Sally, but my name is Ava."

I shook her hand. "Why didn't you expect one of us to takeover Gracie's body?"

"Well, actually, what I meant was . . . I was hoping Gracie wasn't possessed." She shrugged. "She's soulless but a riot to be around. When Aosoth is in town, she favors Gracie over most of the others, hence me staring into your eyes. Aosoth is older than us, so the laser beam is a tad bigger than ours. Also, she seems to always have a certain expression on her face."

"Like what?" I wondered what was taking Aidan so long. I really wanted a cocktail. I could feel a slight itching and constricting feeling inside my arms and chest and hoped maybe the giggle water would relax this body and allow me to stay for a while. I scanned the crowd and couldn't see him.

"I'd try to imitate her, but I don't think I can," she said. "It's a shitty, twisted, arrogant smirk." She curled her lips tightly to the left side of her kisser, showing part of her top teeth. She squinted her left eye and widened the right one. I laughed, because she looked like she had a stick up her ass. "See, I told you I couldn't imitate her," she said, giggling, "but I tried."

I opened the beaded and rhinestone purse hanging across my body and was pleased to find a black cigarette case, matches, a wad of dough, keys, and makeup. "Your attempt was a swell one." I could hear the distraction in my voice and became aware my attention had been more focused on the treasures I discovered in Grace's purse than on Ava. To make up for my rudeness, I offered her a ciggy and lit it for her.

She blew out a tube of gray smoke above our heads. "Anyway, Aosoth is a conniving, backstabbing bitch, so stay clear of her."

I lit my ciggy and breathed in the smoke, then exhaled. The wonderful tobacco brought back a familiar pleasure I was more than happy to relive. Once the cocktail was in my hand, I would surely be in heaven, indulging myself in two of my favorites: alcohol and tobacco.

"How would I know her?" I asked, my gaze landing on Aidan heading our way with a drink in each hand. He had an odd look on his face—a mixture of determination and humor.

Ava took another drag. "By her signature all around pompous, shitty look." She glanced in the direction of the bar. "I need a cocktail." Her gaze swept back to me, eyes sparkling with interest. "Say, who is that cute fella coming our way? I saw you talking to him earlier. Is he your flame?"

I laughed. "No. His name is Aidan. He's my recruiter."

"That I am," Aidan said, catching my last sentence when he approached us. He handed me my drink. "The bartender made you a bee's knees instead of the tuxedo #2 you wanted. He didn't realize his mistake until after he handed me the drink. He told me to tell you he'll make what you want the next time around, and it'll be on the house."

"I don't mind a bee's knees." I took a sip, savoring the sweet honey flavor and the background taste of lemon and gin, thinking about Betty and how much she loved this drink. An aching sadness quivered through my chest, rising to my throat, forming a lump. "Excuse me." I looked away and turned my back so I could collect myself. I took a lace handkerchief out of the purse and used it to dab at the corners of my eyes. I was a bit surprised and embarrassed how a subtle reminder of my girlfriend and the wonderful times we spent together could stir such fierce emotions in a matter of seconds.

"What's wrong?" Ava asked, concerned.

"Of course," Aidan said as if an obvious answer to a simple question struck him between the eyes. A warm hand settled on my shoulder. "I'm sorry, lass. I didn't realize the significance of the cocktail until now."

"What's the matter with . . . Ameerah?" Ava wanted to know.

"The bee's knees reminds her of her girlfriend," Aidan told Ava. He squeezed my shoulder. "Dry up those tears, lass. The past doesn't exist anymore; this is your life now. It's time to move on."

He was right. I was better off burying my feelings for Betty and the memories of us. Besides, I had enough heartache this year, and I'd be damned if I was going to spend one more minute in misery when I could be having a grand time instead.

I cleared my throat, took a sip and then a drag off my ciggy, loving the combination against my tastebuds. I didn't realize how much I missed drinking and smoking until now and was pleased the alcohol seemed to tame the itchy, constricting feeling I had earlier in my upper body.

I faced Aidan and smiled. "Thanks. I'm good now." And I was. I felt much better and ready to have some fun.

He returned my smile. "Excellent. Now will you butt me?"

I handed him a ciggy, and in a quick here-I-am-pay-attention-to-me gesture, Ava lit it, taking that opportunity to introduce herself. I politely took a couple steps back, allowing them to move closer to one another and flirt. I noticed while Ava chatted about Astoria and herself, Aidan's gaze kept skipping to the bar area, like he was expecting someone. Then, he'd focus back on Ava, ask her a question, throw in a few charming words, and once again his eyes would dart to the same spot as before. He was doing his best not to be rude and seemed genuinely interested in what she had to say; however, something else took precedence over his desire to get her in the sack. With each moment that passed, my curiosity grew, and my tongue loosened from the alcohol I ingested into this body.

"If you ever want to hang out," Ava said to Aidan, "I'm usually at this club and–"

"Why do you keep looking over there?" I asked Aidan. Ava swung her attention to me, her expression annoyed at my abrupt interruption, but then she glanced at Aidan. Something must have clicked, because when her eyes shifted back to me, they were inquisitive and anxious.

"Lamar challenged me to a fight," Aidan told us.

"Who the hell is Lamar?" I finished my bee's knees and wanted another cocktail.

"Why would he challenge you to a fight?" Ava asked.

"Lamar is a thieving bastard is why," Aidan said. "He heard about my past when I was human and wants to see if it's true . . . there he is." Aidan pointed to a fella dressed in a gray suit and a black derby hat. I wondered if his biceps were as big as the fella Aidan was possessing or if it even mattered. "He approached me while I was waiting to order your drink. I told him I was on business and had to see how you were doing before I'd make a decision whether to accept his challenge or not. How do you feel, lass?"

"Great," I said. "I think the booze is contributing to my ability to reside in this body longer than I normally would for my second time around."

"What do you mean by your past?" Ava asked.

"I'm from Dublin and an undefeated boxer," Aidan answered. "I don't have time to dive into my human history, but Lamar has a huge ego. He's a boxer and undefeated, as well. Therefore, when he discovered I was here, he decided to challenge me." Aidan took my empty glass.

"Would you like your tuxedo #2 now?" When I nodded, his attention shifted to Ava. "I'd like to buy you a drink if you'd allow me to do so."

A pleased smile crossed Ava's face. "I would love to try what Ameerah is getting. I don't know what's in it, but what the hell,"—she ran her hand slowly up his arm—"I'm up for anything."

"Be careful, lass," he said. "I don't want to be horned up before the fight."

"You're going through with it?" I asked, watching him take Ava's hand. He gestured for me to follow them. "When was the last time you got into a fight?"

"Twelve years ago," he said over his shoulder. "But don't fret, lass. I'm quite handy with my fists."

"I hope you're handy with something else as well," I heard Ava say to him and giggled.

As we maneuvered through the crowd, Aidan whispered something in her ear. She playfully slapped him on the arm and tittered coyly some more. I was thankful the upbeat jazz music was loud enough to where I couldn't hear Ava's squeals or girlish laughs. I didn't mind her company and thought maybe we could even possibly become friends; however, the behavior she displayed with Aidan annoyed me. The immaturity alone scratched down my spine like nails on a chalkboard.

"Aidan, I heard you're going to fight Lamar." A lanky ginger fella in a white linen suit and straw Panama hat stopped Aidan in his tracks. When his brown eyes met mine, a beam swiped across them. He winked and slapped a hand on Aidan's shoulder. "You have my bet."

A chain of watchful faces seemed to float and bob past us—eyes flashing light over irises. Aidan was right. This speakeasy was a haven for dark spirits. Word was spreading rapidly about the boxing match.

"Thanks, pal. I appreciate your support." Aidan mimicked the ginger's gesture, placing his hand on his shoulder, shaking it in good cheer.

"How do you know this is Aidan?" I asked the fella.

"The bartender pointed him out to me," he said. "Besides, most of the time dark spirits either take control over a human with similar characteristics from when they were one, for nostalgic reasons obviously, or they have a penchant for a certain type, and ninety percent of the time they'll choose that one."

"Oh, yes," I said, following Aidan and Ava to the other side of the room. "Aidan did mention something along those lines earlier."

The crowd around the bar parted when we approached, so Aidan could order our drinks. I didn't see Lamar and was surprised at all the attention pouring on Aidan. He must have had quite a name for himself when he used to box, because people were beating their gums in an excited fervor nonstop at him. Ava appeared to be enjoying being Aidan's arm candy, while he participated in lively conversations with the other fellas about bare knuckle boxing. He handed me my tuxedo #2 while laughing with his admirers.

"I'm Calvin," the ginger fella said and waved the ciggy away when I offered it to him.

I stuck it in my mouth instead and lit it. "Ameerah. I'm a newbie. This is my second possession." Something wasn't quite right about Calvin, I noticed. He had a strange gleam in his eyes, like behind his calm facade was a squirrelly madness biding its time.

Calvin raised his eyebrows. "Really?"

I took a drink of my cocktail, tasting the orange bitters and gin, savoring the combination of flavors that create this dry martini and nodded.

"Wow," he said, impressed. "You're a natural. I thought maybe this was your tenth time."

"Nope," I replied, enjoying the buzz I already had increase to where I felt absolutely wonderful. I hadn't realized how much I missed this feeling, but I did. A lot. Also, listening to the jazz music play created an urge in me to burn up the dance floor, but I knew it wouldn't be wise to try until I could spend more time in the body I was occupying.

"C'mon, Ameerah." Aidan gestured for me to follow him and Ava. "It's almost time for me to fight."

I'd never seen a bare knuckles boxing match before and wasn't sure if I wanted to. I couldn't understand why fellas would want to subject themselves to bodily harm. What was the point in it—to get respect?

I stopped Aidan while half the crowd went ahead of him, and the other half were at the bar getting their drinks. "Why are you doing this?"

His forehead wrinkled, and he looked at me like I asked him what shape the sun was. "Because he challenged me."

"Okay, but why?" The alcohol was messing with my brain. I knew what I was asking, but the words weren't coming out right. I took a deep breath and tried again when confusion twisted his features. "Why did you start boxing in the first place? It's barbaric. Why would a fella put himself in a position where he could get his ass beat?"

"I originally fought for the money," Aidan said. "I'll tell ya more about it later. We need to crack on."

I followed him and Ava to the back of the room, contemplating whether I wanted to watch or not. Calvin had disappeared in the crowd while I was chatting with Aidan, which was fine with me. He had a creepiness about him I found a bit disturbing.

Aidan glanced over his shoulder to make sure I was behind him. "Don't worry, lass. I'm not a neddy."

We reached a line in front of an open door and stopped. "What the hell is a neddy?" I asked.

Ava was on the other side of Aidan; she leaned across his chest closer to me. "It means fool." She looked up at Aidan and smiled when he nodded.

"We'll see," I said, moving forward along with them when the people ahead of us entered the doorway.

I took a sip of my cocktail. I had to make a decision quick. We were nearing the threshold, and I could see people going down a flight of stairs.

Chapter Seventeen

Volac

As I descended the stairs, I had a bird's eye view of the concrete basement. It was nothing fancy, only a room to perform more illegal acts in secret. A twenty-two-foot square had been roped off. People were packed onto the sides, mingling while they waited. The constant chatter and excited energy engulfed me, pulling me into the fold.

"Aidan is here," someone hollered.

Conversations piped down, and dozens of faces turned to stare at us. Ava grinned and waved. I lit a ciggy and blew smoke at them.

"These two dames with you?" a short, pot-bellied fella in a black bowler hat asked. I could hear a dull, low humming noise as I moved closer to him. Soulless. Unoccupied. Poor bastard.

"They are." Aidan motioned for me to stand next to him. He finished the rest of his whiskey and water in one swallow.

I moved to his side and kept my hands to myself, refusing to give him the satisfaction of having two beautiful women on each of his arms.

"Can you take this for me, lass?" He handed me his empty glass. "I need to limber up."

The fella in the bowler hat ushered us forward to the ropes. "I'm the referee. I'll be in the ring in a few minutes," he said to Aidan.

Ava hugged Aidan's arm she was attached to and kissed his cheek. "Good luck."

Lamar entered the ring. He was similar to Aidan in stature and weight. I'd guess they were both six feet in height with not an ounce of fat on them. Lamar no longer had his hat or suit jacket on, only a black vest and a white shirt with the sleeves rolled up, revealing his large biceps. He wasn't the real McCoy I decided and became disgusted when a gal on the other side of the ropes handed him a newsboy hat. He seemed artificial in his desperate need to mirror Aidan's style and challenge him to a fight, as if they were still in elementary school. I had no time for people like him and hoped Aidan would kick his ass to possibly bring some humility into his life, which perhaps might knock some sense into him.

"Thanks, lass." Aidan turned his hat backwards, eyes focused on Lamar.

"Be careful," I said while he crouched between the ropes and stepped inside the ring.

He gestured for me to come closer to him. "If for some reason he bleedin' knocks me out, I'll either jump into another vessel or wait around for you."

"Won't you be exhausted?" I would think he'd need to regain his energy before taking over another human, but being a dark spirit was new to me. Maybe strenuous activity had no effect on our spirits.

"Nah." He shook his head, the corner of his mouth curling into a crooked smile. "I've been in plenty of pub fights and managed to continue with my business like nothing happened."

"Don't you think you might be pushing your luck?"

He shrugged. "I'm a fucking chancer." His gaze skipped past me. The corner of his eyes crinkled, then fell back on mine. "I'd like to go ridin' on that harpy tonight. I've been horned up since I've seen her."

I glanced at Ava. She was talking to a fella in a suit and black fedora hat. She caught us looking at her and waved, mouthing the word, *Hi.*

Aidan motioned for her to join us. "Watch this, lass," he said. "She'll be beggin' me to poke her."

"Is everything okay?" Ava asked Aidan, worry creasing her brow.

Aidan reached over the ropes, took her hand, and pulled her into his arms. He kissed her softly at first, but when she threw her arms around his neck and leaned into him, the kiss deepened. Cheers and a series of slow whistles issued from the crowd. They were eating up Aidan's bold display of affection while I wished for another cocktail.

Aidan whispered in Ava's ear. She giggled and said something to him. He grinned, winked, and turned to his opponent. He stretched his muscles, hopped up and down, and shadow-boxed, simulating boxing motions by jabbing the air. On the other side of the ring, Lamar followed suit. Bets circled the room, like vultures honing in on prey.

"Wow." Ava touched her plump lips, still red from necking with him. "Aidan definitely knows how to kiss."

"He sure gave your tonsils a good cleaning from what I saw," I said.

She laughed. "He does have some skill with his tongue, which makes me eager to see how talented he is between the sheets."

"There is only one rule to prizefighting," the referee called, now in the ring between Aidan and Lamar. The room fell silent. Someone sneezed in the back. "Once knocked down, you have thirty seconds to get your ass up. If you don't, you lose the match." He pointed to Aidan. "In this corner, we have Aidan Logan. Ireland's undefeated champion." Ava and I, along with others, whistled and hollered our support while some booed. The ref pointed to Lamar. "In this corner we have Lamar Mintz. Though he's only had a few boxing matches under his belt, no one has been able to take him down." Cheers rang across the room. Ava and I booed as did others. Lewd remarks were being thrown out at both contestants:

"Lamar couldn't punch a hole through his ma's pissflaps when he was born. They had to cut the bastard out of her belly instead."

"Aidan is all wet, a flat tire who thinks he's hard boiled. He's nothing but a lounge lizard with delusions of grandeur."

Ignoring the insults, Aidan and Lamar nodded to the referee. They approached him and exchanged some words, once again nodding to whatever was being said. The referee moved to the far side of the ring out of harm's way. Holding my breath, I shifted my weight back and forth. I still wasn't sure about being here, but Aidan needed my support, so I'd put aside my disgust regarding his barbaric behavior.

Lamar danced around Aidan, making jabbing motions, stepping forward as he did so. Aidan dodged him, hopping from side to side, fists raised. A continuous string of support and badgering comments spewed forth from the crowd. Ava was one of them. When Aidan glanced at her, Lamar took that opportunity and slammed his fist into the side of Aidan's face. Aidan stumbled. The crowd went nuts. Aidan shook his head and recovered quickly. I set our empty glasses on the floor and held my hand over my mouth.

"Oh, my God! That was my fault," Ava said next to me, her hands on both cheeks.

"If you want him to have a chance at winning, keep your trap shut," I told her. She nodded, and we turned our attention back to the fight.

Aidan charged Lamar, ready to strike, but then Lamar dropped to his knees. The referee came between them and counted. Once he reached twenty-two, Lamar rose. The ref retreated to his corner, signaling to begin. Once again, Lamar danced circles around Aidan. When Aidan's fist went forward, aiming at Lamar's face, Lamar blocked it with his left hand and with his right fist, he slammed it into Aidan's nose. Blood flew out of both nostrils. Ava gasped. I closed my eyes and shook my head. What was Aidan thinking? He hadn't fought in years, and Lamar had been recently fighting. Aidan was out of practice and an idiot for accepting Lamar's challenge. I should have talked some sense into him.

"Not everything is as it seems," a male voice said next to me.

I opened my eyes. A tall fella in a black pinstripe suit and white fedora with a black hatband was watching the fight beside me. I ignored him and shifted my attention back on the fight.

Aidan's face was a bloody mess, but the blood appeared to stop oozing from his nose. He stepped closer to Lamar and blocked his punches, causing him to skip backward, but when Aidan pulled his arm back, Lamar dropped to his knees. The referee counted again. Red-faced,

Aidan threw his hands up and shook his head in disgust. The crowd voiced their displeasure in hisses, boos, and ripe language. Aidan was pointing at Lamar, jabbing the air with his finger, saying something to the ref.

"Can't you see what Lamar is doing? This is bullshit!" I hollered. "He's a cheapskate and should be disqualified."

"Ameerah is right!" Ava yelled. "The son-of-a-bitch is a coward. You're not a true boxer, Lamar, and should be ashamed of yourself for pulling this dirty rotten trick! Get off your ass and fight like a man!"

"Yeah!" someone hollered. "Quit being a pussy and dropping to your knees!"

"Do you find this type of activity amusing?" the fella next to me asked.

I looked up, and his pale blue eyes were glowing, which meant he was an ancient dark spirit. Could he be the "old one"? If so, I wondered if he'd be sore at Aidan for his extracurricular activity while he was teaching me how to thrive as one of them. "No, I don't," I answered. I offered my hand, and he shook it. "Ameerah Arrowood. I'm a newborn. Aidan is my recruiter."

A pleasant smile crossed his handsome face. "Volac. Please to meet you, Ameerah."

"Volac," I said. "What an odd name. Is there any meaning behind it?"

"Why, yes," he answered. "Actually, there is."

My eyes darted to the fight. Lamar was now on his feet. He and Aidan circled each other in the ring. The crowd continued to shell out obscenities at both opponents, including Ava yelling next to my ear. I turned my back on her and faced Volac, throwing side glances at Aidan.

"As you probably aren't yet aware," Volac continued, "there's a novelty practiced by some of our kind. We have adopted names of demons known to humans. The rather comical part is we created those names to breed fear, interest, and to help perpetuate control over the masses through religious ideology. Volac means mighty and great and that I govern thirty-eight legions of spirits."

I cocked an eyebrow. "Mighty and great, huh? You think highly of yourself, don't you?"

He chortled. "You're quite the pistol, but to answer your question . . . I wasn't the one who chose my name. It was a vote among my early followers. They felt I should secure a title worthy of my accomplishments and character in our dark world."

"What was your name when you were human?" I thought about the female dark spirit Ava warned me about. Aosoth. I wondered what her story was and the meaning behind her name.

"I'll tell you, but I'd appreciate it if you didn't address me as such."

What he said reminded me of when I asked Slim what his birth name was and how he'd basically requested the same courtesy from me as Volac now did.

"Deal," I said.

He offered me a ciggy he plucked out of his flat gold case. I took one, of course. He lit mine and then his. "Rennir Sorkvirson."

"What kind of–"

"Norwegian."

"Really?" I could hear the surprise in my voice because I knew he was ancient. "How old are you?"

"Have you always been this inquisitive?" he asked good-naturedly.

My attention shifted on Aidan when I caught him from my peripheral blocking blows aimed at his face from Lamar. Aidan managed to shove Lamar back, causing him to stumble, but he quickly recovered and kept a safe distance.

I turned back to Volac. "Yes, I have. Is that a problem?"

He shook his head. "On the contrary, I find your thirst and openness for information appealing."

"Swell," I said and blew a lungful of smoke out. "Otherwise, if my inquisitive nature was a problem, I'd tell ya to scram."

He laughed. "Well, then, since you're not going to send me on my way, I'll indeed answer your question. I was a Viking. A seafarer. I raided, pillaged, and traded, among other things."

My mouth fell open. Wow, I was actually conversing with a Viking. I adored history and had read about his people and culture many years ago. My memory was rusty on the fine details, but I remembered enough to get a sense of the type of world he was born and raised in. Then an extraordinary and exciting thought came to me: The dark spirits who were much older than I were figures from another time. They were there, and I imagined the tales they could tell about that era in their life was the cat's meow. I couldn't believe I hadn't realized this from the start. Perhaps my preoccupation with acclimating into this new existence was why.

"You're taken aback with this bit of information," he stated, sounding pleased.

I nodded. "I am and would love to hear tales about your adventures." I smiled at his amused look. "I've always been interested in history and realized mere seconds ago what an opportunity I'll have to learn from not only you but others about what it was like during ancient time periods."

"You are quite the bouquet of surprises, Ameerah." He puffed on his ciggy. "Tell me what other interest might you have?"

I smirked. "Women, alcohol,"—I raised my hand with the ciggy between my fingers—"these, dancing, books, and . . ."

"And what?"

"And . . ."

Frenzy grew in the crowd, pulling my attention away from Volac to the fight. Apparently, Lamar attempted to try his dirty trick of resting on his knees again, but Aidan grabbed him by the collar and yanked him on his feet. The hard look on Aidan's face was a public sign that he had enough. He wrapped his arm around Lamar's neck in a headlock. Lamar struggled to break free to no avail. Then, with the other hand, Aidan repeatedly hit Lamar in the face with precise, controlled punches.

The crowd went wild. Beside me, Ava screamed encouragements to continue pulverizing Lamar and teach him a lesson. When Lamar's face began to marble, I couldn't watch no more and shifted my gaze to Volac. His ice blues eyes trapped mine, and within a span of a few seconds, I felt as if he peered into my soul by the understanding and warmth pooling in them.

I blinked. "What?" Normally, a situation such as this would be awkward but not with Volac. I felt comfortable and had the desire to know what was going through his mind.

"Would you be interested in joining my league?" he asked. Before I could answer, he continued. "You appear to be adjusting exceptionally well to this new existence, and I predict Aidan will be releasing you from his care at any given moment. He does have other souls to recruit."

The thought of Aidan throwing me out into the choppy waters of this dark world with the sink or swim mentality set my nerves on edge. I wasn't ready to be on my own. Hell, my human death was only twenty-four hours ago. I hoped Volac was wrong, and I would make a point to bring this bothersome issue to Aidan's attention once this night ended.

"What did you say earlier? Not everything is as it seems." I leveled my eyes with his and smirked.

"You are a sponge," he said, amused, "soaking information most people would disregard due to the unsuitable nature of their superfluous interests. But I digress."—he touched his chest and leaned forward in a stately manner—"The time shall arise when you find yourself alone, but fear not . . . my door will be open to you."

His offer had me counting my blessing that by pure luck, I bumped into a charming ancient dark spirit who not only intrigued me but gave me comfort in knowing I could seek his council and possibly form a friendship with him.

"How will I find you?"

The volume of the crowd escalated to where I had to ask Volac the question twice, half yelling it to him. Ava was cheering along with everyone else. Aidan had won. I missed the tail end of his victory. Lamar was on the floor, out cold. The referee grabbed Aidan's hand and raised it above his head. His mouth was moving, but I couldn't hear what he was saying above the noise booming around me.

Volac leaned next to my ear. "Ava is part of my league. She will lead you to me." He bid me farewell and disappeared into the crowd.

I felt a hand on my shoulder. I turned to a huge grin on Ava's face. "He won, Ameerah!" she hollered and hugged me.

I glanced at Lamar. The body was lying on the concrete, appearing lifeless. His head was turned, so I couldn't see the damage Aidan's fists caused, which I was grateful for. I had no desire to see his handiwork and was relieved this nonsensical need to prove one's manhood by crushing another man's face was over with.

Ave frowned. "Aren't you the least bit excited?" She pointed at the crumbled form. "Lamar is a spineless coward. I bet the motherfucker vacated the body in between Aidan's punches. I'm sure before Aidan killed the human."

"I much rather have Aidan standing than that piece-of-shit Lamar," I admitted. "But this show is ridiculous."

"Wow, you don't hold anything back, do you?" she asked, laughing, her spirits high from the jovial mood surrounding us.

"It's who I am. If people don't like it, they can fuck off," I said.

"You slay me," Ava said, shooting glances at Aidan who was still in the ring, but now surrounded by dozens of people, congratulating him. "I admire how candid you are, and it seems Volac does, too. He appeared to be charmed."

"He gave me an invitation to join his group. He said you were part of it and would lead me to him," I told her.

"I am," she confirmed and then caught Aidan motioning with his index finger for her to join him. She grinned and waved. "I'll take you to him whenever you want, but right now, I'm going to have some fun with Aidan." She waggled her eyebrows.

"I'd like to know more about him and the dark spirits in his group," I quickly said, because she was already pulling the ropes up to slip in between them.

"I promise. I'll tell ya everything you want to know later," she answered.

"Have fun. I'm going to get myself a cocktail."

She gave me a thumbs up before entering the ring, and once she was inside, she rushed to Aidan. I turned, uninterested in their dramatic display in a room full of eager onlookers. I weaved my way through the crowd, and while I climbed the stairs that led to the club, I pondered the events that occurred tonight. Volac was an interesting fella who could aid me in my transition into this new life. I had no doubts about him. He was ancient, seemly powerful, and–

A sudden, internal horrible itchy feeling threw me out of my thought process. I wasn't ready to leave this body yet. The alcohol had to be wearing off. I needed more. I wanted more. I hurried up the stairs, now experiencing a squeezing pressure around my chest, throat, and head.

Shit.

Not now.

Not yet.

It was too early for this night to end. I tried to hold on for as long as I possibly could. When I reached the bar, I called to the bartender, who was visiting with another customer. "Hey, tuxedo #2 please." He nodded and got busy making my cocktail. The itchy and constriction feeling around the upper body grew worse. *Hold on, Ameerah. Stay inside*, I chanted in my head. But no mantra in the world could stop the inevitable. Only one thing might subdue it. The bartender handed the cold glass to me. I took a swig, hoping my theory was correct.

Chapter Eighteen

Reenergizing

I had been a couple minutes too late. I was now reenergizing myself deep in the forest in the same clearing as before. If only I'd spent less time chatting with Ava, I'd still be in the human, at the bar drinking and smoking. But there was no sense beating myself over it. I'd done pretty damned well hanging on for as long as I had. Next time would be easier and much longer.

After my spirit vacated Grace, I stuck around the club for a while, observing everyone while waiting for Aidan. The exhaustion, though, became too overwhelming. Besides, watching others while they had a grand time wasn't my idea of fun.

At first, I had no idea how to retrace our steps back to this place. Aidan always grabbed my hand and we'd blink out of where we were and find ourselves where he wanted us to be. Then, it occurred to me how he managed to transport us to our desired destination in a matter of seconds: Think of the place I wanted to go and visualize it, like when I wanted to possess a human. The same principle would apply. If anything else, there was no harm in trying, so I did, and to my delight my idea worked.

Resting my head on the log, I couldn't help but be pleased with my progress. I imagined Volac was probably right about Aidan releasing me soon enough. When he mentioned it earlier, the idea of being on my own in this new existence frightened me but not so much anymore. My confidence was growing, and Volac's offer was like a soothing balm on my blistering worries. Also, my desire for revenge on my parents and others was what motivated me to excel as a dark spirit. They took everything from me, and when the time was right, I vowed to do the same to them. But for now, my first priority was me and me alone.

I could feel the warm, comforting energy working its way from my toes up. Closing my eyes, I sighed, listening to an owl hooting in the distance. I wondered how long Aidan would be. No matter, I was perfectly content here, relaxing. My thoughts scattered, and recent memories from my human life bled into one another. An image of Betty's pretty smiling face popped into my mind, followed by another image of us laughing at a silly joke Abe told us. My heart fluttered. Then, I recalled me dancing at Slim's club in front of a captivating audience. Next, were visions of my parents double-crossing me and the staff member's wicked behavior toward me at Bandbridge.

"What's eating you, Ameerah?" a female said—a voice I didn't recognize.

I opened my eyes and unclenched my fists. A dark-haired gal with bright green eyes stared down at me with a curious look. Beside her, stood Aidan, his arm draped around her shoulders.

I sat up. "Ava?"

She smiled. "Now you know what I looked like when I was human. I have to say, Ameerah, you're a doll."

"So are you," I answered. "I'm surprised to see you here but glad you came."

"Aidan invited me," she said, hugging his waist. "Besides, you wanted to know about Volac's group."

"Volac spoke to me," Aidan said.

"Oh . . . what did he say?" I thought Volac had left after our chat. He must have blended in with the crowd, but what on earth would he have to say to Aidan?

Aidan and Ava sat in front of me. He had a pleasant, satisfying expression on his face. I imagined if he were in human form, his complexion would be glowing. I had no doubt in my mind he had sex with Ava. "I don't know what you two spoke about, lass, but you've impressed him, and he would like for you to run along with Ava and have a chat with him. In the meantime, I'll see about recruiting more souls. When you're done with your little get-together, I'll come fetch you."

"Sounds ducky . . ." I narrowed my eyes, my tone now suspicious. "I thought you were going to cut my apron strings, or are you in a round-about way?" Frankly, I wouldn't give a shit if he did. I'd much rather be on my own than do what he wanted so he could indulge himself. I'd miss his company, and I liked him, but if I discovered he was being dishonest or manipulating me in any possible way, I'd cut the strings myself.

"Jaysus, lass, I may be an arsehole at times," he said, his voice raised, "but I wouldn't beat around the bush with you. The choice will be ultimately yours when you decide to take flight from papa bird here."

I raised my hand, palm facing him. "Settle down. I didn't mean to offend you. I only said that because–"

"Because you don't trust people," he interrupted.

I made a face. "No, that's not what I was going to say . . . Let me try this again . . . I only said that *because* Volac had mentioned since I was doing so well, you'd probably release me soon."

"Oh . . . well," he said, taking his newsboy hat off. He playfully smacked me on the leg with it, "you do have trust issues and rightfully so, and in a way, Volac is correct." He put his cap on and leaned back on his hands.

"What do you mean?" I asked.

"He's saying," Ava interjected, "you're doing fantastic. There is really no need to have Aidan shadowing you. However, he could be on standby, meaning if you needed his help, he'd be there."

Aidan nodded and kissed Ava on the cheek.

"I'm good with that," I told them. "But how would I get hold of you or any dark spirit I become acquainted with when I wanted to?"

Ava rose, and Aidan and I followed suit. "It's simple," she said. "Visualize where the individual might be, and you'll find yourself in that place. If he's not there, surely someone will tip you off to his whereabouts."

"I'm still your recruiter," Aidan said. "Until *you* release *me*. So let's meet up at the club we came from tomorrow night and have a fuckin' good time."

"As long as you don't get into another boxing match, I'll agree," I said.

"What?" Aidan feigned disbelief. "You didn't like watching me shatter Lamar's face?"

"If it was for a reason other than proving your manhood, I would," I answered.

Rolling his shoulders forward, Aidan touched his chest. "Ouch, that hurt."

I smirked and shrugged.

He raised his hands. "Fair enough. I swear on me ma's eternal soul, I will not agree to another boxing match when I'm still your recruiter."

I smiled and indicated my approval with a nod.

"Are you ready for me to take you to see Volac?" Ava asked me.

"Yes, of course," I said, "but before we go, can you tell me more about him? How many followers does he have? What type of leader is he? What are his beliefs?"

Ava twisted her lips and stuck a finger on the corner of her kisser. "Hmmm, followers . . . I honestly don't know how many, but he has a lot. They're scattered across the globe. I'm thinking maybe, ten thousand, maybe more."

"I'd say a hundred thousand or more," Aidan said.

Ava looked at Aidan in surprise. "You think so?"

"I do, lass."

Ava turned her attention back on me. "He's a great leader and by no means a dictator. If there's any squabbling in the group, he handles it in the utmost respectful manner, but if you were to cross him, the punishment would equal your betrayal."

I could understand those principles. I felt the same way. So far, from what I gathered when I met Volac and from what Ava was telling me, he seemed like someone I'd like to have on my side. I wasn't sure if I'd join his group, but what the hell? Maybe I would. From what I'd been hearing about him, he'd make a great mentor, so I'd keep an open mind before I made my decision.

"His beliefs," Ava went on, "are he doesn't like to be under a dictatorship. He values his freedom and gives his followers the same courtesy. Whenever he has a gathering, he doesn't make a final decision without hearing everyone out. He believes in loyalty, honesty among his clan, and he believes a lot of humans are wasted space. He foresees them continuing to reproduce, which will eventually result in overpopulation and them depleting earth's resources, among other things. He has no respect for most."

I could see why he had no respect for them. After what happened to me, I felt the same way. I was sure there were a few good apples in the mix of the rotten ones, but in the whole scope of things, they were a cesspool of sewage upon this earth.

Ava raised her eyebrow, questionably. "Anything else you want to know before we descend upon him?"

"Nope. I'm good."

She turned to Aidan, and they embraced. He leaned her backwards, causing her leg to rise while he passionately kissed her. I looked away, feeling a bit awkward, but thankfully their necking was quick.

"I'll see you at the speakeasy tomorrow night, lass," Aidan said to me, looking bright and cheery with Ava by his side. There was even a smile in his eyes.

"I'll be there." I winked and took Ava's hand, anxious to visit Volac.

Ava blew Aidan a kiss, and we blinked out of there.

Chapter Nineteen

A New Friendship

We were on a pristine beach with a huge rock jutting out of the ocean, at least a couple hundred feet high. Smaller jagged boulders surrounded it.

"Haystack Rock." Ava pointed to the monolith. "Neat, huh? Seabirds like to nest there in the summer. The locals say it's 235 feet high."

"Wow." I'd been on beaches before but nothing like this one. The seashore had a natural beauty both rugged and whimsical with the forested headlands as the idyllic backdrop. The scenery alone would spark the imagination of a creative mind that could spin dark fairytales of what could be lurking within those timbers. To add to my wonderment, dawn broke over the wooded horizon behind us, illuminating the furrowed clouds in blood red. Different shades of pink painted the sky in sweeping brush strokes. The sun rose—a promise for a new start.

"If you think this view is the berries," Ava said, "wait until you stand on one of the bluffs. The scenery is breathtaking."

"I bet." I could stay here all day and be perfectly content, but reality set in.

Humans.

The damned humans would ruin it. Even if I possessed one, I'd have to endure the annoyance of company when all I wanted to do was have peace and solitude here. I'd have to wait until no one was around, like now, to enjoy myself.

"I'm glad you came," said a male voice I didn't recognize.

I turned to the sound. A blond bearded fella approached. He wore brown trousers and a matching tunic decorated in gold and blue braiding around the neckline and cuffs. A leather pouch and knife hung from the belt around his waist.

Volac.

"My curiosity got the best of me," I answered, smiling. "It's nice to see what you looked like when you were human. I like the braids you've woven and tied back in your hair. The style fits the rugged life you led."

He returned my smile. "And you, Ameerah, are ravishing."

"I thought Sylis was joining us," Ava said right when I opened my mouth to thank Volac for his compliment. I closed it and shifted my attention to her instead.

"He'll be along shortly," Volac told her.

"Who's Sylis?" I wondered what Volac had up his sleeve and if his intentions for me being here were for reasons I wasn't aware of.

"He's part of our group," Ava said.

"Our group?" I looked between her and Volac. "I haven't agreed to join forces with you. I'm only here to get to know you better and see what you have to offer. I'm nobody's slave, and I will not live under a tyrant. Been there. Done that. No more." I held a hand up. "No offense, Volac, but I rather you know now what I'm all about than lead you on."

"I appreciate you being forthright," he said, "but I assure you, I myself detest oppression, and I would never shackle my people in chains I myself would not bear."

"Ameerah is a bit touchy," Ava told him in my defense. "She has a lot eating at her, which if you knew her story, you would understand."

"What is your tale?" he asked.

I gave him a brief outline of my life and demise, and when I finished, he nodded.

"As I got older," I said, "I decided to be myself and voiced my thoughts. It was my undoing, but I don't regret breaking free from the mold my parents cast me in. I only wish I would have moved out of the house before they came home." I looked away when a sudden bout of sadness overtook me. I detested it. The people who brought me into their world were the ones who, in the end, wanted me out of it. How could parents discard their child, as mine had done to me?

"If you lament what actions you should have taken," Volac advised me, "you will remain bound to the ones who stole your life."

"Listen to him, Ameerah," Ava said. "I felt the same as you when I first arrived here, but when I took his advice and did what I had to do to get over it, I felt a million times better."

"What happened to you?" I asked, wondering how she died and what her story was.

"I dated a gangster," she answered right away. "I was his moll. I helped him cheat in cards, smuggle hooch, and bump off some of his rivals. But he grew distrustful of me after one of his spies told him he caught me necking with another fella who had double-crossed him."

"Did you?" I asked, visualizing the scene.

Her expression turned into disgust. "Hell, no. I was a loyal girlfriend. His spy was sore at me because I turned his advances down, so the dirty, rotten creep lied to my fella about me."

"What did your boyfriend say when you told him it wasn't true?"

"He didn't believe me." She frowned. "One night, he got tanked. He came home reeking of alcohol and knocked me around, accusing me of being unfaithful. When I reached for a vase to smash it across his head, he was too quick. He grabbed it, threw it across the room, and slapped me, calling me a filthy, two-faced tramp. He then pushed me to the floor, straddled me, and choked me to death."

"So you were bumped off like me," I said more to myself than her.

"I was," she answered. "When I became a dark spirit, I couldn't stop myself from thinking about all the things I should have done. Then, I met Sylis, who eventually introduced me to Volac. They helped me through my regrets, and of course, getting justice. Sylis is a good one for making humans suffer. He takes pleasure in people's misfortune."

"Are you singing my praises again?" A fella with dark shoulder-length hair and dark eyes materialized next to Ava. He slung his arm around her shoulders and gave me the once over. "Who is this lovely creature?"

I folded my arms across my chest, sizing him up. His body language and demeanor shouted a cockiness that I found quite annoying. However, if he could aid me in my quest to unleash hell upon those who betrayed me, I'd tolerate him.

"Sylis," Volac said in a well-mannered tone, "meet Ameerah. She's a new recruit." He turned to me and gestured toward Mr. Big Shot. "Ameerah, meet Sylis. He's been with us for a long spell."

Sylis stuck his hand out. Instead of shaking it, I nodded. He jerked his arm up and laughed, amusement dancing in his eyes.

"Pardon Ameerah's mannerism," Volac said to Sylis, "but from the small amount of time I've been in her company, she's quite the bloodhound." He leaned forward in Sylis' direction and staged-whispered, "She can sniff out the likes of anyone. If she doesn't fancy you, you will surely know."

Sylis took his black top hat off and bowed. "So I've met my match." He smirked. "But let's not get too hasty. Formal introductions are sooo dull." He adjusted his hat back on his head. "I say we get down and dirty and reveal our true nature." Raising his eyebrows, he touched his chest. "I for one will admit I'm a prankster, and I take enjoyment at seeing humans' mishaps and inane abilities that reduces them to squabbling idiots among each other. I also have a penchant for loose women."

I mirrored his smirked. "I'm a lesbian. I like to smoke, drink, dance, and have a good time. I detest most humans, and if anyone double-crosses me, I'll pay them back tenfold. I'm blunt and curious by nature. That's all you need to know for now."

Sylis clapped his hands. "Bravo. I like you already."

"Swell, now I can sleep at night," I said dryly and shifted my gaze to Volac. "Where do I go from here? What do you have to offer me?" I was anxious to get on with my new life and to cause suffering to those who stole everything from me.

"There is no doubt," Volac began, "you're excelling as a dark spirit, but if you join us, we can make your transition a lot easier."

"I'm listening," I said.

"Continue to allow Aidan guide you in possessing humans," he said. "You should be able to stay in the body for longer periods without the aid of an alcoholic beverage. Once you mastered it, I will mentor you."

"You can sometimes fuck with humans through their dreams," Sylis piped up, piquing my curiosity.

"Is that so?" I didn't hide my sudden interest in what he had to say.

He nodded. "When a human sleeps, the astral body withdraws from the physical. Most of the time, the conscious mind shuts down, so they're not aware of what's going on. There are different levels to the astral planes. Close to earth is the etheric plane, which is a dim and misty region. This dimension blends into the astral. Usually when a human is asleep, he remains at the etheric level, and there are parts of this level where we can roam. Once he stumbles into our region, we can enter his thoughts and mind and have a splendid time toying with him." A mischievous grin crossed his face.

I had no idea we were able to perpetrate such a devious and brilliant act upon humans. I loved it. I then realized I still had a lot to learn, and Sylis may be the person who could assist me in my goals. I was certain Volac could as well, but Sylis had a calculating demeanor about him that would serve my purpose.

"I didn't know," I said.

"Of course you wouldn't," Sylis answered. "I'm sure it never crossed Aidan's mind to share that helpful bit of information with you. It doesn't matter, though, because we're here to help you. All we ask in return is your loyalty and reliability."

"What if I decided to go my separate way? Would there be a penalty against me?"

"You're a free spirit," Volac told me. "Punishments are only handed out to those who betray me."

"I don't see why I would," I answered. "If I had a problem, I'd tell you."

"Absolutely." He nodded. "I admire that quality about you."

"Okay, so say I agree to join you . . . you'd be my mentor?" He had said he would, but I wanted him to reaffirm it.

"Don't make your decision until you go to our next meeting tomorrow night. In the meantime, enjoy yourself. Practice the act of possessing a human and dwelling inside the vessel for as long as you possibly can. And yes, I will mentor you if you wish for me to do so."

"Where's the meeting, and will everyone be there?" I imagined hundreds, if not thousands of dark spirits gathered in a vast prairie similar to what I saw at the recruiting station.

"Not everyone will be at the meeting," he answered. "We have messengers who can fill the others in on my plans. In regard to where the meeting will be held, Ava or Sylis will take you there."

"Fair enough," I said, "but I would love for you to tell me about your life as a Viking. I know there are more things for me to learn about being a dark spirit, but to be honest, I'm captivated by your life as a human. I think if you were to share that with me, I'd have a deeper understanding of who you are." I thought my request was a reasonable one. I wasn't about to join his league without knowing some of his history.

"I have loads of tales to share due to my adventurous nature when I was human," he said, "but I'll save those for when I have a glass of fine brandy in hand and a comfortable room in which to chat in. On the matter of who I am as an individual, my human life doesn't necessary define the complexity of my character as it is today."

I thought about how I was as a human, which realistically wasn't too long ago and noted the subtle changes since I made the transition. I was now more apt to voice my thoughts and feelings without fretting over the consequences of my actions. I could see his point. "I understand," I said.

His expression softened. "I knew you would. But to placate your tenacious desire to have a glimpse into my life as a Viking, I'll throw you a few appetizers to satisfy you until the time comes when I can feed you tales of that period in my life."

I wished I had a ciggy and a cocktail—even though I wasn't craving them, I fancied those two things. A sudden need to possess a human so I could enjoy partaking in the pleasures of being one consumed me. I looked at Ava and Sylis, who stood patiently listening to what Volac and I had to say. I knew then what I wanted to do.

"I was a farmer," Volac continued. "I had a beautiful wife and a son who was less than a year old when I decided to cross the vast waters in anticipation of the prospects of riches and trade. Our first raid was on an abbey. We killed monks . . . well, most of them. Some we took as slaves along with the many treasures the church harbored. We did the same with other monasteries and coastal villages. The reason for besieging those holy grounds was quite simple: we as pagans were persecuted by Christians, and our agriculture was reduced by them. Of course, our behaviors were motivated by other ambitions, such as exploration, commerce, and an answer to a better life in our homeland. We would return and resume farming after we collected enough plunder and slaves to live comfortably throughout the winter. Our ships were long, narrow, graceful, and made out of wood. They had oars along almost the entire length of the hulls, and the prow always had a dragon's head to keep evil spirits and sea monsters away."

I had a vivid picture of the life he was describing. I imagined it was a difficult one, with hardships people were desperate to overcome. I could see the allure of promising lands filled with riches, fine clothing, and exquisite food one could only dream of. Not to mention, the excitement of going off on an adventure to break the monotony of your tiresome existence. But to destroy and take from villages that had caused you no harm was unjustifiable behavior in my eyes. I could see why they did so with the religious communities. I would have done the same thing, but what about the innocents? I shared those thoughts with Volac to gain a better understanding of why he and his cohorts performed such acts on those who were blameless.

He thoughtfully rubbed his hand against his chin-length beard. "We pillaged for many reasons," he said. "The terrain and additional resources would give my people a healthier population. It was them or us. We chose us."

"For survival, then," I said, thinking out loud. "Whatever became of your wife and son?"

His eyes captured mine, and they hardened. For a split second, I regretted my question, thinking I'd crossed the line, but he sighed. The tense energy that surrounded him lifted, though his gaze remained icy.

"She betrayed me," he said. "Not too long after, I died in battle and chose to become a dark spirit."

I wanted to ask him about his son and how his wife betrayed him, but I bit my tongue. I didn't want to pry too much. Besides, from what he'd already shared, I was inclined to believe loyalty and freedom were the upmost importance to him. If someone were to break either one, there would be hell to pay. At least, that was the impression I got, and as Volac had pointed out earlier to Sylis, I was pretty damned good at pegging people.

"Well," I finally said after a short silence between us, "I can see why you chose this path."

"Why did you?" Sylis asked me.

Again, I went over my story, which I was getting tired of repeating, and to my surprise, he listened and asked me questions. Never once did his eyes wander; they were focused on me and what I had to say. He shook his head a couple times, showing his disgust when I mentioned the cruelty inflicted upon me.

"I think we need to pay Dr. Stratton a visit," Sylis said, throwing me off guard.

Ava squealed. "Yes, let's teach that bastard a lesson."

I looked between the two of them in surprise. Of course, I planned on paying Dr. Stratton back for the hell he'd put me through, but never in my wildest dreams did I think I'd have others helping me accomplish it. "You both want to lend me a hand in destroying the people who caused me anguish and despair?"

"You're damn right," Sylis said, smacking his fist into his palm.

Ava nodded, then released an excited gasp. "We can see what happened to Betty and Abe. Maybe they were looking for you but didn't get to you in time."

I held up a hand and shook my head, swallowing the sudden lump in my throat. "No, I'm not ready for that."

Sylis looked at Ava and made a disgusted sound. "I doubt they did."

"You don't know," Ava countered. "Not all humans are worthless."

"Maybe not," he said, "but until I come across one worth sparing, I'll continue fucking with them."

I looked at Volac. "What do you think? Is it too early for me to do this?"

"If it were a solitary mission," he answered, "I'd advise you to wait until you were more stable in possessing a human. However, with the aid and guidance of these two, I see no reason to be alarmed." He turned his attention to Sylis and Ava. "I trust you both will take the proper precautions in assisting a newborn and will keep in mind, though she has excelled in dwelling inside a vessel, she still needs more practice."

"Yes," Ava said. "I'm aware and won't let her down." She shifted her gaze to me. "Promise."

"I've already taken that into consideration," Sylis told him, already one step ahead, impressing me. I couldn't resist smiling at the excitement bubbling over inside me. "Before we formulate a viable plan and execute it, I'll have Ameerah spend the day with us in human form. Once I'm certain she can handle herself, we'll proceed."

I thought his idea was a swell one. I'd already planned on finding a soulless woman and taking possession. I longed to be a part of earth, to smell the atmosphere, taste food, and have a ciggy.

Volac nodded. "Excellent." He touched my shoulder and gave it a soft, reassuring squeeze. "You're in good hands. I trust Sylis to do right by you. He has never once failed me. It's why I hold him in high regard."

Ava stepped beside me while Sylis beamed at what I suspect was a sought-after compliment from Volac among his followers. Exercising caution in every step he took, Sylis reaffirmed his loyalty to Volac by pledging to him.

"Wait until you see Sylis in action," Ava whispered to me, grinning. "He's a sly, devious son-of-a-bitch. If I were human again, I wouldn't want him sore at me."

I mirrored her jubilant mood with an equally cheerful expression I knew reached my eyes. Soon, justice would be served. Not by the police. Not by a court of law. It would be by dark spirits who could be a human's worst nightmare ever.

Chapter Twenty

Practice

We spent the day in downtown Astoria, masquerading as humans. It was the cat's meow to fool the world into thinking they were conversing with one of their own when really they were interacting with a dark spirit. The deception made me wonder how many I'd come across and spoke with when I was my former self.

I chose a petite, pretty red-head with large bosoms to possess. I'd always wondered what it would be like to have a short, lithe stature, and big busts were an added bonus. I reveled in the fact I could chose whatever body to dwell in and experience the form in its ultimate glory.

Yes, I loved being a dark spirit.

We had breakfast at a charming mom and pop restaurant where I indulged myself in pancakes, hash browns, bacon, and buttered toast with jam. The coffee was good, and of course, the ciggy was heavenly.

Without the aid of a drop of alcohol, I was able to hold onto the vessel until dusk. Sylis and Ava were great companions and impressed by my ability to stay anchored within the human flesh for as long as I had. I didn't see what the big deal was, but apparently acclimating to this new existence took newborns months, if not years to master.

I learned from Sylis who Nathan Caswell was—an immortal who happened to be a damned good tracker. Nathan had an uncanny ability to stalk dark spirits and create his own incantations, which he used every time he cast one of us out of a human. His spells were more potent than the average ones, Sylis explained, and in effect, his powers caused us great lasting pain. Ava had nodded to confirm what Sylis was saying and added what a shame Nathan was on the wrong team, because not only did he have a calculating side, he also was easy on the eyes. She gushed about his boyish, wholesome looks, tall muscular body, and eyes the color of the ocean, framed my brown hair. Normally, I wouldn't be interested in what a fella looked like, but in this situation I noted the details so I could keep an eye out for anyone with those physical attributes.

That night, Sylis talked me into possessing a male. He thought it would be great to fool Aidan at the speakeasy where I was supposed to meet him. I wasn't too keen on the idea, but my curiosity got the best of me.

What was it like to have a penis?

I asked Sylis, and he roared with laughter, telling me I'd have to find out for myself, so what the hell? I did. I chose a nifty dark-haired fella in a black suit with a matching bowtie at the collar of a white shirt. His eyes were green.

"How do you feel?" Sylis asked after I entered the body. The corner of his mouth twitched from trying not to laugh. I must have had a silly expression on my face or something.

I moved my hips back and forth and grabbed my crotch to adjust it. Good thing we were in the back alley behind the building the speakeasy was in. I wouldn't want to make a public spectacle of myself. "I really don't care for this body." The deep voice that came out of my mouth startled me. Then, my attention shifted to between my legs. The left nut wasn't sitting right. What a pain-in-the-ass. I moved it over so it sat comfortably.

"Are you having troubles?" Sylis asked, still trying to compose himself from breaking into laughter. He had chosen a vessel similar to his likeness, except this one had olive skin and short, wavy hair.

Ava was back in the same human she was in the previous night, and I imagined Aidan would be, too. She giggled. "Sometimes I'll jump into a fella when life becomes dull. I didn't care for it at first, but once I adjusted to the mechanics of the male body, I had a ball."

"You mean two," Sylis said, and they both cracked up.

I frowned. The muscles and skin felt tight and heavy. I rubbed my chin. Smooth. At least this one liked a clean shaven-face.

"Well?" Sylis cocked an eyebrow, reminding me I hadn't answered his question.

"I feel fine," I told him, "but I don't know how long I want to remain. I prefer a vagina over a nut sack and ding dong."

Both Sylis and Ava busted a gut, their laughter surrounding me. I followed them to the front of the brick building, into the barber shop, to the back of the store, and through a hidden door behind a paneled wall. We descended a steep set of stairs and entered another door where we were welcomed with live, toe-tapping music and a smoky room. The club wasn't as crowded as the night before, but it was still hopping.

"There's Aidan." Ava pointed to the fella in the newsboy hat heading to the bar. I was right. He chose the same body as before. "Do you want your usual cocktail, Ameer–" She touched her lips and an Oh-My-God expression entered her face. "What's this human's name?"

"Wesley," I answered in a deep voice I still found bizarre, "but people call him Wes." I pulled a silver cigarette case out of the inside pocket of the suit I was wearing and plucked a ciggy out. "And yes, I would love a drink."

She smiled and winked. "Coming right up, Wes."

"I'm impressed," Sylis said while I handed him a ciggy and lit mine. "Usually, a newbie wouldn't be able to reside so soon in a vessel of the opposite sex, but you're doing remarkably well."

I realized prodding me to enter a male body wasn't about fooling Aidan. Sylis was testing me before we took care of Dr. Stratton. I could see why Volac trusted Sylis to take me under his wing. Clever.

"Aside from not enjoying being inside this monkey suit, I feel nifty," I answered, taking a drag and inhaling deeply. The instant relaxation and euphoric feeling washed over me while I held the smoke in my lungs before slowly breathing it out. The sensation was marvelous.

"Here comes Aidan." Sylis blew a tunnel of smoke in the direction of Aidan and Ava, both carrying drinks. "You might despise your current host's gender, but if you lighten up a bit and not hang up your fiddle, you can have a great time."

Sylis was right. I didn't want to be a wet blanket, and I should at least try to embrace this foreign body to see if I could receive any enjoyment from it.

Ava handed me my glass. "Aidan knows."

"You can't pull the wool over my eyes." Aidan thumped his chest with his fingertip. "Although, I find your ruse fair play." He held his beverage up. "Cheers."

"Too bad," Sylis said, raising his glass along with the rest of us. "I was hoping you'd fall for our hoax."

Ava shook her head. "Not Aidan. He's too sharp."

"How does it feel to have a flute, lass?" Aidan asked me and laughed.

"I find it . . . unappealing," I answered.

"You need to get chubbed up and use it," he told me. "Then, you can thank me later." He gestured to an attractive blonde who reminded me of Betty with her bobbed hair, feathered, sequined headband, and white fringed flapper dress. "That human tramp has been eyeing you."

"How do you know she's human?" Ava wanted to know, a note of alarm in her voice.

"She was at the bar earlier, and I could hear her soul." Aidan wrapped his arm around Ava's shoulders. "No worries, lass. You're my gal, and a fine lookin' one." He dipped her backward and kissed her.

"What do you think?" Sylis asked me, shooting glances from me to the blonde.

I imagined her naked. I didn't know why because normally I wouldn't. A vision of me sucking on her nipples and penetrating her followed. I could feel warmth in my pelvic area, then blood rushing to the penis, the balls tightening. The penis stirred and grew, stretching against my trousers. I turned my back to the doll eyeing me and stared at the bulge in my trousers.

"What's eating you?" Ava asked. Her eyes darted to my crotch, and she giggled. "Wow, you're big."

"It's still growing," I said in horror, "and I can't stop fantasizing about her."

Aidan slapped me on the shoulder. "Way ta go. You're chubbed up. Now, you need to knock the hole off her."

Sexual images and feelings raged within me. The thing grew some more and throbbed. I touched it through the material and shifted my erection to the side so it wasn't as noticeable.

"The male body is hardwired differently than the female," Sylis explained. "When we possess a human, we incur the desires of the human flesh and body, which explains your present situation. Your thoughts and insatiable need to claim her is a byproduct of those things."

"I say you take her to the backroom where they have petting parties and poke her," Aidan said.

I swung around, once again facing the crowd, and locked gazes with the blonde. She smiled and waved, feeding the sexual imagery playing in my mind. Waves passed through my throbbing erection. I was rock hard.

"What are you waiting for, lass?" Aidan nudged my elbow.

"Is there another way to get rid of this?" I didn't dare point to the bulge out in the open, but Aidan knew what I was talking about, because his gaze bounced from between my legs, back to my face.

"Your only other option is to do a vigorous hand job on the ol' boy, which in that case"—Aidan pointed in the direction of the john—"you need to find an empty stall and pray you don't get caught."

"Not true," Sylis chided. "Ameerah can think of a mathematical problem or something repulsive to cure her problem, but why waste something that brings you intense pleasure?"

"She's heading this way," Ava said, sounding amused.

Sylis leaned next to my ear. "The human is a whore. Time to make a decision, but I suggest you take advantage of her, because if you don't, I will."

I attempted to concentrate on counting backward from one hundred, but I couldn't think straight. The yearning to do more than petting with this blonde held me in its grasp. I drained the last of my cocktail and handed him my glass. I broke free from my group and met her halfway between two tables occupied by a lively bunch engrossed in their own conversations.

She looked at me. Her green eyes were hooded with desire. A coy smile played on her red lips. "I was wondering if you were going to make an appearance tonight, Wes," she said, surprising me she knew this vessel. Then, out of nowhere, her name came to me.

Ella.

Unfortunately, I didn't know anything else and would have to play along.

She stepped closer, and I could feel the heat of her sexual hunger for Wes rolling off her in waves. My erection continued to throb and strain against my trousers. "I enjoyed necking with you the other night and was hoping we could finish what we started." She opened her beaded handbag and pulled out a key. She dangled it in front of me. "The backroom is locked, but I know the owner. We won't be disturbed this time. What do you say?"

I took her hand and kissed the back of it. "Lead the way, Ella."

A sensual smile crossed her face. "I want you to know I'm normally not this forward, but since we've known each other for a while now and we kissed . . ." She shrugged. "I can't stop thinking about you."

I cradled her cheek in my hand. "The feeling is mutual." *Let's get on with it. This monster will not stop pulsing!*

She took my hand in hers, and we maneuvered through the crowd to the back. An oak door stood before us. She unlocked it. The room was dark, but once she closed and locked the door and turned on a couple lamps, a soft light flooded the room. There were couches and plush thick rugs scattered about. The glossy wooden walls and art décor made the setting classier than one would suspect, considering what this room was designed for.

She tossed her handbag on a couch, and I didn't waste any time. I had to release this pressure in my crotch and act on the fantasies plaguing me since I saw her. I kissed her, softly at first. But when she stuck her tongue in my mouth, our kiss grew deeper. Her hand went to my crotch, and when she began massaging the hardness between my legs, I thought I was going to burst. The feeling was remarkable. Despite myself, I groaned and followed her lead, sliding my hand between her smooth legs and rubbing her clitoris in slow circles over her damp satin panties. Breaking our kiss, she threw her head back and moaned. The sound almost drove me over the edge. She reached for the belt and buttons on my trousers and undid them. When they fell to my ankles, I was amazed at how big this human's penis was and how it stood straight up and bobbed against my abs. The anxiousness to use it became overpowering. We undressed each other and lowered ourselves onto a thick crimson rug. She lay beneath me, and I was careful not to push all my weight on her while I captured her lips, then trailed kisses down her neck.

"I want you inside me," she murmured.

My lesbian side fought the urge to swiftly take her, so I sucked and nibbled on each of her erect nipples while slipping two fingers between her slick folds and pumping them. Her breaths became fast and thick, and when she arched her back and moaned, I could no longer refrain from not fucking her like this body wanted.

I had to have her.

Now.

With my hand, I guided the penis inside her, and sweet mother of Mary, what a glorious feeling. Her warm wetness and the snug feeling sent off a whirlwind of sensations. Once again, she arched her back and grabbed her breasts, which I found extremely sexy and erotic. More stimulation in the male genital area developed at a rapid speed. I could actually feel the semen rising from the balls, and what followed was a feeling of fullness. How odd, and what a pain-in-the-ass for a fella who would want to prolong the act of intercourse but couldn't. But those were fleeting thoughts, for I was too wrapped up in a foreign sexual high to focus on one thing.

When I moved my hips forward and backward, her moans grew louder, and her vaginal muscles gripped the penis tighter, nearly sending me to the moon. Despite the warm, tingling sensation in my groin, I managed to hold on, to enjoy this new sexual experience. I lifted her legs, placing her ankles on my shoulders, penetrating her deeper. Her continuous moans, thick breaths, and beautiful body, turned me on to the point where I caught myself huffing and releasing pleasurable sounds. When her hand flitted between her legs to rub herself, and she cried out she was going to come, a warmth spread across my crotch. Waves of sexual pleasure sent me on an intense plateau. I felt fluid expelling up my shaft and a euphoric release. At the same time, Ella's body tightened and shook.

Blackness.

Son-of-a-bitch!

I catapulted out of the human and found myself standing next to Wes whose body thankfully slumped sideways beside Ella, his arm slung over her stomach. The image of the spot deep in the forest where I'd been to reenergize my spirit, sprang to mind. The next thing I knew, I was there—alone and frustrated.

Chapter Twenty-One

Revenge

The gang showed up not too long after me. They were in high-spirits, wanting to hear every last detail of my sexual experience in the male form. Being me, I didn't hold anything back, including my disappointment in not experiencing the aftereffects of a mind-blowing orgasm in the opposite gender. Aidan, of course laughed and told me I'd be able to feck the box off another gal whenever I damned well pleased. One of the beauties about being a dark spirit was we could push pause and reenact our same behaviors but in a different host. I had to admit I didn't care for the male body. I found it unattractive; however, using it as a tool to experience a different type of sexual pleasure was the bee's knees. I would definitely be inhabiting another one of those again and hopefully the next time around, be able to enjoy the whole orgasmic experience in its ultimate splendor.

Sylis was proud. I had held onto the vessel longer than he thought, which made up his mind that it was about time to destroy Dr. Stratton, Norma, and Florence. From what I told Sylis, he was able to form a devious plan based on the doctor's religious character. I would show Sylis and Ava where Dr. Stratton was, then conduct surveillance on him until we were comfortable the plan would be foolproof. Then, we'd move on and handle Norma and Florence. In the meantime, Aidan could continue recruiting other souls because truthfully, I no longer needed his guidance. I had Sylis and Volac. However, I decided to keep Aidan on standby and meet him at the speakeasy we'd been going to whenever he was available. I was sure he'd bring his new recruits there like he'd done with me, so he could return to the flesh and indulge in his hedonistic pleasures.

"We need to go to Volac's meeting tomorrow night." Ava reminded Sylis and me after Aidan left, and we were making arrangements to spy on Dr. Stratton.

"I'm aware," Sylis said and waved his hand dismissively. "There's no need to fret over pointless issues."

The moon was bright, almost full, spotlighting its white light around us. The wind must have been blowing because the leaves were rustling, some falling to the ground. I longed to feel the breeze in my hair and was looking forward to possessing another body.

"I know this is a fresh wound," Sylis said to me, "but you need to take us to Brandbridge and to the doctor's office, so we can watch him."

I took a deep breath and nodded. The whole idea of revisiting that hellhole was upsetting to say the least, but my desire to see the fucker burn along with his two bitches trumped the hesitation knotting inside me. I stood from my sitting position against the log and offered a hand to Ava and Sylis. I'd never transported another spirit before, let alone two, but what the hell? There was no harm in trying. Closing my eyes, I held onto their hands, and envisioned Dr. Statton's office. Suddenly, I felt a strange, cold shifting in the atmosphere. A few seconds of blackness followed. The next thing I knew, we were there. Dr. Stratton was sitting at his desk doing paperwork.

"If you don't want to stay, Ameerah," Sylis told me right away. "Go to Astoria, and we'll report back to you."

I was at a crossroads. Seeing the doctor's face made me want to take a gat and blow his brains out, but that would be too generous. He needed to suffer. I wouldn't let him get off so easily. I'd make sure of it. On the other hand, it sickened me to be in his presence. I was weak, and I detested it.

"I'll go back to the speakeasy, possess a human, and have some cocktails," I said, not looking at the doctor, knowing if I did, I'd strangle him. "If I'm not there when you're done, I'll be in our spot in the woods waiting for you." I gave them both a pointed look. "Don't do anything without me. I only want you to observe him."

"I won't," Ava promised.

Sylis took his top hat off, smacked it against his knee, and placed it on his head again. "I can't promise you that, Ameerah." His dark eyes hardened, along with his features.

"Why not?"

"I can't stand idly by and not do a damn thing. He's a piece of human garbage."

"Fine." I sighed. "I'm staying, but let's get a wiggle on. I don't want to ever have to look at his despicable mug again."

Ava went to the stack of papers beside Dr. Stratton and flicked them with her fingers. They scattered and fell to the floor. The doctor pushed his round cheaters up the bridge of his nose, mumbled something under his breath, and bent to collect them.

"I didn't know we can do that," I said, hearing the surprise and delight in my voice. "Teach me how."

Sylis moved to the other side of the desk where a coffee cup sat. "Simple. You imagine touching the item"—he placed his fingertip near the rim—"and put an emotion behind your image"—he moved his hand forward, knocking the cup over, spilling brown liquid on the papers the doctor was working on—"like so."

"Nifty," I said and laughed when Dr. Stratton threw out a few colorful words before busying himself mopping up the mess.

Ava moved next to me and elbowed my side. "Try it."

I went to the footprints picture the doctor was so fond of, hovered above the floor so I could reach it, and followed Sylis' directions. Nothing. I attempted it again with no results.

"You're not putting enough emotion behind your gesture," Sylis told me. "Try it again, but this time think of what an asshole he was to you and envision knocking that horrid picture down."

"It'll become second nature to you once you do it a few times," Ava said. "Don't get discouraged."

I nodded and tried again, determined to succeed. Still nothing. "Why can't I do this?" I asked, frustrated. "It's a simple fucking thing." I jabbed my fingers against the side of the picture frame, and it didn't move.

Ava floated to me. "You need to put some strong feelings into it."

"I have."

"Apparently not, Sixty-four," she said, referring to the degrading way the doctor had the attendants at Bandbridge acknowledge my presence. "What did this bastard call you before . . . morally insane? Then, he committed you to a looney bin. I wonder how much your parents paid him to do that. Or maybe the sick fuck gets his rocks off by toying with innocent young gals, and no payment is needed."

I glared at the doctor reorganizing his paperwork while Ava kept flapping her gums about how he mistreated me and said my relationship with Betty was sinful.

Every rotten thing he'd done to me rose to the surface—fresh and vivid. A fierce anger whipped through me. In one swipe, I knocked the picture frame off the wall. It crashed to the floor, spraying shards of glass around it.

The doctor jumped out of his chair. Wide-eyed, he backed against the same shelves I had when I was human, when I was trying to escape. He began reciting "The Lord's Prayer": "Our father, which art in heaven, hallowed be thy name . . ."

"What a load of rubbish," Sylis said, kicking the trashcan over beside the desk at the same time Ava threw a book across the room. It smacked into the shelf beside the doctor's head.

He flinched and ducked. "Thy kingdom come. Thy will be done on earth—"

Fueled by rage, I wrapped my hands around his neck, and it worked. His fingers flew up to his collarbone, his mouth wide open. Sick, gurgling choking sounds reached my ears.

"How does it feel to be choked to death, you sick fuck?" I seethed. "You and my parents stole *everything* from me." I squeezed harder, enjoying his face turning shades of red and purple.

Dr. Stratton slumped to the floor, opening and closing his mouth like a fish. I could hear his soul. It sounded like sloshing water, and the tempo was slowing down, the noise fading.

He was dying.

The fear and shock in his eyes reflected through his cheaters.

He knew it.

I wanted to prolong his agony, which was my original plan, but the panic and horror on his face in his last moments on earth was the berries. He kept grabbing his throat, squirming on the floor, kicking his feet, knocking them into the chair and desk. Then, his body went limp. I released my grip from his neck, feeling a sense of relief, not only for what he'd done to me, but because now his cruelty would no longer touch another soul in Bandbridge.

I grinned.

"You!"

I turned to the familiar voice behind me and was face to face with Dr. Stratton's spirit, hovering above his dead body's feet. An appalling, frightful expression twisted his features, and he disappeared.

Sylis patted me on the back. "Excellent job, Ameerah. I'm proud of you."

"Where did he go?" I asked.

Sylis shrugged. "Beats me, but at least the bastard now knows he was murdered by you."

"Hopefully, to the Sheol of Glass," Ava said and congratulated me on what a fine job I'd done.

"Aidan told me about the Sheol of Glass," I mused. "It's a dreary dimension with large pockets of darkness."

"I hope you're not sore at me for saying those things," Ava said. "I only did so to stir up those powerful emotions you have, to get you to move the picture. I'm sorry."

"There's no need to apologize," I told her, flashing her a smile. I was on cloud nine and didn't feel the least bit bad about my actions. "Let's go find some soulless humans to possess and have a drink."

"What about the other two?" Ava asked. "What are those bitch's names?"

I frowned. "Norma and Florence, but we can take care of them tomorrow."

"You mean today," Ava said. "It's three a.m."

"Yeah, whatever," I said. "I want a cocktail and a ciggy."

Sylis roughly kicked the doctor's body aside. The limbs flopped like on a ragdoll. He sat in the chair behind the desk. "I'll stay here while you two go for a nightcap. I want to do some investigation and maybe have a little fun." There was a mischievous glint in his eyes.

I had no clue what he was cooking up, but at the moment I didn't care. There was no reason for me not to trust him thus far, and besides, I wanted to have some fun.

"Do you want us to meet you back here?" Ava asked, hooking her arm with mine.

Sylis shook his head. "I'll see you at Volac's meeting, and afterward I'll fill you in on my discoveries."

"Fair enough," I said, anxious to leave and go celebrate my achievement of ridding the earth of one wretched human.

"Do you want to take me to Slim's speakeasy?" Ava asked me.

The thought of going back to Slim's so soon and seeing the gals who I thought were my pals, made me tense. At the same time, I felt a crushing blow to my chest. I wasn't ready to return. In fact, I didn't think I'd ever go there again. What would be the point? They had let me down. All of them. End of story.

Ava patted my arm. She knew, there was no need to answer her. "Back to Astoria it is."

We waved goodbye to Sylis and left.

Chapter Twenty-Two

Volac's Meeting

I entered a white gabled barn, illuminated by lanterns placed between the empty stalls on either side of the room. Upstairs was a large hayloft with loose bits of alfalfa scattered across the floor. Dark spirits were already occupying that area while others such as Ava and I appeared on the lower level.

"Why are we having the meeting in a barn?" I asked her. Never in a million years would I have guessed Volac would conduct a gathering here.

"Remember," she answered, "he used to be a farmer when he was a Viking."

I twisted my lips to the side. "I suppose this makes sense, then."

"It does," she said offhandedly, looking around at what I guessed were familiar faces to her. She smiled and waved to a few of them. "Come along. I want to introduce you before Volac appears."

I followed her, dreading being the center of attention, yet curious to meet everyone. To my surprise, the introductions and idle chatter turned out to be enjoyable. Each had a story to tell and which era it came from. I was delighted and entranced with what they had to say. Then, the lively chatter abruptly stopped.

Silence.

In unison, everyone around me stepped back, giving the black hooded figure the floor. His energy flowed through the room, dominating it. Ava grabbed my hand, pulling me beside her so I didn't look like a dumb Dora standing in the center of the room with their leader. I saw Sylis across from us. I caught his eyes, and he gave me a thumbs up. *What in the world did he do?*

Volac lowered his hood and looked around. When his gaze connected with mine, he gave me a curt nod before addressing everyone. "We have a newborn among us." He motioned for me to step forward.

Are you fucking kidding me? I hated being on display, like some damned china doll in a glass cabinet. Reluctantly, I edged forward, feeling the weight of everyone's stare. I tried to ignore them by focusing my attention on Volac.

"Meet Ameerah Arrowood. She's been doing a marvelous job acclimating to her new existence. In fact, I'm quite impressed by her tenaciousness and ease when faced with a task. I believe she would be a great asset to our league, if she so inclines to join us." He gave me a dismissive wave to return to my spot next to Ava, which I happily did while he resumed speaking to the crowd. "I trust if Ameerah needs your assistance or guidance, you will lend it." He paused long enough to sweep his eyes across the room and was met with nods. Satisfied, he continued. "Now, let's get down to business. As you know, many of us have infiltrated governments around the world. We've been doing so for thousands of years. Our goal is to toy with and test humanity's endurance and intelligence. When the time arrives, we will know who will be worthy to remain on earth. Unfortunately, there are more humans than there are dark spirits. We're outranked, not to mention we have the burden of the immortals on our backs and their meddling paws in our business. Regardless, we have the power to change history, and we're going to do so in 1929."

"Why wait four years?" a fella called from the crowd, earning agreeable sounds from his peers.

Volac shifted his attention in the direction of the questioner. "It's a game of chess. All the pieces have to be strategically moved. You allow your opponent to think he's winning, and at the opportune moment . . . checkmate. We did it with the Great War, and we will do so again."

My mouth flopped open. I knew people who were in the war. Granted, my affection toward humanity ran almost dry now, but learning from Volac that the dark spirits were the ones who enabled the world war, flabbergasted me. I didn't know whether to be impressed or appalled.

"Do you have something to say, Ameerah?" Volac asked, obviously reading the shocked expression on my face.

"I knew people who were in the war. I was only a child at the time, but from what I can recall they were swell," I said.

Loud groans rippled throughout the barn in protest to my seemly admiration for humans.

I held up my hand, palm facing Volac, to silence them, and stepped forward. "You're getting the wrong impression, so pipe down and let me finish before you crucify me."

Volac stuck a finger in each side of his mouth and blew a loud whistling noise. Once the room became quiet, he nodded for me to continue, planting his full attention on me.

"By no means am I sympathetic to most human's misfortunes. *Most.* There are a few good apples within the orchard of rotten ones. So why test them?" When I caught a few dark spirits shaking their heads in disgust, I jabbed a finger against my chest and raised my voice. "I was one of the good ones! And some of you can't convince me you were a bad seed when you were human."

"Why did you choose to be one of us?" someone hollered.

"Because I was betrayed by my own flesh and blood," I shouted back. "I was abused. My freedom. My dignity. My life . . . was stolen from me. I was murdered, and I loathed most humans but not all." I knew whatever popularity I'd gain since I arrived was diminishing. I didn't give a shit. If they didn't like what I had to say or who I was, they could fuck off. I hadn't agreed to join them anyway.

Sylis stepped forward, surprising me by his bold support. "Ameerah murdered a human today," he said in a strong and unyielding tone.

Surprised gasps issued from the crowd. "That's right. A newborn bumped off the son-of-a-bitch who played a huge roll in her demise. There are also others who will incur Ameerah's wrath. So if you have any reservations against her having a soft spot for humanity, you're wrong. I've seen her in action. She's definitely one of us."

Sylis and I returned to our original positions. The tension in the air eased. He stuck his neck out for me, and I wouldn't forget. To start, I'd buy him a drink later to show my gratitude.

"Ameerah is correct," Volac said. "There's an exception to the rules when it comes to humans." He turned to me. "To answer your earlier question regarding testing them, it's all part of our design to take back earth as our own. We need humans to continue breeding so more soulless ones will be available to us. Once the time comes when a mass genocide occurs, those we deem worthy will be unharmed, left to reproduce, and provide countless services to us. Of course, they'll be too dim-witted to realize what will actually be taking place. They'll be too caught up in their own self-centered affairs and gadgets to see the signs or even care."

As he was telling me this, I thought about the immortals and wondered how they would stop us. From what I understood, there were more of us than them. They didn't stand a chance. I thought about mass genocide. I wasn't sure how I felt about it, but then again, exterminating the earth of mankind such as my parents and others who were snobs and had other despicable qualities would be nifty.

"Now," Volac said, addressing everyone, "back to where I was at the beginning of our meeting. In 1929, the stock market is going to crash and bring this nation into economic calamity. Right now, there's rapid growth in bank credit and loans. Humans are having the time of their lives, living high on the hog. A lot of them are borrowing money to buy shares in the market. We predict their confidence in stocks and credit will continue to grow. When 1929 draws near, the market will offer consumers the potential to become millionaires. It will be the new gold rush. People will borrow more money to invest in the stock market. What we speculate will follow is a bubble. The shares will keep rising,

not by the true economy but on paper by the optimism of the investors."
He paused, perhaps to allow what he was saying to sink in. I thought
this was a brilliant plan and knew my father had already invested a lot
of his earnings into the stock market. Then, a grand idea came to me
about how to destroy my parents once and for all. "I'll spare you the
intricate details," Volac continued. "But other factors will come into play
to ensure the collapse of society, such as an agriculture recession, sales in
the automobile industry will fall, lower steel production, and so forth.
It takes years to pull off such a feat, so we must exercise patience and do
our part when our assistance is needed. If you have any questions, you're
free to ask now."

While Volac answered the questions thrown at him, Sylis made his
way to Ava and me. He had a cocky expression on his face, which piqued
my curiosity.

"We need to go to Bandbridge when this meeting ends," he told us.

"Why," Ava and I asked in unison.

There was a devilish look in his dark eyes, and a wicked grin crossed
his face. "It's a surprise I have no doubt you'll be pleased with."

I crossed my arms, annoyed. "Spare me your melodrama. You cannot
dangle a carrot in front of me with the pretentious notion I will follow
without at least one nibble."

"Well said, Ameerah." Ava smiled and looked at Sylis. "Tell us what
you did."

"You're ruining it for me," he said, but when we didn't relent and only
stared at him, he sighed. "You dames are hard to contend with but have
it your way." He moved between us and wrapped his arms around our
shoulders. "I'll tell you everything after the meeting."

"Okay, but don't feed us a bunch of baloney," Ava told him. "We want
to know everything. Right, Ameerah?"

I nodded. "Absolutely."

"We'll go back to the forest, and I'll fill you in there," Sylis said. "I
think I need to reenergize. I'm feeling a bit off."

"A bit off," I echoed, pondering. "So you were possessing a human the whole time we were gone?" I wondered who in Bandbridge was soulless. Aidan had told me Norma and Florence had a soul, so they were out of the equation.

Sylis placed a finger on his lips and directed his attention on Volac, who was ending our gathering. I missed the questions due to being preoccupied with my current situation. I wasn't going to sweat about it, though. I understood the reason for our meeting, and I had a sense of what type of leader and fella Volac was. I liked him and what he stood for. After everyone dispersed, I told him I'd join his league on the condition I could leave if I ever had the desire to do so, ideally without any hard feelings between us. He was pleased and agreed to my terms. I could tell by his genuine smile and his warm demeanor he fancied me, which I took advantage of by mirroring his sentiments in return.

"Are you ready?" Sylis asked me, offering his hand. He looked at Volac. "We have some unfinished business which requires our immediate attention."

"Off you go," Volac said, shooing us away in a friendly manner.

Ava stepped on the other side of Sylis. Even though we could have met him at our spot in the forest on our own, we took his hands anyway, and instantly left the barn together.

Chapter Twenty-Three

Sylis' Discovery

We were deep in the woods, back in our usual spot. Bright stars scattered across the black sky, while wispy clouds ebbed and flowed along the full moon. I sat on the log I always gravitated to, and Ava sat beside me while Sylis stood in front of us.

"Did you know, Ameerah," he began, "we're not free to go where we damn well please on earth in our spiritual form?"

"You're fooling me, right?" Aidan never mentioned anything of the sort, and I found the whole thing ridiculous. I wondered if this was Sylis' way of stalling to give him more time to ponder how he'd tell us what happened at Bandbridge. "You're full of baloney."

"He's not," Ava said. "It's true."

Stunned, I turned to her while catching a glimpse of Sylis nodding. "But we've been to quite a few places without being in the flesh," I argued.

"All of them had some form of dark and negative energy or a soulless human nearby," Ava told me. "This restriction placed upon us is a real bitch and another reason why we love possessing humans, because then we're free to wander wherever we want."

"Astoria is one of many places on earth that has a multitude of accommodating hot spots for our kind," Sylis said. "There's a prophesy the 'old one' swears by, which will take place here in Astoria. It's why he encourages us to stay here or at least visit on a regular basis."

I was intrigued because what he was saying reminded me of the visions I used to have when I was human. "What is it?"

"Give her the short version," Ava said, "because I want to know what sort of trouble you stirred up in our absence."

"In a nutshell," Sylis said, "there will be a young gal with special abilities living in Astoria. She'll have witch's blood running through her veins and will be marked for immortality."

I shrugged. "Okay." I didn't see what the big deal was.

He held a hand up. "I'm not finished . . . anyway, the 'old one' has been looking for King Solomon's ring for thousands of years. Whoever wears the ring and knows his incantations will be able to control dark spirits. Us. This gal will be the only one who will be able to find Solomon's ring *and* his incantations."

"How does Volac feel about that?" I knew who King Solomon was. He once ruled Israel, and I absolutely loathed the idea of being under someone's control. Been there. Done that. Not anymore. I didn't give a shit who the "old one" was. If this prophesy ever came true, I'd do whatever I could to prevent him from getting his dirty paws on those two items.

"Volac will not live under a tyrant, and neither will we," Ava reassured me. "So if this ancient prediction comes to light, Volac will do whatever is necessary to prevent the 'old one' from possessing Solomon's power."

"Good." I was pleased to learn Volac felt the same as I. I shifted my attention to Sylis. "Now, tell us what happened at Bandbridge."

"Long or short version?" he asked with a wicked grin.

"For crying out loud. Just tell us already," I said. "You'd mentioned at Volac's meeting you needed to reenergize, which means there's a soulless human in Bandbridge. Aidan told me Dr. Stratton, Norma, and Florence have a soul."

"He's right," Sylis answered. "They do. I'm talking about a fella who has pale blue eyes and–"

I shot to my feet. "That bastard raped me when I was sedated!" I shouted, furious.

Ava's mouth dropped. "Oh my God . . . you never told us. I'm so sorry, Ameerah."

I didn't want to get into why I hadn't mentioned to them that part of the living nightmare I had starred in. So I directed my attention to Sylis instead. "Do you think a dark spirit was the one who violated me?"

"I don't know. There's no way of telling for sure."

"How do you know he raped you if you were sedated?" Ava asked.

"Because I was in and out of consciousness," I told her, gritting my teeth. "I have a fuzzy memory of him on top of me, spreading my legs, saying something about after he was through, I'd be a converted woman, only wanting dick."

Sylis cracked his knuckles; a dark expression entered his face. "We can take care of him, if you want." He sighed heavily and leveled his eyes with mine. "I don't like humans, Ameerah. I'll admit I can be a cruel son-of-a-bitch, but I would never do such a thing to a woman."

"But other dark spirits would. Am I correct?" I asked, my anger rattling each word.

He nodded. "Some of us are extremely wicked."

"Calvin Hyde," Ava blurted.

Calvin Hyde? My mind raced, trying to place the name and face. Then, it clicked. "The lanky, weird ginger fella who was at the speakeasy the night I met you?"

"Yes," she said. "He likes young boys. Sometimes he kills them, then eats their flesh. It arouses him."

I thumped my forehead with the tip of my fingers. "I knew there was something creepy about him." I shifted my gaze to Sylis. "Tell us what happened while you were at Bandbridge today." I wanted to change the subject, because I hadn't realized until now how evil some of us were and didn't want to get roped into a conversation about it.

"I possessed pale-eyes," Sylis began, "and stuffed Dr. Stratton's body in a closet in his office. I then found Norma doing some charting at the nurses' station. In private, I confided in her that Florence was going to frame her for the murder of Ameerah Arrowood."

"What did she say?" I asked.

"She didn't believe me at first," he said. "In fact, she laughed and played it off like she didn't have a clue what I was talking about. But when I told her in detail what they'd done to you, all the color drained from her face." He laughed. "The bitch was scared as hell. I then fed her a bunch of baloney about Florence telling me how nervous she was when the cops came to investigate Ameerah's death, and more than likely, they'll be questioning her tomorrow."

Ava and I both sat back down on the log, captivated by his tale. I was impressed by how much thought he'd put into this scheme in only a small period of time. He was conniving yet brilliant.

"I went on to tell Norma I overheard one of the investigators talking to the other one, saying something fishy was going on, and they were going to get to the bottom of it."

"What did she say?" Ava wanted to know.

"She asked me why I thought Florence would frame her. I told her because I personally knew Florence, and she was the type of dame who would to do anything to save her own hide."

I should have been sore at him for taking the reins without me, but I was too intrigued by this new development to scold.

"What happened next?" I asked, then pointed sharply at him. "You better not have taken care of those two rotten people without me."

He rubbed his chin and scrunched up his face. "Not exactly." When I raised my eyebrows, he continued. "I led her down and through the tunnels beneath the building. The same place you told me where they had you confined and chained to a bed. She was surprised when I showed her Florence was lying on top of a mattress in restraints and unconscious. She smiled, congratulated me for doing a fine job, and arrogantly informed me how very few people knew about these hidden rooms."

"Holy shit," Ava breathed.

Sylis went on to tell us when Norma wasn't looking, he overpowered her and sedated her, as well. Right now, she was chained to the same bed I was . . . in a drug-induced state. After his deed was done, he went back to Dr. Stratton's office, found some whiskey stashed in a drawer in his desk along with a pack of ciggies, and indulged himself while he read through some papers. "The doctor was planning on performing a frontal lobotomy on you, Ameerah," he told me in a flat, serious voice.

Ave gave him an odd look. "What's that?"

I was too stunned to say anything. I knew what it was. Abe had once told Betty and me all about it. I hugged myself, feeling a sense of horror at how close I was to a fate more unimaginably horrible than the one I already had.

"It's when a surgeon sticks two metal rods in your skull and scrapes away parts of your brain," Sylis answered.

Ava gasped and slapped a hand over her mouth.

Sylis looked at me and frowned. "Your parents knew, Ameerah. In fact, they signed a form giving their consent."

I blinked several times, staving off the waterworks, refusing to cry. It shouldn't surprise me, but the news of their heartless act still stung, nonetheless. "Did you find anything else regarding me?"

"No," he said, "I didn't have enough time to go through everything. I did, however, find a large wad of dough in an envelope tucked away in his file cabinet."

"What did you do with the human you were possessing?" Ava asked.

"I left him in the break room." Sylis looked up at the sky. The dark canvas was fading into a sea blue color with thick reddish, pink clouds hovering above us. "His nightshift will end soon. I suggest we go there right now and have Ameerah do some damage." His eyes darted between Ava and me. "One of you is going to have to take over a male body. There are three soulless attendants there now. Two are male, the other female."

Ava stood, pulling me up with her. "I'll be the fella."

I was grateful for Ava volunteering to be in the opposite sex. I was only in a male body once and didn't feel comfortable being in another one while performing a serious act.

I took both their hands, the rage still ripe inside me. "Sylis, take us to where you think the soulless humans are. I have a plan, but we need to act quickly before the authorities come knocking on the door."

A devious grin crossed Sylis' face. "My pleasure."

And then we were gone.

Chapter Twenty-Four

Karma

I detested being back at Bandbridge and became frustrated when we couldn't find the bastard who raped me. Sylis told me the asshole's name was Chester.

Chester, the molester.

How fitting.

The place was quiet, except for a few moans behind closed doors, and a gal cheerfully singing a good morning song I suspected she made up, because the lyrics didn't make sense. We passed a few staff members and nurses going through their daily routines. None of them I'd seen before.

"Where the hell is he or the other two soulless humans?" I asked as we searched another hall. "He wasn't at the nurses' station or in the break room." I was becoming concerned. What if he left the premises? What if we were too late?

I stopped in my tracks and folded my arms. There he was with the other two.

Jackpot.

Though it was faint, I could hear the dull, low humming noise they emitted. I never thought until now that another dark spirit might have already been occupying them. But for once, fate was smiling upon me. Or was it Karma? I'd go with Karma. Fate was a bitch.

Sylis stood composed, the picture of ease only a master possesses after fine tuning his art. "It's your show, Ameerah. Tell us what to do, and we'll perform."

"Let's get a wiggle on," I said. "Then, we head to Dr. Stratton's office."

I crossed the hall to the female while Sylis and Ava went to the fellas. I was close enough to see the cracks in the makeup beneath the gal's brown eyes. Imagining occupying this plain frump, my entire form tingled. I stepped inside her. Blackness and then light through a semi-blurry lens. Great. She had poor vision. But that was the least of my concerns. I stretched the long limbs and twisted the body from side to side. At the same time, I wrinkled my nose from the scent of old urine and bleach.

"Are you fit as a fiddle?" Sylis asked in a deep voice I recognized with great abhorrence. His hands flew up as if he were protecting himself from a blow to the face. "Easy, I'm not him. I'm on your side."

"You look like you're going to coldcock him," a male voice said.

Ava.

The male attendant Ava was occupying turned out to be the same asshole who cornered me in Dr. Stratton's office.

Lovely.

"Follow me," I said, ignoring the urge to attack them.

I led them back down the maze of halls past empty wheelchairs and gurneys shoved against the walls. One of the nifty things about possessing humans was you obtained their basic memories, so I now knew my way around this facility and what the keys in my apron pocket was for.

"Frieda," a female said when we stopped in front of a metal door. With the key in my hand poised to unlock it, I turned, knowing Frieda was this human's name.

A stalky woman with dark hair pulled into a tight bun approached us. The information about her suddenly came to me. Her name was Maude, and she used to work in the TB ward but was recently transferred to this unit.

"Do you know where Norma is?" she asked a bit frazzled.

"No," I answered. "She wasn't feeling well yesterday. Maybe she called in today."

Maude frowned. "Are any of you not busy? I need another person to help supervise the residents during breakfast. Since Norma isn't here, we're one person short."

I pointed to the human Ava was inhabiting. "Orville can fill in. I'll send him there in a minute."

Maude thanked us and scurried in the direction she came from. She made a right turn, disappearing from sight.

"Here's what I want you to do," I told Ava. "After breakfast, everyone will be herded to the common room. Stay with them. Sylis and I will be there as soon as we can."

She nodded. "Good luck, Ameerah," she whispered, leaving Sylis and me.

Not knowing how much time we had left before the authorities would arrive, I hurried and unlocked the door. In silence, Sylis followed me to Dr. Stratton's office. Once inside, I told him to give me the dough he discovered here yesterday. Without question, he crossed the room to the black file cabinet, opened the drawer, and pulled out a wide envelope. After he handed it to me, I shoved it in my pocket.

"Where are the ciggies and whiskey?" I asked while reaching into my other pocket. I pulled out a couple hypodermic syringes and glass vials filled with medicine. Barbiturates. Frieda had them in case a patient became unruly.

Sylis moved behind Stratton's desk and dug through the drawer, rustling papers until he found the items I asked for. "Heads up." He tossed me a silver flask, then a box of matches. He rounded the desk and handed me a brass cigarette case. "We don't have time to smoke in here."

I unscrewed the top of the flask, took a swig, and nodded. The whiskey was smooth and nice. Really nice. There was a hint of an orange peel taste and something else, but I couldn't quite pinpoint what it was. Stratton sure liked his liquor. Fucking hypocrite. The son-of-a-bitch acted pious the last time we spoke, and here he was practicing the behaviors he condemned me for.

"We better get a wiggle on," I said, glancing at the closet in the back of the room, imaging Stratton's rotting corpse stuffed inside. I smiled and handed the flask to Sylis, offering him a drink before we scrammed.

We were fortunate enough that it was in the early morning, and the staff was preoccupied with getting the patients together for breakfast and meds. We didn't run into any trouble while we crossed the corridors and entered the door leading to the subterranean part of the building. We made our way beneath the facility and through the ominous tunnels to where Norma and Florence were held. The occasional sound of pipes groaning and the smell of rotten cabbage and sewage in parts of the passageways were unsettling, but we pressed on until finally we reached our destination. Sylis opened the door to a hall of hidden rooms, and when we reached the cell Norma was in, I paused. I could hear whimpering on the other side of the door.

"What are you waiting for?" Sylis asked.

"Go to the broom closet. There's a bucket in there. Fill it with water," I ordered.

Sylis didn't say a word. He sprinted down the hall to perform the task I asked of him. I remained rooted in my spot with the sudden realization that the last time I laid eyes upon Norma was when she bumped me off.

Hatred and a furious need for vengeance engulfed me. The bitch would pay dearly for the humiliation and abuse she inflicted. I flung the door open and was immediately met with the pungent smell of urine and feces. She was lying on the floor in her own mess, chained to the bed like I'd been. She lifted her head, eyes unfocused, then blinked, perhaps to clear her vision. She reached for me, as if I were an angel here to save her sorry ass.

I bent over and placed my hands on my knees, mimicking the same gesture she'd done when I was the one in chains. "You're pathetic"—I pinched my nose—"and smell."

"Help me, Frieda," she whined.

I shook my head. "Wrong. I'm Ameerah."

She vehemently shook her head. "No, you're Frieda. Sixty-four is—"

"Not Sixty-four," I said between clenched teeth. "I told you my name is *Ameerah*, and then you and Florence drowned me in the tub."

Her eyes widened, and she wiped her mouth with the back of her hand. "You can't be. I'm hallucinating from the drugs that . . ." She shrieked and pointed past me. "Him! He was the one who double-crossed me. Get him out of here!"

Sylis stood in the doorframe with a bucket of water. I motioned for him to enter and to place it beside me.

"Pipe down," I yelled. "You took my freedom. My dignity. My life. How does it feel to be powerless?"

"I don't feel well." She held her stomach and turned her head, appearing on the verge of tossing her cookies.

I laughed. "Look at you, lying in your own filth. At least, I was resourceful and had the decency to clean myself up."

"It can't be," she whispered in horror. "It has to be the drugs. Yes, the drugs." She sat up and hugged her knees to her chest, rocking back and forth. Then, as if a firecracker had been lit beneath her, she stood, eyes wild, reaching for me. She slipped in her own fecal matter and smacked the floor on her side, howling in pain.

"Have you heard of karma, Norma?" I leaned over her, careful not to step in her waste. "Time to pay the piper." I took the syringe and glass vial out of my pocket and loaded the cylinder with the medicine, relying on Frieda's memory on how to do so. My heart was pounding from the sudden onslaught of adrenaline pumping through my veins. I grabbed Norma's arm, expecting a struggle, but she was too busy mumbling to herself and possibly too weak to combat me. I plunged the needle into her arm. She jerked it back in surprise and made a poor attempt to push me away, but I had a tight grip on her. As the barbiturates were introduced into her bloodstream, she grew limp. I dragged her to the bucket of water and forced her on her knees.

"No. No," she pleaded, halfheartedly. "The cat isn't out of the bag. Leave it alone."

I looked up at Sylis, and he shrugged.

"Karma, Norma," I said and was pleased when Sylis bent in front of the bucket and wrapped his hands around the base to keep it anchored to the floor.

"Ameerah . . . Sixty-four . . . . Ameerah." She shook her head in confusion. "She was a danger to society . . . to the children. The way she dressed. Her impudent, sinful behavior, poisoning . . ." Her body swayed, causing me to tighten my grip on the nape of her neck.

I smacked her cheeks a couple times. "Norma."

"Her eyes are glazing over," Sylis said. "Do it now before she becomes unconscious."

I held her shackled wrists back and submerged her head, listening to her making sickening high-pitched noises. Her body squirmed to break free, but she was too weak to fight. Soon after, she slumped forward. I released her. The sound of the bucket hitting the floor with Norma's head still in it pierced the silence. Water rushed around my shoes, damping the edges. I waited to see Norma's spirit but saw nothing. How odd. Then, a cold draft brushed by me, followed by a disembodied soft voice saying, "The cat isn't out of the bag. Leave it alone."

"How come I didn't see her spirit?" I asked Sylis.

He rose and kicked the bucket hard with his foot, making a loud clunking noise from Norma's head knocking inside it. "Because of the way she died. Each passing is different."

I took two ciggies out, popped one in my mouth, and handed him the other. I struck a match and lit them both. "C'mon, let's go pay Florence a visit."

I was practically bouncing out the room from some of the weight being lifted off me. I didn't have a plan on how I would handle Florence. Maybe I'd drug her some more and leave her here to rot. That would probably be the best thing to do. Of course, I could toy with her for a while and be a total bitch like she was with me.

"Damn it," I said when we entered the room, and I saw her lifeless body restrained to the bed, her head turned on its side, eyes closed. "How much medicine did you give her?"

Sylis scrunched up his face and rubbed his temple. "The same amount I injected into Norma. She must have had a bad reaction and went into a cardiac arrest . . . I apologize, Ameerah. I never considered this would occur."

I moved closer to her. There was no sound. I touched her neck where her pulse would be.

Nothing.

"It's all right," I sighed, trying not to sound or appear disappointed. "You were only trying to be helpful." I took one last drag off my ciggy, then snuffed it out on Florence's forehead. Sylis did the same thing. I rushed out of the room, not wanting to stew over this misfortune. "There's something I need to do before we leave."

"What?" Sylis asked as we retraced our steps through the underground tunnels.

The sound of water dripping and pipes groaning unnerved me. I hated being down here. I didn't answer right away due to holding my breath while we trekked by the smelly areas.

"You'll see," I finally answered when we climbed the stairs that led to the facility.

We made it to the common room without incident, only a few good mornings from nurses and attendants were thrown at us. No one suspected any funny business was going on, which fueled my boldness and determination. Thankfully, I had the presence of mind to be cautious, so my senses were on high alert, my anxiety off the charts. The same patients as before were sitting at the long table in the middle of the room, playing cards, looking at magazines, staring off in a daze. I spotted Elizabeth, curled up in a brown cushioned chair beneath the barred window, her gray gown covering her knees, arms around them. She appeared lost in thought.

Shit!

The horrible itchy feeling I always experienced before I was forced out of the body began to plague me.

"What's eating you?" Sylis asked when I halted halfway through the room and shook out my limbs.

"I'm losing my grip on this human," I said out the side of my mouth, frustrated.

The tall, brown-haired attendant Ava was possessing, Orville, stood across the room, chatting with another male worker. Ava's gaze strayed to us, then back to the fella.

"You need to get your emotions under control," Sylis ordered in a low voice with an edge of authority. "If you fail to do so, your spirit will vacate the body."

My feelings were all over the place—a cocktail mix of anxiousness, excitement, relief, joy, and frayed nerves. I took slow, deep breaths in an attempt to calm myself.

Ava crossed the room in quick strides, and although she was inhabiting a male, I could see her personality shining through Orville's brown eyes. She was excited about something and motioned for us to follow her to a corner by the entrance. "There's a mole in Bandbridge," she told us.

I gaped at her. "What? How do you know? Who is it?" My eyes scanned the room.

"Word is going around," Ava said in a hush voice, "it's one of the male patients on the other ward. He's actually a journalist who pretended to be insane, so he could get admitted here. A family member or friend had him discharged a week or so ago."

"If what you're saying is true," Sylis said, "then it explains why the authorities are nosing around here. What happened to Ameerah probably lit a fire under their asses to begin an investigation."

My stomach tightened when a gut-wrenching thought came to me. If I were still alive, and what Ava was telling us proved to be accurate, there was a good possibility that I could have been vindicated and then released. I would have gotten my life back. But who was I kidding? Betty nor anyone of my so-called pals cared the least bit about me. If they had, they would have suspected something fishy was going on—especially Betty and Abe. They knew how my parents were. Abe–

"Stop it," Sylis said, breaking through my mental tangent. He took hold of my shoulders and gave a light shake. "Stop stewing over what could have been. There's nothing you can do to change it. Most humans are foul creatures who need to be purged from this earth."

"We're no different," I countered, thinking of Calvin Hyde.

He squeezed my shoulders and narrowed his eyes. "We're loyal to one another, Ameerah. It's unusual for a dark spirit to turn on his own. If he does, he pays a heavy price and an example is made of him. It deters our kind from making the same mistake. We're also choosy with who we recruit. We were all human once . . . well, most of us . . . but our behavior as one determines our worthiness to be where we are now."

"We need to leave," Ava said.

"How are you feeling?" Sylis asked me, lifting his hands off my shoulders, scrutinizing me.

The horrible, itchy sensation was no longer there. I overcame it without realizing the feeling went away, until he brought it to my attention.

"I'm ducky," I said, smiling. "I need to do something first." Before they could protest, I hurried to where Elizabeth sat. "You need to come with me."

She looked up. Tears glistened in her golden eyes, her features drawn in sadness. My heart clenched, and I wondered what happened to her. She didn't move a muscle or say anything, instead she was studying me closely.

I offered her my hand. "I'm not going to hurt you. I promise. In fact, I have something for you from Ameerah."

She gasped and took my hand. She jerked me down so we were eye-to-eye. "Ameerah?" Her gaze darted back and forth, and recognition brightened her features. "I see you," she whispered. "The face behind the mask." She began to laugh and cry at the same time, hugging me.

I gave her a gentle push and held her at arm's length. "People are watching. You need to come with me before they get suspicious."

She nodded and straightened her back, playing along. She followed me to the entrance where Sylis and Ava waited.

"What in the hell are you doing?" Sylis said, not hiding his disapproval. "We accomplished what we came here to do. This human needs to be left to her own devices."

I wheeled on him. Through clenched teeth, I spat, "Not her. If you want to leave, then leave. Otherwise, shut your trap."

He sighed. "Very well. Lead the way."

Ava raised her eyebrows in surprise at my outburst but didn't say a word. She eyed Elizabeth, sizing her up, and followed us out of the common room.

"Frieda," a female said as we were making our way down the hallway.

I didn't turn until Sylis stopped and elbowed me in the side.

"Where are you taking Fifty-two?"

My heart stopped, and my mind raced on what to say that would satisfy her curiosity. Nothing came to me. All I could do was give her a blank stare.

"I'm not feeling well," Elizabeth said, holding her stomach.

The dark-eyed women crossed her arms over her lanky frame. "All three of you need to escort her? You know the police are here? We have better things to do than treat an upset stomach."

"Orville and I," Sylis said, "were heading in the same direction, and we thought maybe Frieda might need our assistance in getting things in order at the nurses' station, in case the authorities decide to poke around."

"Is the rumor true?" Ava asked the woman. I hadn't clue what her name was. "We heard—"

"Yes, the rumor is true," she said curtly. "Some of us might not have a job after they're through with us." She shifted her attention to Sylis. "Whatever incriminating evidence you find, get rid of." She turned on her heel and left.

"If she was going to give us anymore grief," Sylis said under his breath when we turned the corner down another corridor, "I was going to break her neck."

"This is a horrid place, filled with vile humans," Ava said in disgust.

She glanced at Elizabeth who was staring at her wide-eyed. "Present company excluded," she added.

Elizabeth shook her head as if to clear it. "I don't understand. This has happened to me before, more times than I can count, but . . . maybe I am mad." She rubbed her forehead, confused. "I don't know . . . I don't know . . . God help me."

"God is not going to help you," Sylis said. "So get that nonsense out of your head. Only you can help yourself."

We approached a heavy metal door, where a recess in the wall blocked us from view. I pulled a key ring out of my pocket and picked through the keys until I found the right one.

"What are you doing?" Elizabeth asked.

"I'm busting you out of this hellhole," I told her. "You don't deserve to be here."

She stopped my hand when I lifted it to unlock the door. "I think I need to stay."

"For fuck's sake!" Sylis spat. "Leave her here, Ameerah. She's not worthy of a second chance. Let her rot with the rest them."

I ignored Sylis and shifted my attention to Elizabeth who was startled by his seething demeanor. "You're not screwy. You have a rare gift. You can see Sammy and you can see me."

She pointed at Sylis and Ava. "I can see them, too. Ever since the fire and loss of my son, when I gaze into someone's eyes, sometimes an image of another person comes to me. It's like all of a sudden another face overlays the one others behold. But I have to really look to see it." She scratched her head, her expression muddled. "If you can make heads or tails out of that."

"Make a decision, *now*," Sylis told me. "We're losing time here."

I unlocked the door and pushed it open, allowing bright sunlight to filter into the alcove. The rays flowed across the white titled floor, highlighting chips and cracks.

I took Elizabeth's hand. Her skin was cold, but her palm was sweaty. "C'mon, I'll explain everything once we're out of this joint."

She resisted. "No, I won't survive on my own. My husband doesn't want me." Tears collected in her eyes. "I have no dough, no possessions, and no transportation. At least in here I'm taken care of."

"She's institutionalized," Ava said as she and Sylis stepped outside. Elizabeth and I remained near the threshold. "Leave her be. She doesn't deserve her freedom or your kindness."

I pulled out the fat envelope stuffed with the dough Sylis discovered in Dr. Stratton's office. "You're not broke. Take this." I tried to give it her, but she waved her hands in the air and stepped back. "Elizabeth," I said, hearing the desperation in my voice, "this might be your only chance for freedom. You won't be alone. I'll help you."

"Ameerah," Sylis said, exasperated. "This human is not worth your generosity. Don't be a sap."

I turned, and with blazing eyes, I shot back, "She was there for me through some of my darkest hours. I. Will. Not. Throw her back to the wolves."

"I've missed you terribly, Ameerah," Elizabeth said, taking slow steps backwards. "When I was told you had a seizure while taking a bath and drowned, I was heartbroken."

"I was murdered," I said, and when she stopped, shock marring her wholesome features, I continued. "After they abused me, Norma and Florence drowned me in the bathtub. Those two bitches are to blame for my demise."

Elizabeth gasped.

I extended my hand. "Please, Elizabeth, we're running out of time." When she resumed backing away, I sighed, disappointed she chose confinement over freedom. "Suit yourself." I crossed the space between us and gave the envelope and keys to her. "Your fate is now in your hands. I suggest you find a good hiding spot to stash these in as soon as you can." I turned away, but then felt her hand on my arm. I stopped and looked at her.

"I'm sorry, Ameerah," she said, her bottom lip trembling. "It must have been terrible what Norma and Florence did to you."

I tried to smile but could only muster half of one. "No sweat. They got what they deserved."

Her eyebrows knitted, and she looked away at nothing in particular before fixing her gaze back on mine. "I don't understand."

"You will." I kissed her cheek. "Take care of yourself."

I left her standing there, staring after me, and closed the door behind me, shutting her inside.

"You're a fucking idiot, Ameerah," Sylis fumed, following me to the west side of the building. "I can't believe you–"

"Get out of that body now," I ordered, halting in a shady area among a group of oak trees. The air had a wonderful woodsy smell, like burnt leaves, a sign fall was just around the corner.

"Why?" he asked, dumbfounded.

I pulled the syringe and another vile out of my pocket and loaded the cylinder. "Unless you want to know what it feels like to be drugged and helpless when I burn this human's dick off."

Ava squealed, which was odd coming from the male host she possessed. "Oh, this is going to be the cat's meow," she said, grinning while she moved closer.

"You can leave the body at your own free will, right?" I asked.

"This whole damn place is a negative hot spot," he answered.

I grabbed his arm, shoved his sleeve up, and raised the hand that was gripping the needle. "I take that as a yes, then."

"You never cease to surprise me," he said, fighting back a smile.

His eyes closed.

The human dropped to the ground like a sack of potatoes.

I kneeled beside him and was about to jab the needle into his arm when Ava caught my wrist.

"You don't need to drug him, just do it," she said, handing me some matches and a ciggy. "He's out cold. If he wakes, all the better."

I looked around to see if anyone was lurking within our vicinity and placed the syringe on the ground, out of Chester's reach. We were completely isolated on this side of the building in the cover of the large trees. A flock of ducks in a V formation flew over, quacking at one another. My heart raced from a sudden bout of anxiety and giddiness. This son-of-a-bitch was going to get what he deserved, and hopefully he would no longer have the means to penetrate another woman again. Then, the horrible itching feeling ensued. I lit Ava's ciggy and then mine. As soon as I took a long drag, held the smoke in my lungs, and released it, I felt fine. Fantastic even. I struck another match and dropped the small flame in Chester the molester's crotch and watched it burn, momentarily memorized by how quickly the material of his trousers ignited.

Chester sat up in horror and screeched, making Ava and I jump. He frantically batted at the flames. Ava grabbed him from behind, pulling his arms back, locking them in her grip. I lit another match and flicked it on his stomach, then picked up the syringe. I jabbed the needle in his arm, releasing the medication into his bloodstream. The flames were spreading down his thighs and up his abdomen. He was squirming something fierce against Ava and hollering.

Kneeling beside him, I took his chin in my hand and yanked it toward me so we were eye-to-eye. "This is for violating women, you piece of *shit*."

The hatred I had for this human exploded within me, and I reveled in the fact he was moaning and jerking his body from side to side. The pain and fear on his face planted a smile on mine. His eyelids began to fall, but before he went into complete unconsciousness, I released his face and punched it several times, blooding his nose and lips.

Ava dropped him and rose, stepping away. She picked up our ciggies tossed to the ground in haste and grinned. "They're still lit." She handed me mine. "You did well," she said to me. We both turned our attention back to the burning body. "Too bad we don't have marshmallows." She laughed, and I joined in.

Chester the molester was no more.

Chapter Twenty-Five

1929

After I had my revenge on Dr. Stratton, Norma, and Florence, I saw no reason to return to Bandbridge nor had the desire to find out what happened afterward. Ava, on the other hand, had an underlining obsession concerning the outcome, painting her reasons for returning there as simply curiosity. I hated when people did that shit, covering up the real reason for their actions with nonsense because for some damned reason they didn't want to spill the truth. I called her on it right away and told her not to insult my intelligence. She then came clean. She was obsessed. Intrigued. She explained it like reading a book. We had left at the climax of the story, and now she needed to find out how it ended. She wanted my permission to go back. I told her she didn't need it but gave my blessing anyway when she insisted.

When she return, she reported all the details. Bandbridge did have a mole. The rumor was true. A lot of the attendants were fired, while others were arrested. The journalist who feigned insanity printed several articles in the newspaper about his stay at Bandbridge. His shocking story had traveled fast across the country, which resulted in further investigation and an increase in the budget for the insane asylum. New staff was brought in, and the passageway to the underground rooms where I was held were sealed off. Ava told me the food and sanitary conditions had greatly improved, as well as patient treatment.

"What about Elizabeth?" I asked one morning over a cup of joe and breakfast at a charming restaurant in downtown Astoria. It had been months since the last time I saw Elizabeth on that fateful day when she'd chosen tyranny over freedom. At times I'd wondered how she was fairing.

"I'm going to level with you," Ava said, making my heart stop. I set my mug down and stared at the pretty blue-eyed, dark-haired woman she was possessing. "Elizabeth hanged herself right after we left her."

An immediate lump formed in my throat, and a wave of guilt came crushing down upon me. I pretended to study the perfect manicured nails that belonged to the brunette I was inhabiting. A tear slipped from my eye. I failed Elizabeth, the one person who had ever shown me compassion in my darkest hours.

Ava reached across the table and touched my arm. "Don't beat yourself up over this. You tried to help her, but she wouldn't accept it. There was nothing else you could have done."

I took a hanky out of my purse and dabbed my eyes and cheeks. "I suppose you're right." I thought about Elizabeth and the hopelessness she must have felt powerful enough to drive her to take her own life. It didn't have to be that way, and I wondered if I hadn't reached out to her, would she still be alive? "Can we find her?"

Ava took a bite of her bacon. "I knew you were going to ask me about it, so I had Aidan check into her whereabouts."

"And?"

"Elizabeth crossed over. Her son was waiting for her." She smiled, the warmth reaching her baby blues. "Your friend is at peace now, Ameerah. She's with Sammy and happy."

I sighed, relieved Elizabeth was okay. Some of the heaviness in my heart lifted. Maybe it was a good thing I tried to help Elizabeth, because if I hadn't, she'd still be locked away from society, a victim of the system. At least now she was with her little boy, I told myself, but part of me wasn't buying it.

"You're a true friend, Ameerah," Ava said, raising her mug and taking a sip. "Even in death and despite your peer's objections, you did everything in your power to help a pal."

"I'm loyal to those who have earned it," I simply stated.

Ava and I finished our breakfast and spent the day masquerading as humans, indulging ourselves in entertainment, fine tobacco, and liquor. And throughout the years, she gained my loyalty as well. Together, we attended meetings Volac held, and we'd hook up with Aidan and Sylis at the speakeasy every weekend. We fell into a routine until Ava and I decided to travel to Europe and live the big life, possessing only the rich and the beautiful. We visited Rome, Paris, Berlin, and London, taking in all the historical sights. I hadn't been this happy since the summer I spent with Betty.

One day, while we were at the Notre Dame Cathedral in Paris admiring the Gothic architecture, Ava pointed to a tall, muscular brown-haired fella wearing a newsboy hat backward. He was only a few yards away.

Nathan Caswell.

An immortal.

The best dark spirit tracker of them all.

I had to admit he was a fine looking fella, but we didn't stick around to find out what he was up to. We hightailed it out of there and continued our fun in London. Little had I known at that time, seventy plus years in the future, Nathan and I would become pals.

Volac was right about 1929. The stock market would crash and my patience paid off because it was the year I would destroy my parents, robbing them of everything, bringing them to their knees, like they'd done to me.

I hadn't been back to New York, nor laid eyes on my parents since the day they double-crossed me. Frankly, I wasn't looking forward to revisiting my once-beloved city. After all this time, the wounds were still fresh, and thoughts of Betty tugged at my heartstrings. A battle raged inside me whether to seek her out or let bygones be bygones.

Volac was my go-to fella as I planned my scheme. We spent several nights in human form inside a white clapboard farmhouse. While lounging in the comforts of the cozy living room on overstuffed chairs and couches, we wrapped ourselves in lively and thought-provoking conversations. Sylis and Ava were there as well. My partners in crime. They knew my history. They'd been with me from the beginning. Sylis' cunning and methodical guile were skills I'd grown to admire and emulate. I never had to worry about Ava fouling things up. She could think exceptionally fast in any given situation and had proven to be a real gem. I told them many times over how I was grateful for their support.

Volac filled us in on what was going on behind the scenes at Wall Street. On October 29th, billions of dollars would be lost in the stock market, which gave us a week to carry out our plan. I reminded all three of them who my father was, where he worked, and the location of my parents' house. My father was a player. He loved money and prestige. So did my mother. They lived in luxury, dined on fine china, and were the envy of their peers.

Based on our ongoing conversations throughout the years, Volac enlisted one of his followers named Stan to possess a broker, gain my father's trust, and eventually convinced him to invest a good portion of his money into the market. All that was left was to persuade my father to invest his remaining assets before the crash. I was thrilled with this piece of news and told Volac I wanted to take part in hooking my dear ol' dad and reeling him in to his ruin.

"Are you sure about this?" Sylis asked, his tone thick with skepticism. "One mistake on your part could cost you the deal."

"I'm aware." I tucked a blonde strand behind my ear and sighed while shifting in the chair to get more comfortable. "I think I can do it." The whole idea of conversing with my parents while pretending to be someone else and having to be cordial, had my stomach in a knot. "Butt me," I said when he plucked a ciggy out of its shiny, thin case.

Sylis rose from the chair across from me. He still had on the gray fedora the human was wearing when Sylis took over his body. I could see the objection in his hazel eyes when he handed me the ciggy and lit it.

"You disapprove." It was more a statement than a question, and frankly I didn't give a shit if he did. I knew myself better than anyone, and if I felt like I was up to the task, then dammit, I was going to follow through. But in all honesty, I had my doubts. I took a couple puffs and looked up at him.

"I do," he answered and returned to his seat.

Ava fixed her gaze on Sylis from the chair next to me. "Maybe you should lay off. If Ameerah thinks she can handle it, then she will."

Sylis smirked. "Are you and Ameerah lovers now? You two have been inseparable since the day you met."

"Quit being an asshole," I said, blowing a cloud of smoke in his direction. "Ava is with Aidan. Besides, for your information, I'm not interested in her in that manner."

"It's none of your beeswax," Ava piped.

"I'd like to put my two cents in," Volac said before Sylis had a chance to reply.

"Of course," I answered, aware of how his presence filled the room when he spoke. Not only because the blond human he was occupying had a tall, well-built frame only hard labor and exercise could create, but also the centuries of knowledge that filtered through his blue eyes.

Volac took a sip of his brandy. The sound of the ice cubes clinking against the glass was sharp against the silence in the room. Thankfully, he continued right away, because the noise grated on my nerves. "I think it would be best if you sit this one out, Ameerah, and I'll tell you why."

I glanced at Sylis smiling and nodding in agreement. Biting my tongue, I turned my attention back to Volac.

"Your parents still have power over you," he said to me in a matter-of-fact way. "I saw it in your eyes earlier. I hear it in your voice when you speak about them. You haven't learned to harden yourself to where you're not a slave to your feelings. I feel if you were to go on this operation, it would be disastrous, and you'd never forgive yourself. I suggest you allow Stan and Ava finish the job." His gaze shifted to Ava. "If she agrees that is."

"Absolutely," she said and faced me. "I think Volac has made several good points, Ameerah, and he's correct about you still being emotionally involved concerning your folks. If it's okay with you . . . if you agree to proceed in this manner, I'd love to be a part of it. I swear I won't let you down, and I'll tell you everything that happens."

Shit. I hated to admit it, but they were right. I stared at my lap and fidgeted with the diamond ring on my finger. I was too weak to be physically involved in this mission, and I hated that fact about myself. For four years, I'd flawlessly grown into my new existence. I'd surpassed Volac's expectations by adapting in a short period of time and learning how to dwell inside a human for as long as I desired without losing my control like I had in the beginning. But the one thing I couldn't overcome was my shattered emotions connected to my parents.

"A great depression has already begun," Volac said, causing me to look at him. "Once it spreads throughout America, humans will be put to the test. If you allow Stan and Ava to carry out this plan, I have no doubt they will not fail you."

I'd spent countless nights like this with Volac and have attended every one of his meetings. He'd opened up to me on several occasions about his life as a farmer and Viking, among other things. He'd secured my trust long ago; therefore, I was inclined to bend. To give in. To accept the fact I wasn't in a position to double-cross my parents face-to-face. So I agreed to hand the baton over to Volac, who in turn, would fill Stan in on our plan and then pass all responsibility on to him and Ava. All I had to do, besides meet Stan, was wait, which I knew would set my nerves on edge. So what did I do while I sat this one out, and they jumped into action and got into character? I met Aidan at the speakeasy and partied with him, numbing my anxiety with alcohol and laughter.

* * *

I was on my third cocktail at the blind pig we frequented. The current place wasn't named because it moved several times in the four years I was a permanent patron. We always found its new location, as if it had a neon sign above flashing, "The Speakeasy." Now that I thought about it, that had to be its only name. Everyone always referred to it as such. No matter. Trivial things I overlooked, unless it demanded my attention.

Anyway, I was at the bar, listening to the high-spirited jazz music, telling jokes with Maxwell, the bartender, and the other fellas in my presence, when an attractive dark-haired gal in a low-cut red silk dress caught my attention. She was waving for me to join her at a nearby table. I had a feeling it was Ava, since the human had an almost eerie resemblance to Ava's true appearance. I excused myself and purposely swayed my hips in a seductive manner, knowing the fellas were watching. Only Max knew of my sexual orientation, and I took enjoyment in toying with hot-blooded human males. They were so predictable and a convenient source of entertainment. Besides, my heart should be hammering in anticipation on what Ava had to say, but instead I was slightly ossified—this human couldn't hold her liquor well—and was reveling in the feel of the fringes on my black flapper dress, in motion with each teasing movement I made.

"Where's Aidan?" Ava asked when I took a seat across from her and set my cocktail down.

"He had to help a new recruit," I said and looked up when a gentleman in a black pinstripe suit and dark fedora approached our table. I recognized him as one of the fellas at the bar.

"Excuse me," he said to me and smiled when I met his eyes. "Would you care to dance? I heard you're one hell of a hoofer."

I returned his smile. "I would love to, except I have business to attend to at the moment."

His eyes darted to Ava, then to me. A pinkish, red color stained his cheeks. "Well, maybe some other time then. Pardon my intrusion."

"Your apology isn't necessary," I said.

He nodded and walked away, his shoulders slightly hunched.

"I think the poor sap lost a bet." Ava pointed to the bar.

The fella who just asked me to dance was shaking his head, while the other ones were laughing and sticking their hands out, gesturing for him to pony up. I caught a few looking my way. I raised my glass and nodded.

"Tomorrow is the big day," I said to Ava, ignoring our surroundings, except for her. "The stock market crash. So tell me everything." I took two ciggies out of my purse, handed her one, and lit them both.

"Your father is a narcissistic ass." She blew a lungful of smoke out, her expression twisted in disgust. "And your mother is no better."

"I told you they were—"

"These drinks are from the gentleman at the bar." A waitress dressed similar to me set two honey colored cocktails on the table.

I looked at the bar, and a blond fella in a black suit and red bowtie smiled and waved.

Ava leaned across the table. "Wow, Ameerah, I should take lessons from you. They're literally eating out of your hand." She laughed, picked up her drink, and took a sip.

I ignored my admirers and turned my attention back to Ava when the waitress left. "I told you they were a bunch of high-hats," I said, finishing my earlier statement.

She agreed and went on to tell me my parents had her and Stan attend a dinner party. She dolled herself up to fit the part as Stan's fiancée and carried herself with the air of elegance and one born of money.

"The house you grew up in is gorgeous, but . . ." Her gaze fell to the table, and her expression turned sad.

"What?" A sickening feeling in the pit of my stomach emerged, but regardless of what she had to say, I wanted to know.

"There were no pictures or evidence of your existence in the house," she said, throwing me an apologetic look. "I asked if they had kids, and your mom squeezed out a couple tears, playing the distraught parent role, but in her eyes I could see nothing but indifference. Your father then told us you died of TB, and it was too difficult for them to have reminders of you in their house."

I ran the tip of my finger along the rim of my glass, staring into the yellow liquid. The cocktail was the bee's knees. Betty's favorite. I had no doubt my parents told everyone they knew, including my close friends, that filthy lie. How could two people bring a child into the world and not love it? Was I not worth loving? A thickness grew in my throat, and my eyes stung.

"Don't you dare cry, Ameerah." Ava placed her hand in mine and gently squeezed it. "They're not worth your tears. You need to harden yourself like Volac said."

I nodded and took a sip of my cocktail. She was right. The people who brought me into the world were selfish, self-centered assholes. I drew the short straw in the parent department. Now it was time to move on and disconnect myself and my feelings from them.

"Do you want me to continue?"

I took a drag and blew smoke above us. "Yes. I want to hear everything that happened."

Ava went on about my father's bloated ego and how she and Stan fed it with compliments, friendly banter about politics, and sports. When the opportunity presented itself, Stan took center stage. He had my father believe he possessed hot information about the stock market and told him he'd double his money, maybe even triple it, if he were to put more skin into the game. My father was easily convinced, but my mother on the other hand was uncomfortable anteing up all of their assets. Ava came to the rescue and confided in Mother. Ava was also going to risk everything she owned, because she *knew* this move would be a lucrative one. Mother finally agreed. They sealed the deal, and my parents went to the bank the following day. A few days later, they gave Stan the dough to buy the stocks he claimed would fly off the charts.

Now, we waited until tomorrow to see if what Volac had been telling us would occur.

Chapter Twenty-Six

A Glimpse into the Great Depression

An extraordinary rush of pleasure sent me on a glorious high when I received news from Volac that my parents lost everything in the stock market crash. I went dancing until sunrise with Stan and Ava to celebrate. Soon, the bank would confiscate my parent's house and belongings, among other things. I imagined my mother on the verge of a nervous breakdown, whereas my father would try to salvage whatever dignity he still had left. Then, Volac reminded me that what was already being called the Great Depression was underway. He told me to sit back and wait. All our planning and hard work to destroy my parents would continue to pay off.

Three years quickly passed. During that time, I got the gumption to revisit New York and spy on my parents. They were living in a shabby apartment in the overcrowded Lower East Side slum of Manhattan, working odd jobs to make ends meet. They were no longer the envy of their peers. In fact, all their friends abandoned them.

I spent most of my time watching from afar. My mother washed dishes and scrubbed floors for a local diner in Manhattan. On her days off, she offered her services in a slave market. She'd stand on the street corner and congregate with both white and black women. She'd wait, hoping a rich white housewife would employ her to perform tasks around her house. Her once glowing and pretty face was now worn, haggard even.

My father took to the bottle, purchasing hooch from a bootlegger and did manual labor wherever he could find work. A lot of times he dawdled aimlessly about the streets, and some days he'd stand in the breadline for hours at Times Square with the collar of his trench coat up, head down, the brim of his fedora shielding his face. Gone were the days of fine clothing and dining on exquisite food for my parents.

One morning, I strolled into the diner where my mother worked. The smell of bacon and fried potatoes wafted through the air, causing my mouth to water. I was in a fabulous mood, dolled up in the latest top of the line fashion and a mink stole to stave off the fall chill. The human I possessed was a gorgeous blonde with chin-length wavy hair and a soft, sultry voice that could turn harsh when provoked. This human was a canary. She could sing the socks off of most people. On the other hand, I couldn't carry a note, so I didn't even attempt to belt out a song.

I sat at a square wooden table and ordered French toast, and a cup of joe from a waitress in a brown knee-high dress, tights, and white apron. She had a pleasant smile and was quite friendly. I noticed she wasn't wearing any jewelry, and her dark hair was neatly tucked back in a bun. Not a strand was out of place, which told me she was required by her employer to wear a uniform and have a polished appearance. I did an internal shrug. I imagined she was grateful to have a job during this difficult era, where people would do just about anything to make a dime.

"Would you like cream and sugar with your coffee?" she asked as she wrote my order.

"Yes, please," I answered. "Can you do me a favor and have Mrs. Arrowood stop by my table? I'd like to have a word with her."

The waitress frowned. "Mrs. Arrowood no longer works here. She was canned yesterday."

My face fell. If only I'd come in here a day earlier, I'd have the opportunity to end this part of my prior life.

Damn it.

I made up my mind right there not to make the same mistake with my father.

Empathy softened the waitress's features. "Was she a friend of yours?"

I looked away and dug in my purse to hide my disgust and halt the obscene laughter that almost barked out of me. If only she knew the truth about my mother, she wouldn't be wasting her compassion on a rotten, life stealing, conniving bitch.

"Please take this," I said, handing her a five dollar bill.

"Oh, my." She looked at the dough in my hand, then at me, not hiding her surprise. She shook her head. "I appreciate your generosity, but I can't accept it."

I placed the bill in her hand and closed her fingers around it. "Of course you can. If your boss has a problem with it, send him my way. I'll straighten him out."

She laughed and tears sprang to her hazel eyes. "I have no doubt, but he's a decent fella. He wouldn't mind."

I smiled, once again feeling chipper. This day had only begun, and I would start and end it on a good note. "It's settled, then," I told her. "You keep it."

She covered her mouth with her fingers. Tears slid down her cheeks. She wiped them away and touched my arm. "I cannot thank you enough for this. You're an angel."

This time I laughed. "Hardly. If only you knew."

"Well," she said, "you are to me and my family." Her gaze swept the room where a few patrons were having their breakfast, and another waitress was filling their coffee mugs. "I'll go put your order in and get you some joe."

She turned and headed toward the long counter, lined with bar stools. Behind it was where the coffee makers were. I watched her make a fresh pot, noticing how more upbeat her movements were. I'd given her hope and another means to feed her family, and I felt damned good about it. I had no qualms with helping humans who were trying and had a good spirit inside them. It was the other ones I detested, the pieces of shit who didn't deserve to be here.

The door behind me opened, and the sound of heavy feet scratching the black and white checkered tile floor, caused me to turn and look. My mouth dropped when my eyes landed on Clyde Kelly, A.K.A. Slim. He looked the same as he had years ago, still wearing a fedora, except this one was gray instead of black, and his broad shoulders sagged a bit. He had a newspaper tucked under his arm and winked at me when his gaze caught mine. I quickly turned back around and watched him take a seat at the next table. The waitress then showed up with my coffee, setting a bowl of sugar cubes and a ceramic creamer beside it. I thanked her and watched her take Slim's order as I doctored my drink.

"I'd like bacon, eggs over easy, hashbrowns, toast, and a cup of joe, please," I heard Slim say.

"How do you take your coffee?"

"Black."

My heart and thoughts were racing. I couldn't believe my good fortune. I never imagined I'd run into Slim. I needed to talk to him, to find out what happened to Betty and Abe. But how would I go about it? I was a total stranger to him. I tried not to gawk and shifted my attention to my mug, watching the steam rising above the rim. The rustling sound of paper had me automatically look up. Slims' face was now partitioned off by the newspaper. I took a sip, savoring the sweet, rich, creamy liquid.

What the hell should I do?

I knew. I had to find a way to approach him and fire the questions at him I desperately wanted to know. What was the worst that could happen? Fear was a bullshit emotion, and I wasn't about to become its slave. Taking a deep breath, I pushed my chair back and rose. My palms were sweating. Discreetly, I wiped them off on my wool skirt before approaching his table.

"Excuse me, sir," I said and smiled when he lowered his newspaper. His golden-brown eyes settled on mine, soft and curious. "Ameerah Arrowood used to work for you. Is that correct?"

He looked away. "I haven't heard her name in years."

"But you know her?" I prompted.

A warm smile crossed his face. "Yes, she was the best hoofer who had ever worked for me."

The waitress approached the table I was sitting at with my order. She set the plate down and smiled. "Is there anything else you need?"

"No, thank you," I answered, and when she left I turned to Slim. "Do you mind if I join you?"

He folded his newspaper and gestured to the empty chair across from him. "It would be my pleasure, doll."

I got settled opposite of him, mink stole slung over the back of the chair next to me, and held my hands in my lap. He stuck a ciggy in his mouth and offered me one. I pushed my food aside and gladly accepted, leaning over the table so he could light it.

"Your food is going to get cold," he said, eyeing my French toast.

I shrugged. "I'm not that hungry. It can wait."

He nodded and took a long drag off his ciggy. He blew the smoke out and asked, "How do you know Ameerah?"

"I knew her in school. We used to write letters to each other," I said, making everything up as I went along. "We lost touch, and I wanted to reconnect with her."

He frowned. "Sorry to break this to you, sweetheart, but Ameerah passed away seven years ago."

I covered my mouth, feigning surprise. The waitress appeared with Slim's breakfast. Her eyes danced between Slim and me. An awkward silence fell among us. I took a sip of my coffee in a subtle attempt to dispel the uncomfortable feeling I was receiving from our waitress. Her shoulders relaxed, and she left after Slim told her everything looked perfect.

"How?" I finally asked, watching him snuff out his ciggy in the glass ashtray and dig into his eggs and bacon.

"TB," he said between mouthfuls. "Her parents took her to see her grandmother and shortly after, Ameerah became ill. She was rushed to the hospital and diagnosed with tuberculosis. From what I understood, she expired a few months later."

I gritted my teeth, because I had the sudden urge to holler it was all bullshit, devised by my heartless, soul-sucking parents. But I couldn't. I had to play the part flawlessly, or he would get suspicious and no doubt bid me farewell before I had a chance to ask him more questions.

I scooted my plate to me and took a couple bites of my French toast. The buttery, maple syrup on the delicious bread was the berries. I used the time to savor the flavors and to calm myself, making sure my expressions showed no hint of the seething emotions that had threatened to spew forth a moment ago.

"I apologize for being forthright regarding this grave news," he said. "Ameerah was your pal. I should have been more sensitive in the matter of telling you what had become of her."

"It's quite all right," I answered with a wave of my hand and pressed forward. "What about Betty and her brother Abe? Whatever became of them?"

He took a sip of his coffee and studied me over the rim. "I have a feeling you know more than what you're letting on."

"They were good friends of mine, as well," I simply answered. "In fact, when I was in town in 1925 during the time Ameerah was dancing for you, I went to your speakeasy to watch her perform."

He nodded, clearly buying my line of bullshit.

I lowered my eyes and rolled my shoulders forward. Rubbing my temples, I said, "This news about Ameerah isn't what I expected." I took a deep breath and looked at him with a woeful expression on my face.

The corner of his mouth turned down. "I'm sorry. I really liked Ameerah. She was one of a kind."

"Please don't tell me Betty and Abe are gone, as well. I don't think my poor heart can take it."

"They're alive," he reassured me. "Abe is living in California with his wife Anyah and their two daughters."

I was on my last bite of French toast, my mouth open, fork poised in front of my kisser when he said that. I paused, both surprised and delighted Abe had followed his heart and married Anyah, despite what others or his family thought.

"Abe is a psychologist. He got his degree at Berkeley."

"And Betty?" I asked, taking a slow sip of my coffee.

He folded his hands on the table and sighed. "After Ameerah's death, she fell apart. She drank and cried a lot. But despite her remorse, she was professional enough to follow through with the costumes I'd hired her to design for my dancing girls. Of course, she wasn't able to fill in when one of my girls couldn't perform." He shrugged indifferently. "I gave her a lot of slack, because I knew how heartbroken she was, and she was doing the best she could."

My throat thickened, and my eyes stung. I blinked several times to ward off the tears, but it was too late. They broke loose, trailing down my cheeks. I took a hanky out of my purse and dabbed my cheeks and the corners of my eyes.

Betty loved me.

It took every ounce of mental strength not to sob in front of Slim. So instead of giving into my sadness, I channeled my feelings into the white hot anger for my parents. The waitress stopped by our table and refilled our mugs as I was handing a ciggy to Slim and lighting my own. I inhaled deeply, feeling the nicotine course throughout my system. It tasted and felt wonderful.

"I don't mean to upset you," Slim said, his tone low and sympathetic.

"You're fine," I reassured him. "I appreciate your willingness to satisfy a stranger's curiosity honestly." I stuck my hand out. "My name is Lillian, but my friends call me Lily. You can call me Lily."

He shook it. His grip was firm and confident. "My pleasure, Lily, to chat with you. It's not every day a beautiful sweetheart such as you is bold enough to encroach upon my meal."

"Oh," I said, picking up my mink stole, my cheeks hot. "I didn't mean to intrude. I'll be on—"

"No, you're not," he quickly said. "Stay. I'm enjoying your company, and I don't mind your questions. What I meant was, not many dames have the nerve to approach me in the manner you did. It's refreshing. Usually, I'm the one who has to initiate a conversation, which gets stale after a while."

I set my stole down and settled back in my seat. I took a drag off my ciggy and smirked. "I'm not like most gals, and I don't have time for silly games. If I want something, I go after it."

He took a long draw off his ciggy and nodded. "I can see what you mean, but I have a feeling there's a lot more to you than you're letting on."

"You're very perceptive."

"I have to be in my line of work."

"Do you still have the speakeasy?"

He nodded. "I do."

"Is Betty still working for you?" I wasn't through with asking him questions about her. I had to know how she was doing, and a huge part of me wanted to go to her. I imagined telling her everything that happened and the life I was living now, but that would only make things worse for her. It was probably best to let her be.

"She's not," he answered. "Abe talked her into moving to California with him and Anya. She has a drinking problem that gets out of control at times, and Abe thought a change of scenery and new life might help her. Besides, he can keep a close eye on her and be there when she needs him."

"He's a swell fella. I've always liked him."

"I agree. He was one of my best and loyal employees. I sure do miss him."

"I heard Ameerah and Betty were . . . *together*," I said, trying to be tactful, because I wasn't sure how he'd react.

"They were lovers, yes." He nodded and took a sip of his coffee. There was no hint of judgment in his demeanor. The more time I spent with him, the more I remembered why I liked him so much when I was alive. He was the real McCoy and a nifty fella. One of the few humans I respected.

An extreme sadness drenched me as if someone dumped a bucket of water over my head. My gut twisted, and I had the sudden urge to scream at the top of my lungs, "Why? Why was this life taken from me? I could be happy and living in bliss with Betty at this very moment. What had I ever done to deserve this? Why me?" It wasn't fair, and even though my parents were getting what they deserved, and I reveled in it, the pain, hurt, and sadness was still there, especially now that I knew Betty truly loved me. The only person in my life who had.

I dug in my purse, grabbed a wad of dough, and placed it on the table. "Thank you for your time. I enjoyed visiting with you and appreciate your openness." I could hear the tears in my voice and cleared my throat. *Don't think about what could have been. Think about what your parents did to you instead.*

He sat up, a startled, confused look on his handsome face. "Did I say something wrong?"

"No, you're fine. I have a plane to catch, and I just noticed the time." It wasn't a lie. Lillian did have a plane to catch, which was a perfect excuse to use. Besides, I had one more thing to do before I was done with this human. Then, she could go live her life in Paris.

Slim insisted on paying for my meal, told me he enjoyed my company, and gave me his card. He wanted me to call him when I was back in town. As I was redirecting my thoughts to my hatred toward my parents, I thanked him again and left. The crushing sorrow lifted from my heart, replaced with animosity and a biting hate that chewed at me. I wandered the streets for hours and looked at the defeated, dirty faces in the breadlines, hoping to find my father. He wasn't there. Finally, by pure luck or karma, I found him and my mother behind a restaurant picking through the garbage for scraps. They stopped and backed away when they spotted me.

"I have a message from your daughter, Ameerah," I said, stepping into their space.

My mother paled and stumbled into Father. He steadied her and glared at me.

"We don't have a daughter," he answered in an unconvincing tone.

I smirked. "Yes, you do . . . or did. You betrayed her and had her admitted to Bandbridge Insane Asylum, where she was mistreated, abused, and murdered."

My mother looked at my father and clung to him.

Typical.

She hadn't changed.

She was weak.

Pathetic.

A despicable human who didn't deserve to breathe the same air I breathed.

I loathed her.

Her cheeks were hollowed from lack of nutrition as if an artist took a putty knife and carved out deep slopes in her face.

My father drew himself up in a poor attempt to intimidate me, using his old tricks that got him nowhere. He hadn't learned a damned thing.

"I don't know who you are." He feigned confusion. "You're clearly mistaking us for someone else."

I laughed. It was an empty, mocking sound that caused them to take a few steps back. "Lies," I said. "But no matter. You know exactly what I'm talking about." I moved forward to where I was toe-to-toe with him and leaned close to his face. "I told you I'd ruin you, and I did."

My mother made a screeching noise and slapped a hand over her mouth, fear swimming in her eyes. My father turned, and in quick strides, he led her out of the back alley.

"You took *everything* from your daughter!" I shouted. "Now it's your turn to pay the price for what you've done to Ameerah, you pieces of shit."

They disappeared from sight. Even though I was satisfied knowing I spooked the hell out of them, and they were getting what they deserved, it did little to make up for the turmoil they caused me. Unfortunately, the damage was done, and I was afraid it would be with me for eternity.

Chapter Twenty-Seven

Stepping in and out of War World II

After the day I confronted my parents, I didn't turn back. I wiped my hands clean from that life, including my dear Betty. She was the love of my life, but I knew it would be a complete disaster if I were to try and reach her or even look after her. As much as it broke my heart, I had to let her and Abe go.

Years passed in a blur of alcohol, fine tobacco, entertainment, and lots of traveling. Sometimes I wandered the globe on my own, other times I had Ava with me or a few other pals I met through the years. I ran into immortals along the way. One in particular was a tall, bald African named Anwar. I managed to evade him and the others, not wanting to risk the chance of being cast out by any one of them.

Whenever I was in Astoria, I'd hook up with Aidan and his new recruits at a bar called Black Beard's Tavern that opened after prohibition ended in 1933. The residents in Astoria were big on beer and so were most of my fellow dark spirits, me not so much. Thankfully there were other options, and I could have my martini and dance the night away on their spacious dance floor. There were other bars and clubs we'd frequent in Astoria, but Black Beard's was Aidan's favorite haunt. I had to admit it was a swell place. The building used to be a cannery before it was renovated with thick, oak beams and dark, polished wood throughout the inside, which I heard was from old sailing ships. The building was on the waterfront, perched above the river, some hundreds of feet off shore. There were times I'd sit outside quietly by myself, drink in hand, ciggy in the other, and watch the whitecaps on the river beneath the bright moonlight while the shipping vessels navigated the waters. I enjoyed those peaceful moments and always made a point not to dwell on the past.

After the stock market crashed, the world went through rapid changes. The Great Depression was another nail in the coffin, bringing countless humans to a bitter end from lack of perseverance, resourcefulness, or stupidity. Those were the people Volac, the "old one," and other dark spirits wanted to weed from the earth. The weak. The idiots. The lazy. I couldn't blame my spirit colleagues and was onboard, but little did they know I did help some humans who I knew were trying, like that waitress in 1932. If my peers had problems with it, they could fuck off. I had my reasons and didn't need to justify them to anyone.

Back in 1934 when I was in Oregon, I became miffed when I realized the gal I possessed never smoked or drank in her entire nineteen years. She was a preacher's daughter, and from what I could gather from the selective memories available to me, she was brainwashed. She believed in the Bible in its entirety—talking snakes and all. I couldn't cure this human of her ignorance and idiocy, but what I did was get her addicted to nicotine and alcohol. Once I stepped inside her and suddenly discovered those things, I became hell-bent on smoking, drinking, and polluting this human's body. She thought she was better than everyone due to her upstanding position in the church and the holy life she led. Not anymore, thanks to me, and honestly, I enjoyed every damned minute of it. Besides, behind closed doors, she was a tramp and loved to play with herself.

Anyway, while I possessed her and was walking along the countryside in Oregon, I came across a couple kids around ten and twelve riding the rails. I watched the train slow and them jumping off the boxcar. I decided to approach the two boys and through a pleasant conversation with them, I learned the oldest was named Jack and the younger boy was

Jimmy. They had run away from home because their families couldn't afford to feed them. Despite their unfortunate circumstances, beyond their dirty faces and grubby clothes, I saw a desire and willfulness to survive. I was so impressed and taken aback that I gave them what money I had in my purse—seven dollars and twenty-one cents. They offered to give me their newsboy hats as payment, but I declined.

"We must give you somethin', ma'am," Jack said.

I bent in front of him and gently brushed his brown bangs out of his eyes. He didn't flinch or back away, only stared at me with a stubbornness I found quite charming. He was serious, and a warm smile crossed my face. "That won't be necessary." When he opened his mouth to object, I held my hand up. Jimmy moved beside him and suggested they'd be my slaves for the rest of the week. I shook my head. "I'll tell you what you can do to repay me," I said, giving them an earnest look. "Don't give up. Keep thriving. Be true to yourself and your friends. Don't be selfish, treat this world with respect, and do your part."

Jack spat on his palm and stuck his hand out. "I promise."

I looked at his outstretched hand, then at him. His green eyes held a determination that spoke volumes for his age. He had to be an old soul, or rather his hardships had forced him to grow up quicker than any child should have. Whatever the reason may have been, I spat on my hand and firmly shook his. I showed the same courtesy to his brother, and before I said goodbye, I told them a couple things. "Listen to me carefully. If you ever bump into me, and I pretend I don't know you, and I'm rude to you, it's *not* me. Who you're talking to right now isn't the gal you're seeing before your eyes."

Both boys screwed up their faces in confusion.

"What in world are you talkin' about?" Jack asked, tilting his head to the side while Jimmy rubbed the side of his nose, looking lost.

"Let's just say I'm borrowing this body and leave it at that."

Their eyes grew into saucers and mouths fell open. I assured the boys there was no need to be alarmed, but for some odd reason I had to tell them. They then began guessing who I really was.

"An angel," Jack said.

"A space alien," Jimmy piped.

"I know." In excitement Jack jumped up and down. "A parasite."

And as they continued throwing out possible answers, their imaginations grew more absurd, comical even, to where all three of us were hunched over in laughter. I finally said to forget it and became serious. The energy that was charged moments ago sizzled. They fell silent and stepped closer to me, like we were huddling before a ballgame.

"In five years, America will be forced to go to war with Germany," I said, knowing this from Volac's meetings. The "old one" had been planning the rise of Adolph Hitler and the Nazi party for decades. In fact, the first war was part of this whole scheme. The Treaty of Versailles was to bring the German people to abject poverty, to shame them and breed resentment toward the Jews and others. He, Volac, and other dark spirits were part of this master plan to exterminate what they considered human garbage. "You'll be at the right age to fight for our country," I continued. "If you decide to do so, be safe." I honestly had no idea at the time how ugly and brutal the war would get. All I knew was the "old one" had his reasons and one of them was to punch holes in the hearts of humans, and of course, to create a mass genocide.

After I chatted with the boys a little bit longer, I left, and to this day I sometimes thought about them. When the war I warned them about went into full force, I wondered if they were overseas fighting for our country.

I'd been following World War II for some time. A lot of the Nazis were dark spirits, but there were quite a few who were human. I had to hand it to the "old one." From the beginning, he'd orchestrated and carried out a clever plan to psychologically brand the minds of Germans by using colorful aesthetical symbols such as the crooked cross and eye-catching red, white, and black. He also used symbols of power and strength. The agenda was to allure and inspire passion into the hearts of the German people. Programming. Of course, his charismatic speeches and passionate ideology brought hope to the downtrodden. Germany would rule the world, and the "old one's" belief of a pure Aryan race would be a cog in the wheel of life he was aspiring to ultimately create on earth. He also wanted to get rid of the mentally and physically disabled. The weak. The inept. Basically, anyone who was a burden to society. Like the thousands of legions of dark spirits he once commanded, he wanted to create generations of Aryan humans who were physically fit and obedient to him and his commanders.

Since the war began in 1939 when Germany invaded Poland, I kept my distance. I had personally told Volac I didn't want to take part in it. I was too selfish. I wanted to continue having fun. Besides, even though I detested most humans, I wasn't sure how I felt about what the "old one" was doing. Volac took no offense to me not participating in the "old one's" plan. He confided he already anticipated my objection to get involved. The brutality alone would trigger memories from my human life, and he didn't want that. He himself was immune to such horrific acts. However, like Sylis, harming women and children was off limits in his eyes, unless they deserved it, of course.

I was in Vegas on December 7, 1941, when the Japanese launched a surprise attack on Pearl Harbor's naval fleet. Like everyone else, I was shocked. Volac never mentioned this devious act would happen in order to get Americans involved in the war, but I imagined the "old one" had failed to mention to him this underhanded part of his plan—unless Volac knew but was sworn to secrecy not to blab. I didn't know nor did I care. All I knew at the time was the United States would now get involved.

I was right.

Wherever I went, I felt American's outrage and panic. A lot of them were fearful the Japanese would attack the U.S mainland. Soon after, they were thrust into the war and everyday life across the country altered. The majority accepted what sacrifices they had to make in order to achieve victory. A rationing program ensued on the American people. Rationing stamps were given to families, used to buy their allotment of food, clothing, gas, fuel oil, and tires. While men went to war, women went to work as riveters and machinists in defense plants; they worked in factories and became welders and electricians. I was indeed impressed by the comradery and patriotic spirit of everyone around me. In fact, their enthusiasm and interest in the war infected me to where I found myself listening to the radio alongside them for updates on the war. In coffee shops and clubs, I conversed with humans about the fighting overseas and what the frontline reports said that day.

One afternoon, while I was at a soda fountain having a vanilla malt at the counter and listening to "Boogie Woogie Bugle Boy of Company B" playing on the jukebox in the background, an attractive dark-haired female with a slick bobbed hairdo strolled in. Her high heels clicked against the linoleum floor as she made her way toward me. She smiled and waved. I glanced around to make sure I wasn't misreading her friendliness that appeared to be directed at me. The young fellas and gals at the counter and tables in the store were busy conversing with each other, paying no mind to her.

"Ameerah, it's Ava," she said, sitting on the spinning stool next to me, eyeing the gooseneck soda spouts. Or was she admiring her reflection in the large mirror behind the counter? I couldn't tell.

"How did you know it was me?" I asked, surprised but delighted to see her. It had been months since we chatted. She'd been in Germany, playing the part of a girlfriend to a fellow dark spirit who was possessing a Nazi.

She ordered a cherry float from the older fella wearing a white button-up shirt and black bowtie. I took a long pull off my straw, enjoying the cool vanilla malty flavor drenching my tastebuds.

"Aidan told me you'd be here," she said.

Of course. I'd forgotten I mentioned to Aidan last night that I'd been craving one of these delicious treats. I even invited him to join me this afternoon and described what type of human I'd be possessing, but he had new souls to recruit.

"So what's it like there?" I asked. "And don't beat around the bush. I want to know."

"It's nasty on both sides," she said, flashing the soda shop fella a smile when he placed her drink in front of her. "Let's go to the table in the corner so we can have some privacy."

"I've been keeping up on the war," I told her after we sat at the round marble-topped table. "I thought about tagging along with you but . . ." I shrugged. "It's not my war. Besides, I have a feeling the plans of the 'old one' aren't as transparent as he'd like the world to think . . . if that makes any sense?"

"I think you're right," she agreed and suddenly turned serious. "Remember Calvin Hyde?"

"The lanky ginger fella who I thought was creepy when I met him? I recall you told me he was one of the evil dark spirits among us."

She took a drink of soda and nodded. "He's now one of the leading members of the Nazi Party in Germany. He's in charge of the entire Third Reich and of the killing of masses. He's responsible for setting up and overseeing the concentration and extermination camps and reign of terror upon the prisoners. So far, he's had millions of Jews, Poles, and Soviet citizens exterminated, including children."

"Undesirables?" I felt a strong sense of sympathy for what those humans went through. I saw no reason in torturing them unless they deserved it, and I found it hard to believe each and every one of them did.

"Yes," she answered. "Do you remember me telling you about Aosoth?"

"The female dark spirit who is a wicked bitch?"

"The very one. She's there and in charge of the female sections of the camps. She's instilled more panic and fear than the SS men have. She beats and tortures women on a daily basis to where they collapse and sometimes lose consciousness. She also trains the female guards to harden themselves and severely punish the prisoners when necessary."

"Are the female guards dark spirits?" I'd never met Aosoth, but what I'd heard about her from Ava and others, Aosoth was a malevolent being without a conscience. Rumor had it she'd never been cast out by an immortal due to her craftiness. I wouldn't put it past her to have the ability to manipulate and brainwash humans to take part in unimaginable behavior toward their prisoners.

Ava frowned. "No. As far as I know they're all human."

I clenched my jaw. Most humans were despicable. Taking prisoners was one thing, but to abuse them like I was in Bandbridge or worse, made me want to take all of those assholes and inflict the same suffering they caused on their fellow man and woman. In fact, now that I thought about it, I was equally disgusted with the dark spirits like Aosoth and Calvin who took pleasure in doing inhumane things to others.

"Are Volac and Sylis mistreating humans?"

"Not that I'm aware of," she said, shaking her head. "I know Sylis was part of a specialized paramilitary unit responsible for murdering countless Jews and those who supported them. He had Russian prisoners of war dig six pits large enough to bury twenty-five thousand people, and the pits were designed to literally allow the victims to march to their own graves, which they did. Then, Sylis and his men shot every last one of them in a mass shooting."

"I had no idea," I said more to myself than her, stunned by those atrocities. "What about Volac?"

She rubbed her brow and made a face. "All I know is he's part of the armed forces, conquering territories, similar to what he'd done when he was a Viking."

"I suppose that makes sense, given his background. I hope he's not a monster like Calvin and Aosoth and others like them. I understand the agenda behind the madness of the 'old one.' However . . ." I trailed off, losing my train of thought due to all of them bouncing in every direction inside my head.

Ava reached across the table and touched my arm. "Don't get uptight. Some of us don't agree with how things are being carried out, and I learned some top secret news last night." She smiled mischievously and scooted her chair around the table, making scraping sounds on the floor as she did so. She was now elbow to elbow with me.

"What?" I turned to her and bowed my head, making a point to lower my voice. "Is the war going to end soon?" It had been years since the U.S. entered the war, and no one had ever told me how long it would last. All I knew was dark spirits not only single handedly created this war, they had also been compelling the masses through propaganda to behave in the matter that suited their devious agendas. The war was only one network of many psychological controls to toy with humans and alter their existence.

"The 'old one' is no longer possessing Hitler," Ava said in a high whisper.

I gaped at her. I didn't expect this piece of news and was floored. "Why would he do such a thing? I thought he would see this war through and destroy as many undesirables as possible."

"No," she answered. "It wasn't his intention to win. He only wanted to perform a genocidal scrimmage, fracture the hearts and minds of humans, and achieve other goals that I'm not aware of. He also didn't take into account the strength of the American people and how they became a collective force here and overseas. Not to mention how the immortals got heavily involved in fighting against them. So now the 'old one' is in Africa searching for King Solomon's ring."

My head spun. I was speechless. My feelings were all over the place.

"Oh, that reminds me." She looked around to double check no one was within earshot. The dull hum of chattering patrons and Bing Crosby playing on the jukebox was a safe bet our privacy was secure. "Remember the hardboiled immortal who is the best dark spirit tracker?"

"Nathan . . . what's his last name?" For the life of me, I couldn't think of it. I was drawing a blank.

"Caswell," she blurted.

I snapped my fingers and pointed at her. "Yes, that's it. What about him?"

"He's fighting in the war as an American soldier. He even fought on the beaches of Normandy."

"I bet the 'old one' lost a lot of troops because of Nathan and the other immortals," I said, imagining them casting the dark spirits out when no one was looking and taking bullet hits and then magically healing from their wounds. I wondered how they were able to pull those things off without alarming the humans. Their strength and speed would surely raise eyebrows.

"You ain't kidding," she answered. "They're a thorn in our side."

"Why would the 'old one' leave the others holding the bag to go searching for Solomon's ring when clearly he knows he's not going to find it? Maybe he doesn't believe in the prophesy about the gal in Astoria being the only one who will be able to locate the king's ring and his incantations."

"Oh, he believes it, but it doesn't mean he can't narrow down where it's at."

"I suppose, but I think it's shitty of him to pass the buck. In fact," I said, raising my chin, making a snap decision, "I'm done."

Ava looked at me in surprise. "What do you mean?"

"I don't want to be part of Volac's group anymore or anyone's for that matter. I'm going to do my own thing." When her face fell, I added, "I'll still pay Volac and the others a visit."

"You've already been doing your own thing," she argued. "What's the big deal in staying with our group?" When I opened my mouth to answer, she continued, "So you have to perform tasks for him from time to time, but what he asks of us is justifiable. Hell, he didn't even squawk when you told him you refused to take part in this war. He supported you in your decision."

"True, but there *will* be a next time, and I shouldn't have to answer to anyone about whatever decisions I make for myself. It's none of their damn business, and I will not be controlled. Period."

Some birds cannot be caged, and I was one of them.

After some lighthearted arguing on Ava's part, she realized I wasn't budging. I smiled, pleased that I finally made the decision to be fully independent and free from the politics in our dark world.

Germany had surrendered on May 7, almost a month after my visit with Ava, and Japan would quit fighting on August 15. The "old one" had accomplished what he was set out to do—not to win the war, but to psychologically change the hearts and minds of humanity. The human world would never be the same again.

Chapter Twenty-Eight

Decades Passed

Volac had politely accepted my decision to leave our group with the promise that I'd pay him visits and seek out his council whenever I desired. He shared with me secrets about our dark world and had been a wonderful mentor throughout the years. Of course I would visit with him again, which I had throughout the decades that followed.

I spent many years drifting from my realm to the human one.

In the dark spirit's realm, the planes of our existences were vast. Each one of us could claim a home where we could rest and experience solitude without being bothered. I chose a light olive green Victorian house with white trim and a gray roof. It had pointed arched gabled windows on the top floor and a turret in between them. The house sat in a valley of rolling hills, framed by a deep forest with black gnarled trees. Whenever I needed to unplug from everything, it was the perfect respite for me. And though the sky was always a purplish gray hue, and the grass and trees were continually cast in shadow, like beauty to the beast, I found comfort in its embrace.

As the years passed, I continued to have fun on earth, possessing soulless humans and toying with them to amuse myself. I adjusted to the changes as each decade passed, like with fashion and slang. The style of dancing changed, as well. In the 'fifties, I learned how to do the jitterbug, the hand-jive, and of course I'd perform the twist when I heard

Chubby Checker playing on the radio, "Let's Twist Again." I was also on American Bandstand, dancing to the top forty music, wearing a poodle skirt and saddle shoes. Then, the Vietnam War happened. I didn't know what the real reason was for America to get involved because I wasn't part of Volac's group anymore, but Ava told me the dark spirits had a heavy hand in the whole operation. It was their way to continue to shift and mold the minds of humans. They wanted to break down the family unit, the cultural standards of morality, and crack the very foundation our forefathers fought for and believed in. She told me an immortal had gone to a congressman and told him about the communist takeover of America. He laid out a manifesto, created by the dark spirits on how they intended to bring their goals into fruition, like take control of the schools, change the curriculum, use current Communist propaganda, and so forth. They planned on infiltrating the press and gaining control of TV, radio, and motion pictures. The immortal went down the list, one by one, but the congressman wouldn't listen to him. In 1963, the Communist Goals for America was entered into Congressional record. The immortal—we had no idea of his identity—was right, and so it had begun.

I partied a lot in the 'sixties and 'seventies. I drank and smoked pot. I didn't dare do LSD because I was told by Volac that the mind-altering drug would cause me to immediately vacate the vessel. I didn't want that, so I was cautious with what I ingested into the body I was possessing.

I went to Woodstock in August of 1969. I saw The Grateful Dead, Creedence Clearwater Revival, Janis Joplin, The Who, and Jimi Hendrix. I possessed a hippy gal with long, straight brownish-blonde hair who drove a beat-up blue and white Volkswagen bus. I had a groovy time, smoking dope, drinking, and dancing in the rain.

When Studio 54 opened in New York City in 1977, I was determined to get inside the exclusive nightclub. I quickly discovered you had to be glamorous to gain access, and a lot of people were turned away because they were deemed to be ugly. Around that time, Aidan had proved himself to join the "old one" and his league and no longer had to be a recruiter, so he accompanied me along with Ava on this silly quest of mine. We were finally able to find some soulless celebrities to possess and had no problems getting into this popular nightspot. We had some wild and fun times and were even there when Bianca Jagger rode a white horse through the club on her thirtieth birthday. Too bad Studio 54 closed two years later for income tax evasion.

In the 'eighties, I decided to do something completely out of character.

"You're nuts," Ava said to me one day when I told her my plan to possess a counselor I had my eye on. We were lounging on the Queen Anne couches in the living room of my Victorian house in our dreary realm. When I made a face, she sat up and waved her hands wildly in the air. "I didn't mean it like that. I know you're not nuts, but–"

"I know what you mean," I said, sighing, "but the female I'm referring to works in a facility in Phoenix, Arizona, that houses troubled humans. It's not an insane asylum like I was in. It's an inpatient and outpatient care clinic," I explained, hoping she wouldn't give me any grief over this. "If I were to occupy her body, one of my main duties would be to discuss with clients their options and goals so the rehabilitation and plans could be developed to that client's needs. I'd also monitor and record the client's progress, among other things."

"Why a counselor? Won't it bring back bad memories?"

I shrugged. "There's only one way to find out."

"Why a counselor?" she repeated.

"Because I want to know what it feels like to be on the other side of the coin," I answered. "When I was in Bandbridge, I was the patient. I want to experience it from another viewpoint." I'd always wondered what it would have been like to have been in Ann's position—the nice nurse who had released me from my restraints and was rudely dismissed by Norma. She could have stood up to that bitch and helped me escape, but she didn't. I know I would have. But there was another reason. The main one, really.

Elizabeth.

I couldn't help her, and I realized she didn't want my help, and she was now with her son, but the guilt still weighed heavily on my heart. She was there for me through my darkest hours, and I failed her.

"That makes sense," Ava thoughtfully said. "Let me know how it goes. I'll hang around Astoria with Aidan, so you can meet up with me later. I'm curious to see what happens. I hope it doesn't backfire on you."

I didn't say anything, only stared past her at nothing in particular, deep in thought. I hoped the same thing, but regardless, I had to try it. Maybe this idea of mine would help me, because maybe I'd be able to help a deserving human who no one else could, like Elizabeth. Or maybe it would make my inner demons worse. There was only one way to find out, and I was willing to take that risk.

Chapter Twenty-Nine

Present Day with Derek

"Hold up, love," Derek said, pulling me back to the present. He snuffed out his ciggy in an art deco brass ashtray stand and continued, "Why in bloody hell would you do such a thing?"

"I told you," I said, hearing the defensiveness in my voice, raising my gaze to the stamped-tin ceiling, suddenly grateful we were alone in his private quarters, away from the crowd in the club. "I wanted–"

"I heard what you said, but the decision was daft, if you ask me."

"Ava thought so, too." I reached for my cocktail on the end table and frowned when I noticed the glass was empty. "But you know how I am. Once I get an idea in my head, I go full throttle."

He rose and went to the mini bar that reminded me of the kind a wealthy man would have in his study back in the day when Humphrey Bogart and Lauren Bacall fell in love. The small bulbs along the top metal base were lit, adding to the vintage feel of this room. "Would you like me to make you a tuxedo #2 for old time sake?"

"I would love one," I said, lighting a ciggy.

He poured gin and vermouth into a glass, then added a dash of maraschino liqueur, bitters, and a dose of absinthe. "Why don't you continue with your story? How did you meet Nadia? I'm guessing she was one of your patients."

"Yes, she was in outpatient care. The human I possessed was well-trained in group therapy and visiting with patients on a one-on-one basis. Thankfully, we have the ability to access basic information from the people we dwell in, but I did have to bullshit my way out of some situations due to the human's knowledge blocked off from me." Derek handed me my drink. "Thank you. Anyway . . . oh, and she had a soul. I was able to possess her, because she had dabbled in the dark arts. That was the first time I'd ever inhabited a person with a soul before."

Derek returned to his spot on the couch across from me, holding a glass of whiskey and water on the rocks. "It's a bit different, isn't it?"

"Yes," I said. "Much harder to hang onto the vessel for a long period of time. There were occasions where I'd get odd thoughts that weren't mine. But I adapted rather quickly.

"Anyway, I shared an office with a psychologist who was my superior. One afternoon, Nadia came in for her three o'clock appointment, like she'd been doing every Wednesday for the past month. This would be the first time I'd personally met her. I familiarized myself with her case beforehand. Like me, she was an only child. Her mother had a fling twenty-four years prior and became pregnant with Nadia. She grew up not knowing who her father was and with several abusive step-dads. Her mother and the men she brought into their lives were on drugs off and on throughout Nadia's childhood. After her mother went through her third divorce and began bringing home strange men, one of them moved in with Nadia and her mother and sexually abused Nadia repeatedly." I clinched my hands into my lap and took a deep breath. I wish I would have known who the bastard was, because I would have killed him like I had Chester. Aside from therapy, Nadia didn't want to talk about him. The subject was too painful for her, so I never pressed the issue.

Derek held up his hands, palms forward. "No need to go into further explanation, love. I know the issue is touchy. So in a nutshell, she had a shitty upbringing."

I took a hit off my ciggy and nodded. "She also lived in poverty and had to fend for herself. I loathed my parents for their elitist and self-important attitude, but at least I never went hungry, and I had nice things, whereas Nadia had shit. Her mother was a lying, thieving cunt. Humans like her need to be exterminated from this earth." My nails were digging into my palms, making half-moon indentions.

Derek raised his glass. "You got my vote. Do you still feel the same way?"

"Hell, yeah," I blurted without missing a beat. A smile crossed his handsome face, his blue eyes twinkling. I went on, not allowing my thoughts to analyze his reaction, except he liked my answer. "Long story short, Nadia was a recovering drug addict and attempted suicide several times. She'd been drug-free for eight months and was undergoing therapy to stay on the straight and narrow. I'll never forget the day she walked into my office. I lost my breath, and my pulse raced from the immediate attraction I had toward this doe-eyed beauty. But she wasn't beautiful in the preprocessed, packaged sense society had labeled and stamped their approval on that had females clamoring to emulate. No, she had a tragic, haunting beauty with her long, Morticia Addams straight dark hair and shy delicate features. She wore a white off-the-shoulder slouchy shirt and acid washed jeans. The human I was possessing was five years older than her and of course attractive. I guess Nadia felt the same magnetic pull as me, because the energy in the room sizzled between us."

"Have you ever felt an instant attraction like it, before?" Derek asked.

"No, this was something I'd never experienced. It completely threw me off my game. I was no longer interested in anything else but her."

I could still see her face in my mind, her eyes fixed on mine; they darted to my silk, cream colored blouse, the buttons opened to the middle of my breast, revealing flesh under a bit of white lace. Her gaze lifted back to my face. Her tongue peeked out between her lips, slowly wiggling across them.

"How did you know she felt the same attraction as you?"

"By the way she looked at me and her body language. The woman I was possessing never met her before. She was given Nadia's case because her counselor was on maternity leave. I introduced myself to Nadia as Ameerah. Why? I don't know, but I had the need to do so. I did, however, advised her that everyone addressed me as Summer McDowell, which was the name of my host. She didn't question it and sat in the chair in front of my desk. I quickly pushed my desires aside and went into professional mode, telling myself I was there to help her, not me. I opened her chart, and we fell into an easy conversation about herself and her upbringing. She made a point to tell me she was going to a community college, getting her prerequisites out of the way. She didn't have a major and had no idea what to do with her life. Maybe run a halfway house for troubled teens. She didn't know. She was lost. She did have a day job managing a movie theater. She contemplated majoring in business, but she was still indecisive.

"After our session, she flashed me a coy, flirtatious smile on her way out. I sat back in the leather chair behind the desk and sighed. I began questioning my plan, myself, and whether I should continue counseling her. Normally, if we were in a different situation, I'd ask her out, but we weren't, and I didn't want to jeopardize Nadia's treatment. But I wanted her. I wanted her badly. So much that I'd contemplated occupying another vessel and seeing if our bodies would respond in the same manner as they had when she walked through my door. I decided against it. I refused to toy with Nadia and made up my mind in that moment to deny my burning desires for her and remain professional while I continued this charade. Besides, I truly wanted to help her and wanted to be the counselor I wished I had when I was in Bandbridge.

"The following session, she was clearly trying to seduce me, wearing a short skirt and making a point to cross her legs so the hem would rise up her thighs, revealing a black garter belt attached to her stockings. I tried to ignore the warmth rushing through my body and the pulsing between my legs. I was there to help her, not give into my desires, I kept telling myself."

"I give you kudos for restraining yourself from seeking out another way to be with her. You must have been smitten hard," Derek said, taking a sip of his whiskey.

"I was," I agreed. "But the third session with Nadia did me in." I closed my eyes and rubbed my brow. "Ava and you were right. I was nuts to have gone through with my plan."

"Ameerah." Derek's soft and caring voice caused me to open my eyes. "I wish we were wrong. I'm seeing a pattern with you, love, but please continue. You have me anticipating what did you in."

A pattern. What in the world was he talking about?

I cleared my throat and went on, knowing he would explain what he said later. "The first two meetings I had with Nadia were preliminary, to gain more of an idea of her history and her demeanor. The third one, she arrived at her normal time, relaxed. She had a smile on her face when she entered my office and took her usual seat on the other side of my desk. There was a cheerful spark in her brown eyes, and I asked her how her week had been . . ." I trailed off.

"What did she say?" Derek asked.

I took a deep breath and locked my eyes with his. This part of my tale was more difficult to share than I thought. Maybe because of what happened in the end and the guilt that weighed heavily on my heart from my actions during that time. Regardless, I was to blame for what transpired, and in order to accomplish what I was set out to do here in this room with Derek, I must continue my story. And so I did, wheeling us both to that time:

* * *

"Excellent," she said. "I got a dollar raise at my job, and I won two hundred dollars from a scratch-off lottery ticket."

I told her congratulations, but she made a face. "What's wrong?" I asked.

She rolled her eyes and sighed. "A guy in my English class asked me out. He's a fox, but I'm totally not into him."

I folded my hands on my desk and thought maybe I was disillusioned by the signals I thought she was sending. "Why not?"

She slowly rubbed the back of her neck and locked her gaze with mine. "I'm not into men."

I'd lie if I were to tell you I wasn't elated by her admission, but nonetheless, I had to remain professional.

"Is it because you were sexually abused by your mother's boyfriend?" I asked.

"No," she said, dropping her gaze to her feet.

The walls seemed to close in. The room stilled. The energy grew thick between us. She was silently contemplating whether to say what suddenly reared inside of her. At least, that was the impression I was getting.

"Is there something on your mind?"

She looked up with a haunting, sad expression on her face. "I was always interested in girls, and he knew it, because he had caught me and my girlfriend making out in my bedroom. One night . . ." She leaned back in her chair, took a deep breath, and continued, "One night, he snuck into my room while I was asleep. He pulled the covers off me and crawled on top of me. He covered my mouth and said he would kill my mother and then me if I made a sound. He told me once I had a real dick inside my pussy, I'd never turn back. He was saving me from damnation, and I should be grateful for his generosity." She looked at me, tears welling. Her eyebrows knitted. "What's wrong?"

I could feel the blood draining from my face. Chester had told me almost the exact same thing when he molested me. I realized then I couldn't do this. I fucking couldn't do it. Ava was right. I should have listened to her. What was I thinking? Well, I knew what I was thinking at the time, but—

No, I was done.

This was too much.

I wanted to help her.

God, I wanted to help her, but how could I help Nadia when I couldn't even help myself?

Abruptly, I stood. "I'm sorry, but I'm going to have to hand over your case to someone else."

Alarmed, she hopped to her feet. "Did I say something wrong? Please tell me. I don't *want* anyone else but you."

She stressed her last sentence in a way that could only be construed as she wanted me for more than just a counselor.

"I apologize if I'm being unprofessional," I told her, "and you're fine. I have issues I thought I could overcome by helping you and others, but clearly I was wrong." I moved to the door, placed my hand on the knob, and said goodbye to her. But then she said something that shocked me to my very core.

Chapter Thirty

Nadia

Derek leaned forward on his knees, his legs apart. "What did she say?"
"She said, 'I know who you are.'"

He gaped at me. "How?"

"Let me finish the story, then you'll know."

The corner of Derek's mouth twisted, and he sat back with his drink. He made a gesture for me to get on with it. I took a sip of my cocktail and lit a ciggy at the same time he did. I blew out the smoke and proceeded with my story of Nadia and me.

* * *

When Nadia said that, I turned around, and she was standing in the middle of the room with an anxious look on her face.

"Excuse me?" I asked back then in 1985.

"I know who you are," she repeated, her tone firm and unrelenting.

"And who do you think I am?" I asked.

"An entity who possesses humans."

I crossed my arms, appearing calmer than I felt. For sixty years of being a dark spirit, never once had I ever run into someone who knew who I was, except for an immortal. It had hit me like a ton of bricks. My blood turned cold. "Are you an immortal?" I asked, reaching behind me for the doorknob, mentally preparing to flee.

She shook her head, pulling her hair back from the right side of her neck, revealing a three-dimensional spiral, in a conch-shell form, the size of a dime. My eyes widened, and I became slacked-jawed. "Do you recognize this symbol?"

"'What do *you* think?" I demanded, my shock quickly turning to irritation. I read her whole history in her medical records, and there was nothing in there about Nadia being tangled in the dark arts. What type of game was she playing? What was her incentive for playing me for a fool, which she did. I should have listened to Ava, dammit.

She frowned. "You're mad."

"'You're damn right I'm mad," I shouted, glaring at her. "You've never mentioned you were once involved in black magic. It's not even in your damn file. What sort of trickery are you up to?"

She pointed to my eyes. "I can see a thin, yellow beam of light move across your iris. It does it every time you get emotional, like now."

I blinked, stunned she could see it. I'd always thought immortals were the only ones who could. I wondered if Volac knew that there were some humans who could see that red flag of ours.

* * *

"Amazing," Derek breathed while I took a drink of my cocktail to combat the dryness in my throat. I could see the same shock I felt at the time reflected in his own eyes. "What was your reaction?"

"I stood up straight, refusing to be rattled," I told him with a smirk. "But let me get back to my story. I'm on a roll now."

"Carry on, then, love."

* * *

I remembered asking her, "How long have you been able to see this?"

"After the immortal cast one of your kind out of me," she said, but then her tone shifted into an almost desperate, pleading sound. "I *know* it's an anomaly, because I haven't been marked for immortality, yet I have the ability to tell when a malevolent being is in my presence. I don't know why, and I'm truly sorry for not being upfront with you about it."

"Do your ears ring when one of us is around you?" I wasn't done questioning her. I wouldn't let her off that easily. The last time someone fooled me was when my parents spun the lie about my grandmother having TB, so they could get me to go along with them, and then had me committed to an insane asylum. The back of my neck burned from the anger boiling inside of me.

"No," she answered. "I can tell you're pissed off because I wasn't honest with you, but you weren't honest with me, either."

I blew up. "That's fucking ridiculous! How in the hell was I supposed to tell you who I truly am? Most of the human population know nothing about us. Instead, they have their own idiotic beliefs about demons and hellfire. For your information, the reason I decided to masquerade as a counselor was so I could do something good for a change and work through my own damned issues I still carry with me from when I was human."

She held her hands up in surrender. "I'm sorry. Please forgive me. I'm not a fraud. What's in my records and the things I've told you about my life are totally true. Please let me take you out and make this up to you." She had that desperate look in her eyes again. I'd never cared for brown eyes before, but hers were gorgeous—deep with flecks of gold. "What do you say? You can't deny the attraction between us, and if you quit this job or possess another body, we can see each other."

I thought of the fucked up life she had and all the people who had disappointed her like the people had in my human life. As those thoughts raced through my mind along with her apology, my anger simmered. Truthfully, she melted my heart, and she was correct. I couldn't deny the heat between us. I wasn't in love with her, but I wanted to be with her. I wanted to help her and still had hope I could.

I sighed. "Fine. Make it up to me then," I said, trying not to stare at her bottom lip she was chewing on. "I'll request to hand your case over to someone else by making up some bullshit excuse." I opened the door wide, signaling for her to leave. "Your time is up."

She nodded with a half-hearted smile on her lovely face. "Do you want me to pick you up tonight?"

"No, I'll meet you there," I answered, determined to get to know her better instead of submitting to my raging hormones.

"That's totally fine," she said, stepping in front of me. I could feel the instant heat between us, so I moved back, not wanting to give into it like I normally would. "Meet me at Black Angus on Metro Parkway at seven. Do you know the one I'm talking about?"

"'I do." I opened the door wider. "I'll see you there."

She frowned, appearing crestfallen. I gathered it was because of my abrupt signal for her to leave and the hard look I felt on my face. My heart clenched. I wanted to touch her arm and tell her things would be okay, but I didn't. I stood by my promise to help her. If I were to touch her, I'd give into my sexual desires, knowing she would in turn give into hers for me. Our actions would sabotage the kind of relationship I was hoping to have with her and had craved since I lost Betty. Nadia was no Betty. No one could ever replace her, but I saw parts of myself in Nadia from talking to her about her life. I was not only physically drawn to her but emotionally, as well.

* * *

"Anyway, Derek, my dear friend, after she left, I went to my superior, had Nadia transferred to another counselor, and left. I went shopping at Metro Center mall and bought a black satin wraparound dress for our date—the kind that has the spaghetti string around the waist. It looked great on the body I was using. Hell, I wanted to do myself when I saw my reflection in the mirror of the dressing room. The outfit hugged my slim hourglass figure perfectly—very sexy and feminine. The light satin fabric felt wonderful against my skin. I was getting aroused while rubbing the material on my thigh. All the pent up sexual energy from today was pushing against the walls of my stomach and pulsing between my legs, demanding to be released. I contemplated masturbating right there in the small changing room, but then I heard women coming in, chatting about a wedding they were preparing for. The doors on either side of me closed to the other rooms. They went on chatting back and forth in excited voices. I had to get out of there and please myself in private. I bought the dress and drove to this human's condo in her white convertible VW bug. Once I entered her home, I tossed the bag on the kitchen table and stripped off my clothes as I walked down the short hallway to her bedroom . . ."

"And?" Derek asked, shifting on the couch. "Come on, love. Don't leave out the naughty details."

He was getting hard. I could tell by the way he moved his palm against his inner thigh, trying to shift it into a more comfortable position. He'd done the same when I told him about Betty and me having sex, but I ignored it then. Not this time. I had to give him shit about it.

"It's obvious you have an erection," I said, pointing at his crotch. "And don't feed me some bullshit line that you don't. Remember, I've possessed men before. I know what it's like." It was a pain-in-the-ass and would sometimes twist in your underwear, which hurt like hell. Not to mention trying to hide it when you didn't want someone to see you were turned on. Females had it much easier.

"You know me better than that," he answered, reaching into his trousers, shifting his member into a safe and comfortable position. "I would never . . ." his eyebrows pulled together in thought. "What was that line Clint Eastwood said in one of his westerns?" He thought some more, staring at the floor.

"I don't know what you're talking about."

He looked up and grinned. "Got it! I would never piss on your back and tell you it was raining." He laughed, stood, and picked up my empty glass. "Would you like another one?"

"Of course," I said.

"Go on. I'm listening."

"I bet you are." I laughed. "But don't distract me. I need to get this out." I took a deep breath and plunged ahead. "When I was done pleasing myself, I took a shower and spent hours getting ready. I twisted the shoulder-length brown hair up and clipped it in a pretty jeweled barrette. I applied makeup, lining my hazel eyes with black liner. I have to admit, I'd always enjoyed preening myself and the sensuous feelings I experienced whenever I got dolled up. But anyway, three and a half hours later, I was sitting at a table across from Nadia at the steakhouse, enjoying the wonderful smells of fried onions and steak. She was wearing the exact same wraparound dress as me, except in a dark blue color. We laughed at the odds of that happening and fell into a nice, comfortable conversation throughout our meal, despite how packed it was and all of the chatter swirling around us. It was almost as if we were in our own bubble, and that was fine with me." I paused when Derek handed me my cocktail. I took a sip, tasting the bitters and hint of gin. It was delightful. "Thank you," I said. "You make a mean tuxedo #2."

He smiled. "My pleasure, love."

"Now, where was I?"

He returned to his seat and sat. "You and Nadia were at the steakhouse, and despite the crowd, it was—"

"Oh, I remember," I said. "Okay, back to 1985 at the restaurant with Nadia."

* * *

"Do you forgive me?" she asked after our waiter had put a large chocolate cake with thick fudge dripping down the sides in the middle of our table for us to share. She stuck her fork in the moist pastry, then placed it between her lips. She closed her eyes. "Mmmm, this is heavenly. Here, you got to try this, Ameerah." She reached across the table and fed me a piece.

"Oh, my," I breathed, allowing the rich chocolate to coat my entire mouth. I slowly licked my lips to ensure there was no syrup or crumbs on them. "This is wonderful, and yes I forgive you."

"'Excellent," she said, taking another bite, smiling. "Since now you know everything—"

"'I don't," I interrupted, anticipating exactly what she was going to say. "You never told me when you were involved in the dark arts, why, and if you're still entangled in it."

She shrugged. "Not much to tell. I was a curious teenager. I played with the ouija board with my friends and by myself. I read a ton of books and got involved with black magic. The end."

She was being evasive, so I pried some more. "What did you discover during that time?"

"I found by fooling with the ouija board and giving permission to have a spirit work through me, I stuck a welcome sign on my body for any interested spirits to possess. I also learned magic is real if you know how to wield it, and most humans are sleepwalking through life, unaware of what's truly going on."

I took another bite and folded my hands on the table. "And that is?"

She laughed. It was light and flirty. "I don't have to tell you, Ameerah." She leaned across the table, and in a low voice, she said, "You're one of them."

"And that doesn't bother you?"

She shook her head and fed me another piece of cake, her eyes focused on my lips. "No. I'm intrigued by you. I want to know more. I say we go to the park near my apartment and talk beneath the stars. What do you say?"

* * *

"So forty minutes later, Derek, we were at a nice park with small rolling hills and wooden bridges spanning across several ponds. That's where I met *her*."

"Who?" he asked.

"Aosoth."

Chapter Thirty-One

Bliss

"I can't stand that cow," Derek said, his features twisting as if he had a foul taste in his mouth. "You hadn't told me when you first met her. It was at the park, then?"

I nodded. "Now you know, but she didn't crawl out of her web right away. She waited. I was sure of it." I fixed my eyes on his. "You know when you can tell when someone is lurking around, watching you?"

"I do, actually."

"Well, I had that feeling while Nadia and I walked around the park, enjoying the warm spring air, the smell of fresh-cut grass, and the bright, beautiful stars above us. The Big Dipper showed like a neon sign through a crystal clear sky. I remember the moon wasn't quite full yet, but the white orb seemed majestic compared to the stars, and I marveled at it. I told Nadia it almost seemed like the moon was god to the stars."

"I like that, love," Derek said. "The moon as a god to the smaller heavenly bodies."

"Yes," I mused, my thoughts drifting to that scene.

"What happened next?"

I blinked. "Oh, right, back to my story."

* * *

She slipped her hand into mine, intertwining our fingers together. I didn't protest. In fact, it felt nice. "Is there a god?" she asked me as we strolled across an arched bridge over a small pond.

"If there is one, I haven't met him," I answered. "There's no such thing as hellfire or a judgment day. I can tell you that much."

We sat on a bench beneath an oak tree and fell silent for the first time that evening, but it was a comfortable silence, not awkward. The sounds of crickets and frogs surrounded us. Nadia was deep in thought, staring at the ground. Three toads hopped by, and we watched them until they disappeared into the darkness. From out of the corner of my eye, I thought I saw movement next to a large tree to my right, but then Nadia released my hand and turned to me, suddenly excited and curious, pulling my attention to her instead.

"Why did you choose this existence? Have you ever regretted it and wondered where you'd be right now if you had crossed over instead?"

I didn't want to get into the whole sordid details of my parents' betrayal and what the assholes did to me at Bandbridge, so I skirted her questions the best I could without divulging those details. "I chose to become a dark spirit, because I didn't want to forget what it was like to be human and the pleasures that came with it, like scrumptious food, sex, alcohol, tobacco, and the opportunity to experience whatever life I desired. I'm the captain of my own ship, instead of subservient to the light walkers or any other higher being."

Her brow wrinkled. "Light walker?"

"'Humans call them angels," I said, "and to answer your other question, I don't regret my decision."

"What's your world like?

"Don't answer that." A female voice said. She stepped from behind the oak tree we were sitting under and approached. She was an attractive blonde wearing black spandex pants and a slouchy red shirt hanging off her shoulder. A white studded belt dipped loosely around her thin waist. When she stopped in front of me, her dark eyes bored into mine. A laser beam of light flashed across them, but it was much thicker than mine. She was older than me. This had to be Aosoth. I didn't know why I thought so, but she looked like she sucked on a lemon by the way she pursed her lips, and her arms were tight across her chest. She had a vibe that screamed bitch.

I wasn't alarmed by her presence and remained rooted in my spot. Nadia stiffened beside me and made a quick move to rise. I placed a hand on her shoulder, halting her. She looked at me in concern and sat back down. Slipping her hand in mine, she stared at the blonde.

"You must be Aosoth," I said, flashing a phony grin. "After all these years, we finally get to meet. Wow. This is my lucky day."

"I know who you are as well." Aosoth flipped her spiraled hair off her shoulder. Her lips tightened, and her eyes narrowed. "Ameerah Arrowood, the star pupil who took to being a dark spirit like a duck to water and had Volac eating out of your hand the very first time he met you. Lovely. If only he could see you now with this *human*." She made a derogatory gesture toward Nadia. "Now, don't get me wrong," she continued in an annoying high-pitched tone. "Humans are great for play toys. I myself have several. But to get emotionally involved with them in a relationship"—her gaze fell to my hand holding Nadia's, and her expression shifted into disgust–"goes against everything we stand for."

"'Everything *you* stand for," I countered. "Besides, it's none of your damn business how I live my life. You and no one else has any right to dictate to me how I can and cannot live."

"On the contrary, but you're too infatuated to even see your own hand in front of your face." She pointed at Nadia, and her eyes danced back and forth between us. "Well, isn't that precious. You two are wearing the exact same dress, only in a different color. How convenient. I guess we have proof you're kindred spirits." She rolled her eyes and made a face. "Now, where was I? Oh, yes. Whatever you tell to them about our kind, about our world is frowned upon. The 'old one' would surely not be pleased, and neither would Volac, if you don't heed my warning to end this *thing* you have."

She was grating on my last nerve. She had no right to meddle in my business. It wasn't like I plastered on a billboard that we exist, and even if I did, humans wouldn't take it seriously. They were too caught up in their own lives to care. "Do you think I give a shit?"

"I know you don't," she answered, her words clipped. "But you should. Don't be a fucking moron, Ameerah!"

I released Nadia's hand and rose, almost toe-to-toe with Aosoth. The bitch didn't flinch or back away, which was fine with me. My temper flared. My hands balled into a fist. I didn't take kindly to people's demands as to what to do with my life or insulting my intelligence.

"Back off, Aosoth. Do I have to spell it out for you? It's. None. Of. Your. Damn. Business."

She glared, and a slow, plastic smile crossed her face. "Have it your way, then." She turned on her heel, and as she walked away, she glanced over her shoulder. "Don't say I didn't warn you."

I clenched my teeth and stared her down. I was fuming. She was going to be a problem, and if my hunch proved correct, I'd have to figure out a way to solve it. In our world, there were few rules we had to abide by. One of them was not to harm another dark spirit, unless you had approval from the "old one" or another elder. However, there was a way I could stop her, and I took comfort in knowing I had that option, if Volac agreed to it.

I felt an arm go around my waist, and I relaxed a little, feeling Nadia's warmth. She told me not to allow Aosoth to ruin our night. Slowly, Nadia's fingers moved up and down my hip bone. The satin fabric of the dress rubbed against my skin in a sensual manner. I'd planned on taking our relationship slow, but Aosoth pissed me off. Who the fuck was she to tell me who to date? So out of spite, I threw my original plan on the ground, stomped on it, and decided right then to give into my attraction toward Nadia.

"Do you want to come to my place and finish this night out?" I asked her.

She turned to me and fixed her eyes on mine, giving me a heated, devilish stare. She knew exactly what was on my mind. "I'd been hoping you'd ask me."

She made a move to kiss me, but I stopped her. "Wait until we get there." I scanned the area, wondering if Aosoth still lingered about. I really didn't give a shit if she did, but I knew if I were to kiss Nadia now, we'd end up doing more than makeout here in the park, and I didn't want that.

"C'mon." Nadia took my hand, and we crossed the grounds to the parking lot where our vehicles were. "I'll follow you," she said and pecked me on the cheek before stepping into her car.

Where I resided wasn't far away, and as soon as I got behind the wheel and pulled onto the highway, I couldn't stop fantasizing about her the whole way there. I wanted to please her like no one had ever done before, and the thought of my intentions caused a pulsating warmth between my legs. I glanced in the rearview. Her headlights shined in the mirror. What was she thinking at that moment? Was she fantasizing about me, as well? I knew she wanted me from the first day we met, and tonight I would finally be hers.

Ten minutes later, we entered the condo. After I closed and locked the door, I turned and found myself face-to-face with Nadia. Without hesitation, she cupped my cheeks in her hands and kissed me with a fierce passion that took my breath away. Gently, she pushed me against the door, deepening her kiss, her tongue dancing with mine. We were huffing in each other's mouths, making soft pleasurable sounds. Her fingers snaked beneath my dress and up my thigh. They found their way between my legs, her lips and tongue now making a trail down my neck. I released a soft moan when her fingers slipped inside me and moved back and forth in a slow pumping rhythm. I thrust my hips against the motion, and she quickened the pace.

"I want you," she breathed next to my ear.

I took her wrist and guided her to the bedroom down the hallway. I turned on the tableside light and undid the string around my waist. The dress slipped off and fell in a puddle on the floor. Nadia's eyes danced over the white lace lingerie I was wearing and trailed below to the garter belt and stockings. A hungry passion entered them, causing my body to warm. A throbbing tightness formed between my legs. She shed her dress from her gorgeous body. To my surprise and delight, she was completely naked. I pulled her down onto the bed and shifted on top of her. She grabbed my g-string, tugged it off, and placed her lips on mine, her tongue in my mouth. I rolled one of her nipples between my forefinger and thumb, and with the fingers of my other hand, I rubbed her clit in a slow circular motion. She broke our kiss and moaned, which I found incredibly sexy. I kissed her neck and collar bone, plunging my fingers inside her slick folds, pumping while I sucked on an erect nipple. Her breathing got heavier, and the more she moaned, the wetter I became. I kissed a path down her flat stomach and position myself between her legs while she rubbed her breast and softly moaned. As I moved my fingers in and out of her, I hooked the tips and pressed on her g-spot while I flicked my tongue against her clitoris. Her breaths came thick and fast.

"Don't stop, Ameerah. I'm going to come," she said.

I moved my tongue and fingers faster. The pleasing sounds she was making almost did me in. I was extremely wet and horny. Her moans grew louder. She arched her back, her breasts two gorgeous mounds in the air. She let out a sound between a moan and a scream, and her whole body shook, then tensed.

"Ameerah," she huffed. "No one has ever got me off like that before."

* * *

I halted my story, because Derek was shifting in his seat again. I could clearly see his erection straining against his trousers.

His eyebrows pulled together. "Why did you stop? I was rather enjoying your romp in the sack with Nadia."

"Yeah, I can see that," I said, staring pointedly at his crotch. "You're as hard as a rock,"

"I can't help it, love. Your story has excited my John Thomas." He smiled and winked.

"Do you want to take care of that? Maybe slap the ol' boy a couple times, as Aidan would say."

"No, carry on. I'll be fine." He stood, readjusted himself, and sat back down. "There. Much better." The left side of his face distorted, scrunching together his cheek and eye. "Maybe not." He rose again, did a little shimmy, and reseated himself with a heavy sigh of relief.

I laughed. "Are you good now?"

He took a sip of his whiskey and gave me a thumbs up.

"Where was I?"

"You were at the part where Nadia declared no one had ever got her off like you did."

I smiled at the memory. "Yes, well, let's just say I wasn't through pleasing her," I said with a teasing smile to see him squirm, which he did.

"You're wicked."

I laughed again, then got serious and fell back into my story.

* * *

Nadia and I discovered that night we were sexually compatible in every way. If I were to tell you our relationship wasn't based on sex, I'd be lying. It was its foundation, but during the weeks that followed, we grew attached to one another. When Nadia wasn't in class, at work, or in counseling, she was with me. We enjoyed each other's company. I taught her how to dance, and we laughed at how left footed she was, but eventually she learned. We went to clubs and danced. One night, we were at a club called City Lights that had an outdoor terrace used for a dance floor with strings of bulbs blinking above it. Nadia and I were among a group moving our bodies to "We Belong" by Pat Benatar, but it started to rain. The crowd took shelter beneath the awnings. Nadia and I threw our hands in the air, shook our hips, and continued to dance while we got soaked, our shirts clinging to our bodies. Afterward, we were met with applause and free drinks for the rest of the night. We gained new friends and always had a fantastic time when we were together. I couldn't remember the last time I smiled and laughed so much.

Two weeks into our relationship, I decided to tell her about how I grew up, what my parents were like, and their betrayal. I broke down in front of her, something I'd never done before with another person.

"Why didn't they love me?" I was curled up on my couch with my knees against my chest, my arms hugging them, sobbing. I hated how vulnerable I became and what a hot mess I was.

She pulled me into her arms and wiped the tears off my face. "It wasn't your fault your parents didn't care for you," she softly said. "They were self-centered assholes and got what they deserved." She cradled my face in her hands, and her eyes poured into mine. "You're a loveable person, Ameerah. I love you."

I realized then I was in love with her, and I asked her to move in with me that evening. She did.

The next day, we were lying in bed naked, facing each other, our feet rubbing together. The smell of bacon and eggs hung in the air from the breakfast I made earlier. I remember thinking how happy I was to have her there with me, but my heart twisted when Betty popped into my mind. This was what she and I could have had every day of our lives. We were so close to making it happen, until my parents ruined everything.

"I heard there's an ancient grimoire bound in human flesh with a spell to trap a dark spirit. Is the story true?" Nadia asked.

Her question alarmed me. How did she know about the highly coveted grimoire Volac had showed me years ago?

I propped myself on my elbow and looked at her. "Where did you hear this from?"

She smiled. "When I was into black magic, I conjured a spirit on the ouija board who told me about it, so I wondered if it was true."

For some reason, I decided to play dumb. Normally I would be honest with her, but something in my gut told me to guard this secret.

"Not that I know of. I think the spirit was toying with you."

She flopped on her back and stared at the ceiling, sighing. "Maybe." She fell silent, and I got the feeling she knew I wasn't being truthful with her. She seemed disappointed and a tad annoyed. She looked at me, her expression curious. "So what's your world like?"

"Dreary," I answered, "but comfortable. I have my own house there. We all do. I'm rather fond of it."

"No sun or bright blue skies?"

I shook my head. "Nope. It's more like living in a Grimm fairytale where the misfits reside."

She turned on her side and smiled. "You're not a misfit."

"Yeah, I am, but I'm okay with it," I said. "I'm not the only one, and I have good friends."

She sat up as if a brilliant idea struck her in that moment. "I want to meet them."

"Not a good idea," I said, shaking my head.

"Why not? Don't you think they'll like me?"

"You already know why," I told her, a bit surprised she asked a question she already knew the answer to. Or maybe she didn't. Maybe she thought not all dark spirits detested humans since obviously I didn't. That was probably it. "They wouldn't approve of our relationship, unless it were strictly a sexual thing."

She frowned, and the energy in the room grew thick and tense. She got out of bed, her gestures stiff and quick. I felt an invisible wall between us.

I sat up. "Don't be mad. You met Aosoth. You heard what she said, and you knew the answer to your question, so why ask me that?"

Nadia was already halfway dressed. It was like she couldn't get out of there fast enough. She slipped a white T-shirt over her head and yanked it down. "I know, Ameerah," she said. "I thought maybe you could put a good word in for me or something."

I laughed. I couldn't help it. Of course it pissed her off even more. "You make it sound like you're trying to get into a sorority. It's not like that."

"Bite me," she said and stormed out of the room.

"Wait!" I hopped out of bed and raced after her. This was our first fight as a couple, and I didn't want her to leave angry. I reached her before she opened the front door. "I'm sorry if I disappointed you, but you have to realize my world is different from yours. My peers would not approve of our relationship, and I don't want to cause problems. It's not that I'm ashamed of you. I want to protect what we have because it's so great. Do you understand?"

Her eyes roamed my naked body, and a teasing smile crossed her face. "I'll be back in an hour or two. I have a meeting with my counselor." She kissed me. It was soft and sweet at first, until she deepened it and brushed her fingers between my legs, causing me to hitch my breath and softly moan. She stepped back and winked. "I'll take care of you later."

She left, and that was the last time I ever saw her.

Chapter Thirty-Two

Fury

D erek stared, engrossed in my story. "What happened?"
I rubbed my temple. "Aosoth killed her."

"Blimey, Ameerah," he said, gaping at me. "How?"

I closed my eyes, took a couple deep breaths, and opened them. "Hit and run. Nadia was walking across the parking lot after her therapy session, when . . . when you know." I didn't want to go into detail about how the vehicle barreled into her from the side, reversed and drove over her body several times, crushing it.

"When Nadia didn't come home, I was worried. I called the theater where she worked. She wasn't scheduled to come in until the next day, but I knew some of her coworkers and thought one of them might have seen or heard from her. None of them had, so I waited. I'll never forget the haunted, hollow feeling in my gut, and a disturbing thought struck me. What if she was one of those people who walked away from a relationship without giving the other party the courtesy to at least say she was through? I knew she'd cut all ties with her mother without confronting her about why she no longer wanted to associate with her again. So with a heavy heart, I'd decided more than likely that was what she'd done. I went to bed, telling myself Nadia's clothes and possessions were in the condo. She'd have to eventually come by to collect them, and when she did, I'd try to work things out with her. I knew she was fragile when it came to relationships, due to her upbringing and all the shit she'd been through. I'd do the best I could to iron things smooth again; however, if she couldn't understand why I wouldn't allow her into my world, I'd be the one who would end our relationship.

"The next day at work, when I was in the break room getting a cup of coffee, my boss told me what happened to Nadia, and I was . . ."

"Gutted," Derek said.

I lit a ciggy and nodded, taking a drag. "Yes, completely. I had my appointments rescheduled for the following week, knowing my patients still had group therapy, and that all four of them were doing wonderfully in their treatment since I decided to possess this human."

"Did it help?"

"Did what help?"

"You helping humans with their problems."

I took another drag and blew out a lungful of smoke, sighing. "I don't know. I suppose. I felt good helping them because I thought they deserved it, but it didn't make me feel better about Elizabeth's situation or my own when I was human, like I was hoping this absurd experiment of mine would do. You see, my desperation to be free from the painful shackles of my human life blurred all reason and prompted me to take action with the humans." My throat thickened. Tears were welling. "Honestly," I said while getting a hanky out of my purse and dabbing my eyes. "Time doesn't heal all wounds. That's a bullshit saying. The wounds are still there. You learn to live with them and to recognize circumstances you find yourself in that cause them to bleed again. Betrayal triggers mine."

"How do you know it was Aosoth who killed her?"

"The bitch left me a note," I answered between clenched teeth, crushing my ciggy in the ashtray. "After I received the news about Nadia, I went home, broken. When I reached my door, I discovered a folded piece of paper taped to it. My heart leaped in my throat, because I thought maybe it was from Nadia. With shaky fingers, I yanked it from the door and stepped inside. I sat on the couch and took a couple deep breaths and opened it." My gaze fell to my fingers in my lap. I was twisting them, trying to maintain my composure. My feelings were all over the place: sadness, rage, annoyance. I chugged down the rest of my cocktail, hoping the alcohol would numb those sensations, grateful the human I was possessing knew how to hold her liquor.

"Don't leave me in anticipation, love. What did the letter say?" His knees were apart, and he was leaning forward with his forearms on them, hands clasped between his thighs.

"It said, 'You didn't heed my warning, so I solved the problem myself. Aosoth.'"

Derek shook his head in disgust, his eyes steady on mine. A pure hatred for Aosoth shone in them.

"I was livid," I said before he had a chance to respond. I had to get this part of my story out. It was crucial for him to know, so he could help me look for a way to get salvation without the help of a light walker. I dived back into my tale.

* * *

I hopped in my car, shoved a pair of sunglasses on my face, and drove to the desert. Through a stream of tears, I screamed, cursed, and pounded the steering wheel the whole way. Once I reached my destination, I stepped out of the vehicle, and though it wasn't quite summer yet, I immediately felt the dry heat on my skin and the bright sun on my face. I knew this place was brimming with dark energy, which would allow me to vacate the vessel I was in. I'd been to that particular spot many times throughout the years, and the familiarity of the reddish dirt, the scrub brushes, cactuses, and rocky terrain, was a welcome sight to behold.

The earth crunched beneath my ankle boots as I walked a few yards away from where I parked. My foot hit a large rock, and a lizard scurried away. Wiping the tears off my face, I traveled on. When I entered the hot spot, a tingling sensation fanned throughout my body. I raised my hands above my head, palms facing the cloudless blue sky, and envisioned Volac on the porch of the beach house the human he'd been occupying owned. I knew this, because I'd been his guest there many times, and he favored the place.

A whooshing noise echoed around me, my stomach flipped, then blackness. Within a matter of a couple seconds, a loud popping sound followed. I then found myself standing on the whitewashed, wooden porch in front of emptied wicker furniture. Half panicked, I turned and scanned the beach for any sign of him. There was nothing, except for the sounds of the waves crashing against the shore and seagulls calling to one another. Then something occurred to me. In my haste to locate him, I forgot I needed to find a human to possess in order to converse with him here, unless of course he was in his spiritual form. What a fucking idiot I was to have spaced this condition of communication! I was fit to be tied and went to my Victorian home in our realm to try to calm myself. A trove of emotionally exhausting feelings of despair, anger, hate, and heartache, assaulted me all at once. Hours later—or maybe a day; I wasn't too sure—Ava found me sitting on the corner of the couch, knees pressed against my chest, arms hugging my legs, my features hard, my gaze stone cold.

"What's wrong?" she asked, concern creasing her forehead. She sat beside me and placed a gentle hand on my arm. "Ameerah?"

I knew what she was thinking. My attempt to heal my wounds by counseling humans, in order to see my situation in a different light had failed. It had. Miserably. But she wasn't aware of the main reason, which was to free myself from the guilt concerning Elizabeth. Now, I not only had that weighing heavily on my heart but Nadia's death, as well.

"Aosoth killed Nadia," is all I said, my tone mechanical due to how numb I felt at that moment.

"Who's Nadia?"

"My girlfriend. My *human* girlfriend," I stressed, sweeping my eyes to meet hers.

I could see the surprise in them. I'd thrown her off guard, and I bristled inside knowing once what I said sank in, her sympathetic demeanor would be replaced with disgust and disapproval. I was ready for it. Prepared to pounce on her, to tell her to fuck off, to get the hell out of my house, and to never come back. But she didn't.

"I wasn't aware," she softly said and sighed. "You know how I feel about humans." She rubbed her forehead, like she would if she had a headache and needed to ease the pain. Then, she spoke again with careful words in a low voice, "I understand the heart does funny things and doesn't give us a choice about whom to fall in love with. A human though, is unacceptable in our world. If word had gotten out you were emotionally involved with one, someone else would have murdered Nadia, and you'd have been punished in some form or another."

"You're taking Aosoth's side?" I glared at her, but the empathy I saw in her face prevented me from being angry. Although she disapproved of my relationship with a human, she felt bad for me.

"Not at all," she quickly said. "Aosoth is a psychopathic bitch, but like I said, if she wouldn't have done it, another dark spirit would have and would probably rat on you, which she hasn't, right?"

"As far as I know." I hopped to my feet and swung around, facing Ava, my anger boiling again. I could feel the heat rising to my face. "I don't give a flying fuck if she did or not, the bitch is going to pay for what she did!"

"You're not thinking clearly," Ava said. "Haven't you listened to what I said? Nadia would have eventually been bumped off anyway, and if you harm Aosoth over this, the result will be a double whammy for you. You might even get sentenced to The Sheol of Glass. Do you want to risk it? Really?"

A lump formed in my throat. "It was my fault Nadia died," I choked out. "If I would have never got involved with her, she'd still be alive."

Ava didn't say anything, only stared at me. What could she say? I was right, and she was a good enough friend not to drive the blade deeper into my heart by outwardly agreeing with me.

At once, everything came crashing down on me. My legs turned to

Jell-O and gave out. I slumped to the floor and sobbed in my hands. I was a piece of shit. I should have known this would have happened. Aosoth warned me, but my hatred for her and my stubbornness got in the way. I still despised her with every inch of my being and made a silent vow that one day she would pay. Somehow, some way, I'd make sure of it. But at that moment, my contempt for her was overshadowed by guilt.

Ava pulled me into her arms, and I clung to her like a weeping child who lost her best friend in an accident she could have prevented. I remembered at the same time feeling relief for not telling Volac about Nadia and demanding to use the grimoire he kept hidden away. I wanted to perform a deadfall spell on Aosoth—to trap and torture her. That was my original plan, which I now knew, thanks to Ava, would have backfired on me.

"Don't be too hard on yourself," Ava finally told me when I calmed down. "Why would you take Aosoth seriously when she warned you? You didn't know the consequences of your actions. I'm sure if you did, you would have ended your relationship with Nadia."

"I knew that every one of you would have disapproved, though," I said bitterly.

"Yes, but you didn't know in the end one of us would have killed her and your involvement with Nadia could have possibly cost your freedom."

She was right, I didn't know, but I still felt like shit. Nadia was dead because of my ignorance. I made a huge fucking mistake, something I could never change, and I had to live with that burden for the rest of my existence–

Until now.

Chapter Thirty-Three

Derek's Help

"Until now," Derek echoed mindlessly, staring at me with a blank look on his face. "What do you mean?"

"Nadia is in the lower world in a confused state of existence," I answered.

"And how do you know this?"

"Paige Reed performed a spell for me," I replied. "I wanted to see if I was forgiven for my sins and to contact Nadia, so I could crossover and be with her. After Paige cast the spell, I heard Nadia calling my name, then a light walker entered the room through a portal that had materialized on the wall."

"Bloody hell, Ameerah," Derek said, shaking his head in disbelief. "One day your antics are going to get you in loads of trouble. Paige Reed is an immortal, who—"

"Who got rid of Aosoth," I said, grinning. "Now the bitch is imprisoned in a different part of the lower world."

"Yes, I've heard about it. It's brilliant, except for one thing."

"What?"

He frowned. "There's a possibility she can escape."

"I know," I said, "but I don't care, because if she does, hopefully I'll have my salvation and be with Nadia in Summerland or a place like it."

His eyes were locked on mine, and he slowly shook his head.

"Why are you looking at me like that?"

He let out an exasperated sigh. "I adore you, Ameerah. You know that, right?"

My heart pounded. The sudden fear of him not helping me twisted my stomach. All I could do was nod.

"You've made a mess of things with your daft decisions, and I don't know if I can help you clean them up." He counted a few of the items on the tips of his fingers. "You had a love affair with a human, you're friends with immortals, and you pissed off Volac because of it."

"I'm only asking for your assistance," I said in a raised voice, "if you *think*, I'll be forgiven and will be able to crossover and help Nadia."

"Nobody can give you salvation," he told me, frustrated. "Only *you* can."

I ground my teeth. "I've tried," I said between tight lips. "I told you my whole damned story, hoping if I released everything that's been bottled inside me, I'd forgive myself, but I don't. In fact, truthfully, I feel worse now." I rose and stood in front of him, jabbing my chest with my fingertip. "Nadia is dead because of me. *Me!*" I exploded into tears, loathing myself even more for breaking down in front of him. I clapped a hand over my mouth and turned away. "My parents never loved me," I choked out. "They betrayed me and had me wrongfully committed to an insane asylum where I was mistreated and murdered. I lost Betty and the opportunity to build a marvelous life with her. I tried to save Elizabeth but failed. My revenge on my parents only gave me a sense of satisfaction and justice, but it didn't heal the wounds they inflicted. Decades later, I met Nadia, fell in love with her, and . . . " I couldn't talk anymore. The tears were flowing, and my voice kept cracking.

"Ameerah," Derek said, his voice soft and empathic. I felt a warm hand on my shoulder. I turned, and he embraced me. I clung to him and silently cried. "There. There." He rubbed my back in slow, soothing circles. "I think I can help you, but you have to listen to me and set aside your ego and stubbornness."

I pulled back, and he wiped the tears off my cheeks and kissed my forehead, then guided me to the couch. I had no idea what he was going to say, but I was all ears. I'd known Derek for a long time. Aidan had introduced us when we were at a club one night, and Derek and I became fast friends. Some of the things I told him tonight he already knew, like me being a lesbian and having visions when I was human, burning Chester the molester alive, and once being part of Volac's league, but other than those things, he didn't know much else. But now that I'd opened my wounds to him and caused them to bleed in his presence, I was both curious and nervous about what he had to say. We sat, and I folded my hands in my lap, looking at him through sore, watery eyes.

"I told you earlier I saw a pattern in your behavior," he began. "What I meant was you don't think things through. You allow your emotions concerning your past to enslave you, which causes you to make daft decisions and in the end does you more harm than good. There's no doubt in my mind your parents were dodgy humans, and I for one commend you on your successful plan to hand their arses over on a platter. However, their lack of the capability to truly love you unconditionally shouldn't diminish your own self-worth and love." He leveled his eyes with mine. "I believe these things I'm telling you now were told to you in the past by Volac and your friends."

I nodded. "They did, but–"

He raised his eyebrows, sending me a I'm-not-done-yet look. "Ego, Ameerah," he said and continued when I smashed my lips together. "I believe Betty was your true love because what you had with her was before your parents betrayed you. You loved yourself, your life, and the promise of a bright future with her. Decades later, you attempted to recreate what you and Betty had with Nadia, and when Aosoth killed her, taking away yet another love of your life, as soon as the opportunity presented itself, you became friends with our enemies and betrayed Volac, all because you wanted revenge on Aosoth. Not good, love." He slowly shook his head in disapproval. "You want salvation?"

"You know I do," I mumbled. Why would he ask me that? He knew the damned answer.

"Then, stop living in the past. Recognize you're not responsible for other people's behaviors. Stop blaming yourself for Elizabeth's and Nadia's demise. In addition, I suggest you try to clear the air with Volac and ask for his forgiveness, as well as disconnect yourself from your new immortal friends."

I dropped my gaze to my lap, twisting my fingers in them. I hated to admit it, but he was right. However, I didn't think I could mend my relationship with Volac, and it might take a while for me to let go of the past. My shoulders sagged. How could I save Nadia if I couldn't even save myself? I was a lost soul and didn't know what I wanted except to rescue Nadia and be with her.

"You said your mother named you Ameerah because it means princess?" Derek asked, breaking the brief silence between us.

"Yes, she did," I answered, wondering why he'd bring that up.

He placed his hands on my shoulders and fixed his eyes on mine. "You're not a princess, Ameerah. You're a *fucking* queen. Start acting like one."

I jerked my head back, startled by how forceful his tone of voice was. "Okay, but it might take me a while to overcome all my issues."

"Bullshit!" he said, rising to his feet. The energy in the room suddenly grew tense and heavy with his anger, causing my pulse to race. I'd never seen him like this. "You've had ninety *fucking* years to overcome your issues. You start now, because if you don't, I'm walking out"—He pointed to the door—"and you can forget about my help." He took a couple deep breaths, and I watched as his expression softened. "I don't want to find out that you were sent to The Sheol of Glass, and if you keep fucking up, love, that's where the elders will send you."

My heart dropped, and my stomach churned uneasily.

I'd never thought about that before. Well, actually, I had, but I was too caught up in my schemes and emotions to allow the reality to sink in that I could be sentenced to The Sheol of Glass for betraying my people.

Shit.

I closed my eyes and rubbed my temples against the dull ache in my head. "I don't want that," I said barely above a whisper, but I knew he heard me, because he sat beside me and placed his hand on my knee. I opened my eyes and stared into his. The hardness in his face cracked when he saw the crushing realization in mine that I needed to buck up or else I'd be toast. "I'm not going to lie," I said. "I don't know if I can salvage what Volac and I once had, but I'll try."

"Exactly what I want to hear, love." He squeezed my knee and smiled.

"You're not the only one who has told me this stuff," I said. "So obviously it's true." I paused before continuing. "I'm the only one who can grant myself salvation, correct?" I knew the answer, but I had to hear it spoken aloud one more time. Just once more.

He nodded. "Yes, love, if you can't accomplish it on your own, the light walkers will help you by having you go through a rehabilitation process in a realm specifically designed for that purpose."

I bristled. There was no way I was going to go through that. I didn't care if it wasn't like Bandbridge or not. Hell, no.

My body stiffened. "Well, you can forget that shit. I won't do it, which means I'm going to have to forgive myself and take to heart everything you and my friends have told me in order to reach salvation." I slumped against the couch and heaved a heavy sigh. "I can do it, but it's going to take time." I covered my face and rubbed my temples again. The dull pain was sharp now. I hated this part of possessing a human—we felt the body's pain. "How in the hell am I going to save Nadia? If I can do that, I believe all the other bullshit I'd been harboring can be easily dealt with, because this . . . this is what's been eating at me the most throughout the years."

Derek was studying me, mulling something over. I could tell by the contemplative expression on his face. "If you had the opportunity to rescue Nadia from her stupor but couldn't be with her straight away, would you still—"

"You're damned right I would," I said, not giving him a chance to finish. "Nadia is there because of my ignorance. If I can help her, and she crosses over without me, so be it. I honestly think, though, she'll want to be with me, because she loves me. Regardless, the truth is this rescue mission is about me wanting to correct the horrible mistake I made, but most importantly, it's about her. If I were in her shoes, I wouldn't want to be living an existence where I was in a state of confusion, would you?"

"No, love," he said, shaking his head, looking past me, deep in thought.

He appeared to be debating something, and a sudden fear that he might not help me caused me to take one more swing at convincing him to do so. "I don't know what's running through your mind, but perhaps if I recount to you what happened the other night at Nathan's house, it might persuade you to assist me, if you're capable to do so, that is."

"Very well, love," he said with a ghost of a smile. "Tell away."

Once again, my pulse raced. Derek was acting odd, and I had no clue why, so I dove into what happened the other night at Nathan Caswell's house:

* * *

I was with Paige at Nathan's lovely A-frame house deep in the woods. The inside was quite striking in a rustic, homey decor. We were in his living room when Paige performed the spell to reach Nadia. Nathan and I sat on the couch, watching her as she threw her hands above her head, palms facing skyward, her beautiful dark red hair hanging behind her.

"In love and pure light, I call forth Nadia to join us here," she said in a strong and commanding voice. "Ameerah would like to visit with you."

The lights flickered and dimmed.

"Ameerah, where are you? I can't find you," a faint, teary voice called in desperation.

My heart jumped to my throat, and I shot to my feet. "I'm here, sweetie." My eyes swept the room, searching for Nadia.

"Ameerah, where are you? I can't find you." The voice repeated in the same tone.

"Nadia. Can you hear me?" I hollered, suddenly panicked because she sounded lost and helpless, all because of me. I looked at Paige. "Help me," I pleaded.

I could see the sympathy in her dark green eyes. Yes, she was immortal, and we were supposed to be enemies, but because of our hatred toward Aosoth we became friends.

She nodded and threw her hands above her head again. "In love and pure light, I call forth Nadia. If you can hear me, Ameerah is anxious to reunite with you."

"Ameerah, where are you? I can't find you," Nadia said once again, but this time her voice was louder and echoed throughout the house.

I paced the room, because I didn't know what else to do. My heart was pounding and breaking at the same time. I tilted my face up and raised my voice, "Nadia, can you hear me?"

Silence.

Panic and frustration gripped me. My heart squeezed, and my chest tightened. I dropped my face into my hands and quietly sobbed. A sudden flash of anger went through me when I thought about Nadia being like this for years. Why? She didn't deserve it. I screamed in my hands, the sound high-pitched, muffled. Furious, I dropped my hands and balled them into fists. Shaking them in the air, I yelled, "Why? Why are you doing this to us? I'm changing my ways. I'm doing the best I can, yet you're still punishing us. Don't you have any mercy or compassion?"

"Ameerah," Paige said.

I shifted my blazing eyes to her. "They're a bunch of assholes," I hissed.

"'You don't mean what you're saying," Nathan said, concern etching his handsome face.

I spun, facing him. "You're damned right I mean it." I spat the words between clenched teeth.

"Ameerah," Paige said again, pointing to her left a few feet away from the fireplace. She moved to the couch where Nathan sat, and I followed.

There was a small wave in the air, like what you'd see coming off a hot asphalt road. A bright blue light appeared in the center and expanded into several rings. The center formed into a coned shape that narrowed inward and widened into a breathtaking scene of a vast gorgeous meadow surrounded by enormous mountains lined in a circular pattern beneath a pale lavender sky. They were covered in lush thick bright green grass and tall trees. The waterfalls cascading from them had prisms of colors dancing along the front. I wondered if this was Summerland, and a deep longing to be there with Nadia tugged at my heartstrings. A tall figure appeared in the meadow–a glowing silhouette strolling toward us, as if he were enjoying a nice summer's day and had no worries.

"'Who is it?" I whispered.

"'I don't know," Paige said, staring in the same direction.

Nathan rose. "We're about to find out."

As he approached, details of this fella's appearance came into focus. He reminded me of a young Bob Dylan with the shaggy brown hair, sideburns, a long nose, and deep blue eyes. His white shirt was unbuttoned enough to reveal a hairless, well-defined chest, and the bottom hem appeared shoved into his blue jeans, making me wonder if he'd been too distracted to properly tuck it in.

"'You know who he looks like?" I asked, glancing at Paige and Nathan.

"'I was thinking of Bob Dylan in the early 'sixties," Nathan said.

I nodded. "I always thought he was adorable."

"I think he's a light walker," Paige mused.

"You're correct," the Dylan lookalike said, entering the room. He had a quiet, gentle demeanor that poured into our space, and his face seemed to glow.

"Where's Nadia? Why can't she hear me?" I demanded, not giving a shit he was a light walker. Despite how his aura made me feel, I had no respect for him. Period.

"She's in the lower world," he answered. "She's in the part where shell shocked souls reside."

I stared at him, dumbfounded. At first I wasn't sure if I heard him correctly.

"What does that mean?" Paige asked.

"Sometimes spirits become confused when they have no recollection of their death and have a strong attachment to earth or to somebody who still dwells on this plane," he said with a note of sadness. "These souls remain there until we can snap them out of their stupor and help them crossover."

"Nadia," I croaked, feeling the color draining from my face.

"We've tried reaching her to no avail," he said. "But take comfort in knowing we never give up. One day—"

"Take comfort?" I said in a raised voice. "How can I take comfort in knowing my girlfriend is aimlessly wandering, trapped in a vicious cycle of confusion, repeatedly calling my name, and looking for me?"

"I understand your grievances, which you have every right to," he calmly said. "But these heartbreaking situations are a drop in a bucket compared to what lies ahead once the veil is lifted from them."

"How can you be so callous?" I seethed.

"I'm not," the light walker answered, still calm. I wanted to slap him. "I understand why these spirits are going through it, and though it pains me to see, I know the end result. I've experienced it myself and can assure you this blemish on these souls will pass."

"Ameerah can help Nadia snap out of it," Paige said.

"Yes, I can. I *know* I can." I took a step forward but stopped when he shook his head. "What? You don't agree? Because if you don't that's a bunch of bullshit."

He looked at me with such compassion and understanding that I thought maybe he had a sudden change of heart and would take me to Nadia.

"It has been determined," he said, "that yes, your presence would crack through Nadia's confused state and bring her to her senses." He paused, but when I opened my mouth, the bastard continued. "However, you still have unresolved issues which need to be addressed and dealt with before you have the capability to assist her."

I couldn't believe what he just said. The blood in my veins ran cold. "But-but I turned my back on the dark ways. Am I not forgiven?"

"The only forgiveness you need to seek is your own," he told me, "and you're not there yet, but I'm here to guide and aid you."

I crossed my arms. "So what you're telling me is until I learn to forgive myself and overcome my *issues*"—I made air quotes—"I can't help Nadia?"

He nodded. "Correct."

I glared at him. "And how do you propose I do this?"

"Rehabilitation," he simply said.

"Oh, hell, no." I stuck my hand out in a halting gesture. "I went through that bullshit when I was human, because my parents double-crossed me."

"This is different. You go through a—"

I pointed past him. "Fuck that. I'll deal with it on my own and then go to Nadia myself. I'm sure Paige can help me."

"There is only one way to get to the lower world without being propelled there. Paige doesn't have access to it; only a higher being can," he said.

"Well, I'll find a way," I half-shouted, hot around the collar. "You're unbelievable. You people should know the hell I went through when I was human, yet you want me to relive it?"

Paige faced me. "He doesn't. If you'll give him a chance to explain how it works, I'm sure you'll see it'll be nothing like what you went through." She took my hand and sandwiched it between hers. "Please, he's trying to help. Please, let go of your anger and listen to him. He's not attacking you. He's on your side."

Despair replaced my anger. My bottom lip shook. Tears sprang to my eyes. If he was truly trying to help he would take into consideration my situation and would help me in a more suitable fashion. But it was his way or no way. Fucking prick.

"I can't do it," I whispered to Paige.

Paige turned to the light walker. I could see the desperation in her face. "Can I go with her if she agrees to it?"

I was surprised she asked that, and my heart warmed at the fact she would stick her neck out to help me. I glanced at Nathan. He was looking at Paige, his eyes wide with shock. He hadn't expected her bold move either, and I wondered if he would try to stop her if the light walker would allow her to accompany me.

"Unfortunately, you cannot," he said. "She needs to do this on her own."

A weird choking sound issued from my throat. I could feel the walls closing in on me, and tears pushed their way out of my eyes. I pulled Paige into a quick hug. "I gotta go. I'll keep in touch." A sob escaped my lips. I released Paige and looked at Nathan. "Thank you, Nathan. You're a good friend, as well. I'll see ya around." I crossed the room and swiped the keys to the jeep off the table next to the front door and left. End of story.

* * *

Derek's face darkened, and for a second I thought he was sore at me for admitting how close I was to Paige and Nathan. I stood and turned my back on him, prepared to hightail it out of there.

This was a mistake.

Another big fucking mistake.

I should have never poured my heart out to him, but I loved Derek. He was my friend, and I trusted him with my life. Now our friendship was ruined. Tears spilled down my cheeks.

"The light walker could have helped you," he said, his voice laced with rage.

"What?" I turned, wiping the tears off my face and cleared my throat. "How do you know?"

He stood, his features cast in annoyance. "I know the wanker. His name is John. He bloody well could have allowed you to confront Nadia, to see if you could reach her, and leave you be, but the bastard didn't."

I blinked at him, stunned. "How . . . how do you know him?"

He closed his eyes and took a deep, disturbing breath. He was struggling with something that I didn't understand. Then, he looked at me. "Because, love, I'm a bloody light walker."

Chapter Thirty-Four

Derek's Secret

I rolled my eyes and almost laughed. "A light walker? Right," I said, snatching my purse off the chair. How could he joke at a time like this? I didn't know what his problem was. Something was eating at him, but to blatantly make up a bullshit lie for reasons I had no idea why convinced me telling Derek my story and asking for his help was another hairbrained idea of mine. I was done. I crossed the room, heading toward the door, wanting to get the hell out of there. "I don't know what sort of game you're playing, but–"

"It's true, Ameerah." His voice was firm, halting me.

I turned and crossed my arms. "I've known you for a long time, Derek. You're no damned light walker. You're a dark spirit."

"I'm a light walker who turned dark," he answered, his blue eyes lit with defiance and purpose. "I grew tired of assisting humans I felt didn't deserve my help, but it was expected of me, along with other things I found insufferable. I also longed to smell the rain, to taste food, drink fine spirits, and to feel sexual pleasure once again. My experiences with those things were only memories, yet when I would aid and guide humans on earth and encounter those things through observation, I became envious of them. I didn't want to reincarnate again. I wanted to be autonomous."

"So you became a dark spirit?" I guessed.

He took his fedora off, scratched his head, and stuck his hat back on.

"Do you know what it takes to be a light walker?"

I shook my head. "Not really." I still couldn't grasp he was what humans called an angel, and I knew I'd have to see proof in order for my mind to accept it.

"Before you can become one," he explained, "you have to reincarnate countless times in order to gain the experience and understanding you'll need to become a higher being. I've been through unimaginable things, but it was an absolute requirement for me to do so. How could I bring comfort to a human who was brutally murdered if I hadn't experienced the same thing?"

My lips twisted to the side as I thought about it. "Makes sense."

"Anyway," he said, suddenly appearing anxious, "let's say I went through the trenches in order to become a light walker. Once I proved my worth and became one, I realized it wasn't for me. Instead I found I shared the same common beliefs as the dark spirits, so I became one."

"How come you never told me, and no one knows about it?" I demanded, perturbed he'd kept this from me.

He rubbed the spot between his eyes and sighed. "The elders know, love, but no one else . . . well, except for you now . . . I'd appreciate it if you kept this information to yourself. As for not sharing my secret with you years ago . . . this part of my existence is something I don't particularly care to revisit. As you said earlier tonight, I'm straddling the line between Heaven and Hell, and no one needs to know."

"Your secret is safe with me," I promised, then an exciting thought entered my mind. "Wait a minute. Have you ever experienced what Nadia's going through?"

A shadow crossed his face, and his eyes tightened. "I have, and it was bloody dreadful, like being woken from a dream, and you have no idea what day or time it is. You're in a constant state of disorientation and confusion."

I cringed, imagining Nadia like that now. Right now. "What brought you out of it?" I asked, my words fast and panicky due to the next question I needed to ask.

"I did," he replied with a faint smile. "While I was aimlessly wandering in the lower world, I tripped in a hole and somehow jarred myself out of it."

"Since you're a light walker . . . or was," I said, "do you have access to the lower world? Can you take me to Nadia so I can help her?" I crossed my fingers behind my back, something I hadn't done since childhood. I may not be able to save myself, but if I could help her, overcoming my issues would be gravy. Besides, Nadia would want to be with me. She was fascinated with my kind and would no doubt become one of us. We'd have a grand time, and I'd teach her how to excel as a dark spirit.

"John, the bloody bastard, could have granted your request," he seethed, his jaw muscles twitching. "His refusal is a prime example of why I chose this path instead."

My face fell along with my heart. He couldn't help me. Therefore, I'd have to figure out another way to reach Nadia or accept the fact that I'd never see her again.

"Why the long face, love?"

I stared at my feet, silently planning on leaving and calling it a night after I answered his question. I'd go back to this human's house, leave her body, and return to my place. "I thought since you were a higher being, you might be able to take me to Nadia, but you're no longer one, so thank–"

"I'm still one, and you bet your sweet arse I'm going to take you to her," he said.

I looked up to a mischievous grin on his face. "Really?" I was almost afraid to believe him, but my heart was pounding something fierce from the sudden jolt of excitement.

He nodded. "You're damn right."

If I were the type of gal who squealed whenever she got excited, this would be the moment for it. But I wasn't that type. Instead, I threw my arms around his shoulders and thanked him repeatedly, telling him I'd owe him one. Big time.

"Once a light walker, always a light walker," he said next to my ear.

He took a small step back and held me at arm's length. "There are some things off limits to me, but the lower world is not one of them."

"How are we going to find her?" I asked, more than anxious to leave but a bit worried all the same. "I imagine there are countless spirits there who are dazed and confused."

"There are," he agreed. "But you've told me enough about Nadia so I'll be able to take us to her straightaway."

"Oh, my God. I can't believe this." I hugged him again, grinning like a silly fool. "Can we go now?"

"Sure, love, but let's park ourselves on the couch in case these humans wake up before we return . . . or I come back." He pulled his cell phone out of the pocket of his trousers and texted.

"Who are you texting?"

"Jared."

"The fella who is manning the bar?"

He nodded without looking up, fingers moving across the small screen. "I'm telling him you and I are vacating these vessels for a short time and to keep an eye on them. If they happen to rouse themselves before I return, Jared will keep them occupied." He sent the text, and we sat on the couch.

"I think you'll like Nadia when you meet her, and she becomes one of us," I mindlessly chatted while we waited for Jared's response. "Like me, she still has family issues she'll need to resolve, so we can help each other overcome them. We don't need to go to no damned rehabilitation realm. Besides, I think I'm almost over mine. Talking with you helped me a lot." I was rambling, I realized, but for some reason, I was a nervous wreck.

His cell phone made a ding sound, and he looked at it. "We're all set." He smiled and offered me his hand. "Are you ready to save your girlfriend?"

"Hell, yeah," I answered, returning his smile, slipping my hand into his.

Chapter Thirty-Five

Curve Ball

A cold, confining darkness engulfed me. My stomach dropped as if I were being lowered deep into the earth. I could hear names being shouted and pleas for help:

"Michael . . . Michael . . . Michael."

"Hank, the house is on fire! Hank, the house is on fire!"

"I want my mom. I want to go home. Please help me. I want my mom. *Mommy*."

Within a span of several seconds, we arrived at our destination. My eyes were drawn upwards to the purplish-gray sky fused with a brilliant red hue that rippled continuously across it. We stood beneath a huge weeping willow tree in an open dry field surrounded by spirits. Aimlessly, they wandered the barren landscape. Some were in their pajamas while others wore fancy to regular clothes. I could guess which era they passed from their attire. There were also men in military uniforms who obviously died in battle. I stood rooted to my spot, mesmerized by this heart-wrenching yet captivating scene, and I found myself trying to guess how each one of those spirits died.

I pointed to a woman who appeared to be in her early twenties. She wore a white bonnet and a long dark green dress. "See her? Look at all of them. This is heartbreaking." Like the rest of her peers, the poor lady appeared lost, searching, turning in circles. She'd walk for a stretch before repeating the same routine. What a nightmare.

"Yes, it's bloody horrible," Derek answered, his tone colored with remembrance.

I scanned the crowd, hoping to find Nadia. When I didn't, I panicked. "I don't see Nadia. Where is she?"

Derek hitched his thumb over his shoulder. "She's that way."

I turned, and there were countless people meandering zombie-like in the same direction, as well. My eyes caught a beautiful woman with long, flowing blonde hair, radiating a golden glow about ten inches from her body. A light walker, I presumed. She stood in front of a young dark-haired lady in a nightgown. They were animatedly talking. The young lady nodded. The golden glow expanded, encompassing them. They both smiled, and in a flash, they were gone.

Derek was staring off in that direction, his expression unreadable. "You used to do the same thing, right?" We followed toward the dark, rocky mountains. The temperature was a bit chilly but not enough to raise goosebumps.

"Yes, among other things," he answered. "What you saw will eventually happen to everyone here, but why prolong this wretched state they're in, if you can break through it much quicker."

I could hear the annoyance in his voice at the last part of his statement. He was still stewing over John, the light walker, not taking me to Nadia. I felt the same way. If he would have granted me my request, it would have saved me a lot of trouble.

"I agree, and I can see why you became dissatisfied with being one of them. I'm sure you had to follow the golden"—I made air quotes—"rules, and you had someone to answer to."

He gave me a sidelong glance. "We dark spirits also have rules to abide by, but they're only a few, not like with this lot." He made a sweeping gesture toward the light walkers who were either talking to those spirits or lingering nearby. There must have been a hundred or more. "Those some call angels have a superior who is the head of the counsel which consists of peers and beings higher than us. The head honcho gets voted in. Most of it is rubbish. Some makes sense. Regardless, though, I'm a square peg who thought he could fit in a round hole."

To my right, a few yards ahead, I noticed a middle-aged fella in army fatigues standing beneath a black gnarled tree. He was talking to a male light walker. They appeared engrossed in conversation, and I wondered what they were discussing. Maybe he still didn't believe his human body was dead, or maybe he'd accepted it but didn't want to cross over until his questions were answered. There were a million things they could be talking about, but those two were probably the most likely ones, I thought.

"Do you know what's wrong with the fella over there?" I jerked my head in the direction of the pair.

"He's . . . confused," Derek answered slowly, like he was speaking to a simpleton.

"Smart ass," I said, elbowing him in the side, making him smile. "What I mean is, do you know how he died?"

"Yes." He nodded. "He was shot in the head in the jungles of Vietnam during the war. The impact happened so quickly that his spiritual transition warped, which resulted in this state of confusion. But not everyone who has been shot or died tragically comes here. It all depends upon the spirit," he added.

"How do you know what he died from?"

Derek flashed me a bitter smile. "We gain instant information on a spirit in this realm. All we have to do is focus, and we know an individual's history. It's quite remarkable, actually."

I stared at the fella. For some reason, he captured my attention, much like when you channeled surf and paused in the middle of a scene in a movie because something in it made you curious. It appeared the fella came out of his stupor, but his shoulders were slouched forward, his head hung low. The light walker placed his hand on the fella's shoulder, telling him something. His radiance surrounded them.

"There she is." Derek pointed to the left, his expression turning to disgust. "Oh, goody. John is there, too," he said sarcastically.

I gasped. "Where?" I scanned the area he was indicating and saw John with Nadia. She was wearing the same clothes she had on the last time I saw her—jeans and a white T-shirt—and she appeared coherent.

She was awake!

John must have brought her out of her stupor.

Holy shit!

My heart warmed at the sight of her and moisture collected in my eyes. The next thing I knew, I was running, calling her name.

Surprise entered her clear brown eyes. "Ameerah?"

"The one and only." I threw my arms around her, laughing and crying at the same time.

"I can't believe you're here," she said. I could hear the smile in her voice. She pulled back, and her eyes danced across my face. "It is you. Wow. John was just telling me how much time I lost."

I looked at John who was frowning at me. "What? You don't approve? Well, too damn bad."

"You shouldn't have done this, Derek," John said to him when he joined us, ignoring my snide comments. "I had this handled."

Derek rolled his eyes. "You bloody well could have taken Ameerah here from the start, when you realized how difficult it would be to bring Nadia back to her present state of mind."

I'd never thought about that before, but he was right. If John would have approached me after Nadia passed away, I would have jumped at the chance to help her. I opened my mouth to give him a piece of my mind, but he spoke first, so I resorted to glaring instead.

The frown was still on his face. "Ameerah has issues of her own to deal with. If I'd brought her here, the situation could have turned disastrous."

Nadia released her arms from me and stepped back. At the same time, I let out a mocking laugh. "Bullshit. I know I can't cross over right now. I know what I have to do to reach salvation. But most importantly, I know we could have prevented Nadia from being in a perpetual state of confusion for as long as she has been . . . if you would have asked for my help that is."

"I'm sorry, Ameerah." John's voice was soft and careful, "but it's against our principles to take action in such a manner."

"Fuck your principles," Derek piped. "Not every situation is the bloody same, and sometimes you have to take risks."

"It was awful," Nadia admitted, rubbing the corner of her eye.

I took her hand in mine and lightly squeezed it. "Derek already explained the experience to me," I told her. "But it's over now, and we're together."

I felt her stiffen, and she released my hand. An immediate, invisible wall erected between us. Now, I was the one confused, and I could feel it plastered on my face.

"I'm going to crossover, Ameerah," she said without feeling.

I gawked at her, stunned, but then I reminded myself that I knew there was a possibility of this happening. No big deal. This turn of events would only motivate me more to do what I had to do so we could be together.

I shrugged. "Okay. I only thought because you were fascinated by us, you'd want to become one, and we could be together."

She shifted her weight uneasily and pursed her lips. Her eyes darted to John, reminding me of Mother doing the same thing to my father when she sought his approval.

Annoyed, I stepped in the way so Nadia couldn't look at him. "Spit out what's on your mind, and don't insult me by giving John the power to answer for you."

"She needs to know the truth, Nadia," he said.

Nadia fixed her eyes on mine. "I used you, Ameerah."

I took a couple steps back, feeling as if she kicked me in the gut. "What?" I was dumbfounded. I shook my head. "No, wait. Our chemistry. All the fun times we had. The night you told me you loved me. It was real . . . all of it was real."

Derek moved beside me and crossed his arms. "I had a feeling your behavior was a bit dodgy when Ameerah told me about you."

"Ameerah," Nadia said, "Our sexual chemistry was real. Amazing even. I also had a blast with you, and I did love you, but I was never *in* love with you."

She did love me. Past tense. She was never *in* love with me.

My god, I'd been a complete and utter fool.

"I told you I knew about the dark spirits," she went on. "What you didn't know was my complete fascination with your kind and world. I thought . . ."

I put my hands on my hips and narrowed my eyes, trying not to focus on the fact that she shattered my heart, and I wanted to curl into a ball and sob. Instead, I swallowed the lump in my throat and allowed my anger to step forward. "You thought *what?*"

She looked away before answering me. There was no hint of apology or remorse in her expression. In fact, she appeared rather indifferent on the matter, which gutted me even more, but I'd be damned if I were going to give her the satisfaction of knowing it.

"I thought eventually," she said, "you'd open up to me about the magic in your world. I was still heavily into black magic, even after the immortal had cast one of you out of me. But now that I had the mark you saw on my neck to protect me from ever being possessed again, and the ability to see the laser beam of light flash across the iris whenever a dark spirit possessed a human, I could use those two things to get what I wanted."

I recalled the last time we were together in bed, when she asked me about the grimoire. I had played dumb and told her the spirit she'd spoken to through the ouija board was toying with her. Afterward, I had the feeling I upset her, that she knew I wasn't being truthful with her.

"The grimoire," I said. "You wanted it."

She nodded. "I had a feeling you were lying to me when I asked you about it, but I wasn't too sure, so I'd have to continue spying on you and earn more of your trust."

I blinked and shook my head in disbelief. "What? Spying on me?"

"Did you honestly think it was a coincidence we wore the same dress on our first date?" she asked, sounding bored.

My thoughts spun on everything she'd told me thus far. Then, the crushing realization sank in that Aosoth was right. I was a fucking moron. My entire form became numb, and I stumbled into Derek. He slung his arm around my shoulders and held me close.

"How could you do this to me?" I asked, hearing the tears in my voice I'd been desperately trying to keep at bay. "I was in love with you."

"Harden yourself," Derek whispered in my ear. "She doesn't deserve your tears."

I glanced at him, and he winked.

"It wasn't premeditated," Nadia answered defensively. "The first day I walked into your office, I felt immediately attracted to you, something I'd never experienced before. When I realized you felt the same way, I'd planned on making a move on you. Then, I saw the laser beam of light flash across your eyes and knew you were a dark spirit possessing my counselor."

"And that's when you devised this cunning plan of yours to use Ameerah to get what you wanted, am I correct?" Derek spat, disgusted, his cold eyes on her face.

Nadia's gaze shifted to him. "That's right."

"Something a dark spirit would do," John said.

Derek barked out a laugh. "Right, mate. Dark spirits are known to court and romance a human. Are you new?"

John shrugged, unfazed by Derek's snarky comment. "I suppose you're right." He refocused on Nadia. "It's time to go."

Nadia took a couple steps toward me, and I held my hand out, palm facing her. "Stay away from me."

She stopped. "What I said about your parents being assholes is true," she said and glanced over her shoulder at John, which once again reminded me of my mother seeking my father's approval. I told her not to fucking do that, yet she went ahead and did it anyway. I could feel the anger boiling inside me, my expression stone cold. I refused to look at John, so I kept my hard eyes on Nadia instead. "John is taking me to the realm of rehabilitation to help me deal with the bullshit of my life . . . you know, with my family and being raped. Sort of like what you went through . . . in a way." She was wringing her hands nervously, probably because of the way I was regarding her with pure contempt. She attempted to smile, but when she risked looking into my eyes, it turned into a frown instead. "Listen, I know you're pissed off, but John was telling me what the rehabilitation realm is like. It sounds pretty narly. You get to sleep in–"

Derek removed his arm from my shoulders and leaned forward, his blazing eyes on her. "Are you bloody daft?"

Nadia backed away and moved next to John. "I just thought if Ameerah knew what it's like, she might change her mind. I know she wants salvation, and if she can't do it on her own, this is another way she can get it. Of course, she still has to do it by herself, but the light walkers will help her."

The whole idea of it all sickened me, like it always had. This situation was fucked. She used me and had toyed with my emotions in an attempt to get what she wanted from me. She was no better than my wretched parents.

A wave of unbridled emotions crashed through me: heartbreak, despair, helplessness, and rage. Derek and the rest of my friends were right about humans. They were despicable creatures who had caused me nothing but heartache. And although a small part of me made allowances for some of them, as of this precise moment, the majority of my entire being loathed them. And then with a shocking jolt of clarity, I realized I had come full circle in regards to the moment when I took my last breath on earth and the thoughts that had accompanied me through my transition. They were virtually the same thoughts I had now. But this time, I would not make the same mistakes I had in the past. I would not allow my emotions that were carried over from my human life to this one to rule me.

No more.

I was done being a sap.

"You can forget it," I finally said to Nadia and John. "In fact, I don't want to crossover." I realized then as the words rolled off my tongue that they were true. I didn't want to, and I liked being a dark spirit. I had friends I could trust. Unlike humans, they had never double-crossed me. Sure there were dark spirits who were downright evil like Calvin Hyde, but I chose not be around them. I loved my friends. I loved who I was, and God help the humans who pissed me off from now on, because I wasn't playing nice anymore. I was a dark spirit, and I could now proudly say, I am Ameerah. I'm a fucking queen.

Nadia blinked at me in surprise. "Really? You totally don't want to move on?"

Instead of answering her, I squared my shoulders, held my head high, and turned my back on them. "C'mon, Derek. I'm way overdue for some hell raising."

Beaming, Derek hooked his arm with mine and said, "It's about fucking time."

And in a blink of an eye, we were gone.

Chapter Thirty-Six

Two Months Later

After that fateful night when my heart was ripped from my chest and stomped on with Nadia's admission that she'd never been in love with me and had basically used me, I'd decided to take Derek's advice to own my bitterness and rage instead of those emotions owning me. For decades I'd done the opposite and received nothing but grief. I felt liberated and became my old self again when I channeled those feelings to do one thing and one thing only: destroy the pieces-of-shit humans on this planet. With the help of Derek and Ava, I was able to attract men and women who were in committed relationships, and nine times out of ten, I was able to lure them into bed with me. It was quite simple, actually.

My first victim was a Doctor Steven Heinz who owned his own thriving family care practice in Astoria on Exchange Street. According to Derek, Steven was happily married with three young kids, went to church every Sunday, and was well respected in the community. But like my parents, he was an elitist who erected a false facade to ensure his foothold on the top rung where the wealthy rubbed elbows. Behind closed doors, Heinz and those like him poked fun of the people below them. Derek was my eyes and ears on this first stunt I pulled. He masqueraded as a lawyer who happened to be soulless and in the same caste system as Steven. Once Derek gave me all the ammunition I needed, I made my move.

Steven was an average looking fella, with short blond hair that was receding. He was tall with broad shoulders and brown eyes. Every Thursday evening, he'd go to a seedy bar in a nearby town, have a few drinks, and cuss up a storm while joking with the patrons he'd normally demonize with his cronies.

Two-faced bastard.

Thanks to Derek, I knew Steven's type: tall brunettes with long hair and blue eyes. I wasn't able to find a soulless human with his eye color preference, but I had the rest of the assets to work with, and I was a pro at it.

When I entered the bar, I spotted him right away with a beer bottle in his hand, leaning an elbow on the worn oak bar, talking to a bald fella next to him. I shimmied his way, loving the feel of the silk fabric of the slinky low-cut black dress against my skin. The atmosphere was low-key with only a handful of people, and the room smelled of alcohol, fried food, and stale cigarettes. A waitress with big forearms and a thick frame was carrying a plate of buffalo wings. She placed it on a table in the back where three middle-aged fellas sat.

As I slid my ass on the barstool next to Steven, I flashed him a coy smile. He did a double-take, his eyes dipping down to the top, fleshy part of my breasts. I crossed my legs, allowing the slit in my dress to part, revealing lace and the garter belt I was wearing.

He fixed his eyes on mine, and a slow smile crossed his face. "Hi. Can I buy you a drink?"

It was like taking candy from a baby.

"Sure." I returned his smile. "I'd like a martini with extra olives," I told the bartender.

"I've never seen you here before." Steven took a swig of his beer and ordered another one. "Are you new in town?"

I smirked. "I don't talk to strangers," I playfully said. I dropped my gaze and peeked at him through my long lashes.

He laughed and pointed at the cocktail the bartender placed in front of me. "Yet you allow them to buy you a drink?"

I slid an olive off the toothpick and stuck it between my lips, sucking on it, and then I rolled it with my tongue. Plucking it out of my mouth, I slowly licked the juices off, hyperaware of him intently watching me.

He shifted in his seat and held his hand out. "I'm Steven."

I noticed he wasn't wearing his wedding ring and shook his hand. "Daisy."

"Like the flower," he said. "Perfect. If I could, I'd plant a whole field of you." He laughed at his own joke.

What a cheeseball.

I played along, pretending to find his lame ass comment comical by touching his arm and nodding. "You flatter me."

The bartender popped off the cap of a beer bottle. It fell to the floor, making a tinging sound. He handed the beer to Steven.

"This is my fifth. I think I better stop."

"I'm only halfway through my martini, and I can already feel a buzz coming on." I winked, enjoying the fact I had this fucker eating out of my hand.

"So you never answered my question." He took a swig of his beer, his eyes darting to my hand rubbing the inside of my exposed thigh along the black lace of my stockings.

I raised my eyebrows, acting clueless, but I knew damned well what he was talking about. "Which was?"

"Are you from here?"

"No," I said, shaking my head. "I'm passing through. I was visiting a friend in Portland. I'm on my way home." I took a sip of my martini, craving a ciggy. It annoyed me smoking was banned in bars. If someone were to tell a person back in my time that one day this would happen, he would laugh his ass off. He wouldn't believe it. It was a stupid fucking law anyway. If you didn't want to go to a bar where people smoked, by all means, don't go. But here was the thing. The nonsmoking bars were losing business to the smoking bars, so the dumbass humans made a law that all bars had to be nonsmoking.

His eyes darted to the side, then rested on me. I could tell from his contemplative expression he was considering something. "You're here for one night?"

I finished my martini and ordered another one. "Yes. I plan to head home in the morning."

"What do you do for a living?" He looked at the bartender making my drink and raised his beer bottle. "I'll take another one." The bartender nodded as he poured gin into the glass.

"I'm a dental hygienist. What about you? What's your profession?"

He leaned closer to me, cupped his hands around his mouth, and staged-whispered, "I'm a mercenary, but nobody knows." He dramatically pressed his finger to his lips.

Fucking liar.

I giggled, pretending to be amused and whispered in his ear, "Your secret is safe with me."

While we finished our drinks, I continued to flirt with him and buff his ego. When he told me about how he loved to rock climb and race cars, I thought about his wife and kids at home. I bet he had fed her some bullshit line that he was buried in charts and was following up with his patients. Soon she'd find out what a cheating bastard he was, and his kids would be better off in the end.

An hour later, we were in a hotel room I'd rented earlier in the day and placed a hidden camera inside a picture on the wall across from the king sized bed. The photo was of a rustic cabin in the woods and mountains in the background. It was nothing fancy or eye catching, which served my purpose. All I had to do to turn the camera on was push the remote button in my purse.

"I was watching you expertly maneuvering the olive with your tongue earlier," he said when I closed the door behind us. "I couldn't help but imagine you sucking my cock with that beautiful mouth of yours."

I turned and slowly kissed him, allowing my tongue to explore his mouth. He tasted and smelled like beer. Not my favorite thing, but his response was immediate, and he was a good kisser. His hand slipped up my thigh and between my legs, but I stopped him and pulled away.

I waved a finger at him, like a parent would when a child was being naughty. "Why don't you take a shower first. Then, I'll show you what my tongue and mouth can do." I reached down and placed my hand on his erection straining against his jeans. I massaged it. He closed his eyes and softly moaned. "I'll be waiting."

He opened his eyes when I removed my hand. "Why don't you take one with me?"

I smiled, placed my palm on his chest, and trailed my finger down it. "There's something I didn't tell you about myself," I said in a sultry voice, purring each word.

His eyebrows knitted, and he took a step back, blanching. "You're not a guy . . . are you?"

I laughed, took his hand, and placed it between my legs. "You can rest assured I'm one hundred percent homegrown female."

He breathed a sigh of relief when I pushed his hand back. He swiped it across his face. "You scared me for a minute. It happened to a friend of mine once when he was in Vegas. It wasn't his proudest moment, I'll tell ya and—"

I kissed him again to shut him up so I could get on with this charade. He pushed me against the door, and his hand cupped my breast. I pushed him back and undid his jeans. He was hard again.

"What I was going to say was I love to dominate my partner," I said. "Do you have a problem with that?"

"No," he answered with a wicked grin. "I've never been dominated before. It's been a fantasy of mine."

"Well, then, get your ass in the shower, wash up, and I'll be waiting for you." I unzipped the back of my dress. The silky material slid off my body, pooling around my ankles.

Steven's eyes hungrily roamed the mesh lace teddy I was wearing along with the matching garter belt and stockings. It also helped that I had on black high heels. Hell, I'd do this human. She was fucking hot. His hand latched onto his erection through his plaid boxer shorts, and he began stroking it.

I encircled my fingers around his wrist and stopped him from pleasuring himself. "No masturbating. That's an order." I turned him around to where he was facing the bathroom. "Now, get to it."

Without another word, he obeyed. Once I heard the shower running, I got busy. I pushed the remote button in my purse to turn the camera on and texted Ava who was on standby. We had rigged it to where she could watch and record us on her laptop or cell phone. I stood in front of the picture, waved, and made an obscene gesture. LMFAO, she texted back. We were in business.

I looked around the room. Plain. Brown walls. Cheesy, thin cream colored bedspread. A flat screen TV stood on top of a particle board dresser directly across from the foot of the bed. Above it was the picture with the hidden camera.

A squeaking noise came from the faucet in the bathroom. The water stopped. I tugged the bedspread and covers off and left them in a pile on the floor. I sat on the edge of the bed, facing the bathroom, leaning on the back of my palms, breasts poking up.

Steven came out of the bathroom, his damp hair slicked back, his cock rock hard, the tip bouncing against his soft stomach. With my finger, I motioned for him to come to me.

"You're gorgeous," he said. "I want to fuck you like no tomorrow."

"Get in the middle of the bed and kneel," I ordered.

Like an eager child, he did what I said. I made him position himself to where he was facing sideways toward the camera, and there would be no doubts about his infidelity. I moved to the other side of the bed and situated myself sixty-nine style beneath him, then wrapped my lips around his throbbing cock. I didn't care for giving blowjobs. I was fantastic at it, but it wasn't my favorite thing to do. I pretended like it was a lollipop and went to town, licking, sucking, while I massaged his balls. I gripped his shaft and ran my hand up and down. From my experiences in possessing male humans, I knew what it felt like and what worked. He groaned between quick breaths. When they got more persistent and louder, I pulled my mouth away, told him to get on his back, and then

I straddled him. No need to take my panties off, they were crotchless.

I was always thinking ahead.

"If you come, I will punish you," I whispered in his ear.

"Don't worry," he said, breathless. "I have it under control."

And he did.

Thanks to my creative imagination, I pretended he was someone else, which made me soaking wet and caused me to moan and cry out when his lips and tongue explored my body.

An hour or so later, he thanked me for a wonderful night. He seemed a bit nervous when he noticed the time and hurried out the door, smoothing his wrinkled maroon polo shirt out.

Did I feel like a dime store hooker?

Not at all.

Besides fulfilling part of my mission, he got me off and was skillful between the sheets, which convinced me he'd been cheating on his wife for quite some time.

The bastard was going down.

Thanks to Ava, she burned two disks of the video for me. The next day, while Steven was at work, I found a different soulless human to possess—an elderly lady in her eighties who was on vacation in Astoria. I didn't care for the achy body or the poor eyesight, but this senior citizen served my purpose. Humans were programmed to respect their elders, so when I shuffled to Steven's front door and knocked, his wife didn't bristle like she would have if I were a young gal. I handed her the DVD disk and told her to watch it.

"What's on this?" she asked, eyeing it curiously.

She was an attractive lady. Her brown hair was pulled into a ponytail, and her dark blue eyes appeared tired and a bit lost. I wondered if she suspected her husband's betrayal, but regardless, she was about to find out.

"You need to watch it right away, my dear," I said, inwardly cringing at how scratchy and worn out my voice sounded. "It'll change your life, but make sure you watch it alone."

Her eyebrows knitted. "Okay."

I turned to leave, anxious to exit this body when her question stopped me.

"Who are you?"

I glanced over my shoulder, peering at her through thick bifocals. "I'm a fucking queen." I smiled, winked, and continued to mosey down her driveway to the waiting red suburban Ava was driving.

We dropped the other disk off at Steven's church. Ava personally handed it to his pastor while I waited for her in the vehicle. She told me he kindly accepted it and promised to view the video within the hour.

A week later, I received word that Steven's wife kicked him out, filed for divorce, and his reputation in the community was ruined. Thanks to me and my partners in crime, he was knocked on his ass, no longer living the highlife. I didn't stick around to find out how his church handled his infidelity, because I moved on to find the next scum-of-the-earth human and proceeded to take similar actions as I had with Steven. During those two months, I discovered that women were just as bad, if not worse when it came to betraying their mates. All I had to do was possess a hot muscular male, flirt with them, and the bitches were all over me. Though I didn't much care for the male anatomy, I did enjoy fucking the women. Because I was partial to them, I spent more time pleasuring each one than I did with the men. I enjoyed their beautiful bodies, the sexy way they moved, and the erotic sounds they made caused by me and me alone.

One afternoon, while I was in spiritual form, seeking out a soulless human to possess, I came across Paige and Nathan. They were sitting on a bench in the park, obviously not aware they were in the middle of a negative area where dark spirits such as myself could roam without the immortals detecting us. I was surprised to see them and noticed they were holding hands. I wondered if Nathan would cheat on Paige or vice versa. There was no way for me to find out, though. They were immortals who would know if I were dwelling inside a human, because the ringing in their ears would alert them, and they'd be able to see the laser beam of light move across my eyes. No matter. It seemed like they were made for each other, though sometimes I wondered.

Both of them were deep in thought, drinking their coffee, watching a couple of squirrels run across the lawn and up an oak tree. They looked well. Paige was beautiful, with her long, straight dark red hair and dark green eyes, and Nathan could be a model for a Calvin Klein ad. He had that look and the muscles to go along with it. If I were straight, I'd definitely be drooling over him. I was about to leave them be until Nathan spoke, and I heard my name. I immediately moved in front of him, noting the troubled look on his face.

"What are we going to do about Ameerah?" He sighed and ran a hand through his hair.

"I don't know," Paige said, frowning. "She's gone over the deep end. We have to do something."

"Maybe we can speak to her. Ya know, talk some sense into her."

I laughed. I had more sense now than ever before.

"We can try. I'm worried about her." Paige turned to Nathan. "Don't you think what she's doing is kinda good in a way? I mean, seriously, those relationships would eventually end anyway."

Thank you, Paige.

"It doesn't matter," Nathan said. "She's meddling in affairs across the globe, ruining lives which aren't yet supposed to be ruined. Also, her actions are not only affecting the couples involved and their families but the communities they reside in, as well. It's the domino effect. We have to stop her."

I left, not bothering to hear Paige's response. If they thought they could stop me, they were fooling themselves.

I am Ameerah.

Some birds cannot be caged, and I'm one of them.

The End.

About the Author

REBEKKAH FORD grew up in a family that dealt with the paranormal. Her parents' Charles and Geri Wilhelm were the directors of the UFO Investigators League in Fairfield, Ohio. They also investigated ghost hauntings and Bigfoot sightings in addition to extraterrestrial cases. Growing up in this type of environment and having the passion for writing is what drove Rebekkah at an early age to write tales dealing with the paranormal. Her fascination with the unknown is what led her to write the *Beyond the Eyes* trilogy, its companion, *Tangled Roots,* and now *Ameerah*, which is a standalone book.

Rebekkah resides in rural North Dakota, in a farming community of about 1,800 people. She loves where she's lives and has been known to call her small town Mayberry. She has an irreverent sense of humor, adores coffee, and yummy food makes her happy. Besides creating stories, she loves books, antiques, animals, connecting with her fans and other authors, and watching her favorite TV shows, among other things.

Other Books by Rebekkah Ford

Beyond the Eyes trilogy
Beyond the Eyes
Dark Spirits
The Devil's Third
Tangled Roots: (a companion to the trilogy)

By Moonlight (Paranormal boxset):
15 novels and novellas from your favorite or
soon-to-be favorite paranormal authors

Where To Connect With Rebekkah Ford

Author Rebekkah Ford: rebekkahford.com
Wandering Thoughts of A Writer:
themusingwriter.blogspot.com
Author Rebekkah Ford's Facebook Page:
www.facebook.com/rebekkahford2012
Twitter: twitter.com/RebekkahFord
Goodreads: www.goodreads.com/author/show/6180865.Rebekkah Ford
Pinterest: www.pinterest.com/rebekkahford/
Google Plus: plus.google.com/102242636096208798568/posts

Subscribe to Rebekkah's monthly newsletter. Get updates on Rebekkah's books, such as new releases, excerpts, giveaways, top secret information, and much more! Your information is kept private. Rebekkah doesn't share, sell, or spam newsletter subscribers. http://rebekkahford.us7.list-manage.com/subscribe?u=06bbb5773fe9e17e6ba0e860e&id=51f0af6e94

Thank you for taking the time to read *Ameerah*. If you enjoyed it, please consider telling your friends or posting a short review. Word of mouth is an author's best friend, and I appreciate your support.